Praise

DELORES FOSSEN

LONE STAR NIGHTS

HQN™

ISBN-13: 978-0-373-78962-7

Recycling programs for this product may not exist in your area.

Lone Star Nights

Copyright © 2016 by Delores Fossen

The publisher acknowledges the copyright holder of the additional work:

Cowboy Trouble
Copyright © 2016 by Delores Fossen

www.HQNBooks.com

Printed in U.S.A.

CONTENTS

LONE STAR NIGHTS

CHAPTER ONE

THE DYING WOMAN'S misspelled tattoo bothered Lucky McCord. Not nearly as much as the dying woman, of course, but seriously, who didn't know the rule about putting *i* before *e* except after *c*?

The tattoo "artist" who'd inked that turd of a misspelling onto Dixie Mae Weatherall's forearm, that's who.

It was a shame the inker wasn't anywhere around to fix his mess so Dixie Mae could finish out her last minutes on God's green earth with a tat that didn't set people's teeth on edge.

While the nurse adjusted the tubes and needles going in and out of Dixie Mae, Lucky stayed back against the wall. Man, he hated hospitals. That smell of disinfectant, lime Jell-O, floor wax and some bullshit—literal bullshit—from his own boots.

Lucky hadn't had time to clean up before he'd gotten the call from the doctor telling him that Dixie Mae had been admitted to Spring Hill Memorial Hospital and that it wasn't looking good. The doctor had said he should hurry. Lucky had been thirty miles away in San Antonio, just ten minutes out of an eight-second bull ride that'd lasted only four seconds.

A metaphor for his life.

The bull ride, or rather the fall, had left him with

a bruised tailbone, back and ego. All minor stuff, though, compared to what was happening here in the hospital with Dixie Mae.

Hell.

He'd always thought Dixie Mae was too tough to die. Or that she'd at least live to be a hundred. And maybe she was pretty close to that number.

Most folks estimated Dixie Mae's age anywhere between eighty and ninety. Most folks only saw her gruff face, the wrinkles on her wrinkles and her colorful wardrobe that she called a tribute to Dolly Parton, the rhinestone years.

Oh, and most folks saw the misspelled tattoo, of course. Couldn't miss that.

When Lucky looked at her, he saw a lot more than just those things. He saw a very complex woman. By her own admission, Dixie Mae subscribed to the whack-a-mole approach to conflict resolution, but she was one of the most successful rodeo promoters in the state.

And hands down, the orneriest.

Lucky loved every bit of her ornery heart.

There'd been so many times when Lucky had walked away from her. Cursed her. Wished that he could tie her onto the back of a mean bucking bull and let the bull try to sling some sense into her. But he'd always gone back because the bottom line with Dixie Mae was that she was the only person who'd ever believed he could be something.

Powerful stuff like that would make a man put up with any level of orneriness.

The petite blonde nurse finally finished whatever she was doing to Dixie Mae and stepped away, but not before giving Lucky that sad, sympathetic look. And a stern warning. "Don't give her any cigarettes. She'll ask but don't give her one."

Lucky had already figured that out, both the asking part and don't-give-her-one part. He didn't smoke, but even if he did, he wouldn't have brought her cigarettes. A shot of tequila maybe, but that would have been to steady his own nerves, not for Dixie Mae.

"She bribed the janitor," the nurse added. "And she called a grocery clerk to offer him a thousand dollars to bring her a pack, but we stopped him before he could give them to her."

"Assholes," Dixie Mae declared. "A woman oughta be able to smoke when she wants to smoke."

Lucky just sighed. It was that way of thinking that had put Dixie Mae in the hospital bed. That, and the other hard living she'd been doing for decades. And her advancing years, of course. Besides, since there was an oxygen tank nearby, it was possible the staff hadn't simply wanted to deny her a smoke for her health's sake but rather because they hadn't wanted her to blow up the place.

"Are you close to her?" the nurse asked him. According to her name tag, she was Nan Watts.

"Nobody's close to me," Dixie Mae snarled. "But Lucky's my boy. Not one of my blood, mind you, but my own blood son's an asshole." She added a profanity-riddled suggestion for what her son could do to himself.

The nurse blushed, but maybe Dixie Mae's cussing gave her some ideas because on the way to the door, Nan Watts winked at Lucky. He nearly winked back. A conditioned reflex, but he wasn't in a winking, womanizing kind of mood right now.

"Boy, you look lower than a fat penguin's balls," Dixie Mae said after the nurse left. She waggled her nicotine-yellowed fingers at him, motioning for him to come closer. "Did you bring me a cig?"

"No." He ignored the additional profanity she mumbled. "Why are you here in Spring Hill?" Lucky asked. "Why didn't you go to the hospital near your house in San Antonio?"

"I was here in town seeing somebody."

Since Dixie Mae had been born in Spring Hill, it was possible she had acquaintances nearby, but Lucky doubted it.

"I'm worried about you," Lucky admitted. He went to her, eased down on the corner of the metal table next to her bed.

"No need. I'm just dying, that's all. Along with having a nicotine fit. By the way, that's a lot worse than the dying." She had to stop, take a deep breath. "My heart's giving out. Did the doc tell you that when he called?"

"Yeah." Lucky wanted to say more, but that lump in his throat sort of backed things up.

He touched his fingers to the tat.

"I know. It bothers you," Dixie Mae said. Each word she spoke seemed to be a challenge, and her eyelids looked heavy, not just from the kilo of electric-blue eye shadow she had on them, either. "Have you thought maybe you're all over the tat because you don't want to think about the rest of this?"

There was no *maybe* about it. That's exactly what it was. It was easier to focus on something else—anything else—rather than what was happening to Dixie Mae.

Lucky nodded. Shrugged. "But the tat really does bother me, too."

She waved him off. Or rather tried. Not a lot of strength in her hand. "I was shit-faced when I got it. So was the tattoo guy."

"*P-e-i-c-e-s* of my heart," he read aloud. Complete with little heart bits that had probably once been red. They were now more the color of an old Hershey bar. And Dixie Mae's wrinkles and saggy skin had given them some confusing shapes.

When he had first met Dixie Mae, Lucky had spent some time guessing what the shapes actually were. Not a disassembled United States map as he'd first thought.

But rather a broken heart.

With the way Dixie Mae carried on, sometimes it was hard to believe she even had a heart, and she'd never gotten around to explaining exactly who'd done such a thing to her. Or if the person had survived.

Lucky doubted it.

"I wish there was time to get it fixed for you." He traced the outline of the heart piece that resembled the map of Florida but then drew back his fingers when he realized it could also be a penis tat. "I wish there was time for a lot of things."

Like more time. This was too soon.

"No need. Besides, it's not even the worst of the bunch. When I was younger, I got drunk a lot. And I went to the same tattoo guy," Dixie Mae admitted. "You should see the one on my left ass cheek. I didn't realize he needed a dictionary for the word *ass*."

It wasn't very manly to shudder, but Lucky just had this thing about misspelled words and didn't want to see other examples of them, especially on her ass. Besides, there wouldn't be many more moments with Dixie Mae, and he didn't want to waste those moments on a discussion about the origins, shapes and locations of bad tats.

Dixie Mae dragged in a ragged breath, one that proved beyond a shadow of a doubt that she was a two-packs-a-day smoker. Unfiltered, at that. "We've had a good run together, me and you. Haven't we, boy? Made each other some money. Had some good times when I wasn't kicking your butt or boxing your ears."

"We've made some money all right," he agreed.

As for the good times, Lucky would have to grade those on a curve.

She'd started sponsoring him in bull-riding events when he was nineteen, just a couple of weeks after his folks had died. When he'd turned twenty-five, Dixie Mae had allowed him to buy into her company. Lucky was nearly thirty-three now, and they were still partners. He did indeed help her run Weatherall-McCord Stock Show and Rodeo Promotions, but he hadn't given up bull riding, mainly because he was better at it than the business side of things.

"I'll miss you," Lucky added. He cursed that lump in his throat again. Because it was true. He would miss her.

"Awww." She dragged in another ragged breath. "That's monkey shit, and we both know it."

"No. It's not. I will miss you." And he meant it. He'd never thought he could love someone this much, not since his mother had passed, but he loved Dixie Mae.

Lucky couldn't be sure, but he thought maybe her eyes watered a bit. Then she was back to her usual self. There was something comforting about that.

"I do have a favor to ask you," she said. "That's why I had the doc call you."

Lucky nodded. "I'm here, and I'm listening."

She patted his cheek. "The girls do like that pretty face of yours, but rust up your zippers a little. Or wear a bigger rodeo buckle. Might slow you down a bit so you can take time to enjoy something other than a woman's secret place. Besides, some of those women you see don't keep their *places* so secret."

"Neither do I," Lucky reminded her. Then he winked. It was a good use of what might be the last wink he'd ever give her.

"Don't get fresh with me, boy. I don't fall for monkey shit like that."

He figured she was saying that just to take away the tension in the room. But then again, it was her normal, surly mood and one of her normal, surly sayings.

"Now, to that favor," Dixie Mae went on. She took an envelope, one that had a couple of cigarette burns on it, from beside her on the bed and handed it to him. Her hands were shaking now. "I got nobody else to ask, but I need some help. And before you think about saying no, just remember this is my dying wish. A man wouldn't be much of a man to deny an old dying woman her last wish."

Yeah, a man like that would indeed have to be missing a pair. "I'll do whatever you want. Anything."

Lucky started to open the letter, but Dixie Mae stopped him by taking hold of his hand. "No. Don't read it now. Save it for later. Let's just sit here, take in the moment together."

And she smiled.

Not that evil smile Lucky had seen her give before she'd thrown something at somebody, threatened them with bodily harm or cursed them out. This smile seemed to be the genuine article. She'd saved it just for him.

"Tell me about your ride today." Her voice was a hoarse whisper, and her eyelids drifted all the way down.

Lucky's own voice didn't fare much better. "Not much to tell, really. The bull won."

"The bull usually does," Dixie Mae whispered. She smiled again, then both her grip and the smile began to melt away.

And just like that, Dixie Mae Weatherall was gone.

Lucky tried to hold it together. Tried not to give in to the grief that felt heavy and cold in his chest. He brushed a kiss on her cheek, gathered her in his arms, and Dixie Mae's "boy" cried like a baby.

CHAPTER TWO

CASSIE WEATHERALL FOUGHT back the tears. Fought for air, too.

Breathe.

She couldn't actually say the word aloud. She couldn't speak yet, but she repeated it in her head and hoped that it worked.

It didn't.

Her heart continued to race, slamming so hard against her chest that she thought her ribs might break. Her throat closed up, strangling her.

This was just a panic attack, she reminded herself. All she needed to do was calm down and breathe.

That reminder still didn't work so Cassie tried to force herself to think this through logically. She had enough adrenaline pumping through her to fight a bear. Maybe six of them. But there were no bears to fight here at Sweet Meadows Meditation and Relaxation Facility. Other than the grizzlies in her head anyway, though sometimes, like now, they felt worse than the real thing.

And speaking of her head, Cassie was no longer sure it was on her shoulders. Too much spinning. Wave after wave of panic. She couldn't let anyone see her like this. Couldn't let them know that she was broken and might never be fixed.

She went old-school and put her head between her knees. Of course, that meant sitting down, and while the path was good for walking and running, the small rocks dug into her butt and legs. Good.

Pain was good. Pain gave the adrenaline something else to battle other than the bears.

Breathe.

It was all about the breathing. All about taking in the right amount of air. Releasing the right amount, too. Cassie managed that part, but then the darkness came. The shaking. And her feet and hands started to go numb. That dumb-ass bear was going to win if she didn't get hold of this right now.

She heard the sound of someone approaching, and Cassie struggled to get to her feet. *Please, you can't see me like this.* But thankfully the footsteps stopped just on the other side of the path. There were thick shrubs between her and the person who'd made those footsteps.

"Miss Weatherall?" someone called out. Not a shout, but a soft, tentative voice.

Orin Dayton. The office manager at Sweet Meadows.

Cassie considered not answering him, but that would no doubt just prompt him to walk the twenty or so feet around the row of shrubs that divided her suite from the running trail. And then he would see her with her head between her knees, sweating, crying.

"Yes?" she forced herself to say.

"Uh, is something wrong, Miss Weatherall?" he asked.

"No. I overdid my run, and I'm a little queasy." The lie was huge. So huge that Cassie looked up at the afternoon sky to make sure a lightning bolt wasn't coming at her.

"All right," he finally said. He used the tone of a person who wanted to believe the malarkey she'd just doled out. "A Dr. Knight from Los Angeles called a couple of minutes ago."

Andrew. He was the only person other than Cassie who knew why she was really here at Sweet Meadows.

"I rang your room," Orin went on, "but when you didn't answer, Dr. Knight said to get you a message. That Dr. Stan Menger from a hospital in Spring Hill, Texas, is trying to reach you."

Spring Hill. Her hometown. But Cassie didn't know this Stan Menger. "What does Dr. Menger want?" Please not something that required her immediate attention. Not while she was battling a panic attack.

Orin paused again. "I'm afraid it's not good news."

Great. First, bears. Now, bad news. Since she'd already used what little supply of air she'd had left in her lungs, Cassie didn't say anything else. She just waited for him to continue.

"There's been a death, Miss Weatherall," Orin said. "It's your grandmother. Dr. Knight said you shouldn't go home, though, that it wouldn't be good for you right now. Dr. Knight said just to stay put and that he'll take care of everything."

But Orin was talking to himself because Cassie punched the last of the bears aside, got to her feet and ran to her room to pack.

DIXIE MAE DESERVED a lot better send-off than this. But considering she didn't have a friend other than him in the tristate area, Lucky figured he shouldn't be surprised there were only four people at her memorial service. Five, if he counted his brother Riley who'd dropped by earlier. Six, if he counted the sweaty-faced funeral director who kept popping in and out.

Lucky decided to count them both.

Dixie Mae's driver, Manuel Rodriquez, was at the back of the room that the funeral home had set up. He was glaring at the flower-draped coffin, and the glare only got worse whenever his eyes landed on the four-foot-by-four-foot glossy picture that Dixie Mae had arranged to be placed beside her. No smile in this one, just a steely expression, as if she were picking a fight from beyond the grave.

Judging from Manuel's glare, he'd likely been on the receiving end of too many of Dixie Mae's fight-pickings.

Other than Manuel, the funeral director and Lucky, the only other guests were two women.

And Lucky used that term loosely.

It was hard to tell their ages, probably in their early twenties. Purple hair, purple nails, purple lips and boobs practically spilling out of their purple tube tops. Yet another loosely used term because the tops were more like Band-Aids.

Since Dixie Mae's only child, her estranged son, Mason-Dixon, owned a strip joint on the outskirts of town, it was possible these two were his *employees*. Perhaps he'd sent them to see if his mom had left him some kind of inheritance.

Good luck with that.

Dixie Mae had probably figured out a way to take every penny to the grave. Or skip the grave completely. Plus, Dixie Mae wasn't exactly fond of her son and would have given her money to his strippers rather than the man she'd called her shit-head spawn.

Lucky hadn't been able to get in touch with Dixie Mae's only other living relative, her granddaughter, Cassie, though Lucky and Dixie Mae's doctor had left her a couple of messages at her office in Los Angeles. Whether she'd show up was anyone's guess.

He heard someone come in and turned, hoping it was a mourner who'd make this memorial service actually look like one. But it was only his twin brother, Logan.

Logan and he were identical in looks, but that was where any and all similarities ended. Logan was the responsible, successful tycoon who ran the family business, McCord Cattle Brokers, and had been in charge of it since their parents had been killed in a car wreck fourteen years ago. Lucky was the screwup. Considering their other brother had been an Air Force special-ops super troop and his sister was the smartest woman in Texas, it meant all the good family labels had been taken anyway.

Screwup suited him just fine.

Fewer expectations that way.

After having a short chat with Manuel, Logan came to the front where Lucky was standing. Even though Logan ran a cattle-brokerage company—and ran it well, of course—there were no bullshit smells coming from his boots that thudded on the parquet floor. With his crisp white button-up shirt and spotless jeans, he looked as if he were modeling for the cover of *Texas Monthly* magazine.

Logan had done exactly that—a couple of times.

"Are those Mason-Dixon's girls from the strip club?" Logan hitched his thumb to the pair in the back.

Lucky shrugged. "Don't know for sure. I introduced myself when they arrived, but the only response I got was a grunt from one of them." He'd been afraid to ask anything else since even the smallest movement might cause those tube tops to explode.

"Did Dixie Mae go peacefully?" Logan asked.

"As peacefully as Dixie Mae could ever go anywhere. Thanks for coming. She would have appreciated it."

"No, she wouldn't have, but I didn't come here for her. Are you okay?"

The funny thing about having an identical twin was being able to look into eyes that were a genetic copy of Lucky's own. The other funny thing about that was despite the screwup label, Logan's eyes showed that his question and his concern were the real deal.

"I'm fine." Lucky patted his back jeans pocket. "Dixie Mae gave me a letter right before she died."

"What does it say?" Those genetically identical eyes got skeptical now. So did Logan's tone. Lucky couldn't blame him. Dixie Mae brought that out in people.

"Haven't read it yet. Thought I'd wait until this was over." Until after he'd had a little more time to deal with her death. A few shots of Jameson, too. "I know it's hard to believe, but I'll miss her."

Lucky didn't see Logan's hand move before he felt it on his back. A brotherly pat. Just one. It was more than most folks got.

"What will you do with the rodeo business now that she's gone?" Logan asked.

"Dixie Mae and I talked about it. She wants me to

keep it going." It was her legacy in a way. His, too, since the name of the company was Weatherall-McCord Stock Show and Rodeo Promotions. "But it's a lot of work for one person." He poked Logan with his elbow. "Want to help me?"

Logan shrugged. "We could incorporate it into McCord Cattle Brokers. That way you could use the administrative staff I have in place. Plus, there's an office already set up for you here in Spring Hill."

Considering that Logan hadn't even paused before that suggestion, it meant he'd been giving it some thought. Well, Lucky had, too, and the rodeo business was his. He didn't know how he was going to run it all by himself, but he wasn't going to be lured back to Spring Hill and be under Logan's thumb.

That thumb might also be a genetic copy of Lucky's own, but it had a way of crushing people.

"I need to get back to the office," Logan added, already looking at the exit. "We've got a cutting-horse trainer coming in today, and I could use some help. Maybe when you're finished here, you can come on home?"

Most of his conversations with Logan went that way. There was always something going on at either the office in town or at the ranch where Logan stashed some of the livestock he bought. And Lucky would indeed make an appearance, maybe try to smooth over things with the horse trainer Logan was sure to soon piss off if he hadn't already. Logan was good with four-legged critters and paperwork. People, not so much.

"I'll be there later," Lucky told him.

After he read the letter from Dixie Mae, he'd probably need to get drunk. Then sleep it off. Of course, after that he had a rodeo all the way up in Dallas. Even though he didn't spell that out to Logan, his brother must have tuned in to that twin telepathy thing that Lucky had never experienced. But Logan seemed to know exactly what Lucky had in mind.

"Also, remember the wedding and the Founder's Day picnic next month," Logan added. "You should at least put in an appearance."

Lucky nodded. He'd make an appearance all right. For both. His brother Riley and his bride-to-be, Claire, were getting married at the family ranch and then having the reception at the picnic so that everyone in town could attend. It made sense since the McCords hosted the event. That not only meant they footed the bill, but that the entire family was expected to show up and have fun. Or at least look as if they were having fun. It'd been much easier to do that when Lucky was a kid, and his mom and dad had been running the show. Now it was just another place for him to have memories of things he didn't want to remember.

Still, he'd be there. Not just because of Logan and Riley, either, but because the picnic was something his mother had started, and despite the bad memories it would bring on, the event was her legacy.

Logan went to the guest book and signed it before he left, his boots thudding his way to the exit. That's when Lucky noticed the purple-tube-top girls were gone. Manuel, too. Heck, even the funeral director had ducked out again.

Lucky sank down in one of the creaky wooden chairs, wondering if he should say a prayer or something. Dixie Mae had left specific instructions with the funeral home that there would not be a service, music or food. No graveside burial, either, since she was to be cremated. The only thing she'd insisted on was the creepy picture of her that would ensure no passerby would just pop in to say goodbye to an old lady. However, she hadn't said anything about a guy praying.

Footsteps again. Not boots this time. These were hurried but light, and he thought maybe the tube-top visitors had returned. It wasn't them, but it was a woman all right. A brunette with pinned-up hair, and she was reading something on her phone. That's why Lucky didn't see her face until she finally looked up.

Cassie.

Or rather Cassandra Weatherall. Dixie Mae's grand-daughter.

She practically skidded to a stop when she spotted him, and he got the scowl he always got when Cassie looked at him. He got his other usual reaction to her, too. A little flutter in his stomach.

Possibly gas.

Lucky sure hoped that was what it was anyway. The only thing he'd been good at in high school was charming girls, but nothing—absolutely nothing—he'd ever tried on Cassie had garnered him more than a scowl.

"You're here," Cassie said.

Lucky made a show of looking at himself and out-stretched his arms. "Appears so. You're here, too."

She slipped her phone into the pocket of her gray jacket. Gray skirt and top, as well. Ditto for the shoes. If those shoes got any more sensible, they'd start flossing themselves.

But yep, what he'd felt was a flutter.

Probably because he'd never been able to figure her out. Or kiss her. He mentally shrugged. It was the kiss part all right. When it came to that sort of thing, he was pretty shallow, and it stung that the high school bookworm with no other boyfriends would dismiss him with a scowl.

He'd considered the possibility that she was gay, but then over the years he'd seen some pictures she'd sent Dixie Mae. Pictures of Cassie in an itty-bitty bikini on some beach with a guy wrapped around her. Then more pictures of her in a party dress, a different guy wrapped around her that time. So apparently she liked wraparound guys. She just didn't like him.

"Is your dad coming?" he asked.

Her mouth tightened a little. Translation: sore subject. "Probably not. He hasn't spoken to Gran in twenty years."

Lucky was well aware of that because Dixie Mae brought it up every time she got too much Jim Beam in her. Which was often. According to her, twenty years ago she'd refused to give Mason-Dixon a loan so he could add an adult sex toy shop to his strip club, the Slippery Pole, and it had caused a rift. Or as Dixie Mae called it—the great dildo feud.

Still, Lucky had hoped that her only child could bury the hatchet for a couple of minutes and come say goodbye to his mom.

"My mother won't be here, either," Cassie went on.

Yet another complicated piece of this family puzzle. Cassie's folks had divorced before she was born. Or maybe they had never actually married. Either way, her mom preferred to stay far, far away from Spring Hill, Mason-Dixon, Dixie Mae and Cassie.

Cassie walked closer, stopping by his side. She

peered at the casket. Hesitating. "That's not a very good picture of her," she said.

Lucky made a sound of agreement. "Her doing. All of this is. She did try to call you before she passed. I tried to call you afterward."

Cassie nodded, seemed flustered. "I was at a... retreat on the Oregon Coast. No cell phone. I didn't get the news until yesterday afternoon, and I caught the first flight out."

"Shrinks need retreats?" Lucky asked, only half-serious.

"I'm not a shrink. I'm a therapist. And yes, sometimes we do." There seemed to be a lot more to it than that, but she didn't offer any details. "Were you with Gran when she died?"

Well, heck. That brought back the lump in his throat. It didn't go so great with that flutter in his stomach. Lucky responded with just a nod.

"Was she in pain?" Cassie pressed.

"No. She sort of just slipped away." Right there, in front of him. With that smile on her face.

Cassie stayed quiet a moment. "I should have been there with her. I should have told her goodbye."

And the tears started spilling down her cheeks. Lucky had been expecting them, of course. From all accounts Cassie actually loved Dixie Mae and vice versa, but he wasn't sure if he should offer Cassie a shoulder. Or just a pat on the back.

He went with the pat.

Cassie pulled out a tissue from her purse, dabbed her eyes, but the tears just came right back. Hell. Back-patting obviously wasn't doing the trick so he went for something more. He put his arm around her.

More tears fell, and Lucky figured they weren't the first of the day. Nor would they be the last. Cassie's eyes had already been red when she came into the room. As much as he hated to see a woman cry—and he *hated* it—at least there was one other person mourning Dixie Mae's loss.

Lucky didn't hurry her crying spell by trying to say something to comfort her. No way to speed up something like that anyway. Death sucked, period, and sometimes the only thing you could do was cry about it.

"Thanks," Cassie mumbled several moments later. She dabbed her eyes again and moved away from him. That didn't put an end to the tears, but she kept trying to blink them back. "Did she say anything before she died?"

Lucky didn't have any trouble recalling those last handful of words. "She said, 'The bull usually does.'"

Cassie opened her mouth and then seemed to change her mind about how to answer that. "Excuse me?"

"I don't know what it means, either. Dixie Mae asked about the rodeo ride that I'd just finished. I told her the bull won, and she said it usually does."

She blinked. "Does it usually win?"

"Uh, yeah. About 70 percent of the time. But I got the feeling that Dixie Mae meant something, well, deeper."

Heck, he hoped so anyway. Lucky hated to think Dixie Mae had used her dying breath to state the obvious.

Cassie glanced at him from the corner of her eye. "So you're still bull riding?"

The question was simple enough, but since it was

one he got often, Lucky knew there was more to it than that. What Cassie, and others, really wanted to ask was—*Aren't you too old to still be riding bulls?*

Yep, he was. But he wasn't giving it up. And for that matter, he could ask her—*Aren't you too young to be a shrink?* Or rather a *therapist.* Of course, her comeback to that would probably be that they were the same age and that she'd just managed to cram more into her life than he had.

"Are you okay?" she asked. "You seem, uh, angry or something."

Great. Now he was worked up over an argument he was having with himself.

"I'm still bull riding," Lucky answered, knowing it wouldn't answer anything she'd just said. "And you're still, well, doing whatever it is you do?"

She nodded, not adding more, maybe because she was confused. But Dixie Mae had filled in some of the blanks. Cassie had gotten her master's degree in psychology and was now a successful therapist and advice columnist. Cassie traveled. Wrote articles. Made regular appearances on TV talk shows whenever a so-called relationship expert was needed.

Bull riding was the one and only thing he'd been good at since adulthood. Ironic since he failed at it 70 percent of the time.

Cassie took a deep breath. The kind of breath a person took when they needed some steeling up. And she got those sensible shoes moving closer to Dixie Mae's coffin. So far, Lucky had kept his distance, but he went up there with Cassie so he could say a final goodbye.

Dixie Mae was dressed in a flamingo-pink sleeveless rhinestone dress complete with matching necklace, earrings and a half foot of bracelets that stretched from her wrists to her elbows. Sparkles and pink didn't exactly scream funeral, but Lucky would have been let down if she'd insisted on being buried in anything else. Or had her hair styled any other way. Definitely a tribute to Dolly Parton.

Too bad the bracelets didn't cover up the tattoo.

"I loved her." Lucky hadn't actually intended for those words to come out of his mouth, but they were the truth. "Hard to believe, I know," he mumbled.

"No. She had some lovable qualities about her." Cassie didn't name any, though.

But Lucky did. "Right after my folks were killed in the car wreck, Dixie Mae was there for me," he went on. "Not motherly, exactly, but she made sure I didn't drink too much or ride a bull that would have killed me."

More of that skeptical look. "Your parents died when you were just nineteen, not long after we graduated from high school. She let you drink when you were still a teenager?"

"She didn't *let* me," Lucky argued. "I just did it, but she always made sure I didn't go overboard with it."

"A drop was already overboard since you were underage," Cassie mumbled.

Lucky gave her one of his own looks. One to remind her that her nickname in school was Miss Prissy Pants Police. She fought back, flinging a Prissy Pants Double Dog Dare look at him to challenge her until Lucky felt as if they'd had an entire fifth-grade squabble without words. He'd be impressed if he wasn't so pissed off.

"You can't tell me you didn't love her, too," he fired back.

At least Cassie didn't jump to disagree with that. She glanced at her grandmother, then him. "I did. I was just surprised you'd so easily admitted that you loved her."

Easy only because it'd dropped straight from his brain to his mouth without going through any filters. That happened with him way too often.

"Men like you often have a hard time saying it," she added.

"Men like me?" Those sounded like fighting words, and he was already worn-out from the nonverbal battle they'd just had. "I guess you're referring to my reputation of being a guy who likes women."

"A guy who sleeps around. A lot." She hadn't needed to add *a lot* to make it a complete zinger.

"Rein in your stereotypes, Doc." While she was doing that, he'd rein in his temper. And he'd do something about that blasted tat.

Lucky grabbed the felt-tip pen from the table next to the visitor's book, and he got to work.

"What are you doing?" Cassie asked.

"Fixing it." Not exactly a professional job, but he made a big smudgy *i* out of the *e* and an *e* out of the *i*.

Cassie leaned in closer. "Huh. I never noticed it was misspelled."

Lucky looked at her as if she'd sprouted an extra nose. "How could you not notice that?"

She shrugged. "I'm not that good at spelling. I mean, who is, what with spell-checkers on phones and computers?"

"I'm good at it," he grumbled. So that made two skills. Spelling and bull riding. At least he succeeded at the spelling more than 30 percent of the time.

Cassie stepped back, looked around the room. "I need to find the funeral director and then call the hospital and find out if Gran left me any instructions. A note or something."

Lucky patted his pocket. "She gave me a letter."

Cassie eyed the spot he'd patted, which meant she'd eyed his butt. "Did she say anything about me in it?"

"I'm not sure. I haven't read it yet." And darn it, the look she gave him was all shrink, one who was assessing his mental health—or lack thereof. "I was going to wait until after the service." Except it was as clear as a gypsy's crystal ball that there wasn't going to be an actual service.

"Well, can you look at it now, just to see if she mentions me?" She sounded as though she was in as much of a hurry as Logan.

Lucky wished he could point out that not everything had to be done in a hurry, bull riding excluded, but he was just procrastinating. Truth was, as long as the letter was unread, it was like having a little part of Dixie Mae around. One last unfinished partnership between them.

He huffed, and since he really didn't want to explain that "little part of Dixie Mae" thought, he took out the letter and opened it. One page, handwritten in Dixie Mae's usual scrawl.

Cassie didn't exactly hover over him, but it was close. She pinned her chocolate-brown eyes to him, no doubt watching for any change in expression so she could use her therapy skills to determine if this was good or bad.

Dear Lucky and Cassie...

That no doubt changed his expression. "The letter's

addressed to both of us." He turned it, showing her the page. "Dixie Mae didn't mention that when she gave it to me at the hospital."

Cassie took it from him, and Lucky let her. Mainly because he really didn't want to read what was there since it hadn't gotten off to such a great start.

"'Dear Lucky and Cassie,'" she repeated. "'I need a favor, one I know neither of you will refuse. I've never asked either of you for anything, but I need to ask you now. Call Bernie Woodland, a lawyer in Spring Hill, and he'll give you all the details.'"

Cassie flipped the letter over, looking for the rest of it, but there was nothing else. "What kind of favor?"

Lucky had to shake his head. He'd figured it had something to do with the rodeo business, but now that Dixie Mae had included Cassie, maybe not. Cassie had never participated in the rodeo, or in her grandmother's finances for that matter.

He was also confused as to why Dixie Mae would have used Bernie for this. Dixie Mae no longer lived in Spring Hill. Hadn't for going on ten years. Her house was in San Antonio, and she had a lawyer on retainer there. Why hadn't she used him instead of Bernie?

"Did she say anything when she gave you the letter?" Cassie asked.

It wasn't hard to recall this part, either. "She said a man wouldn't be much of a man to deny an old dying woman her last wish."

Remembering her words had Lucky feeling another flutter. Not a sexual one like with Cassie, but one that sent an unnerving tingle down his bruised spine and tailbone.

If it had been a simple request, Dixie Mae would

have just told him then and there on her death bed, rather than using her final breath on the bull remark. Instead she'd used the dying card to get him to agree to some unnamed favor, and that meant this could be trouble.

Cassie must have thought so, too, because some of the color drained from her cheeks, and she pulled out her phone again. "I'll call the lawyer."

She stepped away from the coffin. Far away. In fact, Cassie went all the way to the back of the room, and, pacing behind the last row of chairs, she made the call.

Lucky was about to follow and pace right along with her, but his own phone buzzed. Because he was hoping Cassie would soon have some info on the favor, he was ready to let the call go to voice mail, but then he saw the name on the screen.

Angel.

What the hell? He wasn't the sort to believe in ghosts and such, but if anyone could have found a way to reach out from beyond the grave, or the coffin, it would have been Dixie Mae.

Lucky hit the answer button and braced himself in case this was about to turn into a moment that might make him scream like a schoolgirl.

"Lucky," the caller said. It was a woman all right but definitely not Dixie Mae. This voice was sultry, and he was about 60 percent sure he recognized it.

"Bella?" he asked.

"Who else?" she purred.

Well, she hadn't been at the top of the list of people he expected would call themselves Angel, that's for sure. Bella was more like a being from the realm opposite to the one where angels lived. Lucky had met her about three months ago after a good bull ride in Kerrville, but he hadn't seen her since.

"I expected you to call me before now. Naughty boy," Bella teased.

Now, that label fit. They had engaged in some rather naughty things during their one night together. But he'd never intended for it to be anything other than a one-nighter. And Lucky had made that clear, with very specific words—*just this once.*

He glanced back at Cassie. She was still talking on the phone. Or rather listening, because she didn't seem to be saying much at all. Unlike Bella.

"Did you hear me?" Bella asked.

No, he hadn't, but Lucky had his own stuff to ask her. "How'd you get my number? And who's Angel?"

"Angel's my stage name, remember?"

Oh, yeah. Now he did, thanks to her memory jogging. Bella aka Angel Bella was a wannabe actress moonlighting as a cocktail waitress at the Blue Moon Bar.

"When you were asleep, I added my number to your contact list," she explained. "And I put your number in my phone to make sure we stayed in touch. Like now, for instance. I remember you saying you're from Spring Hill, and guess who's passing through town right now?"

Lucky didn't think that was a trick question. "Look, Bella, this isn't a good time. I'm at a friend's funeral."

"Oh." She paused and repeated that "oh" again. "Well, darn. I'd really hoped to see you. Maybe in an hour or two? I could...console you."

He bit back a groan. "Sorry, but I'm just not up to a good consoling."

Especially Bella's version of it. And especially not now. Cassie had started to talk, and though body language could be deceiving, he thought she might be arguing about something.

"I can see you tomorrow, then?" Bella pressed, and even though Lucky couldn't see her face, he sensed she was doing a fake pout thing with her mouth.

Lucky was about to come up with a couple of excuses, but then he saw Cassie slide her phone back into her pocket. She didn't come hurrying to him, though, to tell him about her conversation with Dixie Mae's lawyer. She just stood there, her back to him.

"I gotta go," Lucky said to Bella, and despite the woman's howling protest, he hit the end-call button and made his way to Cassie.

"So what's the favor Dixie Mae wants us to do?" Lucky asked.

Cassie took her time turning around to face him, but she didn't actually look at him. Instead, she tipped her eyes to the ceiling as if seeking divine help.

Then Cassie uttered a single word. A word that Lucky was afraid summed up this mess that Dixie Mae had just dumped on them from the grave.

"Shit."

CHAPTER THREE

CASSIE HATED TO rely on profanity to express herself, but she didn't know what else to say after the conversation she'd just had with Bernie Woodland.

Why in Sam Hill had her grandmother done this?

"Do I want to know what Dixie Mae's lawyer had to say?" Lucky asked.

That was an easy question to answer. "No."

Apparently, though, Lucky wanted her to expand on that a bit. And she would. But first, Cassie had to locate the nearest chair and sit down. Sometime during that conversation with Mr. Woodland, her knees had lost all their cartilage.

Lucky cursed. It was a much worse word than *shit*, and he dropped down in the chair next to her. "Tell me what's wrong."

Cassie nodded, swallowed hard. "There's no need to panic. It's something we can work out, I'm sure."

Though the lawyer seemed to have a different notion about that last part. Still, he was wrong. He had to be.

"What's the favor Dixie Mae wanted us to do for her?" Lucky pressed.

Best just to put it out there and let Lucky work through his own version of panic. Then they could go to Mr. Woodland's office and talk some sense into him.

"Apparently, my grandmother left us custody of some children," Cassie said.

Lucky stared at her. Stared some more. Then he laughed. Not the hysterical laugh of someone panicking, either. He thought this was some kind of joke.

"Custody of some kids?" More laughter from him. It was so hard he appeared to get a stitch in his side because he clamped his hand there for several seconds. "Right. Like I'm daddy material."

Cassie agreed with him on that point. Lucky was about as un-daddy-ish as a man could get. He was more the sort to practice making babies than to tend to them. That was something she hadn't especially wanted to notice about him.

"Never took Dixie Mae for one to pull a prank like this," Lucky added when he finally quit ha-ha-ing.

She hated to say this, but it was something he had to hear. "It's not a prank. Mr. Woodland said Grandmother had him draw up papers, and she signed them the day before she died."

Because Lucky was so close to her, just inches away, Cassie watched that sink in. Slowly. Word by stupid word. It didn't sink in well.

A muscle flickered in his jaw. Then another. It didn't take long for the shock and anger to set in after that.

Lucky snapped to his feet with military precision. "Those darn papers can just be *un*signed. Come on. Let's go to the lawyer and get this straightened out right now."

If he hadn't caught onto her arm and wrenched her from the chair, Cassie might have had trouble getting her legs to work. But Lucky had no such trouble. He lit out of there with her in tow while he fished through his jeans pocket for his keys.

Snug jeans.

That hugged his butt just right.

Cassie was dumbfounded that she'd even noticed something like that. Then again, she always noticed things like that when it came to Lucky. She made a mental note to talk to a therapist about it. Of course, she had plenty of other stuff to bring up considering her grandmother had obviously lost her mind and Cassie hadn't picked up on that until it was too late.

"What kids?" Lucky snapped.

Throughout most of her life, Cassie had gotten accustomed to Lucky giving her heated looks. Or maybe that was just the way he normally looked when his attention landed on a woman. However, that kind of heat was gone now, and in its place was a whole lot of confusion.

"I'm not sure, but according to the lawyer, Grandmother had custody of them for the past several months."

"Impossible. No one in their right mind would give Dixie Mae kids to raise. *Any* kids. What do you know about them? Who are their idiot parents? And why didn't Dixie Mae ever mention anything about them?"

Three good questions. She had fewer good answers. In fact, Cassie had no answers at all.

"Mr. Woodland didn't know. Grandmother didn't give him any details, only that she was transferring guardianship to the two of us. He was going to call us when the children arrived at his office—which should be any minute now."

Just saying the words aloud caused the anxiety to

swell in her chest again. Her nerves were already prickling beneath the surface, what with Dixie Mae's death, and her other *problem*, but the prickling was well on its way to being full-blown panic.

Breathe.

Not that guppy breathing, either. That would cause her to hyperventilate again. Nice, normal, slow breaths. At the end of a few of those, Cassie's head finally began to clear.

"It has to be a misunderstanding," she said more to herself than Lucky, but he latched right on to the idea as if it were a true beacon of hope.

"You're right. And Bernie Woodland will tell us that." Possibly a lie, but she needed a beacon of hope, too.

Lucky practically stuffed her into a sleek red truck and peeled out of the parking lot. Even though she didn't need any proof whatsoever of his bad-boy reputation, she got it right away. He sped down Main Street, violating at least three traffic laws while getting the attention of every single female they passed along the way. Two gave him "call me" hand gestures.

Because Spring Hill was a small town by anyone's standards, it didn't take Lucky long to get to the lawyer's office. Only a couple of minutes. He screeched the truck into one of the tight parking spaces and threw open the door in the same motion that he turned off the engine.

Cassie had to run to catch up with him. Thankfully, that was easy to do since she was wearing her traveling shoes and not her usual heels. She made it in behind him by only a few seconds. During those seconds, though, Lucky had already managed to get the attention of the receptionist, Wilhelmina Larkin.

Wilhelmina was sixty if she was a day but obviously still wasn't immune to Lucky McCord and his crotch-framing jeans. She stood, twirling a coil of her hair around her finger and smiling in a coy way that made it clear she appreciated the view in front of her.

"I need to see Bernie," Lucky insisted. His tone was hard enough, but he returned Wilhelmina's smile as naturally as he drew in his next breath.

"He's busy with a client right now," Wilhelmina said.

The woman actually batted her eyelashes. Good gravy. If Cassie hadn't already had enough to sour her stomach, that would have done it. With the way women threw themselves at Lucky, it could possibly turn out that these children in question might be his offspring after all.

Lucky leaned in, his hands landing on Wilhelmina's desk. "*Un*busy Bernie. We want to talk to him right now. It's important."

Maybe it was because Lucky quit grinning or maybe it was because he no longer sounded like the hot cowboy women drooled over, but either way, Wilhelmina nixed the eyelash batting and actually slid her gaze toward Cassie, apparently noticing her for the first time.

"Oh," Wilhelmina remarked. "This must be about Dixie Mae. What's going on anyway? Bernie wouldn't get into it with me. Dixie Mae's orders, he said. Dixie Mae thought I'd gossip about it. That's what she said to Bernie—that I would gossip about it—so Bernie typed up the paperwork himself. Didn't even know he could type."

Lucky gave her a flat look, and Cassie thought he might repeat his order to see Bernie. He didn't. He stormed passed Wilhelmina, heading up the hall. There were several offices, but Lucky seemed to know exactly which one belonged to Bernie because he opened the door without knocking. Bernie was with someone all right.

Cassie's father.

Mason-Dixon Weatherall.

Cassie stumbled to a stop, her father's and her gazes colliding like two unconnected burglars who'd broken into the same place at the same time. Instant guilt.

Well, guilt on her part anyway.

She'd distanced herself from him years ago because of the way he treated her, and he'd distanced himself from her because of the distancing. Cassie was betting, though, that her father felt no guilt whatsoever about that, what with his my-way-or-the-highway approach to life.

It was the first time she'd seen him in nearly ten years, and her immediate thought—once she got past the question as to why he was there—was that he looked so old. He was still dyeing his hair the color of crude oil, still wearing clothes straight out of the sixties, but there were a lot more wrinkles on his face than there had been during their last meeting.

Her father eased himself to his feet. "Cassie," he greeted.

"Dad," Cassie greeted back with the same caution of those two theoretical burglars.

Lucky volleyed some glances between them. "Does your dad have anything to do with this *shit*?"

"Do you?" Cassie asked her father.

"You'll have to be more specific," he snarled. "I deal with lots of different kinds of shit."

Bernie stood then, tugging off his glasses and dropping them onto the desk. He was about the same age as her father, but it was night and day in the apparel arena. Bernie was wearing conservative clothes similar to hers. Actually, the jacket was identical to hers.

Something that made her frown.

"Mason-Dixon doesn't have anything to do with the letter Dixie Mae left the two of you," Bernie clarified.

"The old bat left you a letter, too?" But her father didn't wait for them to confirm it. "She left me six fucking cats. Six! She arranged to have her driver drop them off at the club this morning. Them, and their litter boxes, which hadn't been cleaned in days. They're going to the pound as soon as I leave here."

"No," Cassie practically shouted, and it got everyone's attention. "Grandmother loved those cats."

Her father's fisted hands went on his boney hips. "Then why the hell did she leave them to me?"

Yet another of those questions that Cassie couldn't answer. Maybe Dixie Mae had indeed gone insane.

"I'll take the cats," Cassie volunteered. "Just give me a couple of days. I've got my own problems to work out." A laundry list of them, and that list just kept growing.

Her father looked at her. Then at Lucky. "Did you knock up Cassie or something?" he asked Lucky.

While Lucky was howling out a loud "no," Cassie fanned her hands toward her clothes. Then toward Lucky's. "Does it look as if we could be lovers?" she asked.

Her father did more glancing and shook his head. "Guess not."

It was yet something else that made her frown. Maybe she needed to start shopping at a different store.

"So, you'll take the cats?" her father clarified.

Cassie nodded but didn't have a blasted clue how she was going to make that happen. Her condo in LA didn't allow pets. Still, the shelter here in Spring Hill probably wasn't no-kill, and she couldn't risk her grandmother's precious cats being put down—even if it had been a lamebrain idea for Dixie Mae to leave her pets to a man who'd been on her bad side since she'd given birth to him.

Her father moved closer and gave her *the look*. The one he'd been giving her since she was a kid. "Just know that I expect something other than cats from Dixie Mae's estate. Whatever she had, I get half."

"I'm pretty sure you won't," Lucky spoke up. "Dixie Mae didn't like you, and she always told me that she had no intention of giving you any money. She wanted her money to go to Cassie."

"Cassie will share," her father insisted. The look intensified, and suddenly she was six years old again and getting sent to her room because she was acting too prissy.

Lucky moved in front of her father, getting right in his face. "I'm thinking that'll be Cassie's decision."

"We'll see about that." Her father started out, then stopped when he was right beside her. "If those cats aren't gone in two days, they're going to the pound. The goddamn things are chewing the feathers in the girls' costumes."

That seemed very minor compared to being given

children, but as Cassie had always done with her father, she held her tongue. And took a few steps away from him. She'd spent her entire adult life trying not to get embroiled with him and his smutty lifestyle, and she didn't want to start now.

Cassie didn't say goodbye to him. She merely shut the door once her father was gone and then whirled around to face Bernie. Now, here was someone she would confront. Except Lucky beat her to it.

"Say it's not true," Lucky demanded. "Tell me that Dixie Mae didn't give us custody of some kids."

Bernie sighed, causing his pudgy belly to jiggle. He pulled open his desk drawer, cracked open a bottle of Glenlivet and downed more than a couple of swigs. "She did indeed leave Cassie and you custody of two children," Bernie confirmed.

Of course, the lawyer had already told her that, but hearing it face-to-face gave Cassie a new wallop of panic. No. This couldn't happen now. She couldn't lose it in front of Lucky. In front of anybody.

Lucky, however, didn't seem to notice that she was cruising her way to a panic attack. He was apparently coping with the anxiety in his own way. By cursing a blue streak in an extremely loud voice.

"How the hell could you let Dixie Mae do something like that?" Lucky yelled. "You should have stopped her."

"Really?" Bernie challenged. "You believe I could have stopped Dixie Mae? Were you ever able to stop her from doing something she insisted on doing?"

"No, but that's beside the point. Dixie Mae and I differed on rodeo stuff. Business. If she'd mentioned giving me custody of some kids, trust me, I would have stopped her."

Judging from the groan that followed, Lucky knew that was a partial lie. He would have indeed *tried* to stop her, but Dixie Mae would have just found a way around it.

The same thing Cassie had to do in this situation.

"Neither Lucky nor I knew that Dixie Mae had anything to do with any children," Cassie started. "When did it happen? *How* did it happen?" she amended.

"I'm not sure of all the details," Bernie answered. "Until Dixie Mae showed up here, it'd been years since I'd seen her. She said she wanted me to do the paperwork because I was local."

Local? Cassie figured there was more to it than that. Maybe Dixie Mae's usual lawyer didn't handle situations like this. Or maybe her grandmother had just tried to be sneaky because her lawyer in San Antonio perhaps would have contacted Cassie to let her know something fishy was going on. And this definitely qualified as fishy.

"Dixie Mae said a couple of months ago an old friend of hers got very sick," Bernie continued. "This friend was taking care of her grandkids and asked Dixie Mae to step in for a while."

All right. There was the out Cassie had been hoping for. "You can contact the grandmother and tell her to resume custody."

Bernie shook his head. "The grandmother died a short time later, and the grandkids' parents aren't in the picture. They're both dead. That's why Dixie Mae took over legal custody."

Lucky shook his head, too. "Well, she must have

hired a nanny or something because Dixie Mae never had any kids with her when she came to work."

"She did have a nanny, a couple of them, in fact," Bernie went on. "But they quit when they butted heads with her so Dixie Mae arranged for someone else to watch them temporarily. She didn't give me a lot of details when she came in and asked me to draw up papers and her will. And right after we finished with it, she got admitted to the hospital."

Cassie latched on to that. "Maybe there's something in her will about Lucky and me being able to relinquish custody to a suitable third party."

Lucky tipped his head in her direction. "What she said. Find it."

But Bernie didn't pull out a will or anything else. "The will didn't address trusteeship of the children, only the disbursement of Dixie Mae's assets. I'm not at liberty to go over that with you now because she insisted her will not be read for several weeks."

Cassie doubted there was a good reason for that. But she could think of a bad reason. "This was probably Grandmother's attempt at carrot dangling. If Lucky and I assume responsibility without putting up a fuss, then we'll inherit some money. Well, I don't want her money, and I'm putting up a fuss!"

"So am I," Lucky agreed. "Fix this."

Bernie looked around, clearly hesitating. "I guess if you refuse, I can have Child Protective Services step in."

All right, they were getting somewhere.

Or maybe not.

"Of course, that's not ideal," Bernie went on. "The children could end up being placed in separate homes, and foster care can be dicey." He scratched his head. "Dixie Mae was so sure you two would agree to this since it was her last wish."

Her grandmother had no doubt told Bernie to make sure he reminded them of that a time or two. Especially after what Dixie Mae had said to Lucky: *A man wouldn't be much of a man to deny an old dying woman her last wish.*

"I smell a rat," Lucky mumbled.

So did Cassie. Dixie Mae had practically duped Lucky into saying yes, and the old gal had figured Cassie wouldn't just walk away, leaving him to hold the bag.

Damn it.

Cassie couldn't just walk away. But that didn't mean she was giving up without a fight. She wasn't in any position to raise children. Especially not with Lucky.

Heck, who was she kidding?

He'd probably be a lot better at it than she would be. At least he wasn't an emotional mess right now and hadn't just checked out of a glorified loony bin. As a therapist she probably should have considered a better term for it, but loony bin fit. Too bad she hadn't had her grandmother there with her so she could have had the chance of talking Dixie Mae into making other arrangements for the children.

"How do we get around this?" Cassie asked Bernie at the same moment Lucky said to him, "Fix this shit. And I don't mean fix it by putting some innocent kids in foster care. Fix it the right way. Find their next of kin. I want them in a home with loving people who know the right way to take care of them."

Good idea. Except Bernie shook his head again. "I

started the search right after Dixie Mae came in. No luck so far, but I'll keep looking. In the meantime, Cassie and you can take temporary custody, and if I can't find any relatives, I'll ask around and see if someone else will take them."

That wasn't ideal, far from it, because "asking around" didn't seem to have a deadline attached to it. "How long would we have them?" she asked.

"A couple of days at most," Bernie said.

Perhaps that was BS, but Cassie latched on to it and looked at Lucky. "Maybe we can figure out something to do with them just for a day or two?"

Oh, he so wanted to say no. She could see it in his eyes. Probably because *he* didn't want to stay anywhere near Spring Hill. It was no secret that Lucky had a serious case of wanderlust. Along with the regular kind of lust.

"Two days is too long," Lucky said, obviously still mulling this over and perhaps looking for an escape route.

Two days, the exact amount of time she had to do something about those feather-chasing cats at the strip club. Cassie tried very hard not to think bad thoughts about her grandmother, but she wished the woman had gone over all these details before she'd passed away.

"You'll need to work out something faster than two days," Lucky insisted. "I've got to be at a rodeo day after tomorrow."

Yes, she had things to do, as well. Things she didn't want to do, but she wouldn't be able to wiggle out of them the way that Lucky was trying to wiggle out of this.

"I can try," Bernie said, not sounding especially

hopeful. Too bad, because Cassie needed him to be hopeful. More than that, she needed him to succeed.

"I'll call the Bluebonnet Inn," Bernie added, "and get the girls a room there."

Lucky seemed to approve of that, but Cassie wasn't so sure. She, too, had planned to stay at the Bluebonnet Inn, mainly because it was the only hotel in Spring Hill. That meant Lucky would likely expect her to be with the children 24/7.

But Cassie wasn't having this all put on her shoulders. Nope. She was packing enough baggage and problems as it was so she'd also get Lucky a room at the inn.

"Where are the children?" Cassie asked.

Bernie checked his watch. "They should be here any minute now." He pushed a button on an old-fashioned intercom system. "Wilhelmina, when the Compton kids arrive—"

"They're already here," Wilhelmina interrupted. "Want me to send them back?"

"Sure." Bernie took his finger off the intercom button and drew in a long breath, as if he might need some extra air.

A moment later, Cassie saw why.

The air sort of vanished when the door opened and Cassie saw one of the children in question. And this time, she wasn't the one to say that one all-encompassing word. It was Lucky.

Shit.

They had apparently inherited custody of a call girl.

CHAPTER FOUR

THERE WERE ONLY a handful of times in Lucky's life when he'd been rendered speechless, and this was one of them.

The "girl" walking up the hall toward him was indeed a *girl*. Technically. She was female, nearly as tall as Cassie, and she was wearing a black skirt and top. Or perhaps that was paint. Hard to tell. The skirt was short and skintight, more suited for, well, someone older.

"This is Mackenzie Compton," Bernie said.

Cassie blew out a breath that sounded like one of relief. Lucky had no idea what she was relieved about so he just stared at her.

"This isn't a child," Cassie explained, relief in her voice, too. "So obviously there's no need for us to take custody."

Right. "What Cassie just said," Lucky told Bernie.

However, Bernie burst that bubble of hope right off. "Mackenzie just turned thirteen."

Maybe ten years ago, she had. But she wasn't thirteen now. "Can she prove that?" Lucky blurted out.

Mackenzie didn't say a word. Didn't have any reaction to that whatsoever. She just stood there looking like a both-arms-down Statue of Liberty who'd been vandalized with black spray paint. She had black hair, black nails, black lipstick and stared at them as if they were beings from another planet. Beings that she didn't want to get to know.

Good. The feeling was mutual.

But thirteen?

"I can prove her age," Bernie supplied. "I have her birth certificate and school records." Bernie handed him a folder. "Her sister, Mia, is four."

Four. Well, hell. Now, that was a child, though he still wasn't convinced Mackenzie was a teenager. Maybe if she scrubbed off that half inch of makeup, there'd be some trace of a girl, but right now he wasn't seeing it.

However, he was seeing something. An extra set of legs. Either Mackenzie had four of them, a pair significantly shorter than the ones wearing that black skirt, or her little sister was hiding behind her.

Mackenzie took one step to the side, and there she was. A child. A real one. No goth clothes for her. She was wearing a pink dress with flowers and butterflies on it, and her blond hair had been braided into pigtails. She had a ragged pink stuffed pig in the crook of her arm.

If there had been a definition of "scared kid" in the dictionary, this kid's photo would have been next to it. Mia was clinging to her sister's skirt, her big blue eyes shiny with tears that looked ready to spill right down her cheeks.

Lucky took a big mental step back at the same time that he took an actual step forward. He didn't have any paternal instincts, none, but he knew a genuinely sad girl when he saw one, and it cut him to the core. He went down on one knee so he could be at her eye level.

"I'm Lucky McCord," he said, hoping to put her at ease. It didn't work. Mia clung even tighter, though there wasn't much fabric in Mackenzie's skirt to cling to.

Mia. Such a little name for such a little girl.

"Do either of them…" Cassie started, looking at Bernie. But then she turned to the girls. "Either of you, uh, talk?"

Mia nodded. Blinked back those tears. Her bottom lip started to quiver.

Well, hell. That did it. Lucky fished through his pocket, located the only thing he could find resembling candy. A stick of gum. And he handed it to Mia. She took it only after looking up at her big sister, who nodded and grunted. What Big Sis didn't do was say a word to confirm that she did indeed have verbal communication skills beyond a primitive grunt.

"The girls have had a tough go of it lately," Bernie said as if choosing his words carefully.

Lucky added another mental *well, hell*. He'd probably said *hell* more times today than he had in the past decade. He'd always believed it was the sign of a weak mind when a man had to rely on constant profanity as a way of communicating his emotions, but his mind was swaying in a weak direction today.

And he didn't know what the hell to do.

"Where have they been staying since my grandmother's death?" Cassie asked. "Gran passed away two days ago."

Good question, but Lucky didn't repeat himself with another *what she said*.

"With Scooter Jenkins," Bernie answered.

Lucky had to do it. He had to think another *hell*.

"You know this man?" Cassie asked him.

"Scooter's a woman." At least Lucky thought she was. She had a five-o'clock shadow, but that was possibly hormonal. "She's one of the rodeo clowns."

Spooky as all get-out, too. While Scooter had worked for Dixie Mae as long as Lucky could remember, she was hardly maternal material. Nor was she exactly Dixie Mae's friend. The only way Scooter would have taken the girls was for Dixie Mae to have paid her a large sum of cash.

"Ten grand," Bernie said as if anticipating Lucky's question. "The deal was for Scooter to keep them until after the funeral and then transfer physical custody to Cassie and you."

Since Scooter was nowhere to be seen, that meant she'd likely just dropped off the kids. Lucky would speak to her about that later. But for now, he needed to fix some things.

Apparently, Cassie had the same fixing-things idea. "Why don't Bernie and I go in his office and discuss some *solutions*?" Cassie said to him. "Maybe you can wait in the lobby with the girls?"

Lucky preferred to be in on that discussion, but it wasn't a discussion he wanted to have in front of Mia. Not with those tears in her eyes.

"Please," Cassie whispered to him. Or at least that's what Lucky thought she said at first. But when she repeated it, he realized she had said, "Breathe."

Oh, man. Cassie looked ready to bolt so maybe her talking to Bernie was a good idea after all. While the two of them were doing that, maybe he'd try to have the kids wait with Wilhelmina so he could join the grown-ups.

Cassie and Bernie went to his office. Cassie shut the door, all the while repeating "Breathe." Lucky went in the direction of the reception area.

Where there was no Wilhelmina.

Just a pair of suitcases sitting on the floor next to her empty desk. But there was a little sign that said I'll Be Back. The clock on the sign was set for a half hour from now. It might as well have been the next millennium.

Mia was holding on to the gum and pig as if they were some kind of lifelines, all the while volleying glances between her sister and him. Since it was possible there'd be some yelling going on in Bernie's office, Lucky motioned for the girls to sit in the reception area.

He sat.

They didn't.

And the moments crawled by. The silence went way past the uncomfortable stage.

Lucky didn't have any idea what to say to them. The only experience he'd had with kids was his soon-to-be nephew, Ethan. He was two and a half, and Lucky's brother Riley was engaged to Ethan's mom, Claire. Too bad Ethan wasn't around now to break the iceberg.

"So, what grade are you in?" he asked, just to be asking something.

Mia held up the four fingers of her left hand—the hand not clutching the gum but rather the one on the pig. Since he doubted she was in the fourth grade, he figured maybe she was communicating her age. So Lucky went with that. He flashed his ten fingers three times and added three more. Of course, she was way too young to get that he was thirty-three, but he thought it might get a smile from her.

It didn't.

He tried Mackenzie next. "Let me guess your favorite color. Uh, blue?" He smiled to let her know it was a joke. The girl's black-painted mouth didn't even quiver.

And the silence rolled on.

Oh, well. At least Bernie had said this so-called custody arrangement would only last a day or two, and they weren't chatter bugs. Mia's tears seemed to have temporarily dried up, too. Plus, Cassie was likely jumping through hoops to do whatever it took for them not to have to leave here with these kids. Lucky was all for that, but he wasn't heartless. He still wanted to leave them in a safe place. Preferably a safe place that didn't involve him.

What the heck had Dixie Mae been thinking?

"Bull," someone said, and for one spooky moment, Lucky thought it was Dixie Mae whispering from beyond the grave.

But it was Mia.

Those little blue eyes had landed on his belt buckle, and there was indeed a bull and bull rider embossed into the shiny silver. Lucky had lots of buckles—easy for that to happen when you rode as long as he'd been riding—but he had two criteria for the ones he wore. Big and shiny. This was the biggest and shiniest of the bunch.

"Yep, it's a bull," Lucky verified.

Mia didn't come closer, but she did lean out from sour-faced Big Sis for a better look.

"I ride bulls just like that one." He tapped the buckle, and hoped that wasn't too abstract for a four-year-old. Of course, she had clearly recognized it as a bull, so maybe she got it.

And the silence returned.

"So, what was it like staying with Scooter?" he asked.

That got a reaction from Mackenzie. She huffed. Not exactly a sudden bout of chatter, but Lucky understood her completely. What he didn't understand was why Dixie Mae had left them with Scooter in the first place. But then, there were a lot of things he didn't understand about Dixie Mae right now.

"How about you?" he asked Mia. "Did you like staying with Scooter?"

She pinched her nose, effectively communicating that Scooter often smelled. Often kept on her clown makeup even when she wasn't working. The only thing marginally good he could say about the woman was that her visible tattoos weren't misspelled.

"Do we gotta go back with Scooter?" Mia asked.

Lucky wasn't sure who was more surprised by the outburst of actual words—Mackenzie or him. It took him a second to get past the shock of the sound of Mia's voice and respond.

"Do you want to go back with her?" he asked.

"No." Mackenzie that time. Mia mumbled her own "No." Judging from the really fast response from both girls, and that it was the only syllable he'd gotten from Mackenzie, he'd hit a nerve.

A nerve that affected his next question. "So, where do you want to go?"

Now, this would have been the time for both girls to start firing off answers. With friends, relatives, rock stars. To a goth store, et cetera. He got a shrug from Mia and a glare from Mackenzie.

What had he expected? Bernie had already told him their parents were out of the picture. Orphans. Something that Lucky more than understood, but he'd been nineteen when his folks died. Barely an adult, but that had *barely* prevented him from having to stay with a clown.

Though there were a couple of times when Lucky had called Logan just that.

More silence. If this went on, he might just take a nap. Lucky went with a different approach, though. "Is there a question you want to ask me?"

Mia looked up at her sister, and even though Mackenzie's mouth barely moved, Lucky thought he saw the hint of a smile. The kind of smile that had some stink eye on it.

"Have you ever been arrested?" Mackenzie asked. Yeah, definitely some stink eye. "Because Scooter said you had been."

"I have," he admitted. "Nothing major, though, and I never spent more than a few hours in jail."

Except that one time when there'd been a female deputy who'd come on to him. But that time he'd stayed longer by choice. Best not to mention that, though. In fact, there was a lot about his life he wouldn't mention.

"What'd you get 'rrested for?" Mia asked.

Lucky smiled, not just at the pronunciation but the cute voice. Cute kid, too.

"Drinking beer." Like Bernie had earlier, Lucky chose his words wisely. At any rate, beer or some other alcohol had usually been at the root of his bad behavior.

Mackenzie made a *hmmp* sound as if she didn't be-

lieve him. Lucky didn't elaborate even though there
was no telling what Scooter had told them.

"Don't drink beer," Mia advised him in a serious
tone that made him have to fight back another smile.

The little girl came closer, leaving her sister's side
and not even looking up for permission. She climbed
into the seat next to him, tore the gum stick in half and
gave him the bigger of the two pieces.

"Thanks," Lucky managed to say.

Mia then offered half of her half to her sister, but
Mackenzie only shook her head, grunted and deepened her scowl. Much more of that and she was going
to get a face cramp.

"Is Lucky even your real name?" Mackenzie again.
"Because if it is, it's a stupid name."

Such a cheery girl. "It's a nickname. My real name's
Austin, but nobody ever calls me that."

Heck, most people didn't even know it.

"My grandpa McCord gave me the name when I
was just three years old," he explained. "I somehow
managed to get into the corral with a mean bull. And
despite the fact I was waving a red shirt at him so I
could play matador, I came out without a scratch."

Lucky, indeed. His grandpa could have just called
him stupid considering the idiotic thing he'd done.

"What about the lady doctor?" Mackenzie asked,
clearly not impressed with his story. She folded her
arms over her chest. "Has she been arrested, too?"

"Can't say," Lucky answered honestly. "But I doubt
it." Though something was going on with Cassie.
Those *breathe* mumblings weren't a good sign.

"Is she gay?" Mackenzie continued.

"No," he said, way too loud and way too fast. He paused. "Why do you ask?"

"Her shoes and clothes," Mackenzie quickly supplied.

Lucky groaned. "It's never a good idea to stereotype people." That was the second time today he'd given such a warning, though Mackenzie probably didn't have a clue what that word meant. She didn't seem the sort to work on building her vocabulary.

He cursed himself. Huffed. He needed to take his own advice. Yeah, stereotypes weren't a good idea.

"Are you two together, then?" Mackenzie asked. "The lady doctor and you?" she clarified, though her question needed no such clarification.

Lucky almost preferred the silence to this. "No. I was business partners with Cassie's grandmother, Dixie Mae, and Cassie and I went to high school together."

"I know who her grandmother is," Mackenzie snapped. *"Was,"* she added, also in a snap. She didn't offer more on the subject of Dixie Mae, but since Mackenzie didn't complain about her, maybe that meant she'd gotten along with the woman.

That would be a first, but hey, miracles happened. Lucky had found a way to love the woman so maybe Mackenzie and Mia had, too. Or rather just Mia, he amended when Mackenzie's scowl deepened.

"I just thought you and the lady doctor were..." Mackenzie said, but she waved it off. "It was just something Dixie Mae said."

That got his attention. "What'd she say? Specifically what'd she say about Cassie and me? Because if this is Dixie Mae's way of matchmaking from the grave—"

He stopped. Wished he hadn't said it because of the look it put on Mia's face. Little name, little girl. Whopping big ears. She'd already been shuffled around too much, and she didn't need to hear that she might go through another shuffling all because Dixie Mae wanted her granddaughter and her "boy" to end up together.

Something that wouldn't happen.

Cassie had already made that plenty clear.

"We need to get one thing straight," Mackenzie continued a couple of seconds later. "If you hurt my sister, I'll punch you and the lady doctor right in your faces."

"Kenzie doesn't mean it," Mia whispered behind her hand. She unwrapped her piece of gum, tore it in half again. One piece she put in her mouth. The other, in her pocket.

"I do mean it," Mackenzie insisted. "Nobody hurts my sister. *Nobody.*"

"I understand. I've got a kid sister of my own. Her name is Anna." Because he thought it might give them some common ground, he started to tell her about Anna, that she was a college student in Florida, that he'd walk through fire for her. But Lucky stopped.

And he silently said another *hell.*

Had someone hurt Mia before? Was that why Mackenzie had doled out that threat? And for the record, he did think she meant it.

Mackenzie clammed up again, and even though he looked at Mia to see how she was dealing with all of this, she was swinging her legs, humming to herself and rolling the silver foil from her gum into a little ball. Lucky would have pressed Mackenzie for more info, or rather *any* info, but he heard the footsteps coming up the hall.

Finally.

He stood, moving in front of the girls in case Cassie and Bernie had to tell him something that wasn't meant for those big ears. But selective muteness must have been catching because Bernie sure wasn't talking, and Cassie dodged his gaze.

"Well?" Lucky finally prompted in a whisper. Probably not a soft enough one because Mackenzie and Mia weren't doing any gaze-dodging at all. They had their baby blues pinned to him.

"We reached a solution," Cassie said.

"Good?" And, yes, it was a question. One they didn't answer. "All right, where are they going?"

Bernie and Cassie exchanged uneasy glances. "Home," Bernie answered, looking right at Lucky. "With you."

CHAPTER FIVE

"HOME, WITH ME?" Lucky said.

All in all, Lucky took the news about as well as Cassie had expected. He added, "No." And he kept on adding to that no. "It's crazy there now what with Riley and Claire's wedding coming up. They're getting married in the house."

She knew Riley and Claire, of course. Had even heard about Riley leaving the Air Force and getting engaged to Claire. But Cassie hadn't known about the wedding planning. Still, their options were limited here.

"It'll only be for a day or two," Cassie reminded him. She also tried to keep her voice at a whisper, but there wasn't much distance between them and the kids. It didn't help that Mackenzie was glaring at her.

"You don't know that," Lucky argued. "*He* doesn't know that." He flung an accusing finger at Bernie. "I'll get us all rooms in the Bluebonnet Inn—"

"I've already tried," Cassie explained, "and they're all booked for the high school reunion, class of 1948." Some might cancel because they weren't spring chickens and might not be able to make it, but Cassie couldn't count on that.

"We can all go to Dixie Mae's house in San Antonio, then," Lucky suggested.

Cassie really hated to be the bearer of more bad news. "She's already sold it. The new owners apparently closed on it earlier today."

"When did Dixie Mae arrange that?" he snapped.

Cassie had to shrug. Apparently, her grandmother had been up to a lot of things that Cassie and Lucky hadn't known about, but from what she could gather, these buyers had agreed to purchase the place months ago and had already done all the paperwork in advance.

Lucky stayed quiet a moment, but the quietness didn't extend to his eyes. There was a lot going on in his head right now, including perhaps a big dose of panic. "Another hotel, then. Or are you going to tell me every hotel in the state is booked?"

"Told you they wouldn't want us," Mackenzie mumbled.

Good grief. This was exactly what Cassie was trying to avoid so she took hold of Lucky's arm to pull him down the hall. "Watch the girls," she told Bernie.

Lucky didn't exactly cooperate with the moving-away-from-them part. "That's not true," he told Mackenzie, surprising Cassie, Mackenzie, maybe even himself. "This isn't about wanting or not wanting you. It's about, well, some other stuff that has nothing to do with you and Mia."

Cassie tugged his arm again, and this time she managed to move him up the hall and hopefully out of earshot. "All right, what's the real problem here?" Cassie demanded. "I mean, other than you don't want to be home, and this would require you to be. Is it because I'd be there, too?"

He looked at her as if she'd just spontaneously sprouted a full beard on the spot. "What?"

Since that question could cover a multitude of things, Cassie went with the one most obvious to her. "I've resisted your advances for years, and you hate me. Now you don't want me anywhere around you."

More of the sprouted-full-beard look. "I don't hate you, and you might not have noticed, but I quit *advancing* on you a long time ago."

Ouch. Well, that stung, a lot more than it should have. And it was stupid to feel even marginally disappointed. But there had been something about Lucky's attention that had made her feel attractive, especially in those days when no other guy was looking her way.

"I don't hate those kids, either," Lucky went on. "In fact, the little one's a sweet girl." He paused, not exactly hemming and hawing, but it was close.

"Is it because there aren't enough rooms in your house?" Cassie asked. "Because it looks huge to me."

"It is huge, and there are plenty of rooms. That's not the point." But it still took Lucky a while to get to what the point was exactly. "Logan's at the house," he finally said. "His loft apartment in town's being renovated so he'll be staying there until it's finished. Heck, he's probably there right now."

She waited, hoping for more of an explanation. Cassie had to wait several long moments.

"Logan and I don't exactly get along," he admitted.

"Okay. That's a valid argument. I understand not getting along with relatives." Mercy, did she. "But there are advantages to being here in Spring Hill, since it's where Bernie is. We could be right in his face every day to make sure he's doing everything he can to resolve this."

Lucky kept staring at her. Then he turned the tables on her. "What's really going on here with you?"

Perhaps all those years of seducing women and being seduced by them had honed his perception. Or maybe he had ESP. This definitely wasn't something she wanted the girls to hear so she pulled Lucky back into Bernie's office.

"Dixie Mae told Bernie that she thought Mackenzie might be suicidal." Cassie didn't add more. Didn't want to add more. She especially didn't want Lucky or anyone else to see that just saying those words felt as if someone had clamped on to her heart with a meaty fist and wouldn't let go.

Breathe.

"If she's suicidal, why isn't she in a hospital or someplace where she can get help?" he asked.

"Because she doesn't have an official diagnosis. That was only Dixie Mae's opinion. I've asked Bernie to try to get Mackenzie's medical records, but that'll take a while. By then we should have found their next of kin or made other arrangements." God, she hoped so anyway.

"There's something you're not telling me," he pressed.

Yes. Something she wouldn't tell him, either. Cassie somehow had to get past this so she could try to work out things in her head. If that was even possible.

"I just don't want Mackenzie to slip through the cracks," Cassie added. That was true, but it had nothing to do with what she was holding back. "No matter how she dresses or how she acts."

Though the dressing part did push Cassie's buttons. Again, old baggage, because it reminded her of her trashy-dressing mother.

"Agreed," Lucky said right away. "But stating the obvious here, I don't know squat about kids. Much less ones who might or might not be suicidal."

Cassie knew more about the suicidal part than she wanted to admit. "If you have another option about where to take them, I'm listening."

Lucky had no doubt already gone through the options, and it wouldn't have taken him that long. Because other options didn't exist. With no next of kin, that left foster care, and while it could be a good thing for some kids, it could spell disaster for someone like Mackenzie, especially if she got placed in a separate home from her sister. Worse, once Cassie signed over the temporary custody, she wouldn't even have any legal right to check on the girls and make sure they were in good homes.

The muscles in Lucky's jaw started stirring. "And you really think it'll only be a day or two at most?"

"I sure hope so. You're not the only one who'd rather not be here."

His eyes met hers, and she halfway expected him to ask if he was part of the reason she didn't want to be there.

He was.

Lucky had a way of stirring things inside her that shouldn't be stirred. Along with heating parts of her that should remain at room temperature. She had enough bears chasing her without adding Lucky Mc-Cord to the furry mix. But adding him was something she was apparently going to have to do.

At least for this guardianship facet of her life anyway. No heating or stirring allowed.

"With the Bluebonnet Inn booked, I don't have a
place to stay," Cassie added. "And I need some office
space. I have a client I have to see. It can't wait, and
she'll be flying in to San Antonio in the morning. I can
have her come to the house, or I can leave you with the
girls while I go to San Antonio and meet—"

"You're not leaving me with the girls. Especially
when one might be suicidal. You can have your meeting at the house. There are two offices. My brother Riley's been using one, but the other one should be free."

"Thanks." Of course, office space was really only a
minor part of this. "You'll need to keep the girls away
from this particular client."

That put some concern on his face. "What kind of
client is this?"

"The worst kind. A person who's a celebrity only
because she's a celebrity."

Lucky really didn't show any interest in this client anyway, but he probably would when she arrived
tomorrow.

"Other than being with this client, you're not to let
Mackenzie out of your sight. Agreed?" Lucky pressed.

"Agreed. Well, except that I'd like to go back over
to the funeral home and say a proper goodbye to my
grandmother."

Certainly, he couldn't deny her that. Even though
he looked as if he would do anything to avoid being
alone with the girls.

"All right," he finally said.

"I also left my rental car there," she added. "My
suitcase is in it."

"I can have one of the ranch hands pick it up if you need it before you can make it back over to the funeral home."

So, they had worked out the immediate details, but maybe this pact wouldn't have to last long. And there were some things she could do to make sure it didn't. Like hiring some private detectives to speed up the hunt for the girls' next of kin.

"I'll call ahead to the housekeepers and tell them to get a couple of guest rooms ready. I'll also need to get another vehicle since my truck won't hold all four of us. And I need to cancel out of the rodeo I'm supposed to be leaving for in the morning." He reached for his phone but stopped when they heard the voice.

"Uh, we got a problem," Bernie called out.

"What now?" Lucky grumbled, and he hurried toward the reception area with Cassie right behind him.

Bernie wasn't in the hall where they'd left him. He was at the front door of his office, and he had a thunderstruck look on his face.

"The girls are gone," he said.

"HURRY UP," Mackenzie told her sister.

But Mia didn't listen. She was poking along, looking back over her shoulder at the lawyer's office. "Lucky was nice," Mia insisted.

Sometimes, her sister could be so dumb. "It's an act," Mackenzie said. "He's only being nice because he has to be, because he wants to get money or something."

"How'd he get money or something?" Mia asked instead of hurrying.

Mackenzie ignored her. It wouldn't be long now

before the lawyer looked out and spotted them. Well, it wouldn't be long if he ever managed to finish that text he'd been pecking out on his phone. Sheez. Old people and their fat, slow fingers!

"How'd Lucky get money or something?" Mia repeated, and since she probably wouldn't shut up—or hurry—until she got an answer, Mackenzie ducked into an alley with her so they'd be off the sidewalk.

"Dixie Mae had money, stupid. Lucky and the lady doctor will probably get it if they have us. People leave that sort of stuff in wills."

She nearly said *shit* instead of *stuff*, but Dixie Mae had said it wasn't a good idea to cuss in front of little kids, that it could make them get into trouble. Dixie Mae had said that it happened to her. Since Mia was a little kid, Mackenzie had tried to cut back just in case Dixie Mae was right.

"I'm not stupid," Mia protested.

Great. Now she was about to bawl again. "I didn't mean it. Just quit asking so many questions and keep walking. Your feet don't move fast when you keep saying things."

"Where we going?" Mia asked less than two seconds later.

"Away from here. We're not staying where we're not wanted."

Of course, they hadn't been wanted in a long time, not since their grandmother had gone to heaven—and Mackenzie was sure that's where she'd gone. Maybe Dixie Mae had, too, but maybe it was a different part of heaven from where Granny Maggie had gone because Dixie Mae probably wouldn't like living with angels, nice people and shit. Plus, she wouldn't be able to smoke up there and cuss.

Mackenzie led Mia to the other end of the alley and was about to cross the street when she spotted the Spring Hill Police Department. She definitely didn't want to go in that direction, and if the lawyer had finally finished that text, he might have noticed they were missing. He could have already called the cops.

Or maybe he wouldn't call anybody at all.

Those three beep-heads—that wasn't the name Mackenzie really wanted to call them, but she was trying to think with less cussing, too—anyway, maybe the three would be glad Mia and she were gone so they wouldn't have to upset their pretty little lives.

Mackenzie waited a sec to make sure the police weren't going to come storming out of the building. No storming so far, though. But just in case that happened, she took Mia up the street and to the right, away from the police department.

She'd paid attention when Scooter had driven them in from San Antonio to Spring Hill, and there was a bus station just on the edge of town. If they could get there, she had enough money for two bus tickets to San Antonio. From there they could get to Dixie Mac's house. As big as the place was, they could hide out there until Mackenzie could come up with something better. With the cash she had stuffed in her shoe, they could get by for maybe a whole week as long as they ate just French fries.

They passed in front of the grocery store, and Mackenzie tried to keep her head down, tried not to get noticed. But people noticed all right. Probably because of her clothes. Nobody dressed like her in this hick town.

Too bad she hadn't had anything else to put on. All her clothes were black.

Just ahead, Mackenzie spotted something that balled up her stomach. A cop wearing a blue uniform. And he had a gun. Jail might be better than going with Lucky and the doctor, but being locked up would probably just make Mia cry. A lot of things made her cry.

Mackenzie turned around, took a side street and tried to remember how to get to the bus station. She didn't dare stop and ask, but maybe there was a map or sign or something.

"Looking for somebody?" a man asked from behind them.

"Just walking," Mackenzie answered without even looking back at him. But he was walking now, too, and it didn't take him long to catch up with them.

Her heart jumped so high she felt it in her throat.

Because it was Lucky.

Except he'd changed clothes real fast because he was wearing a suit jacket, and he didn't have on that big rodeo buckle that had caught Mia's eye. And he was standing in front of a big building. Probably once it'd been somebody's house because it sort of looked like Dixie Mae's place, but this one had a sign on the front of it.

McCord Cattle Brokers.

Mackenzie didn't know what a cattle broker was, but McCord was Lucky's last name. Maybe it meant he owned the place.

Mackenzie thought about taking off running, but he looked fast. A lot faster than Mia would be anyway. Mackenzie could get away on her own, but there was no way she'd leave her little sister behind.

"Are you ladies, uh, girls, lost?" he asked as if he didn't even know them.

Mia looked at Mackenzie, probably for her to explain this. Maybe Lucky had got hit on the head or something and had amnesia, like what happened on the TV show that Dixie Mae watched.

"We were just headed to the bus station to meet one of our friends," Mackenzie explained.

"What happened to the bull?" Mia asked before Mackenzie had even finished the lie.

"What bull?" Lucky asked.

Yeah, amnesia all right. Or maybe he could just be pretending that he didn't know them so he wouldn't have to take them. Grown-ups played all kinds of stupid games to get out of doing things they didn't want to do.

"The shiny bull that looks like this." Mia opened her hand and showed him the silver ball she'd made from the gum wrapper.

Lucky got a funny look on his face. He also glanced around before he tipped his head to the big building. "Why don't you come in, and I'll draw you a map to show you how to get to the bus station."

Mackenzie didn't like the sound of that at all. She'd met Lucky, but he was still a stranger, and if he got her into the house, he might call the police. Or try to do something even worse.

She stepped in front of Mia. "I already told you I'll bust your face if you try to hurt my sister."

Lucky held up his hands. "Wouldn't dream of it." He mumbled something Mackenzie didn't catch. "Let me guess—you two know my twin brother, Lucky?"

Twin? Mackenzie eyed him, trying to figure out if

that was true, but she didn't have time to decide because someone called out her name.

The lady doctor.

She was running toward them, and she wasn't alone. Lucky was with her. At least it was a guy wearing a shiny bull buckle. Maybe there were three of these men who looked alike.

"Why did you run off like that?" the lady doctor asked at the same time Lucky asked, "What the heck were you thinking?" Both seemed to be aiming those questions at Mackenzie.

"So, you do know my twin brother, Lucky," the other man grumbled. "Please tell me you have this, *whatever this is*, under control," he said to Lucky.

"No, I clearly don't." Lucky knelt down in front of Mia. "Are you okay?"

Mia smiled and handed him the silver ball. It was just a gum wrapper, but it also made him smile. People usually smiled around Mia. But Lucky didn't give Mackenzie a smile when he stood back up. Didn't give his twin one, either.

"Remember that letter Dixie Mae gave me?" Lucky said to him. He didn't wait for an answer. "Well, Cassie and I need to take these girls for a day or two."

"Cassie," the twin said in the same friendly way some people said hello. He didn't look angry at her, only at Lucky.

"We need to take them to your house," Cassie explained. "But they slipped out of Bernie's office while we were trying to make arrangements to get them there."

The twin glanced at all of them, like he was the boss or something. Even the boss of Lucky. He pulled

Lucky aside, the way the lady doctor had at the law-yer's office.

"Are these your kids?" the twin whispered to Lucky. He probably thought he was saying it soft enough, but Mackenzie had good ears.

"We're not," Mackenzie told the question-asking twin.

But Mia must have heard it, too. "Our daddy and mommy die-did," Mia said.

"Died," Mackenzie corrected. She huffed.

The twin had actually thought they were Lucky's? No way. Of course, Lucky seemed to feel the same about them. In addition to her good ears, Mackenzie had also learned to pick up on that kind of stuff.

The boss twin studied them a few seconds longer as if trying to decide if that was true or not. Then he finally tipped his head to a fancy silver car next to the fancy building. He took some keys from his pocket and handed them to Lucky.

"Use my car," the twin told him. "I'll have some-body drop me off at home later. Good to see you again, Cassie. I'm sorry for your loss."

Lucky made an I'm-watching-you gesture with his fingers, pointing to his eyes first, then aiming those pointed fingers at Mackenzie. He stooped down when he made eye contact with Mia.

"Will you promise me you won't run off again?" he asked her.

Mia nodded. Smiled, even. "Yes, I promise."

Lucky turned to Mackenzie next. "And now I need that same promise from you."

She hated having to do what anyone said, but she

wasn't in a good position here. Not with these two staring at her.

"Say it, Kenzie," Mia pressed, giving her skirt a tug.

So Mackenzie did because she knew if she didn't that Mia would just keep at it. "I won't run."

It wasn't a lie. Next time she wouldn't run. Mackenzie would somehow get a ride to the bus station or else just walk. But first chance she got, she was getting Mia and herself out of there.

CHAPTER SIX

THREE CARS AND four trucks. That's how many vehicles Lucky spotted in the large circular drive that fronted the ranch and house. Obviously, he was not going to be able to make a quiet entrance with Cassie and the girls.

"It's really big," Mia said, looking up at the place as Lucky drove closer.

Yeah, it was. Too big. Or at least it had been after his folks died and after both Anna and Riley had moved away. Of course, Lucky had moved even before that, and despite the pretty exterior, he didn't see a home, not anymore. It was just a house where he used to live with his family.

Oh, man.

He tried to push all that back down into the pit of his stomach. It would churn there, but it was better than dealing with it now. Especially when he had a crap-load of other stuff to deal with.

"You told them we were coming?" Cassie asked.

Her nerves were showing. Her mouth was tight. She was gripping her purse. Of course, the nerves likely had more to do with all the things ahead of her rather than walking into what appeared to be some kind of gathering. Things like him. Dealing with Dixie Mae's death. Their temporary custody of these kids.

But especially him.

Cassie had always had this oil/water thing when it came to him, and she wasn't going to like being under the same roof. Lucky wasn't going to like it much, either, not because she was under the same roof with him, but because he was under this roof, period.

"I told the housekeeper Della we were coming," Lucky answered.

Della and her sister, Stella, had started working for his family when Lucky was just a kid, and the pair would make sure those guest rooms were ready. Lucky just hoped that the rooms wouldn't be needed that long. Two nights max. He didn't want this drawn out. Mia and the Runaway Goth Girl had been jacked around enough and needed some place permanent to stay, and this definitely didn't qualify as permanent.

From the looks of it, Cassie had been jacked around, too.

"As soon as you're settled into your room," Cassie said to the girls, "we can talk. Would that be okay?"

Of course, Mia nodded right away. Mackenzie was practicing her "I suck lemons frequently" face. The thick makeup helped with that because it appeared to be cracking in places like meringue on a pie. It was amazing she'd perfected both the expression and the art of pancake makeup at such a young age.

"We gonna talk about Miss Dixie Mae?" Mia asked.

Cassie seemed a little surprised by that. "Would you like to talk about her?"

"Sure. I miss her. She was sparkly."

Yeah, she was, and it only reminded Lucky that he had something else on his plate: grieving for Dixie Mae. He'd planned on having a date with some hundred-proof by now to help ease his pain, but booze would apparently have to wait. Although he might need a shot to get through this next hour.

"Dixie Mae die-did," Mia said, sounding as sad about that as Lucky felt.

"Yes, she did," Cassie confirmed. Heck, she sounded sad, as well. Lucky hoped they didn't start crying, or there'd be several sets of wet eyes in the car. Mackenzie's wouldn't be one of them, he was betting. But his sure would be.

"What about you, Mackenzie?" Cassie asked. "Do you miss Dixie Mae?"

The look on her face intensified to "I suck lemons, and limes, too."

"She misses her," Mia said. "She just doesn't like to say it."

Wise words from such a little one. Too bad this package deal hadn't included only Mia because Lucky wouldn't have minded spending a day or two with her.

Okay, and maybe Cassie, as well.

That blasted attraction was still there, and he was positive now that it wasn't just gas. Too bad. Because attractions like that usually got him in trouble.

"Lady Doctor?" Mia said, reaching up to tug on Cassie's sleeve. "Will you be staying with us?"

"Yes. And call me Cassie." She stopped. "Or maybe Miss Cassie. All right, just Cassie."

It wasn't a good sign that she still seemed to be waffling about what the girls should call her considering they had some whopper obstacles in front of them. Like finding the girls' next of kin. And getting enough washcloths to remove all that makeup from Mackenzie's face.

He parked Logan's car right in front of the house.

Like Logan, the Jag had too many bells and whistles, and it took Lucky several minutes—yes, minutes— to figure out how to pop the trunk to get to the luggage. However, before he could even step from the car, the front door of the house opened, and Della and Stella came out. Judging from the gleeful looks on their weathered faces, they were excited about the possibility of kids staying with them. Or maybe they were just excited about the possibility of Lucky being responsible for the kids.

Responsible for anything, for that matter.

"Cassandra Weatherall," Della greeted, pulling Cassie into a hug. "You haven't changed a drop. Well, except you're dressing more comfortably these days. Nothing wrong with that."

Cassie frowned when she looked down at her skirt and shoes. Something she'd done several times in the past hour. Of course, her clothes were catwalk-ready compared to Mackenzie's.

"I was so sorry to hear of your grandmother's passing," Della added to Cassie. "Dixie Mae always did treat Lucky all right, so that made her all right in my book, too."

"Thank you." And Cassie repeated the process when Stella hugged her and offered her own condolences.

Lucky hadn't been aware that the housekeepers would even remember Cassie since to the best of his knowledge, Cassie had never been to the house. Still, it was Spring Hill, where everybody knew everybody.

Along with everybody's business.

By now, what had happened would be all over town—along with some embellishments to the gossip. Lucky didn't care about that gossip when it came to himself, but he doubted Cassie would appreciate it, what with her status as a celebrity therapist.

"It's about time you came home," Della said, looking at him.

That was the only scolding he got because Della turned her attention to the car's back door when it opened. She gave a big, welcoming smile when Mia stepped out. As did Stella. He could practically see the fantasy they were weaving in their heads about him, Cassie and the cute kid.

Then Mackenzie stepped out.

Della and Stella actually dropped back a little, and just as fast as their mental fantasy had come, it went. Good thing. Lucky didn't want anybody playing matchmaker here, and Della and Stella were prone to that since they often said he didn't choose wisely when it came to female companionship. Which he didn't. And he intended to keep on choosing unwisely.

"Uh, I thought you were getting sisters," Stella said. "Children sisters," she clarified.

"They are children," he assured her. He still intended to check Mackenzie's birth certificate, though. "This is Mia Compton," Lucky said pointing to her. "And that's her sister, Mackenzie. This is Miss Della and Miss Stella. They pretty much run the place." Something they managed to do even when Logan was there.

Della recovered from the shock before Stella did, and she managed an inkling of the smile that she'd had before her eyeballs had been widened by Mackenzie's appearance. "Well, welcome to the McCord Ranch. I hope you feel right at home here." She extended that to Cassie.

Then to Lucky.

It was a nice chain-yanking kind of reminder that he should come home more often. Lucky expected to hear that a lot in the next twenty-four hours. He grumbled that he wasn't very pleased about it, but then because he knew it would make her smile, he winked at her. It worked. Stella smiled, then giggled.

"What's with all the vehicles?" Lucky asked, hauling out the girls' suitcases.

"Wedding stuff. Claire, Riley, Ethan and Livvy are here. Plus, Riley's having a meeting with the horse trainers in the office. Oh, and there are two fellas from a magazine, and they're taking some pictures and talking to Riley about an article they're doing on Logan."

The latter seemed to be a monthly occurrence, but maybe the other things were temporary. In other words, maybe they'd all be leaving soon.

"Riley is Lucky's brother," Della went on, talking to the girls now. "He's marrying Claire, and Ethan's her little boy. Claire's a wedding photographer."

Mackenzie showed no interest whatsoever, but Mia seemed to hold on to every word.

"She's got a little boy?" Mia asked.

Della nodded, tapped Mia's nose. "Cute as a button, just like you."

"Right," Mackenzie grumbled. "Because all buttons are sooooo cute."

Since that sounded like something Lucky would have said twenty years ago, he tried not to laugh.

"Oh, and Livvy's here," Della added. She glanced at Cassie. "She's Claire's business partner."

Livvy was also one of Lucky's ex-lovers, and with the side glance that Cassie gave him, it seemed she'd already picked up on that. Then again, she would probably give him a side glance because she thought he'd slept with every woman in town but her. He hadn't, but that particular gossip thread had been exaggerated at lot.

"Are they nice ladies?" Mia whispered to Lucky.

"Very nice. But they might make you eat vegetables. Is that okay?"

Mia gave it some serious thought. Nodded. But it garnered some disapproval from Big Sis. "She doesn't have to eat anything she doesn't want to eat," Mackenzie declared like gospel. "And I don't want her compared to a stupid button."

Lucky had no idea how he was supposed to respond to that, but *sounds good to me* probably wasn't the way to go here. Even though that had been his philosophy about life for a while now. Don't eat anything you don't want to eat. Don't do anything you don't want to do.

Don't be like his brothers.

It kept things simple and meshed with his smart-ass outlook on life.

Lucky braced himself for the chaos he was sure to find inside. Good thing because there was indeed chaos. The moment he stepped in, Ethan zoomed past him, running so fast that he was practically a blur, and it took Lucky a moment to realize the toddler was chasing a cat. Judging from the looks of it, it was the same cat Lucky had given him three months ago. It had grown almost as much as Ethan.

He saw Livvy next. She was teetering in needle-thin heels on a stepladder. She was as skinny as a zipper except for those massive boobs. Today, her hair was turtle green with tiny gold star decorations scattered over her head. Most women couldn't have pulled off the look, but Livvy had the personality to pull off anything. Including his clothes.

Something that wouldn't happen again, of course.

Now that Riley and Claire were getting married, it seemed too risky to sleep with a woman so close to his brother's wife. A two-night stand was one thing, but a long relationship had a hundred percent chance of failing, and Lucky didn't want any bad blood lingering around that he'd have to face every time he came back to town.

It took Lucky a couple of seconds to spot Claire. She was holding some kind of chart-looking thing while studying the layout of the living room furniture. "I think we're going to have to move everything out of this room."

Livvy made a sound of agreement, went up another step on that ladder and clicked off some pictures with her camera phone. But there was another guy there, too, taking pictures—of Riley and one of the horse trainers—and he had a real camera, not just his phone. The man chatting with them had to be a reporter.

"Well, looky who's here," Livvy called out. "Lucky McCord, you look good enough to—"

But she froze when she saw Cassie. Maybe because Livvy thought they were together. Or maybe she stopped because of the girls. In any case, it probably wasn't a good idea for Livvy to finish saying what she thought he looked good enough to do.

"Lucky!" Claire squealed when she saw him. She hurried to him, waving her hands in the air until she reached him, and then she hugged him. "Welcome home."

Leave it to Claire to make it feel as if that welcome were marginally true. Riley was getting one in a million with Claire, and Lucky was glad his usual fool of a brother had come to his senses and seen that. Of course, Riley had had to get out of the Air Force to make all this happen, and Lucky still wasn't sure how he was dealing with that, but once he had Claire wedded, things would all fall into place.

Riley was definitely the marrying sort. Anna, too. Logan was more in the to-be-determined group. And Lucky fell into the no-way-in-hell category. At least with Riley and Anna, Della and Stella would get those "grandbabies" they were always clamoring about.

Lucky had to give it to Claire, she didn't step back or look shocked when her attention landed on the girls. She greeted them, even Mackenzie, and Cassie with the same warm smile she'd given him.

"Cassie." Claire hugged her just as Della and Stella had done. She offered her condolences, too. Since Claire had lost her own grandmother only months earlier, Lucky was sure she knew how Cassie must feel.

"Sorry about all of this," Claire said. "We'll be out of your way soon. I hope," she added when she glanced at Riley. He didn't exactly look comfortable with whatever the reporter and photographer were saying to him. "It's his first big interview."

But not his last. Lucky knew Riley had gotten sucked into Logan's hamster wheel of building McCord Cattle Brokers, making it as big as could be.

"So, when is this wedding again?" Lucky asked. Though he already knew the date. "And am I invited?" he added with his customary wink.

"Of course, you're invited. It's next month, the same

day as the Founder's Day picnic. It'll be small, informal," Claire added.

"Semi-informal," Livvy corrected. "I talked Claire into doing the princess dress."

Claire made a face. "That was a compromise, but I nixed the tiara and the glass slippers."

"Nixed for now," Livvy said. "But there's plenty of time to change your mind about those. Also about the wand and hair glitter."

The look on Claire's face let Lucky know there'd be no reconsidering those things.

"You gonna be a princess?" Mia asked Claire.

"For an hour or so anyway. Want to be a princess, too? You can be a princess flower girl if you want, and wear the tiara. The hair glitter and slippers, as well. Ethan's going to be a *car boy*. Instead of rose petals, he'll be dropping toy cars from a basket." Claire paused, seemed a little worried. "We'll have to work on him not throwing them at the guests, though."

"I could be a princess?" Mia pressed, sounding in awe and hopeful at the same time.

"Of course. All of you are invited," Claire added looking at Cassie and Mackenzie. "And you can be one, too," she said to Mackenzie.

"We're not staying here that long," Mackenzie grumbled.

"Oh. Well. I'm sorry to hear that. If you have a change in plans, though, the invitation stands." Claire sounded genuine about that. "And what about you?" she asked Cassie.

"I'm afraid I'll have to miss it. I'll need to be back at work as soon as we've figured everything out with the custody, but I'm sure the wedding will be lovely.

I always thought Riley and you would make a great couple."

Mackenzie huffed. Why, Lucky didn't know. Maybe because she'd gone more than a minute without doing it. Sort of like a pressure cooker letting off steam, but in this case Mackenzie was letting off some surliness so that she wouldn't explode.

"She's got stars," Mia whispered to her sister. She nudged Mackenzie and pointed to Livvy.

That was Livvy's cue to pluck one from her hair. It was apparently a stick-on, and she gave it to the little girl. "It's magic," Livvy declared. "But it'll only give you one wish so use it wisely."

Mia looked as if she'd just been handed a miracle, one that she'd have to give a lot of thought.

"I like your shoes," Mackenzie said to Livvy. And she actually sounded, well, human. Human enough to be envious anyway.

"These?" Livvy pranced around like a ballerina. "Want to try them on?"

Mackenzie hesitated. Nodded. But then shook her head, probably because she sounded interested, which would have been equal in her mind to committing manslaughter. "No thanks."

Livvy made a suit-yourself sound. "I buy them on-line, and I'll give you the website." She plucked another gold star from her hair. She offered it to Mackenzie, but the girl only shook her head.

"I don't believe in magic," Mackenzie declared.

"Too bad. Because magic's how I got these." Livvy glanced down at her massive boobs. Then at Mackenzie's rather flat chest.

Mackenzie didn't take the gold star, so Livvy stuck

it in the girl's spiky black hair. Livvy looked at Cassie next. No offer of a gold star, but she did extend her hand for Cassie to shake.

"I'm Livvy Larimer, and I've seen you on TV," she said. "All those hot celebrities. Would love to get you drunk and see what kind of secrets you'd share."

"No secrets," Cassie assured her. Now Cassie's gaze drifted to Lucky. Perhaps she was implying that extended to Lucky himself, but Livvy didn't seem to be buying it. Livvy gave him a thumbs-up, apparently approving of a choice that Livvy thought he'd made. A choice to get in Cassie's pants.

Cassie glanced down at Livvy's shoes. "Though I would like the website for those."

"Sure. Of course. I'll email the link to Lucky and he can give it to you."

Great. Now he was involved in the fuck-me-heels buying loop. A loop and link he'd never share with Cassie.

Thankfully, Della saved the day. "I'll show the girls to their rooms," she offered.

"We'll go with you," Lucky said at the same time Cassie said, "I'll go, too."

Mackenzie rolled her eyes because she no doubt knew this was about the running-away thing, and she took both her and Mia's suitcases from him. "You can't babysit me all the time," Mackenzie grumbled, and she made it sound like a threat.

Lucky made a mental note to make sure someone did indeed watch her 24/7.

"You can spend some more time with your family and friend," Cassie said to him. "I'll go up with Della and the girls. I need to make a phone call anyway, and maybe I can do that in the guest room."

All of that sounded, well, like something a visitor might say, but there was something wrong. Something other than the obvious. But Lucky couldn't quite put his finger on it.

While Della led the three of them—Mia, Mackenzie and Cassie—up the stairs, Lucky was about to say goodbye to Claire and Livvy and head toward his own room just off the hall. But he didn't get far because someone else called out his name.

Riley.

His brother stepped away from the others and went to him. Livvy and Claire must have realized a brother talk was about to happen because they suddenly got very busy with a discussion of where to move the furniture. Riveting stuff, apparently, judging from the speed at which the women moved away from him.

"Am I about to get lectured?" Lucky asked Riley right off.

"Not by me. Maybe by Della or Stella, though. By now they've probably figured out this doesn't mean you're settling down and moving back home."

Probably. Of course, the pair would just come up with another dream of marrying him off. Hard to do that, though, whenever they went by his bed and saw the saddle he kept there. Lucky didn't actually use the saddle, didn't bring his lovers to the house, either. For that matter, he didn't sleep in the bed much at all but he liked to keep the saddle there as a reminder to Della and Stella that he wasn't into conventionality.

"You don't seem surprised by any of this," Lucky said.

Riley shrugged. "When I heard Dixie Mae had left

you a letter, I figured something was up. I was thinking you were getting the cats, though. Word around
town is that she had a dozen or more."

"Just six. And no, Mason-Dixon got those." Lucky
was the one shrugging now. "Cassie might end up with
them, though, before the dust settles."

Which made him wonder why Dixie Mae had left
them to her son in the first place. Certainly she must
have known he wouldn't keep them. Maybe this was
like leaving a nickel tip to a bad waiter? Mason-Dixon
would know she hadn't forgotten him but had simply
not been pleased with the sour direction their relationship had taken. Still, it was a crappy thing to do.

The photographer walked closer, his attention on
his camera, and he held up one of the screenshots for
Riley to see.

"I think that's the photo we'll use for the magazine,"
the photographer said. "We can put you side by side
with the shots that we've already taken of your brother.
That'll be the cover."

"Cover?" And yeah, Lucky put some smart-ass attitude on that.

It earned him a jab on the arm from Riley's elbow.
"It's good for business." And he nodded to the photographer. "Thanks."

"Are you okay with all of this?" Lucky asked him
when the photographer stepped away. Both the reporter
and he started packing up to leave.

"Yes. I am. Surprised?

"A little." A lot. Just months ago Riley had feared
that working the family business would make him ordinary. That he would be selling out, even. Clearly,

that had changed. "Having Claire has probably made things a little sweeter."

Riley looked in his fiancée's direction. Smiled. Yeah, nothing ordinary about that look on his brother's face. The look extended to Ethan when the boy zoomed through the room again in pursuit of the cat. He had a gold star in his hair, too. No doubt a magic gift from Livvy.

If Lucky thought for a second they actually worked, he'd ask for one for himself.

"Definitely. Claire has made everything sweeter," Riley said. "And Ethan. He's a good kid." Riley's gaze drifted toward the stairs. "How about them? Are they good k-kids?" He stuttered on the last word. Or maybe he choked.

Since it was pretty much the same reaction Lucky had had when he first saw them, he couldn't fault his brother. "I'm pretty sure Mia is. I'm not sure about the older one, Mackenzie."

Riley made a sound of agreement. "Mackenzie reminds me of you."

"Me?" Riley couldn't have surprised him more if he'd hit Lucky with a magic wand. "I never dressed like that."

"Same attitude. Except you winked and smiled more than I bet Mackenzie does."

It would be hard to wink with all that mascara. Her eyelids might permanently stick together.

"I'm nothing like her." Lucky shook his head. "Too bad, though, because if I were I might know what to do. At this point about the best I can hope for is that she continues to mope and doesn't do anything stupid."

And Lucky knew a little about stupid because he'd managed to do some stupid things in his life.

That still didn't mean Mackenzie and he were anything alike. Heck, she probably wasn't even good at spelling.

Riley gave him a pat on the back. Unlike with Logan, Riley gave him two. It also didn't feel as if Riley couldn't wait to get off to some appointment and therefore get away from him.

"You'll do okay," Riley assured him. "Kids are a lot tougher than they look. Besides, it's just for the night, right?"

"Maybe two. Bernie's looking for their next of kin."

Riley made another sound, not of agreement this time, and even though he didn't explain the sound, Lucky knew what it meant. In fact, he could have an entire conversation with himself about it, but the bottom line was this—Why hadn't the next of kin already come forward? According to Bernie, Dixie Mae had had the girls for a couple of months after their grandmother passed. Certainly, Dixie Mae had searched for their next of kin. Lucky hoped Bernie had better luck than Dixie Mae.

"The girls might end up in foster care," Lucky had to admit. That'd been a hard enough pill to swallow before he'd met Mia. Now it was like swallowing a pregnant elephant.

Another sound from Riley, also not one of agreement. "I'll ask around and see if anyone in town is looking at adoption."

"Thanks." And Lucky meant that. However, it did feel as if he was trying to get out of this guardianship deal ASAP.

Which he was.

The less time he was with the girls, the less chance there was of screwing this up. It was okay when he screwed up his own life—that had become the norm for him—but it was a different thing for that to spill over to two kids who obviously needed a heck of a lot more than he could give them.

Lucky heard the footsteps on the stairs, and he turned to see Mia making her way toward them. Not poking along, either. She was running.

"Come quick, Mr. Lucky," Mia insisted. "It's Miss Cassie. I think she's about to die-did."

CHAPTER SEVEN

OH, GOD. THE BEARS were back, and judging from the way Cassie's heart was thudding in her chest, they had brought along some friends.

Cassie opened her purse. Or rather she attempted to. Her hands were already shaking too hard, and all the shaking caused her to drop it. The contents, including the bottle of meds, scattered across the floor of the guest room. She'd left the door open just in case Della had a question about the girls. It had seemed a good idea at the time, but that open door meant anyone could see her losing this fight with the bears.

And someone did.

Mia.

She appeared in the doorway of Cassie's room. Cassie shook her head, trying to tell the little girl that everything was all right, but the only thing that came out of her mouth was hot air. Literally. Heaven knew how bad she must have looked and sounded to Mia because the little girl took off. Maybe running for cover rather than running for help. Cassie didn't want help.

She crawled across the floor, her spotty vision nailed to that amber bottle of meds. The bears got in the way, of course, blurring her vision even more and thinning her breath to the point she thought she might pass out. Heck, passing out would be a relief right now. And unavoidable, she quickly realized. When you couldn't breathe, you passed out.

The world just floated away from her.

But not for long.

"Cassie?" Lucky said. He tapped her cheeks. Then he shook her. "Call an ambulance."

That got through the bear fuzz in her head just fine, and Cassie forced open her eyes. "No ambulance. I'm fine."

Considering she was sprawled out on the floor, it was no wonder Lucky gave her a skeptical look. But thankfully Mia and Della, who were in the doorway, didn't jump to call that ambulance he'd requested. This was already bad enough without word spreading around town, and if an ambulance came, it'd be all over the state, perhaps the entire country, before she even got to the hospital.

Cassie maneuvered herself into a sitting position. Pulled down her skirt when she realized her panties were showing. It was a true testament to how concerned Lucky was about her that he didn't even seem to notice that. Or maybe compared to the gold-starred, busty Livvy, she wasn't even worthy of a notice.

Which was a good thing, Cassie assured herself.

"I'm fine, really," she repeated when the trio just kept staring at her.

Soon, though, it wasn't just a trio. It was an octet. Lucky, Mia, Mackenzie, Della, Stella, Claire, Riley and Livvy. The woman who'd almost certainly been Lucky's lover. The fact that Cassie would remember that was an unwelcome thought.

It meant she'd given way too much thought to Lucky's love life.

And it wasn't as if she didn't have her own life to think about. Especially right now. Somehow, Cassie had to convince the octet that she hadn't gone bat-shit crazy. While she was at it, maybe she could convince herself of that, too.

"I usually wear much better shoes than this," Cassie said.

All right. That wasn't going to convince anyone of her sanity. But she did own some beautiful heels. Nothing like those stilts that Livvy was wearing, but still nice ones, in fashionable styles and colors. She had a pair in teal for heaven's sake.

"Uh, you want that ambulance now?" Lucky asked her.

"No." Cassie couldn't say that fast enough. She considered lying and saying she'd had an epileptic seizure. People usually seemed more open to that. Not so much to panic attacks, though, especially ones coupled with chatter about shoe choices. "I just need a minute."

Cassie didn't say she wanted that minute to be solo, but Lucky seemed to pick up on that. He stood, motioned for everyone to leave the room.

"Please keep your eyes on them," he said to Della and Stella while motioning to the girls.

And Lucky shut the door. What he didn't do was go into the hall with them. He stayed right there in the room with Cassie. Not only that, he picked up her medicine bottle, handed it to her and sank down on the floor next to her.

Breathe in, breathe out, she reminded herself.

In doing so, she took in Lucky's scent. That didn't help.

Cassie also added some nonsense sayings like, *Take*

it one second at a time and you'll get through this. Of course, she had to take it one second at a time. She couldn't time travel and take it from a second at a time to a minute at a time. And as for the getting through this—of course, she would.

It just didn't feel like it at the moment.

"Panic attack?" Lucky asked.

Cassie wasn't sure if she'd actually used the words *panic attack* when she was prone on the floor or if it was just a good guess on his part.

"One of my ex-girlfriends used to have them," he explained. So not really a guess after all. "It happened every time she… Never mind."

Maybe it was because she wanted to focus on something else, anything else, but Cassie latched right on to his "never mind."

"Did it happen during sex?"

"Uh, no. It happened during bad weather, especially lightning strikes. Why would you think it would have anything to do with sex?" But he waved that off. "You think the only thing I do is have sex. Well, it's been three months. Satisfied?"

He looked as thunderstruck at having admitted that as Cassie had at her shoes revelation. Of course, Cassie probably looked thunderstruck, too. Heck, why had she brought up anything like that with Lucky?

"Why would you think I'd be satisfied over the fact that you've been without sex for a quarter of a year?" Cassie hadn't intended to ask that question aloud, but what with the breathe mantra and the other stuff whirling around in her head, it had just slipped out.

Lucky lifted his shoulder. "Some people like to think of me being brought down a notch or two."

"Not me." She hadn't intended to say that, either. Especially not in a breathy voice. It sounded like some kind of invitation for him to do something about that dry spell. With her.

Cassie took a pill while she waited for him to question her about that breathy invitation. He didn't, though.

"So, how did your ex get through a panic attack?" she asked.

He smiled. It was what the girls in high school had called his pantie-dropping smile. Thankfully, she was immune to it.

"Sex," he answered.

"Of course." What else? He probably used it as a cure for all sorts of things, but apparently he hadn't needed such a cure in the past three months.

"Sex wouldn't work for me," she assured him.

He made a sound that could have meant anything. Or a sound that meant he didn't buy that for a second.

"Since I'd like to stop you from having any more panic attacks without the use of my man parts," he said, "why don't you tell me what triggers them?"

The last question was easy to answer. "Stress triggers them." And memories. But it was the stress brought on by the memories that flipped her switch and sent her from being Cassandra Weatherall, therapist, to an asthmatic-sounding woman sitting on the floor with a bad-boy bull rider.

"Stress, huh?" He scrubbed his hand over his face. "Well, you don't have much of that right now, do you?" He nudged her arm. Winked.

There it was. The bra-dropping wink. It was an example of the charm that'd coaxed many women into bed. Onto floors, too, probably. And up against walls.

It was a lethal combo, with that smile, his looks and that scent. He must be wearing some kind of phero-mone aftershave.

"We'll get all of this worked out," he went on. "The girls will land in a good home, and we'll both go back to doing whatever we normally do."

The first two parts of that were the absolute right things to say. The last part not so much. Cassie wasn't sure she could go back to what she'd normally been doing. Not without it triggering more of these bear attacks anyway.

"Don't tell anyone about the panic attack please," she said.

"I won't," he agreed, "but that doesn't mean it won't get around."

Yes, even without an ambulance ride, that was pos-sible. Likely, even. All it took was a slip of the tongue, and there were plenty of tongues that could slip since the octet had seen her at her worst.

"I know it sounds silly," Cassie went on, "but I have this image I have to keep so I don't want people to know I get like this."

Lucky looked at her. "What kind of image?"

"Someone not on the floor having a panic attack." And someone who didn't talk about having a panic attack. Or about shoes. Cassie groaned. "I have to get myself together. That client's coming in tomorrow. Plus, the girls. And I need to go to the funeral home."

All those things were true, but Cassie left off one big item. The main reason that she was actually having panic attacks. No way could she tell Lucky about that.

"I can stay with the girls while you go to the fu-neral home," he said.

It was a huge offer, and they both knew it. The kids terrified him as much as they did her. "Why are you being so nice to me?"

Lucky slipped his arm around her. "We both lost Dixie Mae. So did the girls."

Cassie made the mistake of turning her head to look at him, and since they were sitting side by side, that meant their mouths were way too close. And Lucky noticed, too. He glanced at her mouth. Then it became more than a glance. It became a lingering look.

It became a mental kiss.

Oh, mercy. She felt it, too, all the way to her toes. And it didn't help with the remnants of the panic attack. She was losing some of that breath she'd just started to gather.

Cassie stood and started gathering the things that had fallen out of her purse. "I'm okay now," she lied. "Just give me another minute to make that call to a PI I know, and then I'll join you and the others downstairs."

Lucky got up from the floor as well, and he did it without taking his eyes off her. For a moment she didn't think he was going to leave, but he finally started for the door. But there was a knock before he even reached it. A very soft knock. When Lucky opened it, she saw Mia standing there.

"Did Miss Cassie die-did?" she asked. She now had the gold star stuck in her hair.

"No, sweetheart. I'm fine." Cassie went closer to show her, and she reminded herself to smile.

Mia studied her face but didn't look totally convinced she was telling the truth. Still, she took Cassie's hand and dropped something into it. A piece of a cookie. She gave another piece to Lucky.

"Ethan gave it to me," Mia explained. "But you might wanna eat it later because I'm supposed to tell you that you gotta come downstairs now because we got some trouble."

"What happened?" Cassie asked, but she didn't wait for an answer. Good grief, had Mackenzie run away again?

Lucky no doubt thought the same thing because he hurried after her, but when Cassie reached the bottom of the stairs, she saw Mackenzie right away. The girl hadn't run after all.

Then Cassie saw the *trouble*.

A cop. One she recognized. Deputy Davy Divine. She'd known him in high school, and he hadn't changed a bit. Still very thin. Still very much resembling his nickname of Davy Dweeb.

"10-23," Davy said to whoever was on the other end of the walkie-talkie he had in his left hand. "That means I arrived at the residence of the perp," he clarified for them, though no one asked him for that information. The person on the end of the line didn't respond, either.

"Cassie," Davy said, adding a crisp nod. "Lucky." Davy was holding a pair of handcuffs. "I'm here to arrest one Mackenzie Compton."

"You're not arresting anybody," Riley insisted. Lucky echoed the same when he stepped in front of Mackenzie.

Davy tapped his badge, one that Cassie was certain he polished daily if not more often. Some people were just born to be cops. Sadly, Davy wasn't one of those people, but the badge gave him some of the respect that he'd never gotten in school. At least he seemed to think so.

"Why are you here?" Lucky asked Davy.

"I already said—to arrest her." He used the cuffs to point at Mackenzie. "She committed a 211."

This time someone did ask what the heck that was. "Robbery," Davy said as if the answer were obvious.

It wasn't. They all just stared at the deputy.

"She stole money from Wilhelmina Larkin's purse," Davy added.

All of them turned to Mackenzie, but the girl just shrugged. Definitely not a denial of guilt.

"Did you take the money?" Lucky asked her.

Another shrug. And Mackenzie suddenly got very interested in staring at the floor.

"Of course she stole it. Wilhelmina said she left her purse under her desk when she went out for her break, and that the only people in the room were these two." Davy pointed to Mia and Mackenzie. "Wilhelmina's pretty sure she's the one who took it." This time, he only pointed to Mackenzie.

"Did you take the money?" Lucky repeated to her.

"Of course she did." Davy, again. "Wilhelmina said she's missing five twenty-dollar bills, and that I'll know it's her money because there are red devil horns on the corners of the bills."

All of them turned from staring at Mackenzie to staring at Davy.

"The bills are her alimony payment from her ex, Tommy," the deputy explained, "and he always pays her in cash, always draws horns on the twenties with a magic marker. Sometimes, he writes voodoo curses on them, but she said he didn't do that this time. That he just drew the horns."

And here Cassie thought *she* had a complicated relationship. A relationship that Lucky likely didn't know about. She should probably mention it to him in case someone blabbered about it before she got a chance to explain.

Since Mackenzie hadn't answered Lucky, Cassie decided to give it a try. She was about to ask again if she'd taken the money, but then Cassie remembered the girl's reaction to Livvy offering to let her try on those heels. Mackenzie had wanted to do it, Cassie had seen that in her eyes, but she'd declined.

"Is the money in your shoes?" Cassie asked.

Silence.

All except for a huff from Davy. "I have the right to search her," he insisted.

"No, you don't," Lucky insisted right back. "She's a minor, and besides, Mackenzie's going to give back the money. Aren't you?" he added through clenched teeth.

The next couple of seconds crawled by. Finally, Mackenzie mumbled some profanity and pulled the money from her right shoe. All five twenties did indeed have devil horns on them. Devils, too. Apparently, Tommy Larkin had spent some time preparing his alimony payment.

Davy put away the handcuffs so he could put on a pair of latex gloves before he took the money and counted it. Twice. Then he put the bills in a plastic evidence bag that he'd taken from his pocket.

"I still have to arrest her," Davy insisted. He shoved the bag and gloves back in his pocket so he could take out the cuffs again.

"You're not taking a thirteen-year-old to jail," Cassie insisted.

Davy just stared at her in disbelief. "If she's thirteen, I'm a camel."

"Then you're a camel," Lucky said, his voice flat.

Livvy mumbled something much worse—"You're a dickweed." Cassie agreed with her but hoped the girls hadn't heard that. Claire apparently had because she pulled her business partner aside.

"Duckweed," Claire whispered, tipping her head to Mia, then to Ethan, who had apparently finished his cat-chasing adventure and was now falling asleep on the floor.

Livvy nodded, apparently agreeing with the kid-friendly word substitute.

Davy volleyed glances between Mackenzie and the cuffs. "I can arrest minors," he said.

Livvy was about to say something else, but Claire took hold of her arm and moved her away.

Mia stepped forward, maneuvering her way through the group to get to the deputy. She plucked the gold star from her hair and offered it to Davy. "It's magic, and I want to use my one wish so that my sister don't have to go to jail."

Oh, mercy. Could the child get any sweeter? It was as if she'd sucked up all the sweetness from Mackenzie, who wasn't doing anything remotely sweet at the moment. She was glaring at all of them.

Of course, later Cassie would need to clarify to Mia that there was no such thing as magic. She didn't want Mia trying to use that gold star to get out of a serious situation, only to learn the hard way that it was just a piece of foiled plastic with a sticky back and came in packets of a hundred.

Davy did more of those volleyed glances at all of them, obviously not sure what to do about that. But Lucky did.

Lucky knelt down to face Mia. "Save your magic star for something else," Lucky told her with a smile, but he wasn't smiling when he stood again and turned to Davy. "Here's how this will work. You will return that money to Wilhelmina, and I'll call her and explain that this will never happen again."

Davy shook his head. "Wilhelmina's pretty upset."

"Then I'll go see her," Lucky snapped.

Davy still shook his head. "She was really upset." In Davy's world *really* was clearly a step up from *pretty*.

"Then I'll go see Wilhelmina *now*," Lucky amended. He took hold of Davy's arm, leading him out the door. "Watch the girls," he added over his shoulder to no one in particular. He also took the time to fire off one last scowl to Mackenzie. "And watch Cassie." Again said to no one in particular.

Cassie wanted to tell him that she didn't need watching, but that would have required her to talk about the panic attack. No way did she want to discuss that.

"You need help?" Riley called out to his brother.

Lucky shook his head. "I'll be back as soon as I smooth things over with Wilhelmina."

Cassie figured that would require him to semipimp himself with some flirting and winking. Perhaps even a coffee date. She wasn't usually in favor of that sort of thing, but she couldn't see much benefit in Mackenzie being hauled off to jail. Although it would keep her from running away. Still, Mackenzie didn't need that kind of trauma in her life and neither did Mia.

Davy reached his cruiser, and he aimed his parting comment at Cassie. "If Lucky's silver tongue turns out to be brass, I'll be back. And none of you will stop me from making that arrest."

He drove off with Livvy's shout coming through even over the sound of the car engine. "Duckweed!"

LOGAN SIPPED HIS whiskey and stared out the bay window of his suite. Definitely not his usual view from his town loft. Or at least it hadn't been for a long time now. But since this had been his childhood room, it was a view he knew well.

The pastures, the barns and the white fences to contain it all. Since the place had been his father's design, everything was aligned just the way it should be. The pastures had even been leveled out so that the fences were in a perfectly straight line. No dips or peaks. His father hadn't been a fan of the rolling-hills effect.

There was something reassuring about that. Everything in its place. Too bad Logan couldn't do that with the family.

If his dad were alive, he would have said Logan had failed.

And he had.

Riley was back now, and happy—to Logan that was equally important, though his dad would have been content with him just being back. Anna would soon return, once she'd finished her degree and her fiancé finished his military commitment. And Anna would get married and continue with the next generation of

McCords. So would Riley. A generation to build on what their father had started thirty-five years ago.

That left Lucky.

Logan's biggest failure.

His twin brother was filled with anger, and Logan hadn't been able to do anything about it. The more Logan pushed, the more Lucky backed away, and when he didn't push, Lucky kept backing further away anyway.

Keep the family together.

That was one of the last things his father had said to him. Logan had been nineteen and had come home from college for reasons he couldn't remember. It had been an ordinary conversation, one he'd had with his dad countless times since he was more likely to listen than Lucky was. However, Logan hadn't known that it would be their last—that less than twelve hours later both his parents would be dead from a car accident. One that could have been prevented.

But that was an old scabbed wound that he didn't want to pick at tonight.

Still, he couldn't push it completely aside. His father had told him to keep the family together. Maybe because he'd had a premonition about his death, maybe because he was feeling down about Lucky and him going off to college. Either way, those words had become Logan's fuel.

And the source of plenty of sleepless nights.

Probably the source of the migraines he'd been having, too. That also was a different problem for a different day. As long as a migraine wasn't chasing him right now, he could put it out of his mind. But he couldn't do that with family. It was always there, always on the front burner, right where his father had put it.

If he couldn't draw Lucky back into the family with work, then he needed to find another angle, because losing his brother wasn't an option. That was the problem with a mandate from a father who was now dead. The mandate couldn't be changed, and Logan was as stuck with it as the rest of his siblings were.

"Are you ever coming to bed?" Helene asked.

Thanks to the moonlight spilling through the window, Logan had no trouble seeing his longtime girlfriend, Helene Langford. Her long blond hair, spilling onto her creamy white shoulders. Her smile. The way she touched her tongue to her top lip when she looked at him.

She was naked, but she had the white sheet clutched to her midsection. Her long bare legs were on top of the cover. Her head was tilted to the side as she studied him. All in all, a beautiful sight.

Perfect.

Everything aligned as it should be, and he wasn't just talking about her face and body. Helene was the perfect woman for him, right down to her double degrees in business and interior design. She could make things pretty and organized, just the way he liked them.

They'd been together for eight years now. Since Logan's twenty-fifth birthday when Anna had set them up on a date. Soon, he'd propose, and they could start on their own next generation of McCords. First, though, Logan had to make sure everything was in place.

"I mean, are you coming to bed to sleep?" Helene clarified, smiling. Because he'd already been in bed with her but had gotten up after they'd had sex.

"Soon. I'm waiting on an email from the PI."

"Another one? You've been exchanging emails with him all night."

Yes, and he might have to exchange even more tomorrow and the day after. "The PI's still doing the background checks on this situation."

No need to explain what that situation was. Helene was well aware of this custody mess Dixie Mae had dumped on Lucky and Cassie.

"Any red flags yet?" Helene asked.

The whole thing was a red flag as far as Logan was concerned. Still, he knew what she meant. "Dixie Mae did have temporary guardianship of the girls prior to her death. The girls' grandmother had her lawyer do the paperwork, and it all looks legit to the PI."

"But?"

Logan had to shrug. "There might not be any buts. If this is some kind of scam, the PI isn't finding the angle."

"What about Cassie's father?" Helene asked. "Mason-Dixon could have orchestrated this."

He nodded. Definitely. "The PI hasn't found any connection between Mason-Dixon and the girls. No connection between him and their parents, either. Their dad died the same year the younger one was born. Accidental drowning. He was drunk and drove his truck off a bridge."

"So, not father-of-the-year material," Helene mumbled.

That was only the tip of the iceberg when it came to the man's father-of-the-year status. He'd had several other arrests, most involving alcohol or theft, and he'd never paid a dime of child support.

"And their mother?" Helene asked.

"Not mother-of-the-year material, either. Gracie Compton. She died of a drug overdose last year. That's how her mother ended up with custody."

Of course, that hadn't lasted long because the grandmother had then died from cancer. The girls had really been through hell in their short lives, and while Logan wasn't untouched by that, he also didn't want someone using this situation as a chance to scam them or his brother.

Helene patted the spot beside her. "Come to bed," she insisted. "And if you do, I'll make sure to work extra hours to finish the renovation on the loft so we can get back into our own bed by next week. I'll work some extra hours on the Founder's Day picnic, too."

She was already working extra hours. Because that's what Helene did. She worked as many hours as Logan did, maybe more, and her only downtime seemed to be the Friday and Saturday nights she spent with him—in their bed.

Well, a bed that she'd picked out anyway.

Actually, six years ago Helene had picked out everything in the loft when he'd first had it repurposed from guest rooms to his private suite. Since the company offices were on the ground and second floors of the Victorian house, it had made sense for him to have a place to sleep there, too. It wasn't home exactly, but it was better than being alone in the empty place.

Too many memories here. And those memories seemed to come tapping on his shoulder whenever he stayed the night.

But for now, Helene was doing the *tapping*. She

patted the bed again and gave him a look he had no trouble interpreting—Did he want seconds?

He sure did, and Logan was headed in that direction when his phone dinged. It was the email from the PI, and hopefully this would be the last report on the matter of the guardianship issue. However, it wasn't the girls' name or even Dixie Mae's on the background check from the PI.

It was Cassie's.

Logan had asked for any and all information, and the PI must have thought that included Cassie. He thumbed through it, not expecting to see anything that would surprise him.

He was wrong.

Logan did see something.

Hell.

CHAPTER EIGHT

LUCKY WASN'T EVEN sure sleep would help. He thought he might be past the point of return on that. Every muscle in his body, especially his butt, was aching, but all that was a drop in the muscle-aching bucket when it came to his head.

Oh, man.

He needed a handful of aspirin and a faster solution to this whole temporary-custody situation.

Of course, sleeping in the hall on the floor hadn't helped, but it'd been necessary to make sure Mackenzie didn't try to go on the run again. Lucky had gotten especially suspicious that she might try that when she'd insisted on Mia and her sharing a room. And when Mackenzie had asked for an umbrella when it had started to rain. Lucky had made sure all the doors were locked up. And the umbrellas. But for insurance, he'd slept outside their room.

Outside Cassie's, too, since hers was right next to the girls'.

Cassie had agreed to stay at the window all night to make sure Mackenzie didn't try to slip out and shimmy down the gutter. Which meant Cassie, like Lucky, was getting little to no sleep.

This was not a situation of misery loving company, though. Lucky didn't want a repeat of Cassie's panic attack so he hoped she'd managed to get in at least a couple of catnaps. In case she had, he'd stayed right next to the girls' door so he could hear if there was any moving around in there.

He hadn't heard anything, thank goodness.

That was one thing off his list. Make that two. The day before, it'd taken Lucky hours of talking to fix the problem with Wilhelmina—and the promise to take her for a drink at Calhoun's Pub. Only then had she agreed to drop the charges against Mackenzie. However, dropping those charges was contingent on one more thing.

Mackenzie's apology.

Thankfully, Wilhelmina hadn't required that apology to be face-to-face. Probably because the woman was a little afraid of Mackenzie, but that meant Mackenzie would have to write it, and Lucky would have to deliver it personally to Wilhelmina. Lucky only hoped Mackenzie could write a convincing apology. Again, he was stereotyping here, but she didn't look like star-pupil material.

Lucky had given Mackenzie until morning to produce the apology. Whether she would do it was anyone's guess, and he was too tired to guess anyway. If she didn't do it, he might have to teach her a really bad lesson and let Davy arrest her. For a couple of minutes anyway.

He heard footsteps on the stairs. Smelled coffee. And even though it was Logan approaching him with a cup in each hand, Lucky didn't even mind an early-morning encounter with his brother if it meant one of those cups was for him.

Both were.

Logan handed him the two cups and sank down on the floor next to him. His brother was already dressed for work in his jeans, cowboy boots and dress coat. He probably wasn't taking any pictures for magazine covers today, but he looked ready for a photo op.

"Anything I can do to help you resolve this?" Logan asked.

Lucky didn't doubt it was a genuine offer. The coffee proved that it was. But Lucky was never sure what Logan's motives were. For Logan, it was all about the family business. That was his bottom line. And somewhere along the way, Logan had forgotten about the family part of family business.

Of course, Lucky was no better.

It was a cow-eat-cow world when it came to McCord Cattle Brokers and the McCord brothers.

But Lucky got the feeling that Logan's offer had more to do with avoiding bad publicity. It had to be all over town now about Mackenzie stealing that money, and the embellished amount was probably in the thousands— and might include diamond jewelry. Maybe even a black-market kidney.

People in Spring Hill had good imaginations when it came to gossip.

"If the girls are going to be here much longer, I'd look into getting a security system," Lucky grumbled. Though it was the first time he'd ever considered it. Unlike gossip, the crime rate in Spring Hill wasn't anything to worry about.

"I could arrange something temporary," Logan suggested.

Even something temporary would take time to install, and Lucky preferred the energy to be spent on finding the girls' next of kin. "Thanks, but no. What would help, though, is some aspirin for this headache," Lucky said. "Got any?"

Logan fished through his pocket and came up with a bottle of meds. Not aspirin, though. This was prescription stuff. Logan took out one of the pills and handed it to him. Lucky washed it down with the coffee.

"Should I ask why you have headache meds like this?" Lucky threw out there.

"No. And I won't ask you if you plan to keep your hands, and other parts of yourself, off Cassie."

Lucky made a face. "Why would you care what happens between Cassie and me?"

Logan didn't answer. He took out something else from his pocket. Not his meds this time but rather a folded piece of paper. "Last night I had background checks run on the girls so I could help look for any of their relatives. I also had checks run on Dixie Mae and Cassie, just to make sure there wasn't anything... out of place."

Uh-oh. Lucky had heard Logan use that term before. *Out of place.* It meant he was digging for dirt.

"And before you start lecturing me about their privacy and such," Logan continued, "I just wanted to make sure these girls weren't part of some kind of scam. That maybe there wasn't someone out there using them to get anyone's money. Yours, Cassie's or Dixie Mae's."

Since Lucky had already opened his mouth to lecture him, he closed it. Because Logan was right. It was something he should have already checked on. Dixie Mae had a good BS meter, but that didn't mean she couldn't have been duped and then unknowingly passed that duping onto Cassie and him.

"The girls are legit," Logan went on. "It was just as Bernie told you. Both their parents are dead. Grandparents, too, and that's why they'd been staying with Dixie Mae and then Scooter. But according to one of the late grandmother's neighbors, there's an aunt, the mother's half sister, who I'm trying to track down. The neighbor didn't know the half sister's full name, but her first name is Alice."

An aunt. That was definitely a close enough blood relative. Lucky had figured they might have to resort to looking for distant cousins.

"The girls never mentioned an aunt," Lucky said.

"Because I doubt they know about her. Neither did Dixie Mae. That's why the custody agreement reads as it does. She wanted the girls to go to a suitable relative, if one could be found. If not, they're to remain with Cassie and you. But this aunt could be the fix to all of this."

"Thanks." Lucky paused. He apparently wasn't the only one who hadn't gotten any sleep. Neither Logan nor the person he'd paid to do these checks had, either. "But what does all of this have to do with me staying away from Cassie?"

Logan tipped his head to the paper.

Lucky wasn't sure he wanted to know what was there, and he didn't get a chance to read it. That's because Cassie's door opened, and she came out into the hall with them. Logan immediately took one of the cups of coffee from Lucky and handed it to her. He also glanced at the paper that he'd given Lucky, and even though Logan didn't say a word about it, Lucky got a clear signal—don't let Cassie see that yet.

Cassie had a big sip of the coffee, as if it were the cure for everything, and it was only after she had several more sips that she mumbled a "Thank you."

"A reporter from LA called the local newspaper," Logan told her. "He talked to Marlene Holland and was asking questions about you."

Cassie didn't seem especially surprised about that. She just sighed. "What did he want?"

"I think he was sniffing for a story, that's all, but Marlene did say he wanted to know about the girls. She didn't have any facts to give him, but he wanted her to call him if she learned anything."

Cassie didn't ask how a reporter hundreds of miles away would have found out about their custody situation. Probably because she was aware of how fast and far gossip traveled. Added to the fact that Cassie was a celebrity of sorts, and it would make a juicy story if the LA press picked up on the fact that she was a temporary guardian to someone who looked and dressed like Mackenzie.

"I instructed Marlene to call me if the reporter contacts her again," Logan added. "I think this guy's running background checks on all of us. Someone is anyway, and I need to find out who." He glanced at his watch, stood. "I have to leave for work, but if I hear anything more about the girls' aunt, I'll let you know."

"Aunt?" Cassie said, looking at the paper. "Did Logan find something?"

Evidently, but Lucky didn't want to share what was on that paper until he'd had a chance to read it. "Lo-

gan's looking for their mother's half sister." And Lucky
had no doubts that he'd find her.

As long as Mackenzie was in the house, there was
potential for bad press, something that Logan would
want to avoid. For once, though, Lucky was glad his
and his brother's agendas meshed.

"Good." Cassie had more coffee, and since her attention kept going to the paper, Lucky stuffed it in his
jeans pocket.

Out of sight, however, didn't mean out of mind,
since Cassie's gaze just went in that direction. Which
meant it went in the direction of his crotch. She quickly
looked away, but not before it got Lucky to thinking.

Why would Logan warn him about getting involved
with Cassie?

And why did that warning only make him want to
get involved with her even more? Because he was stupid, that's why. Of course, he hadn't needed a warning
to make him remember the attraction.

Not with the attraction sitting right next to him.

Even though Cassie probably hadn't slept, she still
managed to look amazing. Hair done, makeup. But that
was just surface stuff. Beneath that, she was beautiful,
always had been. That wasn't only limited to her face.
Her body was a sizzler, too. Not overly curvy but more
than enough to catch and hold his attention.

Especially those legs.

She was wearing a skirt again today, a slim white
one. It hit several inches above her knees, and with
the way she was sitting, the skirt had ridden up even
more. Not as much as the night before when she'd had
the panic attack, but he could see plenty of her long

legs and had no trouble imagining where those legs stopped.

"You're wondering about the shoes," she said.

Uh. No.

But he would take to the grave what he had been wondering about.

However, she was indeed wearing shoes. Heels about four inches high and pale pink, about the same color as her mouth.

"This isn't about what happened yesterday with Livvy," Cassie continued. "I really do wear shoes like this—often."

Lucky had no idea how to respond to that so he just nodded. That was enough of a cue to keep Cassie talking.

"I only wear those flat shoes when I'm traveling. Because I twisted my ankle once while running to catch a flight. And that gray outfit I had on yesterday? Again, just for traveling."

Of course, that only made him notice her legs again. And the fit of her top. Snug in just the right places.

"Anyway, I thought you should know," she added. Cassie drank more coffee, fast, as if trying to give her mouth something else to do other than talk.

"Wanna know something?" he asked.

She didn't jump to answer that. Cassie stayed quiet for a while, studying his face and no doubt trying to figure out what this was about. She finally nodded.

"You'd look good in anything," Lucky admitted.

"Oh," she said. Yeah, that was definitely a surprise. Because it threw the attraction right out there. And there was no doubt about it now—there was an attraction. If there hadn't been, she wouldn't have cared what he thought about her clothes and shoes.

"Oh," Cassie repeated, tearing her lingering gaze from his. "Well, thanks. Now, to what we really should be talking about. The girls," she clarified. Probably because he looked at her breasts, she clarified even more. "Mia and Mackenzie."

"What about them? Mia and Mackenzie?" he clarified, too.

"I don't have any experience counseling or dealing with troubled children, but I have a friend who does. Dr. Sarah Dressler. I called her last night and asked her to come. She might not make it here before it's time for the girls to leave, but just in case this lingers on..."

No need to finish that. If this lingered on, they'd need help and lots of it. Lucky wasn't about to turn down anything or anybody, especially when that anybody might know how to deal with Mackenzie.

"I suspect Mackenzie's acting out because she has abandonment issues," Cassie added. "It's fairly common with children who've lost their parents. They challenge authority, break rules, run away. They run because they fear abandonment again, and they believe running will fix the problem. If they don't stay in one place, they can't be abandoned."

Lucky replayed all of that. Word for word.

Well, hell.

Was Cassie analyzing him now, or Mackenzie?

"There's no quick, easy solution," Cassie went on. "She'll need lots of love, reassurance. She'll need to believe she can fit into a new life where someone will love her... What?"

"What?" Lucky repeated.

"You're looking at me funny," Cassie said.

Lucky quickly tried to fix that. "Just thinking, that's all." And comparing.

But he ditched the comparison. He was nothing like Mackenzie despite what Cassie had just said. Despite, too, what Riley had said the day before about Mackenzie reminding him of Lucky.

Cassie stared at him a while longer. "Anyway, I thought maybe you could talk to her about what it was like to lose your own parents."

This would have been a good time for him to nod and agree. He didn't. "I don't think it's a good idea to dredge up all of that."

More staring at him. "Okay." Lucky figured what she was doing was using a therapist's ploy: waiting for him to spill more.

He wouldn't.

"Why don't you check on the girls?" he asked. It was time to get to his feet and head out. "I'll see about getting us some more coffee and some breakfast." Lucky walked away, hoping that was the end of the subject for Cassie.

It'd never be the end of it for him, though.

Lucky had plenty of memories of that night he'd become an orphan, and he didn't intend to share them with Cassie or anyone else. He hadn't been able to save his mom and dad.

They had both died in a car crash that could have been prevented.

And it was all his fault.

CASSIE WATCHED AS Lucky walked away. She didn't need any psychology degrees to know something was bothering him. Maybe something on that piece of paper that he'd shoved into his pocket.

Something he clearly hadn't wanted her to see.

For just a second she had considered trying to talk him into showing it to her, but it was his own business and had nothing to do with her. And it wasn't as if she didn't have anything else to do. She had to deal with the girls, and that started with her knocking on the door of the guest room where they were staying.

No answer.

It wasn't exactly late, just after eight, but she couldn't imagine the girls—well, Mia anyway—ignoring a knock. Cassie knocked again. Still no answer, and she was about to test the knob when the door opened. Relief flooded through her when she saw Mia. Panic came just as fast, though, when she didn't see Mackenzie.

"I can't tie my shoes," Mia said. She tried to stick out one foot and nearly lost her balance. Cassie caught onto her to stop her from falling.

"I'll tie them for you. Uh, where's your sister?"

"Bathroom. It takes Kenzie a long time to do stuff in there."

Yes, it had to take time to spackle on that much makeup. The bathroom was en suite, but the door was closed and Cassie didn't hear anyone moving around. Since there was a window in there, it was possible Mackenzie had used it to get away. But Cassie re-thought that. She wouldn't just abandon Mia. Well, she wouldn't if Cassie's theory was right.

Of course, that theory was just as likely to be wrong. It wasn't as if she had a stellar track record when it came to doling out diagnoses.

Cassie set Mia on the bed so she could tie her shoes.

She hurried, too. All in all, the little girl had done a good job dressing herself in a pair a pink overalls with a white shirt beneath.

"I pulled up my own panties," Mia volunteered. "And I didn't get 'em bunched up."

Cassie wasn't sure if that was a big accomplishment or not for a four-year-old, but she said, "Good girl," and made her way to the bathroom door. She leaned in, pressed her ear against it and almost fell when Mackenzie threw it open.

"I'm still here, all right?" Mackenzie snarled. "And I wrote that stupid apology to the old woman at the ugly lawyer's office."

Since it had worked with Mia, Cassie went with another mumbled "Good girl," though it didn't have the same effect on Mackenzie. Mia had smiled at Cassie. Mackenzie was sporting her usual scowl and a fresh slathering of makeup. Sheez, considering the amount she used, her entire suitcase had to be filled with the stuff.

Mackenzie thrust a Post-it note at her. "Take it. It's the apology."

Cassie did take it and saw the two words scrawled there. "I'm sorry."

"I told Kenzie to say it like she means it, and that'll make the lawyer lady feel better," Mia said.

"I do mean it!" Mackenzie growled. "I mean it because I want to get everybody off my back."

It probably wasn't the heart-wrenching regret and promise that she'd never do it again that Wilhelmina would be looking for. Hopefully, it would be enough to keep the woman from going through with filing those charges, though. Cassie hated to think that Lucky might have to kiss Wilhelmina, or something more, just to get Mackenzie off the hook. There was also the added problem of Mackenzie not learning anything if Lucky paid for her crimes.

Of course, Lucky wouldn't want to have to pimp himself out to pay for those crimes, either. It wasn't as if Wilhelmina were a tasty morsel like Livvy.

"Cat!" Mia squealed.

Cassie whirled around, expecting to see Ethan's yellow cat, but this one was black. And it was one that Cassie recognized.

Oh, no. He hadn't.

Cassie hurried toward the stairs and encountered another cat. Yet another one she recognized. Both of them had belonged to Dixie Mae, which meant her father had dropped them off.

Or rather he was still dropping them off, she realized, when she spotted Mason-Dixon in the foyer.

He was in the process of letting a third one out of a kitty kennel. The moment the Siamese was free, she shot toward the hall. Her father stood there, smiling, the trio of kennels now at his feet. And he wasn't alone. Della was there.

"Mason-Dixon let himself in," Della said, sounding about as pleased with this visit as Cassie was. "I should have locked the door after I brought in the newspaper."

Her father offered no apology for that. "This'll teach Dixie Mae," he said. Which was a stupid thing to say.

"Gran's dead," Cassie reminded him. "You can't teach her anything now. Besides, you gave me two days to find homes for the cats, and it hasn't even been twenty-four hours."

"What's going on here?" Lucky asked, coming into the foyer.

He was holding the folded piece of paper, the one he'd had in the hall earlier, and he stuffed it back into his pocket. Judging from his expression, whatever was on it was bad news. Or maybe the expression was simply for the bad news right in front of them.

Her father.

"I'm delivering the cats." Her father looked as if he wanted to add some profanity to that, but he must have changed his mind. Maybe because he spotted the kids who'd followed Cassie down the stairs, but it was more likely because Lucky was giving him a "make my day" kind of glare.

"You could have called me first," Cassie scolded. "Or at least knocked."

"I'm tired of being polite." Laughable since Mason-Dixon was rarely polite. "I was also tired of waiting for you to do something about this mess your idiot grandmother made."

"I've been busy," Cassie grumbled.

"Yeah, I can see that." Her father's attention landed on Mackenzie. "Dixie Mae left you a mess, too."

That was *not* the right thing to say. Lucky stepped forward as if he might slug him. Cassie wouldn't have minded that so much—Mason-Dixon deserved a good butt-whipping—but she didn't want that to happen in front of the girls.

"Just leave," Cassie told her father. But then she paused and glanced at the three kennels again. "Where are the other three cats?"

Her father smiled.

Oh, no. That couldn't be good.

"Here's how this will work," he said. "You get the rest of the cats, and I get half of whatever Dixie Mae leaves you. Up front. I don't want to wait weeks for her will to be read. Find out what she left you and write me a check for half. I'm giving you two days. If not, you'll never see the other three cats again."

Cassie glanced at Lucky and Della to make sure she'd heard her father correctly. Apparently, she had, because they looked just as bewildered as she felt. Well, Della did anyway. Lucky looked ready to start that butt-whipping.

"You're holding the cats for ransom?" Lucky asked.

"You're damn right I am. Dixie Mae didn't give me a choice. She's the one who started this by giving me those cats. Well, I'm the one finishing it. Pay up."

Cassie shook her head. "It's possible that Gran didn't leave me any money in the will."

"Oh, she left you plenty all right. And if she didn't leave it to you, she left it to him." Mason-Dixon shot Lucky a glare. "Either way, I want to get paid, and I want it to happen sooner than later."

Lucky stepped closer. "Or?"

Mason-Dixon smiled again. "That's the thing, Cassie won't know what the *or* will be. And I know she wouldn't want to see anything happen to her grandmother's precious cats."

"I'll call the sheriff," Della volunteered.

But that only caused her father to laugh. "Dixie Mae left those cats to me. They're mine now. The sheriff can't take my property without cause, and for now I'm not giving him any cause." He headed out the door and down the porch steps. "Pay up," her father added in a growl as he left.

Lucky started to go after him, but Cassie took hold of his arm. "Don't give him the fight he wants. I'll figure a way to work this out." Though at the moment she couldn't think of how to do that.

So much was hitting her at once, and all Cassie wanted to do was curl up somewhere and calm down before she had another panic attack.

Thankfully, Lucky didn't go after Mason-Dixon. They all just stood there and watched her father drive away while the cats darted around the room. Cassie shut the door to keep them from darting outside, and when she turned Mia was there, her hand outstretched. She had the gold star that Livvy had given her in her palm.

"I can use my wish to make you happy," Mia said.

It was such a touching gesture that it brought tears to her eyes. Of course, she'd been on the verge of crying all morning—heck, all night—so just about anything would have set her off. Still, it was an amazing thing from an amazing little girl.

"Thank you," Cassie told her. "But you keep it. Use it on something for yourself."

It probably wasn't a good thing for her to continue to let Mia believe the star was magic, but Cassie was too drained to change that now. Maybe Mia wouldn't be too disappointed when it didn't work.

"You want me to make some calls to see if anyone is willing to give at least one of these cats a good home?" Della asked.

Cassie nodded. Thanked her, too. Cassie would have loved to have kept the cats herself, but she couldn't. Not unless she moved. And changed her work schedule to stay home more. If she did that, she'd basically have to quit her job, which would mean she would have no income.

"So, you gonna pay him or what?" Mackenzie asked. She didn't seem especially concerned one way or another.

"No," Lucky answered before Cassie could say anything. "You're not paying that duckweed a dime. I'll find out where the other three cats are and...negotiate to get them back."

Since he paused before the word *negotiate*, Cassie was concerned. "What does that mean exactly?" she asked.

Lucky looked her straight in the eyes. "It means I steal them."

Cassie was about to give him several reasons why he couldn't do that. Well, one reason anyway. He'd be arrested. But the sound of the approaching car stopped her, and she hurried to the sidelight window to look out. Maybe, just maybe, her father had had a change of heart—or to be more accurate, acquired a heart—and had decided to give her the rest of the cats.

But it wasn't her father's yellow Cadillac. It was a taxi, and it came to a stop directly in front of the house.

"Are you expecting anyone?" Della asked.

Cassie nodded. But certainly not this early. She wasn't ready to deal with...

Too late.

The taxi door opened, and the woman stepped out. Marla Candor.

"Hey, I've seen her on TV," Della said. "She's on one of those reality shows. A skanky one."

Yes, she was. She was also Cassie's client.

Marla had followed in the paths of other reality stars

to achieve fame. She'd done a sex tape, then made sure it was leaked to the press. When that hadn't given her the desired results, she'd made six more tapes. She also had a laundry list of mental issues that probably couldn't be addressed with a lifetime of therapy, much less the weekly session she scheduled with Cassie.

And her real name was Wendi Myrtle Stoddermeyer.

Marla wasn't alone on this particular visit. But then she never was. She had a cameraman with her who would film every minute of the session so that the best parts could be edited and included in the TV show. Of course, the "best parts" would be when Marla talked about her so-called sex addiction. Cassie wasn't convinced that sex was her addiction so much as her need for people to hear about her having sex.

"Della, would you please take the girls to the kitchen?" Cassie asked.

Thankfully, Della scurried them away.

"You should go, as well," Cassie said to Lucky.

But it was too late. Marla's attention had already landed on Lucky. Her eyes widened. She smiled, and while she didn't exactly lick her lips, it was close.

"Cassandra," Marla purred after she told the taxi driver to wait. But the purr was really for Lucky. So were the massive boobs she thrust in his direction. "I need to see you right away. It's been days since I had an orgasm, and I'm about to explode. And I see the very person who can help me with that."

"Play along," Cassie whispered to Lucky.

To save him from Marla's clutches, and the rest of the horny woman, Cassie leaned in and kissed him.

CHAPTER NINE

LUCKY HAD BEEN so focused on their guest—and he used that term loosely—that he hadn't seen the kiss coming. A first for him. He could usually spot the beginnings of a kiss at fifty paces, but here Cassie had been elbow-to-elbow with him and it had still taken him by surprise.

Not the surprise of the kiss itself.

He knew it was fake. No doubt meant to stop Marla from jumping him right there in the foyer so she wouldn't "explode." But the surprise came from the fact that for a fake kiss, it sure packed a wallop.

Oh, man.

This wasn't good. Fake kisses weren't supposed to taste like that. Or feel like that. He hadn't exactly had a barn full of fake kisses, but Lucky had some pretty realistic expectations in that area. This kiss had shot those expectations to smithereens.

"Oh," Marla said, making her way up the steps. "So that's how it is."

Cassie pulled away from Lucky, and he couldn't help but notice that she was breathing a little harder than she had been ten seconds ago. So maybe it had exceeded her expectations, too.

"Yes," Cassie insisted. "Marla, this is my *friend*, Lucky McCord."

That perked Marla right up. "A friend who shares his benefits?"

"No," Cassie said without hesitation. "His benefits are exclusively with me for the time being."

That didn't perk up Marla at all. "So, what about—"

"Come on," Cassie interrupted. "We should get started with the session. I'm sure you're anxious to get back to LA."

Marla looked far more anxious to examine his benefits, but Cassie hurried her out of the foyer and in the direction of the office she'd already scoped out.

"You gotta watch her hands," the cameraman whispered to Lucky as he trailed along behind them.

It was obvious Cassie was trying to keep Lucky well out of reach of Marla's hands. Also obvious that she hadn't wanted Marla to finish whatever she'd been about to say.

That might have something to do with the note Logan had given him.

Soon, he'd need to talk to Cassie about that, but for now he had a cat issue to deal with, and he also needed to call Bernie to see what progress had been made on finding the girls' aunt or some other next of kin.

Lucky made his way to the kitchen, dodging two of the cats along the way. Since he doubted Mason-Dixon had brought litter boxes, he moved that particular task to the top of his list. He called the grocery store and asked someone to bring over cat supplies and lots of them.

He didn't have the number of the one stripper that he did know at Mason-Dixon's club, but it didn't take him long to get it from a ranch hand. Lucky made the call to find out if she'd spotted the other three felines, but the call went to voice mail. Lucky left her a message.

He found the girls at the kitchen table eating breakfast. At least that's what Mia was doing. Mackenzie was poking her fork at a pancake as if testing it for signs of life.

"Miss Della made shapes," Mia announced, proudly showing him the remains of what appeared to be a heart-shaped pancake. Mackenzie's had probably been a heart, too, but it was hard to tell with all the punctures.

Della smiled, dished up a pancake for him, but Lucky frowned when he looked at it. It definitely wasn't a heart even if he squinted. "No shape for me?" he asked, hoping he didn't sound too disappointed.

"Round is a shape," Della reminded him. She dropped a kiss on the top of his head and put a jar of peanut butter on the table. His favorite thing to eat with pancakes, so he thanked her.

"So, is the skank staying?" Mackenzie asked.

Lucky debated if he should correct her for saying *skánk*, but it seemed a G-rated enough word, especially considering Mackenzie could have used something much, much worse.

"No. She'll leave after her therapy session." Lucky hoped. The taxi was waiting for her out front, so that was a good sign.

"And what about the cats? Are they staying?" Three questions in under a minute. A record for Mackenzie.

"I'm still working on that."

"I want 'em to stay," Mia declared before cramming more of the pancake in her mouth.

Since this might be his best chance at having a real

talk with them, Lucky dived right in. He dived right into the pancake, too. "Tell me about your aunt Alice. Is she a nice person?"

He might as well have asked what it was like to walk on the moon because both girls gave him a blank stare. "We gotta an aunt Alice?" Mia asked.

Lucky tried not to groan. He'd hoped that since the woman was their mother's half sister they had at least met her. It would have even been better if they'd known her and been excited about the possibility of living with her. But no dice.

"Did your mom ever talk about her sister?" He aimed that one at Mackenzie since he wasn't even sure Mia would remember their mom.

Mackenzie continued to put fork holes in the pancake. "Is that who you're trying to pawn us off on?"

Honestly, yes. But he wouldn't dare say that to them. Besides, they wouldn't be going with the aunt unless he was sure she would give them a good home. And just because they didn't know her, it didn't mean she wouldn't be a good guardian.

"A lot of people are trying to find your next of kin," he explained. "Your aunt Alice is just one possibility."

"What's a poss-a-bilty mean?" Mia asked at the same moment her sister demanded, "Who else?"

Lucky glanced at Della to see if she could help, but she gave him a "you're on your own" shrug.

"A possibility is someone who might get the chance to take care of you and love you." That part was for Mia. Lucky turned to Mackenzie for the rest. "Right now, only your aunt Alice is on the list," he admitted. "But we're working on others. My brother Logan is making some calls. So is the lawyer. I'll also be making some myself."

He'd barely finished the explanation when he heard a sound. A moan of some kind. The sort a water buffalo might make when in heat. And it was coming from the office at the back of the house where Cassie was having her therapy session with Marla. When there was a second one, even louder than the first, Lucky hurried back to make sure someone wasn't having a seizure.

"Is everything okay?" he asked when he reached the door.

"Why don't you come in and see," Marla said, giggling. And moaning.

The door opened, just a fraction, and Cassie poked her nose in through the narrow opening. "She can have orgasms by just thinking about it. My advice, don't come in here. Oh, and watch out for her hands."

Lucky was so intrigued by the double hand warning that he almost wanted to go in there just to see what it was all about. Almost. But he'd moved out of the curiosity-killing-the-cat stage about the time he'd sprouted his first chest hair.

"It won't be much longer now," Cassie assured him. "Once she's finished this orgasm, she'll be ready to go." And she shut the door.

This sure seemed like a long way to come for an orgasm, especially one Marla could have just by thinking about it. But maybe she needed Cassie coaxing her or something.

Which, of course, totally interested him.

Lucky blamed that on the fake kiss. It had heated up some things inside him.

He started back to the kitchen so he could keep an

eye on the girls, but he'd hardly made it a few steps when the office door opened again, and Marla came waltzing out. She looked a lot happier than she had when she'd gone in even though there hadn't been much time for mental foreplay.

She smiled when she saw him, continued waltzing. Except she grabbed his balls when she went past him.

Well, hell.

It not only shocked him, it also hurt. That's what the warning was all about. The grab wouldn't hinder his chances of fathering children should he ever plan on doing that, but he might walk funny for a while.

"I did warn you," the cameraman said, and that's when Lucky noticed that the guy was keeping his distance. And walking funny.

Cassie followed the pair, but she stopped once they'd cleared the kitchen. Probably because she didn't want Marla around the girls. Lucky agreed with that.

"You want to talk about this?" he asked Cassie.

"No," she said without hesitation. She checked her watch. "I guess I can get started with some calls about the cats."

"Not just yet," Lucky said. Since the girls were still at the breakfast table, this might be the best chance he got to talk to Cassie alone. He pulled her back into the hall and out of earshot of anyone in the kitchen.

"If this is about that kiss…" she started.

"It's not." Best to leave that subject alone. He had a lot of experience with lust clouding his judgment, and that kiss had fallen into the lust category for him.

"Then if it's about Marla grabbing you—"

"That's not it, either." Lucky took out the note. "It's about what's in this."

"That's the paper you had in the hall earlier. Is it about the girls' aunt?" But she froze. No doubt because of the expression on his face. "It's about me."

Cassie groaned and would have moved away from him if Lucky hadn't taken hold of her.

"Let me guess," she snapped. "Logan went digging into my life."

Since that about summed it up, Lucky nodded.

"He had no right," Cassie insisted.

"I agree with you, but it's just something Logan does. He wanted to make sure none of this was a scam. And yeah, his digging into your life probably started to make sure you weren't part of that theoretical scam. But no scam."

However, it was something much worse.

"Let me see the note," she demanded.

He handed it to her, but Lucky figured she wasn't going to like some of it. Mainly because it wasn't just a note. It was a one-page report from a private investigator Logan kept on retainer.

Lucky watched as her eyes skirted over the first part. Her bio and work history. No surprises there, but her eyes stopped skirting on the section that had caused him to pause, too.

Involuntary commitment to Sweet Meadows Meditation and Relaxation Facility in Oregon.

There weren't many other details, only her commitment date, which was a week ago. But Lucky figured that "involuntary commitment" phrase said it all. There was also the name of the person who'd had her committed, but that was all that the PI had apparently been able to get.

It was enough.

"The only reason I showed you that," he said, "was because I want to make sure you're okay."

"Yes, I'm okay!" she snapped. But then almost immediately she sagged against the wall. Just that short outburst seemed to have exhausted her, and Cassie gave a weary sigh. While still clutching the paper, she covered her face with her hands. "Obviously, I'm not okay. You saw what happened to me."

Lucky wasn't sure how to approach this, whether he should question her more about that or not. She certainly hadn't seemed eager to discuss the panic attack. However, while he was having a mental debate with himself, Cassie must have taken his silence as an opening to explain herself.

"The panic attacks started last month," she said. That seemed to make her angry. Maybe at herself. Maybe at him. Maybe at Logan for uncovering this. "I missed some of the signs with a patient. I screwed up big-time."

Lucky took her hands from her face so he could make eye contact. "You want to talk about it?"

She scowled, maybe because he sounded a little like a therapist. Not intentionally. He just wasn't sure where to go here. When women started crying, he usually found some excuse to get the heck out of there, but that was part of his old baggage. Cassie might need him to ditch that baggage for a while and listen to her.

Or not.

"I'll check on the girls," she said, and she would have darted right out of there if he hadn't stepped in front of her.

"The girls are fine." He hoped. But he wasn't so sure

about Cassie. "Look, I can handle them and the cats. If you need to go back to that place in Oregon, then go."

Her eyes narrowed. "I'm not crazy."

Lucky held up his hands in defense. "I didn't say you were." But this would have been a good time for him to say something else, something reassuring, instead of letting his gaze drift to the paper that she had wadded up.

Because he was right in her face, Lucky saw the exact moment that she got it. That he was concerned about those two words.

Involuntary commitment.

Cassie backed up, huffed. Then sighed again. "I had a bad attack and ended up in the ER. Someone convinced the staff that I needed help, and that's how I ended up at Sweet Meadows."

Lucky got the feeling that was the toned-down version of what had happened.

"Someone?" he repeated. And he knew the name of that someone because it was on Logan's report. "Who is this Dr. Andrew Knight who had you sent to that place?"

More huffing and sighing. "I meant to mention all of this earlier, but it slipped my mind. He's my boyfriend. More or less."

Well, that was a mouthful. This was the first he was hearing of a boyfriend, even one that she considered more or less.

Whatever the heck that meant.

"Andrew overreacted," she added. "He does that sometimes, and we're having a cooling-off period because of it."

Translation—she was pissed because he'd put her in

that place. Lucky didn't blame her. He would have been pissed, too, and there would have been more than just a cooling-off period. He would have dumped the jerk.

And, no, that didn't have anything to do with the fake kiss Cassie and he had shared. It had more to do with the real moments they'd gone through in the past twenty-four hours.

"Andrew's a shrink?" Lucky asked.

She nodded. "But he knows he made a mistake sending me there, and he signed my release papers as soon as I told him I needed to come home to attend my grandmother's funeral."

"What a prince." Lucky didn't bother to take the stank off that, either.

Cassie didn't huff again, but she did fold her arms over her chest and stare at him. "I'll discuss Andrew with you if you'll explore in great detail why you haven't had sex in three months."

She probably thought there was no way he'd chat about something like that. Well, she was wrong.

"Dixie Mae's the reason I haven't had sex. She wasn't spending much time at work so I took over things she normally does."

That was close to the truth anyway. He wouldn't get into the fact that Dixie Mae's failing health hadn't exactly put him in a romantic frame of mind.

"I could feel her slipping away, and there was nothing I could do about it." Lucky hadn't intended to discuss all this. Too similar to another death.

His mother's.

"Oh," Cassie said. The tone of a woman who'd just been put in her place. Something that Lucky hadn't intended.

"You were there for her, and I wasn't," Cassie admitted.

Hell's flipping bells. The tears watered her eyes again. "You weren't there for her because that clown Andrew put you in a nuthouse."

She shook her head. Cried. Yep, no stopping those tears now. She was in a full boo-hoo mode. Lucky had no choice but to pull her into his arms.

"I swear, I didn't know Dixie Mae was that sick," Cassie added through the sobs.

"Because she didn't want you to know. She knew how busy you were, and she didn't want to disrupt your life."

"She disrupted yours," she pointed out just as quickly.

He would have used his shoulder to shrug if Cassie hadn't been crying on it. "I didn't mind. Dixie Mae got me through some hard times. She's kept me under her wing ever since my folks were killed."

"Yes," she whispered.

It was just one word, but it seemed to him to mean a whole lot more. Lucky eased back so he could look at her. That look was enough of a prompt for her to continue.

"I remember when they died," she said.

Again, there was a whole lot more that went with those additional five words.

Of course she remembered. Everyone in town over the age of twenty-five probably did. It'd been talked about, gossiped about, for years. And Lucky was pretty sure that somewhere in all that gossip, there'd been talk about him. About what he'd done.

Or rather what he hadn't done.

"All right," Lucky said. "If we keep on this subject, you'll have to talk about Andrew."

As expected, that hushed her. Cassie gave the tears another wipe. "I'll just freshen up before I see the girls," she insisted, and she ducked into the powder room that was across the hall from the office.

Lucky didn't know all that'd gone on with this Andrew, but it had to be damn bad for her to back off the conversation like that. Especially since she probably wanted to know what'd actually happened the night his parents were killed. Yes, most folks over the age of twenty-five knew about the car wreck, and those same folks wanted the dirty little details. But Lucky figured that was something he might have to take to the grave.

Talking about it just wasn't an option.

He decided to wait for her before facing the kids again. Mainly because he needed a couple of seconds, too. He didn't want Mia picking up on his suddenly sour mood. As sweet as she was, she'd probably want to use her magic star to cheer him up. But even magic wouldn't work on this.

His phone rang, and he saw the name on the screen. Sugar Monroe. One of the calls he'd been waiting for. And nope, Sugar wasn't her stage name. It was the name her mother had given her at birth, and maybe it had been what had set her on her present career path.

As a stripper at the Slippery Pole.

"Lucky," Sugar said the moment he answered. "I got your voice mail, but I'm a little confused. Were you actually asking about cats or was that a G-rated way of asking about p—"

"Cats," he quickly supplied. No sense letting Sugar get the idea that this was a hookup call. He hadn't hooked up with her in years and had no plans to re-hook. And Lucky hoped no single, unattached straight man ever knew he'd had a thought like that.

"You mean those cats that Mason-Dixon inherited from his mama?" Sugar asked.

"The very ones. There should be three of them, and I need to know where they are."

"Last time I saw them, they were in Mason-Dixon's bedroom. Well, it's really more of a dump, but he sleeps here sometimes if he can coax one of the girls into joining him."

Not a pretty picture. And especially not one that Lucky wanted in his head.

"Can you check and see if they're still there?" he asked.

"Sure. Anything for you, Lucky. I'm at the club to pick up some stuff and I'm walking over to Mason-Dixon's room now. Say, when are you coming back here? It's been a while since I've seen you."

"I've been kind of busy."

"Right. What with Dixie Mae dying and all. And what with inheriting those kids. Mason-Dixon said the older girl could work for him soon."

Over Lucky's dead body. Over Mason-Dixon's dead body, too. "She's only thirteen."

"You're sure? Because Mason-Dixon said she was—"

"Sugar, if you don't mind, I'd rather not hear what he has to say about her. Because I'd have to beat the shit out of him. Understand?"

"Yeah, I guess. Okay, I'm outside Mason-Dixon's room, but it's locked. Hold on a second, and I'll put my ear to the door and listen for anything or anybody moving around in there. Yeah," Sugar added several seconds later. "I hear cat sounds."

"Uh, you're sure it's cats and not Mason-Dixon?"

"It's cats all right," she verified. "Mason-Dixon's a moaner, not a meower."

Yet something else Lucky didn't want in his head. "Any sign of Mason-Dixon?"

"Not yet, but he'll be here any minute. He usually comes in around this time."

Not good. "How late will he stay?"

"Late," Sugar verified. "Again, it goes back to if he's able to coax one of the girls to his room. Won't be me, mind you. Don't shit where you eat. That's my motto."

Apparently, that was a motto that Mason-Dixon didn't embrace. "Is it possible he could end up staying there all night?"

"If he hooks up with Cherry, yes. She's an all-night kind of girl."

Hell, he'd need a shower after this conversation. Lucky suddenly felt as if he'd just had a bucket of scum poured over his head.

"So yeah, if he goes with Cherry," Sugar went on. "That's not her real name, by the way. It's Jennifer. Anyway, it'd be the wee hours of the morning before Mason-Dixon leaves."

Lucky hated to plan this around Mason-Dixon's *love life*, but he didn't have a choice. Cassie's father likely carried a gun, and even if he didn't, Lucky preferred not to get arrested.

"If you're wanting to come by when you know for sure Mason-Dixon's not here," Sugar added, "then I'd say stop in around nine in the morning."

"You think the cats will be okay until then?" Lucky asked.

"I can make sure they are."

Good. "Thanks. And I have another favor. Can you be at the club tomorrow morning to let me in?"

"Sure. But if I scratch your back, you can scratch mine. Deal?" He could almost see her smiling.

"Deal," he agreed.

Damn. First Wilhelmina and now Sugar. If he kept owing women all these favors, he wasn't going to have time for anything else. Whatever Sugar wanted to do with him, it wouldn't lead to sex, he'd make sure of that, but it might mean hours and hours of keeping her at bay.

"I'll be there at nine in the morning," Lucky told her.

And after that, he'd be able to add "cat thief" and "bay-keeping gigolo" to his resume.

CHAPTER TEN

CASSIE HAD NEVER stolen anything in her life. Not even another girl's boyfriend, but she had no doubts that this theft had to happen. With the state of mind her father had been in, he could hurt the cats. Or else just lock them up somewhere and not bother to take care of them. No way did Cassie want that to happen.

A theft probably seemed extreme to some people, but the cats were her last living link to her grandmother. And no, she didn't count her father. It'd been a long, long time since Mason-Dixon had been a son to Dixie Mae, and he had such a mean streak that he might do something to the cats just to get back at his dead mother. And back at Cassie.

"I can still do this solo," Lucky offered. "You can wait in the car."

It wasn't his first time offering. Right from the start, he'd insisted she not go with him, but there was no way she was going to let him do her dirty work. Though she'd had a moment's hesitation when Lucky had reminded her that if they got caught they could be arrested.

And locked up by Deputy Davy.

Lucky had added that if he went in alone, at least she'd be there to take care of the girls for the half day or so it would take him to get out of jail. Cassie wasn't comfortable with the possibility of being arrested, but if they did get caught, she had already decided that she would take the fall so Lucky wouldn't land in jail. That way, he'd be the one there for the girls.

The only thing they had to do now was hurry. Della and Stella were watching the children, but Cassie didn't want Mackenzie using this as an opportunity to run away again. That's the reason Lucky had called in reinforcements.

In this case, Livvy.

Livvy had agreed to call Mackenzie with the promise that she'd bring by some of her shoes later for the girl to try on. Maybe the shoes would have high enough heels that if Mackenzie did decide to run, the heel height alone would slow her down.

Cassie reminded herself to give Livvy a huge thanks for this.

Lucky drove out of town and to the outskirts where it didn't take long, less than a mile, for her to spot the Slippery Pole. The exterior was just as tacky as the name. It was flesh pink, and it had a neon sign of a woman with massive breasts. Since it was daylight, the sign wasn't on, but Cassie knew that when it was, the woman's nipples blinked in invitation.

Her father probably thought that was classy.

There was only one vehicle in front of the place— an older-model red Mustang. It was pocked with dents and rust spots, but despite that the vanity plates were gleaming with one word.

Sugar.

Thank goodness the stripper was there to let them in.

Lucky pulled the car to the back of the building and

parked out of sight. The car itself was another sneaky ploy since it wasn't a vehicle her father would recognize should he drive up. Lucky had left his truck at the ranch and used one of the vehicles from the family's garage instead.

The moment they got out, the back door opened, and a red-haired woman stuck out her head. According to Lucky, this was Sugar Monroe, one of her father's employees. The woman hurriedly motioned for them to come in, but the hurriedness didn't extend to the long look she gave Lucky.

Good grief.

This happened wherever they went, and the woman just kept giving him the look until they were inside. Then she kissed him. A loud smack right on the lips.

"Looking good as always," she purred.

Lucky stepped back, and since the overhead lights weren't on, it was hard to see his expression, but Cassie thought he might have blushed. Of course, it could also be a flush of arousal.

Not that she cared.

Okay, she did, but it was stupid because the kiss that Lucky and she had shared was a fake one. The one the stripper had given him was likely the most recent of many.

"Sugar, this is Cassie, Mason-Dixon's daughter," Lucky said, making introductions.

Until then Sugar hadn't noticed Cassie in any way. That happened a lot, too, whenever Cassie was around Lucky, but Sugar acknowledged her now. "Don't you breathe one word to your dad about this," Sugar warned her. No lovey-dovey look for Cassie. "I could lose my job."

Apparently, that was a big deal to Sugar, though Cassie couldn't imagine this being a job worth keeping. The place smelled like a urinal mixed with other bodily fluids that Cassie didn't want to identify. There were always rumors that her father was pimping out his girls, but to the best of her knowledge, he'd never been arrested for it.

"This way," Sugar said. "But you need to hurry. No telling who could come walking in here."

Sugar herself didn't exactly hurry. She fell into step alongside Lucky. "How much longer are you gonna be in town?" she asked.

"I'm not sure." Unlike Sugar, he seemed focused on the task. "Cassie and I have been busy with the girls."

Sugar glanced back at her, giving her a head-to-toe examination in the span of a couple of seconds. Apparently, she didn't approve, but Sugar's narrowed eyes relaxed when she turned back to Lucky.

Cassie had only been to the strip club once in her life, and that was when she'd been trying to mend fences between her father and grandmother, but she'd never been to this back hallway. Only to her father's office just off the front of the building. At the time, she'd thought his office had to be the worst part of the place, but she'd been wrong. This was.

It was a tangle of dressing rooms and rooms with unmade beds. Junk was strewn everywhere, including outside the door where they stopped. There was a pair of red thong panties on the floor and someone had used a black marker to scrawl Mason-Dick on the door.

"Mason-Dixon keeps this locked," Sugar explained, but she plucked a bobby pin from her hair and had the lock open in a snap.

The moment Sugar opened the door, Cassie heard the cats. And smelled them. She hadn't thought anything else could cut through the Slippery Pole smells, but she'd been wrong about that, too. Apparently, her father hadn't changed the litter box, though at least there were bowls of food and water. That still wouldn't earn him any favors in her eyes. He simply didn't want his "investments" to starve to death.

All three of the cats started meowing, and the Persian—her Gran's favorite—began to coil around Cassie's legs, looking for attention. Cassie gave all three a quick pet, but they had to hurry now. She and Lucky put the three into their kennels and started back out.

They didn't get far.

"Sugar?" her father called out. Judging from the sound of his voice and the footsteps, he was headed straight toward them.

"Oh, God," Cassie whispered, something that she was fairly sure was said often in this place. Not as a prayer, either.

"Sugar?" he repeated. "What the hell are you doing here so early?"

"Go," Sugar insisted, closing the door to her father's room and locking it. She started toward those footsteps. "Hurry."

It was really good advice, but it came a few seconds too late. Her father was right there, and Cassie braced herself for a confrontation, but thankfully he had his attention fixed on Sugar.

Lucky pulled Cassie into one of the junky rooms, but he didn't stop there. He yanked her to the floor on the other side of a bed, and he threw some clothes over the kennels. Probably so her father wouldn't be able to hear the cats should they start meowing.

The covers worked. Maybe it was the sudden darkness, but the cats stayed quiet. Cassie's breathing, not so much. That's because in the scurry to hide, she had ended up with Lucky on top of her. With her head right next to a box of condoms. If she believed in such a thing as fate, she might have thought it was trying to tell her something. But Cassie didn't believe in that kind of fate.

However, she did believe in basic animal attraction. Lucky was an animal. So was she, and she was attracted to him. Along with seemingly every other female in town.

For some stupid reason, she remembered the part about him not having had sex for three months. Maybe that made his body more attentive to hers. And vice versa. Maybe it was because he'd just risked jail to save the cats when he didn't even like them.

Maybe it was because she herself hadn't had sex in such a long time.

Whatever the reason, Cassie found herself thinking about kissing him. No. She thought about having sex with him, which, of course, would have included kissing.

She couldn't be sure, but Cassie thought maybe he was thinking about it, too. He shifted a little. The right kind of shift to align the parts of their bodies required for sex.

And yes, he was *interested*.

The alignment gave her proof of that because she could feel the beginnings of his erection. It was stupid to be flattered by that. Even more stupid to make him harder, but that's what she did when she shifted her hips a little. Just enough so that if they'd been naked, they would have had accidental sex.

A hoarse sound rumbled in Lucky's throat, and when his eyes came to hers, he had a "what do you think you're doing?" expression. Or maybe "two can play this game" one. He shifted, this time moving his erection against the vee of her thighs. Then *into* that vee.

Cassie made her own hoarse sound.

And shifted again.

Good grief, this was what horny teenagers did to get off. Not that she'd ever done it, but she was fairly sure now that with some kisses it would work. Of course, just because it would work didn't mean it *should*.

She could hear Sugar and her father talking, figured what they were saying might be important for Lucky's and her escape. Still, Cassie couldn't get her mind completely off what was happening with Lucky's erection and her vee.

Then Lucky kissed her.

It wasn't really a kiss, though. He was breathing heavy now, and it was hitting against her mouth. Against her neck, too. Coupled with the shifting, Cassie thought she might be within seconds of having an orgasm. A rare event for her.

And then it all vanished.

The footsteps started again, coming closer to the door of the room where Lucky and she were shifting and veeing.

"You're sure you haven't seen them?" her father asked Sugar.

"Trust me, if I'd seen Lucky McCord, I would have

remembered," Sugar answered. "Say, are Lucky and your daughter doing the nasty?"

"Not a chance," her father growled. "She's not his type."

Cassie's eyes narrowed because that was almost certainly an insult. Well, apparently she was Lucky's type because there were only a few millimeters of fabric stopping her from *doing the nasty* with him.

"Remember, if you see my daughter or Lucky anywhere near the place, I want you to call the cops," her father added to Sugar.

"Will do. Well, everything's locked up back here. I was just headed to the front door."

There were a few footsteps, but then they stopped. "What were you doing back here anyway?" Mason-Dixon asked.

Cassie felt her breath freeze, and this time it didn't have anything to do with Lucky's body pressing hard against hers. Almost anyway. She didn't want Sugar to get fired, and that's exactly what would happen if her father went into his room and realized the cats were missing.

"I was picking up some makeup I left—"

"Well, clear out," her father snapped, cutting off Sugar. "I've got some company with me."

Cassie's heart dropped even more when she heard a woman giggle, and she didn't think it was Sugar's giggle, either.

"Is that one of the Nederland sisters?" Sugar asked.

"Not that it's any of your business, but yeah. Now, clear out."

Cassie knew the Nederland sisters. They were all

the size of tree trunks, and it wasn't a good idea for her father or any other man to play around with them.

That's because the Nederland sisters had brothers.

They were double the size of tree trunks, and they used their limb-size fists to pulverize any man they thought was disrespecting their sisters. Since men "disrespected" the sisters a lot, the brothers got to do a lot of pulverizing. She was surprised that her father would choose one of the sisters for a lover, but maybe he wanted to add some variety to his life. Could also be that all the strippers were just plain fed up with him and had turned him down.

"You're sure you want to take a woman into your room?" Sugar asked. "Even with the door closed, it smells really bad. Can't imagine how bad it is in there. Why don't you use the costume room instead? There's a chaise in there and some fun toys."

"Fine," her father barked, though his bark couldn't hide that he thought the costume room was a good idea. "Now, leave."

She heard the sound of his footsteps again, headed to the front of the building this time. Sugar's ploy had worked.

"I owe Sugar big-time," Lucky mumbled, not sounding very happy about that. "This might require more than back-scratching."

Cassie wasn't sure she wanted to know what he meant by that, and there wasn't time to find out. Lucky threw the covers off the kennels and they hurried out of there. The moment they were in the car, he sped away.

"How much time do you think we have before my father figures out the cats are missing?" she asked.

"How long does it take to screw a Nederland?" he countered.

Cassie suspected not long, but it sounded like the start of a joke that she didn't want to hear.

"We can't take the cats to the house," Lucky continued. "That's the first place Mason-Dixon will look. We'll take them to my office instead."

Cassie had no idea what he meant by that until Lucky pulled to a stop in the parking lot of McCord Cattle Brokers. "Logan had offices done for Riley, Anna and me, and the cats can stay there for a while. I'll bring over food and a litter box for them later."

Lucky grabbed two of the kennels, Cassie took the third, and with the cats howling now, they raced inside. Of course, they'd have to tell Logan they were there so he didn't think strays had gotten inside the building. Logan's car wasn't in the lot, but there were two others plus a work truck loaded with paint and supplies. No doubt part of the redecorating effort.

There was evidence of that redecorating as soon as Lucky and she went inside. A man on a tall ladder was painting the high ceiling. There was also a tarp covering the floor.

Lucky led her to an office, one totally different from her father's. For one thing, it was clean and perfectly decorated with a high-end desk and bookcases. The windows all overlooked a rose garden. Even his name was on an etched copper plate on the door. Considering the way everything was placed and arranged, she doubted he'd even stepped foot in the place. And he didn't even step foot in it now. He turned the cats loose from the doorway and was in the process of closing it when someone called out his name.

Helene.

Looking more like a cover model than some cover models, Helene breezed toward them. Cassie didn't really know her. Helene's family had sent her to private schools in San Antonio, but of course, Cassie had seen her around town and shopped in her businesses. Helene owned both the antiques store and the clothing boutique, as well as an interior decorating business.

"Cats?" Helene asked, getting a glimpse of them just before Lucky shut the door.

"A temporary fix," he assured her. "I'll be back later with supplies."

"No need. I can do that for you. I understand you have your hands full with Mia and Mackenzie."

It wasn't a question, which meant Helene likely knew all about it. Of course she did. Cassie had heard Della buzzing about Helene staying the night before so certainly Logan would have discussed things with his girlfriend.

Oh, God.

Did that mean Helene also knew about the background check Logan had done on her? Or rather what he'd learned in that background check, about her being sent to Sweet Meadows? Cassie hoped not because she didn't want it getting all over town. If the press picked up on it... Well, Cassie didn't want to think about that.

But she thought about it anyway.

She definitely wouldn't be asked to be on any other talk shows and she'd lose the few clients that she had. She wouldn't mind saying goodbye to Marla, but if she lost the others, she'd lose her source of income.

"I take it you'd like to keep this a secret?" Helene

asked. She tipped her head to the office, but she also gave Cassie a lingering glance.

Yes, Helenc knew. Things passed between them—woman to woman—and Cassie tried to plead her need for silence without actually saying anything. She didn't want to open this up for discussion.

"Definitely keep it secret," Lucky insisted. "And especially don't tell Mason-Dixon. If he comes here—"

"He won't get anywhere near your office," Helene assured them. "Anything else I can do to help?"

Lucky shook his head and turned to leave but then stopped. "Has Logan been having headaches?"

Cassie certainly hadn't expected the question and apparently neither had Helene, and Cassie didn't think the woman's surprise was because she didn't know the answer. "Have you asked Logan about it?" Helene responded.

"Is there something to ask?" Lucky fired right back.

Judging from Helene's sigh, this could go on for a while. "It's not my place to say anything." She tipped her head to the cats. "I'll see about getting them whatever they need." And with that, Helene glided up the stairs.

Lucky stood there a moment as if he might call her back, but his phone buzzed before he could say or do anything. He cursed the moment he looked at the text message that popped onto the screen.

"It's from Della," he said, holding it out so she could see.

But it was hard to read it since Lucky started running toward the exit. Cassie caught up with him, but she didn't get a chance to read it until they were in the car:

We got some problems. Two of them. Get home fast.

"Don't speculate," Lucky warned Cassie. "It could be just about the cats."

Though he doubted that would have prompted a text from Della. Heck, Lucky hadn't even known she could text. But he figured it had to be something urgent for the woman not to call him and give him some details. And that something urgent was likely to be that the girls had run away again.

That wasn't even the worst thing he could come up with, though.

After all, there was the possibility that Mackenzie was suicidal. Had she done something to hurt herself?

Lucky cursed, again. He shouldn't have left them. He should have had some friends deal with the cats at the Slippery Pole, or even paid the Nederlands to do it.

Cassie didn't speculate about the possibilities of what Della's text could mean, at least not out loud. But the moment the house came into view, they spotted two cars in the driveway, and one of them was a Spring Hill police cruiser. Maybe Della had already called out a search party. At least there wasn't an ambulance, but Lucky had a sickening thought—maybe the ambulance had already come and gone, and Mackenzie was at the hospital.

Two days.

That's all it had taken for him to have the "lying in a ditch" fear that he'd heard his mother and other parents go on about. Not that he was a parent, but he now had an inkling of what not knowing could do to a person responsible for a child.

Lucky was right behind Cassie when she bolted out of the car, and he raced into the house fully expecting Della to be standing there with the bad news. But it wasn't Della.

Mia and Mackenzie were in the foyer.

Mackenzie didn't appear to be hurt. Neither was Mia. And he was so relieved to see them that he hauled them into his arms. However, Lucky hadn't seen Cassie moving closer to do the same thing, making it a group hug. Mackenzie went stiff, but Mia hugged them right back.

"I thought you'd left," Lucky admitted. He wouldn't mention the other bad thought he'd had. "I'm glad you didn't. But when Della texted and said there was a problem—"

"Two problems," Mackenzie interrupted. "The deputy's here, and he's searching for the other cats."

Della came out from the living room to finish that explanation. "Apparently, Mason-Dixon called him about fifteen minutes ago, and Davy came rushing right over."

Well, it sure hadn't taken Mason-Dixon long with the Nederland sister.

"I'm gonna find those cats," Davy called down from the top of the stairs. "And when I do, I'm gonna have to arrest you, Lucky, because I know you're the one who took them."

Cassie huffed. "And how would you know that? I had more motive to take them than Lucky. They're my grandmother's cats."

"You're not a troublemaker like Lucky." Davy gave his head an indignant wobble and hooked his thumbs over his equipment belt. "Go ahead, ask him how many times he's been in jail."

This wasn't a subject he wanted to discuss in front

of the girls, but since Davy had brought it up, Lucky went with it. "And how many times have I been in jail because I stole something?" He made a goose egg with his fingers.

That caused Davy to come back down the stairs. "That doesn't mean you didn't take 'em. Where have you been for the past half hour?"

"With me," Cassie jumped to answer. Which, of course, wasn't much of an answer at all.

Davy came into the foyer and stared at them, clearly waiting for more. And Cassie gave him more all right. She hooked her arm through Lucky's and got very close. Shoulder to shoulder. Hip to hip.

"Lucky and I wanted a little time alone," she added. Not exactly a lie, but Cassie probably didn't understand where this would lead.

To gossip and lots of it.

In an hour it would be all over town that Cassie and he were sleeping together, and it didn't help that this attraction was whirling all around them. No doubt leftover lust from that "cuddling" session on the floor of the Slippery Pole. Lucky was certainly still feeling the effects of that. It might take a week for him to go fully soft again.

Davy's gaze whipped back and forth between them as if trying to decide if Cassie was telling the truth. He must have decided that she was because the deputy headed for the door, already taking out his phone. "If those cats don't turn up soon, I'll be back," he warned them.

Davy would, and that was a reminder for Lucky to move the cats, maybe out of town.

"We could blackmail my father," Cassie suggested.

"We know he was with one of the Nederland sisters, and we could threaten him with that if he doesn't back off."

Lucky had to nod. No way would Mason-Dixon want that to get around since then he'd have to deal with the Nederland brothers.

"Blackmail?" someone said. It wasn't a voice Lucky recognized. Nor did he recognize the dark-haired man who stepped out of the living room. The guy was tall, moved like a dancer. Sort of looked like one, too, in his blue suit. The wrong color blue to be from around Spring Hill. That suit had big city/expensive tailor written all over it.

"Remember I texted you that there were two problems," Della said. "Davy was one." She hitched her thumb to the visitor. "He's the other."

"Andrew." Cassie's voice was hardly louder than a whisper, but there was plenty of emotion in it. Mainly surprise. However, Lucky thought he detected some other things, too. Things he couldn't put his finger on.

It took Lucky a moment to make the connection. Dr. Andrew Knight was the person who'd committed Cassie to that "relaxation" place.

And he was her boyfriend.

More or less.

Andrew came closer, and without even acknowledging that Cassie still had her arm looped through Lucky's, he took hold of her and pulled her into his own arms. Cassie had a similar reaction to Mackenzie's, from when they'd shared that group hug earlier. She went a little stiff, but maybe that didn't have anything to do with an absence of attraction. Maybe she was just uncomfortable because her more-or-less boyfriend had caught her hugging up another man.

"Andrew," Cassie repeated when he finally let go of her. "Why are you here?"

"Blackmail?" he repeated. He spared the girls a glance. Finally, he spared Lucky one, too. "It sounds as if I got here just in time." He stepped away from Cassie, extended his hand for Lucky to shake. "I'm Dr. Andrew Knight."

"Lucky McCord."

"Interesting nickname," he said, managing to sound like a pompous ass with just those two words. Lucky's opinion of him didn't improve when Andrew opened his mouth again and continued with, "I understand you ride bulls for a living?"

Yeah, definitely pomp with plenty of ass thrown in.

"Among other things," Lucky answered.

It would have been so easy to get into a pissing contest with this ding-dong. After all, Lucky co-owned a rodeo promotion business. A successful one. Plus, he was a McCord. That came with trust funds and shit.

Especially the shit.

But even if Lucky hadn't had those things, it still didn't give Andrew the right to look down on him. Or the girls. Though that's what he appeared to be doing when he turned his attention in their direction.

"And you two must be Mia and Mackenzie," Andrew said.

"Must we?" Mackenzie fired back.

Lucky tried not to laugh. Failed a little. It earned him a nasty side glance from Dr. Dickhead, and the man certainly didn't laugh. He sighed. The kind of sigh a person might make when trying to convey, *I've got my work cut out for me.*

"I'm here to help you," Andrew said to the girls.

"Uh, I called Sarah," Cassie interrupted. "Child psychology is her area of expertise. Where is she?"

"She won't be coming. Sarah called me after she spoke to you and wanted me to take some of her clients while she was here. I told her that wasn't necessary— that I'd already cleared my schedule and was booking the flight as we spoke."

Cassie shook her head. "But why?"

His next sigh was more of an *Isn't it obvious?* "Blackmail?" he repeated as if it were some big deal. Maybe to him it was, but Andrew didn't know Mason-Dixon. At least Lucky didn't think he did. Come to think of it, Lucky had no idea just how involved Dr. Dickhead was in Cassie's life.

Hell, she could be in love with the guy.

That notion didn't settle well in his stomach.

"I think it's obvious you have other things you need to be doing," Andrew said, speaking to Cassie now. "I expected you to be back at Sweet Meadows by now."

She flinched as if he'd spit on her. Probably because she hadn't wanted him to air her dirty laundry, especially since he'd been the one who'd created the laundry by committing her to that place. Sweet Meadows didn't exactly sound like a loony bin, though, so perhaps Andrew didn't think he was doing her any harm.

"My grandmother died," Cassie reminded him. "And she made us guardians of the children."

"Yes, I heard all about that when I called your grandmother's lawyer. You were only supposed to take the children for a day or two at most. It's been two days."

That was true, but two days hadn't been nearly enough time to find their next of kin. Of course, in the back of Lucky's mind, he'd known it wouldn't be, but he'd still held out hope. Now he was just hoping that it'd be resolved in a week.

"Plus, you should know there's a reporter who's been asking about you," Andrew went on, still talking to Cassie. "Theo Kervin. But reporter is too generous of a job title for him. He's actually a paparazzi from LA."

This had to be the same guy who'd called Marlene at the newspaper. Thank God this Theo wasn't in town to get the latest scoop. What with the gossip about Mackenzie and now the cat thievery, Cassie's reputation could be hurt. Of course, if Theo had also gotten word about Cassie being committed to that place, he might be digging for dirt on that, too.

"There's no story here for a reporter," Cassie insisted, but Lucky knew that was wishful thinking on her part.

"You need to make sure it stays that way—no story. I can handle whatever else needs to be handled so it'll take some of the pressure off you," Andrew said. "I understand you're looking for their next of kin. Well, they can be sent to foster care until you find him or her."

Lucky had held his tongue. Until now. "No. They're not going to foster care."

Clearly that didn't please Dr. Dundernuts. "And what makes you qualified to raise these children?"

Before Lucky could answer, Mia tugged on his shirtsleeve. "What does quala-fried mean?"

Andrew jumped to answer that. "It means *Lucky* should know how to deal with and talk to children." The doc said his nickname as if it were a persistent toenail fungus. "He doesn't. I do."

Lucky wanted to ask him what qualified him to do that, but he was afraid this jerk would have a good answer—like a bunch of degrees and tons of experience.

"I happen to agree with Lucky about the girls not going to foster care," Cassie spoke up. Good thing she'd finally found her backbone. Sheez. Couldn't she see that Andrew was a bully just like her father?

Maybe Andrew saw some of that backbone because after he stared at her awhile, he finally nodded. Then he patted her arm. The next sigh he added had a "just keep calm and don't go nuts again" tone to it.

"All right, no foster care," Andrew agreed, "but I think it's ridiculous not to use a system that's already in place to handle situations exactly like this."

"They're not a situation," Lucky said, stepping in front of them. "And besides, we have a lead on their next of kin. We should hear back from her soon."

Lucky had no idea if that was the truth, but Logan was working on it. If this Aunt Alice was anywhere on the planet, Logan's PI would find her. And soon. Because Logan didn't like unfinished business, either.

Andrew looked at Cassie, silently asking if that was true, and she nodded.

The doc smiled. "Well, good. Then it's practically settled." He seemed plenty gleeful about something that was far from settled.

Andrew looked at the girls. "Since I'm here, I might as well go ahead and have a session with the children.

Is there some place quiet where I can talk with them in private?"

That question elicited a variety of responses.

Cassie: "Uh…"

Mia: "What's a session?"

Della: "There's an office."

Mackenzie: "I don't want your stupid help."

Lucky was in Mackenzie's corner on this. Or at least that's what he wanted to be able to tell the doctor. But the truth was, the girls did need help.

Especially Mackenzie.

And having them see a counselor was something he should have already arranged. He'd gotten so caught up with the details that he'd forgotten the devil that was in them. And the devil in this case was that Mackenzie could be suicidal, and Andrew could help.

"A session is where you talk to somebody," Lucky explained to Mia. "It's supposed to make you feel better."

"Like a magic gold star?" Mia was wearing it on her right earlobe today. Lucky hoped the glue kept sticking so she didn't lose it.

"Better than a magic gold star," Lucky assured her. Possibly another lie. But it made Mia smile.

Now, to Mackenzie.

"It might be a good idea if you talked to him," Lucky said to her. That required him to eat some crow since he'd spent the past ten minutes mind-bashing Andrew.

Mia nodded, of course. Always eager to please. Maybe too eager. Now it was Lucky who was sighing, and his had an "I'm in over my head" tone to it.

Mackenzie just stared at him.

"Please," Cassie said, taking the word right out of Lucky's mouth.

"If nothing else, consider it payment for the money you took," Lucky whispered to her. Yeah, it was another version of blackmail, but Mackenzie did deserve some consequences for the theft.

Though it was a little like the pot calling the kettle black since he'd just stolen some cats. Of course, Lucky figured he'd have plenty of consequences to face for that. Mason-Dixon wasn't just going to drop this, and Lucky would eventually have to offer him enough money to get him to back down.

Mackenzie finally huffed, took hold of Mia's hand. "All right." But before she followed in step behind the doctor and Della, who was ready to lead them to the office, Mackenzie stopped next to Lucky. "You want me to make this bad for that idiot?" she whispered.

It was tempting. God, was it tempting. But Lucky couldn't pass up the chance to do something that might actually help Mackenzie. Mia, too.

"Just talk to him," Lucky settled for saying. "Tell him whatever you want to tell him, and if he offers any advice, consider taking it."

If Andrew heard any part of that, he didn't acknowledge it. He was checking his watch, but he did glance back at Cassie as Della was leading the girls and him to the office.

"After the girls and I talk," Andrew said to Cassie, "then you and I need to have a chat, too. We can do that on the way to the San Antonio airport. I've booked us on a three-o'clock flight."

CHAPTER ELEVEN

CASSIE OPENED HER mouth to say something—*anything*—but Andrew had already walked away from her.

"You're leaving today?" Lucky asked.

She shook her head.

"Well, he thinks you are. Did he tell you he was booking that flight?" Lucky pressed.

Cassie had to shake her head again. Andrew was a take-charge kind of person. There were times when that could be a good thing. Like when she'd been falling apart. But it wasn't a good thing now.

"Don't worry," Cassie told Lucky. "I won't leave you holding the bag with the girls. I'll stay until we find their aunt."

"You're sure? Because Dr. Wonderful will likely try to bulldoze you into leaving on that afternoon flight."

Yes, he would. And worse, there was a time she would have let him. But not now. It was her fault for giving Andrew power over her. Power to make decisions when she'd been too troubled to make them for herself. However, she couldn't let Andrew put her or anything else ahead of the girls.

Lucky was staring at her, and Cassie could tell he thought significantly less about her than he had just an hour ago. He no doubt thought she'd already lost the little bit of spine she'd found when she'd confronted her father.

"I know it's hard to understand," Cassie said. She moved into the living room and sank down onto the sofa. "But Andrew was the only one there for me after... Well, after."

After her client, Hannah Carpenter, had committed suicide.

"I'm not sure exactly what you were going through, but he was the only one there for you only because you didn't tell anyone else," Lucky argued. "If you'd told Dixie Mae or me—"

Her look stopped him. A reminder that there was no way she would have told Lucky because he wasn't on her emotional radar at the time. And as for Dixie Mae, Cassie had called her shortly after it'd happened, but then her gran had gotten sick, and Cassie hadn't wanted to burden her any further with it.

Lucky glanced in the direction of the office. Then at her. "Will he be okay with the girls, or will he act like an asshole to them, too?"

"He'll be okay. Andrew is actually really good at what he does." At relationships, though, not so much. He used every conversation as an attempt to fix rather than listen.

Lucky made a sound of disagreement. "He committed you to that place."

She had to nod. "I could have fought it. I could have stopped him from doing it. But I didn't."

Cassie hadn't meant to tell him that. It was one of those things she wasn't exactly proud of, but Lucky had already seen her at her worst—in the throes of a panic attack, and her wimpiness when dealing with Andrew and her father.

"So why didn't you stop Andrew?" he asked. "Is it because you're in love with him?"

"No." Cassie blurted that out way too fast and much too loud. Which meant she had more explaining to do. And that explaining certainly wasn't going to paint her in a good light, either. "I loved him. Once. When we were in college together. But he's changed since he became a psychologist."

"Good. I'd hate to think he's always run roughshod over you like this."

Oh, he'd always done that, but Andrew had added a lot more honey in those days so that the *shod* hadn't felt so *rough*. Plus, she had tolerated more from him when they'd still been lovers.

"Andrew and I haven't been together like that in a while now." Over a year. "But he still feels responsible for me."

And now more explaining was required.

"Let me guess," Lucky said before she could continue. "He dumped you, and he's feeling guilty about that, so now he's watching out for you."

"Close," she admitted. Actually, it was spot-on. "He can be a jerk, but I'm not sure I would have made it through these last months without him." Cassie paused. "I had a client named Hannah Carpenter."

Lucky didn't say anything. He just sat down on the sofa next to her. Not even that close. And he didn't look at her as if waiting for her to continue.

"As you've probably guessed from Marla, my clients don't usually have serious problems. They're more like small mental glitches. And in some cases, there aren't any problems at all. The client just wants to be in therapy because all his or her friends are. I call it the lemming effect."

"Sheez," he mumbled.

Her sentiments exactly. "They're semicelebrities with semiproblems," Cassie added. "And I thought I wasn't doing any harm by seeing them and letting them talk through whatever issues they thought they had. But I missed the cues with Hannah. I knew she was depressed and was on meds that her doctor had prescribed. I thought she was making progress."

"She was your patient for a long time?" he asked.

"Just a couple of months. We met on one of those advice TV shows where we were both guests, and she asked to continue seeing me."

And she had. Eleven visits total, and Cassie could remember almost everything they'd talked about. Everything except for that last visit.

"I'd been in a hurry during that final session with Hannah," she continued. "I was distracted thinking about another TV appearance. My mind kept going back to the notes I'd made for that, and I... Well, I messed up. I clearly didn't see how much distress Hannah was in, and later that night she took an overdose of sleeping pills."

Lucky stayed quiet, but he did ease his arm around her, and he inched closer. She figured this was the point where most people would have added a horror story of their own to try to make her feel better. Especially since rumor had it that Lucky did have a personal tragedy. Something he felt guilty about.

Something to do with his parents' car accident.

There wasn't a general consensus regarding Lucky's

involvement, but some said his parents had been so upset about something he'd done that it'd caused them not to be attentive enough to the other car. Others claimed Lucky had been in the other vehicle. So far, Lucky hadn't publically confirmed or denied anything, which only kept fueling the old gossip. However, he had told Dixie Mae, and that's how Cassie knew the rumors were wrong.

"And the panic attacks started after Hannah died?" he continued.

Cassie nodded. "But they're getting better. I haven't come close to having one since night before last."

"You're sure?"

Only then did Cassie realize her breathing was off. Way too fast and shallow. The classic beginnings of a panic attack. "I should probably take my meds just in case."

"Or we could try this."

Cassie didn't even see the kiss coming, but she certainly felt it. *Wow.* That was her first thought anyway, and the *wow* just kept repeating in her head. Maybe because of all the heat his mouth was generating. Perhaps it had melted her brain.

If so, Cassie didn't care.

Suddenly, this seemed a lot more important that having a functioning brain.

Of course, she had shared a kiss with Lucky before. The fake kiss. But this wasn't fake. Or if it was, it felt a lot less fake than the other one, and the other one had packed a wallop. This one packed three wallops, and she had to mentally up it to eighty million wallops when Lucky deepened the kiss.

Ever since Cassie had first noticed Lucky and the

effect he had on her gender, she'd wondered what it would be like to kiss him, to have him weave that testosterone spell around her. Well, now she knew. The spell was warm, golden and delicious. Just like Lucky, and in those couple of seconds she understood exactly why he'd managed to attract every girl in high school.

And every girl since.

How she'd ever resisted this, she didn't know, and worse, she didn't want to keep resisting it. Cassie wanted to continue this kiss until it led to something much more. Something that would relieve this ache that was suddenly in the southern regions of her body.

But that didn't happen.

Cassie heard a sound. One she didn't want to hear because it was someone clearing their throat. She pulled away from Lucky just as he pulled away from her, and their attention flew to the doorway.

Where Della and Wilhelmina were standing. And watching.

"I was having a panic attack," Cassie blurted out. Good grief. Where had that come from?

"Okay," Della said, sounding as skeptical as she should be. "Are you better now?"

"Yes." And it was true. There were no signs of the panic attack, though her body was obviously prepping itself for something it wasn't going to get.

It wasn't going to get lucky. Or get Lucky for that matter.

"What about you?" Della asked, turning to Lucky. "Were you having a panic attack, too?" With the deserved chain-yanking, she smiled and lifted her hand to Wilhelmina. "We have company."

Wilhelmina definitely wasn't smiling. Nor was

she batting her eyelashes at Lucky today. And Cassie knew why.

"I'm so sorry," Cassie told the woman right away. "I know we were supposed to bring over Mackenzie's apology, but things have been so crazy."

Wilhelmina gave her a flat stare. "No, *Lucky* was supposed to bring me the apology and take me out to lunch."

Lucky nodded, got to his feet. He glanced at Cassie, maybe to see if she really had escaped that panic attack. Or perhaps just because he couldn't believe he'd kissed her like that. Cassie was certainly having some trouble believing it herself.

"We'll still have that lunch," Lucky assured the woman. He took the Post-it note apology that Mackenzie had written and handed it to her.

That didn't help Wilhelmina's mood any. "No longer lunch. You have to take me to dinner instead."

Cassie huffed. "Do you really think Lucky should have to pay for this with his time? With dinner?"

"Yes," Wilhelmina readily answered, looking not at Cassie but rather Lucky. "You can pick me up Tuesday after work, and I want to go to someplace fancy."

Since there wasn't any place that qualified as fancy in Spring Hill, that meant Lucky would have to take her into San Antonio. Here he was pimping himself, and even though it was for a good cause—to keep Mackenzie out of lockup—it still didn't sit right with Cassie.

"And don't bring her on our date." Wilhelmina shot Cassie a glare before she walked out.

"You should have told Wilhelmina that you were impotent," Cassie grumbled.

Lucky shook his head. "Someone started a rumor about that when I was in high school, and nearly every girl in the senior class wanted to cure me."

Della chuckled. "I remember that." She patted his cheek. "What you should do is let everyone know you're off the market." And her gaze drifted from Cassie, to him, back to Cassie again.

"Oh," Cassie said. "Because of the kiss? Well, Lucky's not off the market. That was just, well… That just was."

"Yeah," Lucky agreed, though it was obvious none of them, including him, had any idea what he was agreeing with.

"You're sure?" Della pressed. "Because that kiss looked like—"

"Don't you have something to do in the kitchen?" Lucky interrupted.

"No. I have something to do right here." Della handed Lucky a note. "It's from Logan," Della explained. "Next week, he wants either Riley or you to go out and check on the park and see how the booths are coming along for the Founder's Day picnic."

Lucky stared at the message as if debating what to do.

"Riley's tied up with ranching and wedding stuff," Della reminded him. She gave his arm another pat. "I know it'll be hard for you. It always is. But maybe if you see the place before the crowds get there, it'll be easier."

"I'll go," Lucky said, his response too fast, as if he wanted to cut off anything else Della had to say.

He handed her back the note, leaving Cassie to wonder what was going on in his head.

"Maybe you can go with him?" Della asked her. It sounded as if Lucky needed that so Cassie nodded.

"Good," Della went on. "If you want to take the girls, too, I can do up a picnic basket for you. Might do you all some good to get out of this house and away from…things." Her gaze drifted toward the office where Andrew was.

Cassie definitely wouldn't mind getting away and catching a moment to clear her head, but then she heard the loud knock on the door. It didn't really even qualify as a knock, more like a pounding. Followed by several jabs on the doorbell.

"We might as well just leave the door open what with everyone coming and going," Della grumbled, heading in that direction. Lucky and Cassie were right behind her, and Cassie hoped this wasn't the deputy returning to search for those cats.

But it was her father.

"Where are those goddamn cats?" he yelled.

Lucky stepped in front of both Della and her, and he blocked her father from actually entering the house.

"They're not here," Lucky insisted. But his attention wasn't exactly on her father's face. It was on Mason-Dixon's arm. "Is that a misspelled tattoo?"

Considering the sheer ire in her father's expression, the question seemed odd. But then she remembered Lucky's extreme reaction to Dixie Mae's misspelled tat.

Mason-Dixon looked down at his right bicep where there was indeed a tattoo, one that Cassie had never seen. Regret Nothing. Except it was inked as *Reget* Nothing.

She was betting her father regretted something—that misspelling.

"Did you go to the same inker as your mom?" Lucky wanted to know. "Because if you did, give me his address so I can send that moron a dictionary."

Her father pulled down his sleeve. "You're getting off the subject, trying to distract me. Well, it won't work." His voice got louder with each word. "Davy said he looked and couldn't find those fucking cats. That means you have them stashed somewhere, and I want to know where. Those are my property."

Lucky tore his attention from the now-covered tattoo. "Property you were using to blackmail Cassie. I know that wasn't what Dixie Mae had in mind when she arranged to have them dropped off at the strip club."

Cassie agreed, but she had to admit she still didn't know what Dixie Mae had in mind when it came to that. Heck, when it came to everything the woman had arranged. If this was some kind of matchmaking attempt on her part, Cassie would hunt her down in the hereafter and have a "chat" with her about it. But for now, she needed to finish dealing with her father.

"What kind of bottom line are you looking at here?" Cassie asked. "Give me a number of how much it'll take for you to back off, and then you'll have enough cash to fix that misspelled tattoo."

"What's going on here?" Andrew asked.

Maybe because her own voice level had been way too loud, Cassie hadn't heard Andrew come into the foyer. The girls were right behind him, and thankfully Della swooped in to lead them back into the kitchen. Cassie definitely didn't want them to be around for what would be a profanity-laced tirade on her father's part. Heck, maybe on her part, too.

"My father wants money for cats," Cassie said.

"Cats that she and Lucky stole!" her father added. He was still shouting, and the veins were bulging in his neck.

"Cassie." Andrew didn't shout. He sounded horrified, though. "Are you trying to shred what's left of your reputation?"

That was not the right thing to say, and it set her teeth on edge as much as the Reget Nothing had riled Lucky. "Actually, I was trying to save my grandmother's cats."

"Cats that Dixie Mae left me," her father said. His attention was on Andrew, and Andrew's attention was on him. "You know how Cassie is. She can get all wound up when it comes to this sort of thing. She let Lucky talk her into doing something stupid."

Because Cassie was seething over the "wound up" remark, it took her a few seconds to pick through what her father had just said and find a little nugget that didn't belong there.

You know how Cassie is…

Lucky obviously picked up on it, too. "You two have met?" he asked Andrew and her father.

Silence.

Not the kind of silence one would expect from two men who didn't know the answer, but rather that of two men who didn't want to share said answer with her and Lucky.

"We've met," Andrew finally said, and judging from the way his mouth tightened, he wasn't too happy about revealing that.

Welcome to the club. For her part, Cassie wasn't happy being left out of this particular information loop.

"I'm going to want an explanation to go along with that," she said. "Because you know how wound up I can get about such things."

Andrew reached out as if to take hold of her, but Cassie stepped away. "Tell me," she insisted.

"It's nothing, really," Andrew answered after several tortoise-crawling moments. "I was just looking out for you. I knew if it got out that this was your father, then it wouldn't be good for your reputation."

Mason-Dixon shrugged. "Hey, I never asked him for a dime. I just asked him if it'd be a good idea if I talked to those reporters and talk-show hosts who are always interviewing you."

Oh. My. God.

Lucky looked at her, silently asking her if she knew anything about this. But she didn't.

"You gave him money?" she asked Andrew.

"Yes." He seemed surprised that she was upset. "Some," he clarified when he seemed to realize that she was past the upset stage.

"I never asked for it," her father repeated.

"You blackmailed him," Cassie shouted. She snapped toward Andrew. "And you paid him without telling me. Don't you dare say it was for my own good."

Judging from the way Andrew suddenly got very quiet, that was exactly what he'd been about to say.

"How much?" Lucky asked.

Andrew shrugged, glanced around as if he expected to find the answer in the hardwood floor.

Lucky snapped to her father. "How much will it take for you to drop this whole cat issue? And don't you dare say you want part of whatever Cassie inherits. Give me a figure."

Cassie was so frustrated and flabbergasted that it took her a second to find her voice. "You aren't going to pay him off."

"It's the only way to get rid of him," Lucky answered. "Clearly, he's got a track record for this sort of thing."

"Hey, I have a lot of expenses from the club," Mason-Dixon snarled. "And here my own mother denied me a loan."

Lucky groaned. "Yeah, yeah. The great dildo feud. I know all about it."

Cassie was really confused now, but she wasn't sure she wanted to know the answers to some parts of this conversation. Especially the dildos.

"Then you know Dixie Mae owed me," her father insisted.

"In your warped fantasy world maybe. So, how much to give Cassie all six of the cats?"

Her father smiled, and it was that sick smile that she'd seen way too often. "Give me your half of the rodeo business."

Cassie actually gasped. It was like asking Lucky to give up his firstborn child or his penis. She wasn't waiting for Lucky to answer.

"No way," she told her father. "You're not getting the business that Lucky and Gran built. And you're not getting anything else from Andrew, either. Here's how this will work. You'll give me the cats and in exchange I won't tell the Nederland brothers that you're sleeping with their sister."

Mason-Dixon made a sound that was part gasp, part huff. "You don't have any proof of that."

She took out her phone. Not that there was anything on there to show him, but she was pissed enough to make an empty threat. "Oh, no? Well, if you believe I could sneak into the club and steal cats, then why would it be so hard to believe that I took a picture of you and Becky Nederland having sex in one of the dressing rooms at the club?"

Cassie wasn't even sure it was Becky. She couldn't tell the sisters apart. But it was highly likely her father couldn't, either.

Her father volleyed glances from the phone, to Andrew, to Lucky and back to her before starting the volleying loop all over again. He finally cursed and turned to walk away.

"This isn't over," he warned them. "When Davy finds those cats, he'll arrest both of you."

Cassie felt as if she'd survived a storm. Part of one anyway. The rest of the storm was there in the foyer with her.

"I don't want either of you paying off my father. Or my mother," she added in case that came up.

But it apparently already had. Cassie could tell from the way Andrew got interested in the flooring again that he'd given her mother money, too. Good grief.

"I know my parents are less than stellar," she said. Such a huge understatement, but Cassie was making a point here. "But I don't need to be protected from them."

However, she might require some bail money if her father managed to get the theft charge to stick. Still, she didn't want this kind of protection from Andrew, Lucky or anybody else.

"Want my advice?" Andrew said, but he didn't wait for her to answer. "I say we leave right now. We'll go to the airport, have some lunch, and with you out of sight, you'll soon be out of your father's mind, too."

That caused some veins to bulge in Lucky's neck.

"I can't leave," she told Andrew. "Did you forget that Lucky and I have guardianship of Mia and Mackenzie?"

"Of course not. I just counseled them, remember? But I also know you can't help them. Especially Mackenzie. She's beyond help if you ask my opinion."

"I didn't ask," Lucky snarled.

"Well, you're not exactly qualified to have an opinion about this. Plus, if Cassie stays here, her reputation could be ruined to the point that no one would ever hire her. She could lose everything. Is that what you want?"

Cassie couldn't stop herself. She screamed. At the top of her lungs. It felt surprisingly good.

"At the moment I don't care what either of you want for me," she snapped. "You're not paying off my father, and I'm not leaving Spring Hill until the girls' situation is resolved."

Lucky shrugged. Nodded.

Andrew didn't shrug, and he certainly didn't nod. He looked about as happy with her as her father had. "Fine. But if you're staying, so am I. I can work from here just as well as you can." He glanced at Lucky. "Why don't you have your housekeeper get a guest room ready for me?"

Lucky looked ready to tell him hell no. Or at least that's what Cassie hoped Lucky would say, but he didn't get a chance to say anything. That's because a loud female squeal suddenly sounded from the front porch.

"Lucky!" the woman called out. She was blonde, busty and clearly very excited to see him.

"Angel," Lucky mumbled, not sounding nearly as excited.

"A friend?" Cassie asked.

Lucky appeared to be on the verge of a shrug when the woman launched herself into his arms and tongue kissed him.

CHAPTER TWELVE

ANGEL HAD NOT been a welcome interruption. It had
taken Lucky a half hour to convince her that this visit
wasn't going to happen and to send her on her un-
merry way. That half hour had involved six more attempted French kisses and a successful crotch groping
that she'd managed to get past him.

Of course, Cassie and Della being there hadn't
helped. And Andrew had thoroughly enjoyed the debacle happening on the front porch.

But Andrew had then gotten his own comeuppance.

Della had made it clear to Andrew that there were
no available guest rooms in the house. She'd been fudg-
ing a bit on that, though. There was an extra guest
room if they wanted to keep Mia and Mackenzie in
the same suite, but Lucky had wanted them to have
the option of their own space. Just in case the guardianship lingered on.

Which it seemed to be doing since they were now
a week into it.

Of course, Della could have put Andrew in Riley's
room since he was practically living at Claire's now.
Heck, Riley had even taken the family pet, Crazy Dog,
to live there. Or Della could have given Andrew Anna's
old room. But that had seemed like a big-assed accom-

modation to make for someone who was being such a big ass himself.

So, Della's news of "no rooms available" had prevented Lucky from getting ugly with Andrew and telling the ass outright that he didn't want him under the McCord roof. With Lucky's mood raw and his nerves on edge, it might have done him some good to tell the man to go to hell instead of just telling him to go to the Bluebonnet Inn—which now had open rooms because the reunion was over. What would have really felt good was for Lucky to punch him.

To punch Mason-Dixon, too.

But starting a brawl didn't exactly seem like a life lesson he wanted to teach the girls. Instead, Lucky and Cassie had called a truce and had spent the rest of the day and the following one with Mackenzie and Mia. Well, they'd spent it with Mia anyway. Cassie and he had played games and watched movies with her and had even taken her out for a ride on one of the gentler horses.

Mackenzie had spent her time scowling. It was possible her scowl was now permanent.

Lucky was hoping some sunshine would help with the scowl. Or at least melt off some of Mackenzie's makeup. That was why he'd suggested they all go to the park, taking along the picnic basket Della had generously fixed. This was a "killing two birds with one stone" kind of thing because he could also tick off that errand for Logan—checking on how the setup for the Founder's Day picnic was progressing.

For Lucky that meant driving all four of them to a place he didn't want to go while having thoughts he didn't want to have. At least Andrew hadn't tagged along, though he'd been calling Cassie practically every fifteen minutes. Thankfully the man had some live-chat therapy sessions and would be tied up most of the day.

Lucky still wanted to punch something, still would have loved to have gotten out of this particular chore of checking on the Founder's Day picnic, and at this point the best he was hoping for was just to get it over with while the girls got a little time outdoors.

Heck, it might help Cassie, too, since her mood didn't seem any better than his. Of course, she'd learned her ex-boyfriend had paid off her parents. But—here was the part he didn't understand—she hadn't demanded that the extortion-obliging moron leave Spring Hill and never come back. Nope. In fact, she'd given him the number to the Bluebonnet Inn. Obviously, she wasn't ready to let go of the head doctor just yet.

Even after she and Lucky had shared that kissing session on the sofa.

He was accustomed to having women kiss him and having it not mean anything. Hell, that was how it'd gone most of his life. Most women just wanted to be with him to see if he matched up to the hype. He had no idea if he did, but for some stupid reason he'd thought that kiss with Cassie had meant something.

Live and learn.

"This sucks," Mackenzie said. "You know that, right?"

"Which part?" Cassie asked. She was leaning her head against the window, but she lifted it enough to look in the backseat where the girls were sitting.

"All of it. I don't do fresh air and sunshine."

Yep, it was the fear of her makeup melting. Or maybe it just seemed like the ornery thing to say.

Of course, with his equally ornery mood, Lucky agreed with her. It did suck. The alternative, though, would have been leaving the girls with Della and Stella again, and they'd already watched them during the cat robbery. And he hadn't wanted to pawn this duty off on Riley what with all the wedding plans still to be finished.

"Do we have to see that idiot doctor again?" Mackenzie asked. "Because that sucked, too."

Neither Lucky nor Cassie had asked about the sessions, and despite how he felt about Andrew, Lucky hadn't wanted it to suck. Especially since Cassie and he didn't seem to be making any progress with the girl.

"I don't like the man doctor," Mia piped up. "But I like brownies and Frisbees, and Miss Della put some in the basket."

Yes, she had. And even though Lucky hadn't checked the other things Della had put in there, it would no doubt be filled with goodies. Other than the sunshine, that might be the only bright spot of this entire outing.

"You don't have to see Andrew again," Cassie assured them. She didn't say the same for herself, though. "But if you think you'd like to talk to someone, I have another friend I can ask to come over."

"I don't want to talk to anybody," Mackenzie snapped.

"Why we gotta talk to somebody?" Mia asked.

"You don't have to," Cassie answered. "But sometimes it makes some people feel better to talk." She slipped Lucky a side glance with that.

Lucky slipped her one right back. Yeah, he had

some demons chasing him, but at least he didn't have a more-or-less girlfriend. What he did have, though, were more-or-less dates with Sugar and Wilhelmina. Cassie might have considered that an even-steven kind of thing, but it wasn't.

Lucky pulled to a stop beneath one of the many shady oaks. They'd need every drop of that shade today because it was Texas hot. A well-hydrated camel with an AC unit would have had trouble in this heat, and he felt sorry for the workers who were putting up the booths.

It didn't look like much now, what with work trucks, equipment and supplies all around, but in a week and a half, it'd be ready for the stream of visitors who would come to eat, listen to music and celebrate. Lucky would be there, too.

But not to celebrate.

Hell, he had way too many memories of this place. It had been his mother's and his thing.

"The banner's already up," Cassie pointed out.

It was a new one. Logan's or Helene's doing probably. This one was shiny silver and copper and had McCord Founder's Day Picnic on it. It was stretched across the grounds above the booths being constructed. It should have read Betsy McCord Founder's Day Picnic.

"Why don't you suggest that?" Cassie asked.

At first Lucky wasn't sure what she meant, and then he figured out he'd said that last part aloud. Too bad. Because it put a new layer of trouble on her already troubled face.

He didn't want Cassie worrying about him. He didn't want anyone doing that. So, maybe it was time to do some "Lucky" stuff. Go out with a woman—not Wilhelmina or Sugar, either. But a woman he could take to Calhoun's Pub for some tequila shots and a long enough make-out session to create some gossip. He'd do that as soon as this situation with the girls was worked out. As soon as Cassie returned to wherever she would be heading with her more-or-less ex.

Yep, that's what he'd do.

"Do what?" Cassie asked.

Shit. Had he done it again? Had he blurted out what he was thinking? But this time it was a false alarm because Cassie was talking to Mackenzie while she was spreading out a blanket on the ground. Mia was helping her. Mackenzie wasn't. She was glaring and pouting.

"I said I don't want to hang around here and eat out of a basket," Mackenzie snapped. "I don't want to share my food with ants and sit in bug poop. I want to go for a walk."

Lucky was instantly suspicious, but his suspicions lessened a bit when Mackenzie strolled off and left Mia, who was still helping Cassie. If Mackenzie was planning on running, she wouldn't have left Mia behind.

"Stay where we can see you," Lucky called out to her just in case.

Whether Mackenzie would or not was yet to be determined, but with the road behind them, there weren't many places for her to go. Especially in those heels. They were clearly a gift from Livvy since they were higher than some stepladders.

"Della included this in the basket," Cassie said, handing him a note.

Curious but reluctant to read what was on the paper,

Lucky hesitated. And then he unfolded the note. It read, "It's okay, Lucky. Your mom would be so proud of you. Della."

That was bullshit, and Lucky paused a moment to make sure he hadn't said that aloud. He hadn't, but Cassie was watching him while Mia started in on one of the sandwiches Della had packed.

"Bad memories here?" Cassie asked, sitting down next to him. They both kept their eyes on Mackenzie.

"Some." Plenty. Of course, there were bad memories all over town because everywhere reminded him of his mother, of her death. Every place but Calhoun's Pub. To the best of his knowledge, his mother had never gone in there. "All of this was my mom's idea."

"I remember hearing that. I remember her being here, too, every year. She loved it."

Yeah.

The silence settled between them. Before long, Lucky saw something that got his attention and changed his mood from sullen to suspicious. Mackenzie had stopped her strolling and was talking to Brody Tate, who was showing her the mechanical-bull-riding stations he was setting up. That got Lucky on his feet.

"You know that boy?" Cassie asked.

Lucky nodded. "He's Elgin Tate's son."

That got Cassie on her feet, as well. Elgin had been their year in high school but had dropped out when he knocked up his girlfriend. And his girlfriend's best friend. And the best friend's sister. Rumor had it that there were a couple more knock-ups in there, as well. If Brody was anything like his father—and rumor had it that he was—Lucky might have to kill him, or at least superglue his zipper.

"Come on." Cassie took hold of Mia's hand. "Let's go check on your sister."

"Is she in trouble?" Mia asked.

No, but her getting in this kind of trouble was exactly what Lucky intended to stop. It was time for some bud-nipping. Especially when Lucky saw that Brody was leaning in closer and closer to Mackenzie. Lucky recognized sweet talk when he saw it. Heck, Lucky was the Spring Hill king of sweet talk.

By the time they reached Mackenzie, Brody had escalated things to nudging the girl's arm with his. Crap. This was moving fast, and it didn't help Lucky's anxiety when he saw a truly horrifying sight.

Mackenzie smiled.

At Brody.

The girl hadn't come close to a real smile since Lucky had first laid eyes on her, and now she was smiling at a turd who no doubt wanted to lay something more than eyes on her.

"Mr. Lucky," Brody said when he spotted them. He wisely stepped away from Mackenzie. "We were just talking."

Maybe Brody had added that preemptive explanation because Lucky's eyelids were narrowed to slits. Of course, Mackenzie did her own eyelid-slitting when she looked at Cassie and him. She clearly wasn't pleased with the interruption.

"Talking about what?" Lucky asked, and yep, he sounded like a cop or a father or something.

It wasn't a tone he'd ever used, but he'd heard Logan dole it out often enough. Since Logan and he were identical in looks and that tone got him results all the time, Lucky figured it was his best shot at letting Brody know that any sweet-talk shit was about to stop.

"Bull," Brody and Mackenzie answered in unison.

At first Lucky thought they were sassing him, but then he realized the mechanical bull was only a few yards away in the booth behind Brody. It was already all set up with the bull in the center of a hay-strewn area that had been made to look like a barn. Beneath the hay was the padded mat to break the riders' falls.

"Where's his legs?" Mia asked, sounding alarmed.

Lucky could see why she sounded that way. This looked like a real white-faced Hereford with sloping horns—minus the legs. It was as if someone had chopped them all off.

Yet something else Lucky would do to Brody if the boy touched Mackenzie.

"He's not real," Mackenzie grumbled. She rolled her eyes. "It's a fake bull."

"Not like that one," Mia said, pointing to Lucky's belt buckle.

"That one's not real, either." Mackenzie again, complete with another eye roll.

"But Mr. Lucky docs ride real ones," Brody explained. And he sounded, well, nice. Maybe he was doing that to get on Lucky's good side, but it was working on Mackenzie, too. She quit cye-rolling long enough perhaps to realize that Brody wasn't snapping or snarling at Mia's questions.

"The real ones got legs?" Mia clarified.

"They sure do, four of them," Brody jumped to answer. "In fact, I've watched Mr. Lucky ride, and he's real good at it."

More sweet talk, but Lucky had no intention of letting it sway him into trusting this son of a baby maker. Besides, he was only "real good" at it 30 percent of the time.

"I was thinking about bringing in a rodeo clown this year," Brody continued. "Thought it would be fun—"

Lucky swiped his finger across his throat in a nix-that sign. "Logan hates clowns. Not a phobia exactly, but close. Since he's the one actually paying for this, I'm thinking that's not a good idea."

"Right," Brody agreed, and there was even more eagerness in his tone.

"You gonna ride this bull?" Mia asked Lucky.

"Why don't you ride it?" Brody suggested to Mia before Lucky could answer.

Mia's eyes lit right up at the possibility, but then she looked at Big Sis, Cassie and Lucky to see if it was all right. Cassie turned to him, probably because she didn't have a clue if it was safe or not. It was, for the most part, but Lucky intended to add his own safety precautions.

"Put it on the greenhorn setting," he instructed Brody, and he helped Mia onto the bull. "To win, you need to stay on it for eight seconds." Lucky looked at Brody again, a silent warning that she would stay on that long or longer, and he wouldn't do any speeding up or joggling that would make her fall.

"Hold on to the rope," Lucky instructed, and since this wasn't a competition, he added, "with both hands."

Lucky stepped back only when he was sure Mia had a good grip, and he stayed close enough to catch her. Brody waited until Lucky gave him a signal before he hit the greenhorn setting. Mia probably would have gotten more movement from a wave in a kiddie swimming pool, but she laughed with each gentle rocking motion.

"One," Brody counted. And he just kept counting while Mia laughed.

Lucky couldn't help it—he laughed, too. So did Cassie, and she moved beside him, maybe to help in case of a fall, or perhaps just to get closer to that very happy kid. After all the crap they'd been through in the past couple of days, it wouldn't have mattered if Mia had lasted eight seconds or not. It felt as if they'd won. But she did last eight seconds, and at the end of it, she slid off as if she'd been born to do this.

She hadn't been, of course.

No way would Lucky ever let her get on the back of a real bull.

"Now it's your turn," Brody said, looking at Mackenzie.

It was hard to tell with the makeup, but Lucky thought she might have blushed. "Not me. Cassie."

Cassie didn't blush, but she looked intimidated. Then she looked down at her skirt. So maybe not intimidation after all, but concern that she was going to pull an "I see London, I see France."

"Here, use my hat," Brody said, tugging his off. "Hold it on your lap."

Lucky didn't know whether to thank the boy or slug him for even thinking about Cassie's underpants.

Hell.

He really did need to rein in some of this jealousy and fatherly twinges. Cassie wasn't his, and he had no right to be jealous. No right to feel fatherly about Mackenzie and Mia.

Cassie got on the bull, placing the hat strategically

in front of her pantie region. It was somewhat of a bal-
ancing act, but she managed to hold on with both hands
while still pinching the hat between her legs.

That lasted about a second.

The moment Brody turned on the bull, he realized
his mistake. This wasn't the greenhorn setting. This
was more the expert-on-steroids notch, and Cassie let
out a shriek as she went flying. Thankfully, she landed
on Lucky. Not in his arms, though.

On. Him.

They fell onto the padded mat in the exact position
a couple might need to be in to have accidental sex.
With the hat no longer in front of her pantie region,
that particular part of her landed right against his dick.
All in all, it was bittersweet. Bitter because it hurt like
hell. Sweet because his dick thought it was about to
get some action.

Cassie scrambled to get off him. Lucky scrambled
to get his hands on Brody's soon-to-be-broken neck.

"Gosh, I'm real sorry, Mr. Lucky and Miss Cassie.
The switch must be messed up or something."

Lucky stood, met him eye to eye and looked for
any sign whatsoever that the faulty switch thing was
bullshit. But Brody seemed genuinely shocked and
sorry. Especially sorry. Now Brody was blushing.
Mackenzie was still blushing, as well. Cassie was
flushed, however, and the flush went up a notch when
her gaze drifted to his zipper.

"Are you okay?" she asked.

"Other than perhaps losing any possibility of ever
fathering children, I'm fine."

Brody laughed. Not a good idea. But he must have

realized that because he shut up and backed away several inches. Then a few more.

"Why can't you father children?" Mia asked.

That caused some more snickering, and Lucky was on the verge of fighting his own snickers when Mia added some words that nearly stopped his heart.

"You could father us," Mia said. "And Miss Cassie could mother us. Y'all could do it together."

It suddenly got quiet. Too quiet. Lucky couldn't be sure, but he thought maybe even the summer breeze had stopped dead in its tracks. Cassie joined in on that quietness, though her mouth was slightly open, as if she were trying to come up with an answer.

"Bull riders like Lucky can't be daddies," Mackenzie finally told her sister. It was either the wisest assessment on earth or the biggest insult. Lucky wasn't sure which.

Thankfully, he didn't have to decide. Or try to add more to Mackenzie's explanation. That was because he saw Riley and Claire approaching them. Lucky was so glad for the interruption that he had to stop himself from hugging them.

"Bull-riding lessons?" Riley asked, but then his attention dropped to Cassie's pantie zone and Lucky's zipper.

Until then, Lucky hadn't realized he still had his hand on Cassie's hip, and Cassie probably hadn't realized that the side of her skirt was hiked up to her pantie leg. If the kids hadn't been around, it would have looked as if Cassie and he had just had a getting-dirty session.

"Lesson's over," Lucky explained, and he made the mistake of helping Cassie with her skirt. He just ended up groping her, and by the time she finally had it straight, he was aroused despite his "injury" on the bull mat.

"Ethan!" Mia squealed when she spotted the boy, and they took off chasing each other in circles.

Mackenzie and Brody seized the moment to step away from the adults, but Lucky gave them the eyes-on-you gesture.

"What brings you out here?" Riley asked.

Lucky had no trouble hearing the concern in his brother's voice. Or seeing the concern in Claire's eyes. Damn. Had everyone in his extended gene pool remembered that coming here would be tough for him? Even the bull looked as if it were in on this shit-filled old baggage.

"Doing a favor for Logan and having a picnic," Lucky answered. "What about you? Why are you out here?"

"Doing a favor for Logan."

At first Lucky thought that was code for checking on him, but then Riley handed him a piece of paper that he'd taken from his pocket. "Logan thought it best if I delivered the news in person."

What now? Because if it was good news, a phone call would have worked. Lucky hoped Cassie and he weren't about to be carted off to jail for those cats.

But it wasn't about the cats. Or jail.

"The PI located the girls' aunt," Logan had written. "Her name is Alice Murdock. She's out of the country on business but will come to Spring Hill next week. She said for us to have the girls' things ready to go, that they'll be leaving with her as soon as she gets here."

MACKENZIE STARED AT Brody from the back car window as Lucky drove away from the park. Brody waved, gave her the call-me sign, and she smiled.

She made sure no one saw it, though.

She'd also made sure no one saw when Brody had written his number on her right hand. He'd done that when Lucky had been talking to Riley and Claire. At the time Mackenzie had thought it was a lucky break that they hadn't had their nosy eyeballs pinned to her. But Mackenzie should have known her luck sucked and that the only breaks she'd be getting were the ones she'd always had.

Bad ones.

Mackenzie looked at her hand again. At Brody's number. He'd drawn a heart around it. Her first heart. Her first boy's number. And no boy had ever given her the call-me sign. No one, boy or girl, had ever looked at her the way he had. Of course this would happen now, just when she wasn't going to have time to do anything about it.

"Will Aunt Alice be nice?" Mia asked.

Even though Mia used her mousy-whisper voice, Lucky and Cassie must have heard it because Cassie glanced back at them. Lucky glanced in the rearview mirror, his eyes meeting Mackenzie's.

Considering Cassie and he had just gotten the best news of their lives—no sucky luck for them—they weren't acting all happy and everything. Probably because they were still mad about the bull throwing Cassie and her landing real hard on Lucky's privates.

But that hadn't been Brody's fault.

At least Mackenzie didn't think so, but even if it had been, Lucky and Cassie didn't have a right to be mad. They just didn't want her to be happy, that's all. Nobody did.

Of course, maybe they were all mopey because they were going to have to keep playing mommy and daddy for another whole week. They'd made it clear right from the start that they'd wanted to ditch this job, and now they couldn't. Yeah, that had to be it. They weren't happy because they were stuck with Mia and her—her more than Mia—until their aunt showed up.

"Well?" Mia pressed, tugging on Mackenzie's arm. "Will Aunt Alice be nice?"

"How the heck should I know? Neither one of us has met her, have we?"

"No. But you think she'll be nice?"

"Sure."

Mackenzie didn't think that at all. If the woman was anything like their mom, then she might use stuff, get drunk and sleep around with men. Mia was too little to remember a lot of that, but Mackenzie had no trouble remembering. And her kid sister wasn't going through something like that again. Heck, *she* wasn't going through that again.

Brody was fifteen, two years older than she was, and he had a job. A summer one anyway. Maybe he could lend her some money so she could get Mia out of there. Of course, getting out of there would mean never seeing Brody again. Unless…

Maybe she could talk him into taking Mia and her somewhere?

After all, Brody said he had his learner's permit, so that meant he could probably drive. And he had given her his number. Had smiled at her and talked to her as if she was, well, special. Yeah, that was it.

Brody made her feel special.

So maybe he could keep on making her feel that way by helping her. And soon. Because Mackenzie had to make sure she had Mia far away from Spring Hill before "Aunt Alice" showed up.

CHAPTER THIRTEEN

IT WAS WRONG on so many levels to stare at Lucky's crotch, but that's what Cassie found herself doing. Why, she didn't know.

Yes, she did.

It was because of those leather chaps he was wearing. They just sort of framed his crotch and acted like a neon sign that said, *Look here, look here!*

So Cassie looked.

At least now her tongue was no longer on the ground, though that's where it'd landed when Lucky had first called out for her to come watch him ride. She had stepped out of the house, expecting to see him in his usual jeans, boots and shirt. But instead, she'd gotten this.

The chaps, leather vest, denim shirt, spurs, gloves and the bull rope he had looped over his shoulder.

Her eyes had instantly gone to his crotch, but her mind had taken an even dirtier side trip. He looked just as ready for some BDSM as he did a bull ride. Not that she was into BDSM, or bull rides, either, for that matter, but it was an interesting image to add to her fantasies.

She only got to enjoy the fantasy a whole couple of seconds, though, before her phone buzzed and Cassie saw Andrew's name on the screen. He'd no doubt finally listened to the voice mail she'd left him.

"Another week?" Andrew snapped, his disapproval coming through loud and clear from the other end of the line.

Even though Cassie couldn't see his face, she figured the disapproval was in his expression, too, and that was why she wouldn't mention that she'd put off telling him for two days that that was how long it would be before the custody issue was resolved. Thankfully, Andrew had been so busy with his therapy sessions that he was conducting online from the Bluebonnet Inn that he hadn't pressed Cassie on nailing down a specific time for them to leave.

Well, they had a specific time now.

A week, or rather only five more days, until Aunt Alice arrived. It was exactly what Lucky and she had been waiting for ever since they'd gotten the girls, but it somehow felt like a hollow victory. Mackenzie was still sullen. Still hurting. Still needed help that she might not get with her aunt. At least Mackenzie was talking to Brody, a lot, and that was better than her moping around the house and labeling everything and everyone as sucky and stupid.

"The aunt might get here sooner," Cassie continued. "The week was just a general estimate. She was out of the country on business, but when she gets back home, she'll be coming from Phoenix."

"Well, she must be infirmed or hobbling because it doesn't take that long to get from there to here."

"No, but I suspect she had some things to take care of first. Like maybe getting the girls' rooms ready and such."

At least Cassie hoped the woman was making those

kinds of plans, and making them in blissful anticipation of getting Mia and Mackenzie.

Because the girls deserved that.

"Certainly *Lucky* can handle those *children* until the aunt arrives," Andrew insisted. He'd said *children* and Lucky's name as if they'd caused a rash on his tongue.

"Lucky's very busy. He's co-owner of a rodeo promotion business, remember? In fact, he's testing out a new pair of bulls that were delivered to the ranch earlier."

Something Cassie fully intended to watch.

Lucky probably didn't know that she had seen him ride once before when she'd been visiting her grandmother. He hadn't worn chaps and the vest that day, though. No bull rope, either. Cassie had watched him climb onto that bull and then had held her breath when it'd bucked.

That day, Lucky had won, not the bull.

And Cassie had been forced to admit that she saw in him what other women saw. A great butt. Great face, too. Now here she was watching him again from the barn as he was preparing to ride.

The ranch didn't have an actual setup for bull riding, but several of the hands had helped build a makeshift shoot and gate where the bull was being held back. Cassie didn't have a good view of the bull from where she was standing, but she could see Lucky straddle the top of the fence, looking down at the animal. He was talking to the bull as if getting acquainted with it. Strange, it was like chatting up someone who wanted to sling your internal organs out of your body.

"Are you listening?" Andrew said, snapping her back to reality.

She hadn't heard a word in the past fifteen seconds or so, but Cassie didn't let him know that. "I'm just a little distracted, that's all. I've got a lot on my mind." And on her eyes. She could feel the adrenaline start to pump through her and figured it was a drop in the bucket compared to what Lucky had to be feeling.

"I know," Andrew agreed. "It's those *kids*." That tongue rash sounded as if it had gotten worse. "They're too much for you to handle."

No, he didn't know. At the moment, it certainly wasn't the kids distracting her. Lucky looked back at her, snaring her gaze, and gave her a smile that could have melted chrome.

This was so stupid. She shouldn't be getting warm in all the wrong places. She was watching him prepare to ride a bull. He wasn't stark naked and—

"I'm canceling my afternoon appointments and coming over there right now," Andrew insisted.

"No." Cassie couldn't say that fast enough. It always turned ugly whenever Andrew was around Lucky, and she didn't want to deal with ugly today. "I'm really busy. I wouldn't be able to spend any time with you, and besides, you can't let your clients down like that."

"Busy with the girls?" he asked, suspicion in his voice.

"Of course. What else?"

It was a lie. Mia was at Claire's having a playdate with Ethan, and Livvy had taken Mackenzie on a shopping trip into San Antonio. For the first time in days Cassie actually had a free afternoon, and here she wanted to spend part of it watching Lucky climb onto the back of an ornery two-thousand-pound Angus bull.

"You sound funny," Andrew added.

"Do I?" She quickly tried to sound unfunny. "Must be because I'm still distracted. I should go now, but I'll call you later."

She hung up before he could protest or make any more obvious observations about her sounding funny. Of course she sounded funny. She was lying and breathing hard. Watching Lucky get ready for the ride was better than foreplay.

Cassie groaned.

She'd let that "foreplay" distract her. Instead of agreeing to call Andrew, she should have insisted he leave town. Of course, Cassie had been doing that for two days with no results. Andrew would leave Spring Hill when he got good and ready, and arguing with him about that would only make him dig in his heels more. She owed him, she really did, but Cassie was too drained to deal with Andrew right now.

Not too drained to watch Lucky, though.

He slipped down off the railing, easing onto the bull. Even from where she was standing, she could see the muscles ripple beneath Lucky's shirtsleeve. Normally, Cassie wasn't into muscle rippling, but she apparently was now.

The ranch hand opened the gate, and the bull charged out. Snorting and bucking. Its massive head was down while the animal spun around, trying to hurl off the rider. But Lucky held on. He squeezed his legs around the bull's sides, the chaps reacting to that pressure.

Cassie reacted, too.

And she thought about how it would feel to be that bull right now. Oh, yes, she was worked up all right.

The bull bucked even harder, slinging Lucky

around, but Lucky just adjusted, his long, lean body
sliding into the bucking moves. His left arm stayed
high, dipping and lifting only when his body did. It
was like watching some kind of dance. With a guy
wearing chaps and spurs.

Cassie completely lost track of time. Eight seconds
or an hour could have passed for all she knew, but then
Lucky threw his left leg over the bull's head, and he
jumped off. Lucky landed on his feet and hurried to
get out of the corral before the bull came back at him.

He laughed.

And that's when Cassie realized she was holding
her breath. Possibly drooling, as well.

Lucky looked at her again, their gazes connecting
and holding for a couple of seconds. Cassie didn't believe in ESP, but something passed between them. He
said something to the hands who were still watching
the bull, maneuvered off the railing and came toward
her. She had another chance to assess that ESP thing,
but this time she knew what it was.

A really hot look.

Lucky walked toward her, the spurs jangling and
the chaps swaying to give her another *Look here! Look
here!* moment. Cassie tried to look unaffected by all of
this and failed so badly that she just gave up.

"Yeah," Lucky said, his voice dousced with testosterone. He bit down on the fingertip of his right glove
to remove it. Then did the same to the second one. "It
has the same effect on me."

This probably would have been a good time for
her to play innocent and say *oh?* or maybe a *huh?* But
after watching what he'd done to those gloves, her innocence was shot to Hades.

Lucky kept coming closer, and the moment he reached her, he slid his hand around the back of her neck, hauled her to him and kissed her.

Cassie said *huh* all right, but for a different reason. Because she hadn't been expecting to feel the slam of heat. It was as if that bull had just rammed into her.

Lucky didn't stop with just one bull-walloping kiss, though. He deepened it, pulling her closer and closer until she was plastered right against all that warm leather.

And his erection.

The chaps made it easier to feel that, too.

"Are you always like this after a ride?" she asked.

"Only when I see you afterward," he answered.

Mercy, that was probably a line he used all the time, but the problem was—it worked. All of it worked, and that's why Cassie melted right into the kiss.

Lucky didn't break the kiss when he pulled her to the side, maybe to get them out of the line of sight of the ranch hands, but it also landed them against the barn wall. She'd never considered barn walls before, but the hard wood had a wonderful effect when Lucky pressed her back against it. All that hardness at her front and back was creating some amazing pressure. Friction, too, when Lucky's body moved against hers.

"What about the ranch hands?' she asked.

"I told them I had to talk to you about the girls. They're so interested in the bulls they won't come in here."

Cassie tried to make herself remember that Lucky had done this too many times with too many women. That should have put her off, but she was so hot now that she reasoned that all his experience would just make this better.

And worse, of course.

Because they shouldn't be doing this.

She was leaving town soon, and she didn't need to pack a broken heart to take back with her to LA. So the rationalization started. This was just a kissing session. A very good one. But it wouldn't lead to anything more.

That's when she realized she was moving.

Or rather Lucky was moving her. He dropped some kisses on her neck, at the base of her earlobe. Then her ear.

Good grief.

How had she not known before now how sensitive of a spot that was for her? And how had Lucky known that it was?

Soon, those questions and all logical thoughts flew right out of her head.

Lucky led her to a ladder, and Cassie wasn't sure how he managed it, but he continued to kiss her as they made their way up the steps. One rung at a time. With more of those body-melting ear kisses. By the time they reached the top, Cassie was so worked up that she didn't even notice where they were at first.

A hayloft.

That gave her just a moment of hesitation. It was one thing to kiss in the barn. No threat there of having full-blown dirty sex—because in her mind, it would be dirty with Lucky—but here they had privacy. And with privacy came the threat of sex, that broken heart and some serious complications added to her already complicated life.

"Do you take a lot of women up here?" she asked.

He was breathing through his mouth when he eased back and looked her straight in the eyes. "You're the first."

That was probably more bullshit than was in the bull pen.

Still, Cassie wanted to believe him even if she knew she shouldn't.

"Let's take it one step at a time," he said. Was his voice always like this? All low and husky. If so, she was surprised he hadn't seduced her whenever he'd said hello. "Just say yes or no. I'll stop at the first no."

The rules were easy enough. Cassie thought she could manage the breath to give a one-syllable answer. Of course, the rules were tested with Lucky's first move when he gave her another of those ear kisses.

"Yes," she eked out.

The next kiss landed on her throat. Or at least that's where it started. But with the dexterity of a magician, he opened the buttons on her shirt, and without breaking the next kiss, his mouth went lower, lower.

Until he had her right nipple in his mouth.

"Yes!" she said a little louder and more enthusiastically than she'd intended.

Lucky lingered there a moment, all the while easing her lower until they landed on some hay on the floor.

Heck, she said yes to that, too.

And Cassie kept saying yes when Lucky undid the rest of her buttons, pulled down her bra and kissed the living daylights out of her.

"If you want me to stop," he reminded her, "just say no."

No was the last thing she wanted to say, but Cassie had to hang on to what little sense she had left.

"You know we shouldn't have sex," she said.

He didn't even pause. Lucky just kept trailing kisses lower and lower until he circled her navel with his tongue. "What's your definition of sex?" he asked.

The question seemed like something that would require a lot more functioning brain cells than she had at the moment, but Cassie gave it a try. "The F-word."

He smiled as if charmed by her inability to say a word that she heard daily. After all, if she couldn't say the word, then she probably shouldn't be doing the act.

"Okay, no F-word," Lucky agreed. "But I can still kiss and touch you. Remember, just say no if you want me to stop."

There was that single brain cell that wanted her to stop, but the other cells were clamoring so hard for the kissing and touching that it got drowned out.

Lucky's mouth came back to hers for the kissing part, and he moved on top of her for the touching part.

Or so she thought.

But the touching part was a whole lot more than that. He unzipped her, all the way down, and he slid his hand into her panties. He didn't stop there. Lucky kept kissing her, kept moving his hand until it reached the most sensitive part of her body.

Oh, yes.

This was that lightning bolt of pleasure. The one she hadn't experienced in so long that Cassie had forgotten what it was like to have a man touch her like this. Lucky's fingers slid right through all that slickness and just kept on sliding. Over and over again. Until Cassie thought she might literally, truly explode.

But she didn't.

Just when she was nearing the climax of the one and only hand job she'd ever gotten, she heard something she didn't want to hear.

Her name.

And it wasn't Lucky saying it, either.

"Cassie?" Andrew called out. "Are you up there? The housekeeper said you were out here in the barn."

Judging from the sound of Andrew's voice, her more-or-less ex was heading up the hayloft steps.

CHAPTER FOURTEEN

HELL IN A HANDBASKET.

What was Dr. Dundernuts doing here?

Lucky wasn't opposed to Andrew learning that Cassie and he had the hots for each other, but he didn't want Andrew or anybody walking up that ladder while he had his hands in Cassie's pants.

"Oh, God," Cassie mumbled, and scrambled away from him. Scrambled to fix her clothes, too.

Lucky didn't have anything unbuttoned or unzipped so there was nothing to fix. Nothing but his hard-on, and scrambling around wasn't going to help that.

"Cassie?" Andrew called out again. The man sounded even closer than before.

"Lucky?" someone else said. Livvy. Heck, she was close, too, and that meant Mackenzie probably was, as well.

"They're around here somewhere," one of the ranch hands explained. It was Zeke Daniels, and he'd been the one who'd helped rig the riding arena for Lucky to test the Angus. "Maybe they went into the other corral to check out the second bull. Come on this way."

Lucky wanted to kiss Zeke for giving them a chance to get down the hayloft ladder without an audience. Lucky didn't mind Andrew knowing what they'd been doing. Or even Livvy. But it was best that Mackenzie be kept out of this particular information loop.

Cassie scurried to the ladder and looked down. She craned her neck and body so much that she nearly fell right out of the loft. Lucky caught onto her, moved in front of her and went down first. At least if anyone was still in the barn, they might think he'd been up there alone. Considering he still had a partial hard-on, though, they might be wondering what he'd been doing.

Once he was down the ladder, he helped Cassie and then put his cowboy hat in front of his crotch. It wasn't a second too soon.

"There you are," Livvy said. At least it sounded like Livvy, but the woman walking toward them was dressed like Mackenzie. In fact, exactly like Mackenzie, right down to the black lipstick and black spiked hair.

Mackenzie was trailing along behind Livvy. Andrew, too. And Zeke.

"I wanted to try a different look," Livvy said, twirling around. She looked like a character in a Tim Burton movie. "And tomorrow I'll try a different look, one where people can see my actual hair color." She winked at Lucky.

Not a flirty wink but one that was perhaps meant to let him know that she was teaching Mackenzie a lesson— that it was okay to look normal every now and then. But the wink sort of got stuck in Livvy's eye when her gaze skirted over them.

"Hay in the hair," Livvy whispered almost frantically.

That sent Cassie and him into a frantic hair search, with them raking at their heads with their fingers.

Livvy didn't help at all. In fact, she picked up a handful of hay and, giggling like a loon, tossed it at them.

Okay, maybe Livvy helped after all, because to the others it might have appeared they were in the middle of a hay fight. Of course, such a fight wouldn't make sense to a normal, sane person, but Livvy wasn't known for doing normal, sane things.

Andrew and Mackenzie stopped right in front of them. Mackenzie was giving them her bored look while Andrew took notice of everything around him. Particularly of the placement of Lucky's Stetson. Lucky hoped the guy didn't ask to try it on.

"Chaps and spurs, huh?" Livvy asked, tossing up another handful of hay.

"Lucky was riding the bull," Cassie explained. Which sounded dirty because she'd hesitated slightly after the word *riding*.

Livvy picked up on it, of course, and threw more hay, causing Andrew to cough and fan his hand in front of his face. Maybe the sudden allergy attack would get him moving so Lucky could have a few more seconds before he attempted to walk.

"That's something I would have loved to watch," Livvy declared. "Any chance you can ride the bull again so we can get a look-see?"

"I don't think that's a good idea right now," he managed to say. "Maybe later."

However, if he did ride the second bull, he'd make sure Cassie wasn't around. Bull riding had always given Lucky the mother of all adrenaline highs, but this was a first for making him horny as hell. Naturally, Cassie was responsible for that. There had just been something about seeing her standing there while he'd been getting his brains scrambled, and he hadn't been able to resist her.

But then she hadn't resisted much, either.

At least she hadn't in the hayloft, but Cassie was definitely putting some distance between them now. That was partially thanks to Andrew. He'd slipped his arm around her waist and was trying to inch her away from the rest of them.

"Cassie and I need to talk," Andrew finally said. "It's important," he added. "It's about Hannah."

Until he tacked on that last part, Cassie had been holding her ground. But what he said caused her gaze to meet Andrew's. Lucky was betting there was no way she'd pass up any and all news about Hannah, her client who'd committed suicide, and he was right. Cassie nodded and stepped away with Andrew. Far away. They went out of the barn and headed toward the backyard.

Livvy glanced at Cassie and Andrew. Then she glanced at Lucky. Then the hayloft. Then Mackenzie—no doubt to see if she was picking up on any of this, but the only thing Mackenzie was picking at was some hay that'd landed on her black top. After all the glancing, Livvy looked at Lucky and raised her eyebrow.

Lucky understood the question. *What's going on?* But since Lucky didn't have an answer to that, he just shrugged. And changed the subject.

"How'd the shopping trip go?" he asked.

Mackenzie kept picking at the hay. Thankfully, Livvy was more accommodating, especially since Lucky needed a distraction. He kept looking at Cassie and Andrew, and every time he did, they were looking at him. He would have just moved this conversation into the house and out of their line of sight, but that would have meant walking right past them. If Cassie had wanted him to hear what Andrew and she were discussing, she would have asked him to join them. Or just stayed put.

"We bought drugs," he heard Livvy say.

That caused Lucky's and Mackenzie's attention to snap back to Livvy, who now had a gotcha look on her face. "Just checking to see if you were listening."

"Well, I am now. What'd you buy?" Though he didn't think for a second that it was drugs.

"The shopping bags are in the house," Livvy went on when Mackenzie didn't say anything. "Don't worry. We didn't max out the credit card you gave us, but we got some things for Mia. Some things for Mackenzie, too, of course. Tops, shoes and…other things."

Now Mackenzie looked at him.

"Other things?" Lucky pressed. He had to tear his eyes away from his latest glimpse of Cassie and Andrew so he could look at her.

"A dress," Mackenzie finally said. "To wear to Riley and Claire's wedding."

At first Lucky didn't see a problem with that. Then he did. The timing of Aunt Alice's arrival, and the woman's insistence that she wanted the girls to leave with her right away.

"Mackenzie and I were thinking that it would be fun for Mia and her to stay for the wedding," Livvy suggested. "Thinking along those same lines, we also got Mackenzie an outfit for the picnic."

The truth was that Lucky wanted the girls at both events. After all, Mia had gotten close to Ethan and Claire, and Mackenzie had apparently gotten close to

Livvy. But Lucky had to shake his head. "I'm not sure it'll be up to me."

"Oh, you can sweet-talk Aunt Alice into letting them stay," Livvy insisted. "I mean, especially after Cassie and you stepped up to take custody of her nieces. Heck, the aunt could go to the picnic and wedding, too."

It was true about the sweet-talking part. He might be able to pull that off, but there was something fishy going on here, and Lucky was pretty sure what that fish's name was.

"I know Brody will be at the picnic," Lucky tossed out there, "but I'm guessing he'll now be at the wedding, too?"

Mackenzie nodded and had the decency to mix a little sheepishness in with her insolence. "I asked Claire to invite him, and she said she would. I'd also like to go on a date with him."

Lucky had hesitated about the wedding and picnic possibilities, but he didn't waste a second responding to this part. "No way. He's too old for you."

"Only by two years," Mackenzie protested after a loud huff.

That was more than enough. "Look, Mackenzie, Brody doesn't come from a good family."

"Neither do I!"

The jury was still out on that, depending on Aunt Alice, but Mackenzie had a point. Her mom and dad hadn't been stellar examples of the human race. Aliens looking for higher life-forms would have skipped right over those two. Still…

"No date," Lucky insisted, and he tried to make sure it sounded like his bottom line. Because it was.

"You're too young. He's too old. And that's not a good combination."

There. Bottom line, finished, and Lucky punctuated it with a firm nod.

But Livvy shrugged and did some hemming and hawing. "What if I chaperoned the date?"

Clearly, Livvy hadn't picked up on the bottom line. "My answer's still no. I like you, Livvy, but if I looked for a picture in the dictionary next to 'responsible adult chaperone,' you're not going to be there."

That didn't seem to hurt her feelings. Livvy just shrugged again. "Then what if Claire and Riley chaperone? I've already asked," she quickly added, "and Claire said if it's all right with Cassie and you, then Riley and she would do it."

"And it would just be a date to the dance at the civic center," Mackenzie begged. "We could even put a time limit on it—like two hours. Miss Claire and Mr. Riley could drive us there, stay with us the whole time, and then drive us back."

Apparently, Livvy and she had already worked out their own version of a bottom line. And Lucky could feel himself wavering. Damn it. That's because Mackenzie actually looked happy for the first time since she'd arrived at the ranch. But he was still wavering.

"Here's a different scenario," he suggested. "I'll talk to Cassie about it, but if she agrees—and that's a big *if*—" he hoped she would "—then Cassie and I will chaperone. And there won't be any slow dancing."

Of course, with Brody's fifteen-year-old body fueling his every thought and move, just laying eyes on Mackenzie would work him up.

Some of Mackenzie's glee went south, but she finally nodded. Now all Lucky had to do was convince Cassie. And if he managed to do that, it'd sort of be like a date for him and her, too.

Sort of.

Other than that, there was one other silver lining here. With Mackenzie leaving town soon, there wouldn't be much time for a romance to develop between Brody and her. That was something at least.

Lucky glanced at Cassie again, but she was no longer talking to Andrew. However, she was chasing him, and Andrew was storming right toward Lucky.

"Lucky McCord!" Andrew shouted. "What the hell did you do to Cassie in that barn?"

CASSIE HAD TO run to make it to Lucky before Andrew got to him. Not because she thought Andrew would punch Lucky or anything. But she didn't want Lucky to blurt out something before he understood what'd prompted Andrew's question.

"Lucky didn't have anything to do with that," Cassie insisted.

Andrew didn't pay any attention to her, and Lucky just looked confused. Because he thought Andrew was asking about what had gone on in the hayloft.

Her ex just kept charging like a bull toward Lucky, and she could see Lucky already posturing for a fight. A fight that wasn't going to happen.

"Lucky doesn't even know," Cassie tried again. She managed a burst of speed at the last moment and darted in between Lucky and Andrew.

"Of course he knows," Andrew argued.

Lucky was still looking perplexed, no doubt because he thought this had something to do with her near orgasm. Of course, Cassie knew Lucky would have had no trouble actually making that happen if they hadn't been interrupted. But it was best not to think about that right now.

Even though it was difficult with Lucky still wearing those crotch-framing leather chaps.

"Uh, what do I know?" Lucky asked.

"You somehow talked Cassie into wanting to quit her job," Andrew accused.

"No, I didn't," Lucky said at the same time that Cassie repeated, "Lucky didn't know."

Cassie huffed and continued while she looked at Andrew. "In fact, I didn't know I was thinking about quitting until just a few minutes ago when I was talking with you."

"You're quitting?" Lucky asked.

Andrew came with his own quick follow-up, not to Lucky's question but to Cassie's comment. "You can't quit. Being a therapist is who you are."

Lucky cleared his throat to get her attention. "Does this have anything to do with, well, anything?"

Since Mackenzie was standing there, Andrew perhaps thought Lucky was referring to the children, but Cassie suspected it had more to do with their near sex. Hopefully, Lucky didn't think she'd seen that as some kind of commitment.

"No. Nothing to do with…anything," Cassie assured him. "I just… Well, I think that maybe I'd like to try something different."

"Hogwash," Andrew spat out. The ranch setting must have rubbed off on him because to the best of her knowledge, he'd never said anything like that. "What would you do if you couldn't be a therapist?"

Cassie had to shrug. She wasn't sure, but she wouldn't mind having a job where people didn't die because she'd botched things. Or a job that didn't spur a panic attack just thinking about it.

And no, it didn't have anything to do with Lucky and the girls.

Andrew huffed and snorted, sounding like a smaller version of the bull Lucky had ridden. He opened his mouth a couple of times as if to dole out the perfect words to make her change her mind. But perfection must have escaped him because he turned to walk away.

"I'll talk to you tomorrow," Andrew said. "By then maybe you'll come to your senses and won't even be thinking about making the biggest mistake of your life."

"Is he right?" Lucky asked her. "Would this be a mistake?"

"Tell you what," Livvy interrupted before Cassie could answer. "Why don't Mackenzie and I go inside and try on those new clothes?" She slipped her arm around the girl's shoulder and led her toward the back porch.

Cassie thanked Livvy for picking up on the cues that this wasn't a conversation Cassie wanted to have in front of Mackenzie. In front of anyone, really. However, she couldn't help but notice that Mackenzie seemed less sullen than usual. The girl actually seemed happy.

"Yeah, she's smiling," Lucky verified. "You probably don't want to hear why since you're going through your own personal crisis right now."

Of course, that meant she had to hear. "Mackenzie's smiling because of a personal crisis?"

"No, I'm the one having the crisis. She's smiling because she's happy that I lost my mind and just agreed to let her go on a supervised dance date with Brody. Claire and Riley volunteered to chaperone."

"You agreed to that?"

She was about to tell him that nothing would have made her give consent for a date between those two. But then she remembered Mackenzie's smile. Yes, that's why he'd done it. And while Cassie wasn't exactly comfortable with it, she knew how persuasive teenage girls could be.

"I'm thinking it might be a good idea if we go to the dance, too," Lucky went on. "Maybe we can hang back near the wall. I could bring binoculars. Maybe a stun gun. A shovel in case we have to bury Brody's body."

Cassie couldn't help it. Despite her blue mood, she smiled, too.

"There it is," Lucky said, joining in on the smile. His was a lot better than hers, though.

She mentally caught hold of that smile for a couple of moments, bracing herself for the nonsmiling conversation to follow. Lucky didn't keep her waiting, but it wasn't exactly the subject she'd been dreading—the one where she'd been thinking about quitting her job.

"Mackenzie wants to stay for the wedding," Lucky went on. "For Brody, of course."

"Of course," Cassie repeated. "You think the aunt will agree to that?"

Lucky lifted his shoulder. "You think she'll agree to let us see the kids after she takes them? I don't mean right away or even that often. I'd just like to check on them every now and then."

"So would I."

But she wasn't even sure if the aunt would grant them any concessions. Or if legally Lucky and she could insist on visits. Cassie seriously doubted temporary custody would trump blood kin.

However, that led her to her next thought. She did want to keep tabs on the girls. Mackenzie likely had a tough road ahead of her, and Cassie wanted to give Mia and her at least the option of calling from time to time. And to think, a week ago Cassie would have been glad to get rid of them.

"Your wanting to quit your job is about Hannah," Lucky concluded. "How serious are you about it?"

"I'm toying with the idea." She was terrified about it, too. "And it doesn't have anything to do with the hayloft," Claire added. "And I'm not thinking about quitting all of it. Just the clients part. I could still do the TV and radio shows."

Lucky stayed quiet, staring at her. She stayed quiet as well, and tried not to stare at him. Mainly because her gaze kept drifting to those chaps. Talk about fueling a fantasy.

"All right, then," Lucky said. "I'm sure you'll figure out what you want to do." He paused. "And the hayloft?"

Cassie figured the right answer wasn't to say she wanted to go back there and have him finish what he'd started. No, definitely not the right answer. They had the girls for six more days at the most, and after that Cassie would leave. Lucky would leave, as well. And if they decided down the road that there should be other trips to the hayloft, then they could make their decision without so much hanging over their heads.

It was the adult thing to do.

Or…

She could offer Lucky a one-night stand. Or even a six-night stand.

Nothing bad could happen from that, *right?*

Plenty of good could come from it, though. Like a minimum of six orgasms.

But the other little voice in her head reminded Cassie that in her messy emotional state, she might not be able to deal with any more emotional mess. She wouldn't die from the broken heart she would get because of Lucky, but she might not recover from it, either.

Cassie wasn't sure she would have shared that info with Lucky anyway, but thankfully she didn't have to. Mia came running out the back door of the house, and she was waving a piece of paper in her hand.

"I got a letter!" she said as if someone had just handed her the leprechaun's pot of gold. "It's got my name on it."

Cassie smiled at first, but then realized it could be from the aunt. Maybe a letter to say she was coming even earlier than expected.

Lucky scooped Mia up in his arms when the little girl reached them. "Who's it from?" he asked.

"Miss Dixie Mae. Miss Livvy said it comed from the grave." Mia's forehead bunched up a little. "What's a grave?"

"A place where people don't send letters from," Lucky mumbled, looking at the envelope. "But that's Dixie Mae's handwriting."

"Course it is," Mia verified. "She wrote me a letter from the grave. She wrote one for all of us. Yours and Miss Cassie's letters are in the house."

CHAPTER FIFTEEN

LUCKY WASN'T SURE how he got from the corral to the house. His feet were working just fine, but his mind was solely on what Mia had just told him.

The last time he had gotten a letter from Dixie Mae, she'd left Cassie and him temporary custody of the girls. Lucky hated to think the worst of someone who was dead, but he wasn't exactly sure he wanted to read the letter that Della was holding up when he stepped into the house.

Cassie took her letter, not opening it but rather holding it to her chest. Lucky put his in his pocket. He'd read it, later, but he thought he first might like those Jameson shots that he'd been promising himself for days.

"Read mine! Read mine!" Mia insisted. She was bouncing up and down as if she were on a trampoline.

Mackenzie, however, was of a like mind as Lucky. She crammed hers in her pocket, too. Livvy had apparently already left, and there was a stash of bags in the entry. The cats were trying to get into them. Mackenzie gathered those up and went upstairs. Lucky would need to check on her soon, to make sure whatever was in that letter hadn't upset her even more. Mackenzie certainly wasn't smiling now.

Unlike Mia.

"Read mine!" she repeated. And Lucky hoped that joy would continue afterward. Of course, he couldn't imagine even Dixie Mae squashing the joy of a four-year-old.

Since Lucky's legs weren't feeling too steady—probably from the bull ride—he went into the living room and sat down, with Mia scooting into the space right beside him. Cassie sat on the other side of her. Mia had already opened the envelope so he took it out and hoped for the best.

He unfolded the letter and saw the date. Dixie Mae had written it a week before she died. So not from beyond the grave after all. And it meant she'd given the letters to someone so they could be mailed. Bernie, probably.

"'Dear Mia,'" Lucky read aloud. "'I know you're being a good girl for Lucky and Cassie, but they'll still like you even if you mess up every now and then.'"

"Will you?" Mia asked. A two-word question coupled with a worried look that squeezed his heart.

"Of course," Cassie said. Lucky echoed the same. It was something Lucky should have already figured out a way to tell Mia.

"'You're like Lucky's twin brother in some ways,'" Lucky continued to read from the letter. "'But being perfect all the time gets on people's nerves and takes just as much of a toll on the body as messing up all the time. Understand?'"

Mia shook her head. It was well beyond her four years. But Lucky got it all right. It was the story of his life. The story of Logan's, too.

"'Just live your life, sweet girl,'" Lucky read on,

"'and keep making people smile. That's your gift. Love, Dixie Mae.'"

Mia stayed quiet a moment. "She loves me?"

Considering that short letter had been filled with things that must have been confusing to a young child, it surprised Lucky that Mia picked up on that one thing.

Love.

Talk about him feeling another heart squeezing. Too bad Dixie Mae hadn't told him about the girls sooner because it would have been nice to have seen her with them. It was obvious from this letter that Mia had given her some happiness in those last days of her life.

"Dixie Mae loved you," Cassie assured her.

Mia smiled. "I loved her, too. She was sparkly."

Yeah, she was. But since Dixie Mae had gotten so truthful with Mia, Lucky had to wonder what was in his letter.

And Mackenzie's.

Hell, if Dixie Mae was going to hold up a mirror to Mackenzie's face, Lucky didn't want her alone when she read the letter. He stood to go to her room, but the front door opened before he even made it to the stairs.

Logan.

"Got a minute?" Logan asked, and he specifically looked at Lucky, which meant he had something that he wanted to discuss privately.

"I'll go up to Mackenzie," Cassie volunteered, and Mia and she went in that direction.

"Trouble?" Logan asked.

Lucky patted his pocket. "Dixie Mae sent the four of us letters."

That put some extra concern on Logan's face. "Trouble?" he repeated, no doubt remembering what'd happened the last time Dixie Mae had done something like this.

Lucky shook his head. "I think it's just her way of saying goodbye." Heck. He hoped so anyway.

"Do you think you're too good sometimes to compensate for me being too bad?" Lucky asked.

Logan gave him a blank stare, and Lucky decided it was a good question to wave off. "You said you wanted to talk," Lucky reminded him.

Logan nodded and seemed relieved about the wave-off. "The reporter Theo Kervin is in town."

Lucky was certain he also had some concern on his face now. "Where?"

"Staying at the Bluebonnet Inn in the room next to Andrew. The clerk said now that she's put a name to a face she's pretty sure she saw him hanging around not long after Cassie arrived."

Crap on a stick. Maybe Andrew wouldn't let anything slip about Sweet Meadows. Lucky wasn't at all convinced that Cassie would quit being a therapist, and having something like that on her "résumé" wouldn't be good. Of course, Andrew had protected her by paying off Mason-Dixon and her mother so maybe the doc would make sure to protect her now by not spilling anything.

"Theo will talk to people," Logan went on. "I can't stop him from doing that, but I've put out the word that he's looking to paint Cassie and maybe you in a bad light. That might cause folks to watch what they say."

Or else it could make them chatterboxes. This was some of the shit that went with being a McCord. The money and power made some people want to take them down a notch.

"I've also told the hands to keep an eye out for Theo in case he tries to come here to the ranch," Logan went on. "If Cassie wants to talk with him, it's probably best if she does that elsewhere so that the ranch and the business won't be brought into it."

That was Logan, always thinking about McCord Cattle Brokers, but in this case his concern might be warranted. Lucky was also betting there was no way that Cassie would want to speak to this reporter, especially if the guy had any info about her stay in Sweet Meadows.

Cassie appeared at the top of the stairs. "Mackenzie isn't going to read the letter so she and Mia are going to watch a movie in their room." She gave Logan an uneasy glance. "Is everything okay?"

"Fine," Lucky assured her. "I'll come up in a bit." And then he'd tell her about Theo, along with deciding what to do about reading his own letter.

"A couple more things," Logan said. "Helene wanted me to ask you if you wanted her to find homes for the cats."

"Not just yet. Though it might come to that if Cassie can't take them with her to LA." That was a reminder Lucky didn't want, but he had to be realistic here. Cassie would leave soon. Even if she did go for a different career, it wouldn't be here in Spring Hill.

Logan nodded. "Now to Riley's bachelor party. He wanted to keep it local so I booked Calhoun's Pub. It'll be two nights before the wedding. I thought maybe you could arrange the entertainment, though."

"Sure. But there'll be no strippers from the Slippery Pole." He'd had enough dealings with Mason-Dixon. Still, he'd have to find something bawdy and inappropriate—which Logan no doubt thought was Lucky's specialty.

"Whatever you decide is fine," Logan assured him. But his attention wasn't on Lucky or the conversation. It was on the back windows. Logan watched as the hands moved a bull from the corral area into the pasture.

"I heard about the bulls," Logan said. "A project of yours?"

"Just testing them before I buy them," Lucky said as he made his way to the door and headed out into the backyard.

"How much does one cost?"

"The buyer is asking thirty grand each."

"Are they worth it?" Logan said without hesitation.

"The Angus is worth more than that. He's been trained well and will draw a crowd. Not sure about the Brahma. A lot of riders steer clear of them."

Logan still didn't seem to be listening, and Lucky thought he knew why. Logan was seeing dollar signs, and it didn't take long to confirm that. "How much does it cost to buy an untrained bull and make him worth thirty grand?"

"Bulls are like relationships. Lots of factors to consider, but you could get a young bull from a good bloodline for about ten grand, maybe less. After you add in training and care, you're probably looking at an average profit of ten to fifteen thousand tops."

That was chump change considering what Logan made off his cattle brokering deals and what Riley made from the cutting horses, but his brother was no doubt thinking in bulk. Once, Lucky had as well, but somewhere along the way the rodeo promo business had eaten up his time.

"I'm not going to buy and train bulls for you," Lucky let Logan know right off. But then he frowned. Saying things like that to Logan was practically a knee-jerk reaction.

"Of course. I knew you wouldn't be interested, but I was thinking I could get someone else. Maybe even use the ranch for holding and training them. There's plenty of space and acres of pastures we don't use. A couple of the corrals could be converted into training areas."

It was a good idea, and instead of completely nixing it, Lucky just put it on the back burner. It was possible he wouldn't have any time to take on even a smaller version of a project like that now that Dixie Mae had passed and he didn't have any help with the rodeo promotion.

Logan stayed quiet a moment, and Lucky figured he was already working out profit margins and such, but that wasn't all that was on his mind.

"You asked Helene about my meds." A muscle flickered in Logan's otherwise unruffled jaw. "I have migraines, but I don't want it to get around."

Lucky couldn't imagine why someone would want to keep that a secret, but he wasn't in Logan's head. Maybe Logan thought it would make him appear weak.

"Mom had them," Lucky reminded him.

Lucky figured he was giving his brother old news. Apparently not, judging from the look of surprise. Maybe Logan had been too busy working the ranch with their dad to notice when their mother had taken to her bed for hours on end. But Lucky had sure noticed.

"That explains why Dad was worried," Logan commented.

Now, that was news to Lucky. "Worried?"

Logan nodded. "It wasn't anything he said specifically, just a gut feeling I got."

Lucky wished he'd had gut feelings about his parents' car accident. Hell, he wished he could go back in time and undo what'd happened to them.

Since that put a damper on his already dampered mood, Lucky was about to excuse himself and go back inside. But his phone buzzed, and when he saw the name on the screen, he stopped in his tracks.

Alice Murdock.

The girls' aunt.

Lucky took a moment, gathering his breath before he answered it, and since Logan had been responsible for finding her, Lucky put the call on speaker.

"Mr. McCord," she greeted. "How are Mia and Mackenzie?"

It was the right question to start with, but it still caused his chest to tighten.

"They're okay." Since he wasn't sure what Logan's PI had told her, Lucky decided to keep it at that.

"Good. Could you please give them my number so I can chat with them sometime?"

"Of course. Any idea when you'll be arriving?"

"I'm finishing up a project now so it shouldn't be much longer. I'm a field director for a nonprofit group that provides medical care in third-world countries, and once I have all of the staff back safe, I'll catch the first flight to Texas."

So, she had a job, one that sounded as if she hadn't followed in her drug-using sister's footsteps.

"Unless you think it's critical that I come now?" she added.

"No. Like I said, the girls are fine." Lucky paused, then proceeded to ask the question he'd had from the beginning. "Why don't they know you? Why didn't you come and get them when your mother died?"

Alice paused, too. "Because I didn't know. My sister and I had a parting of the ways years ago. I just couldn't be around her when she was using, and my mother enabled her. Not by buying her drugs or anything but by refusing to admit she was killing herself. I would check my sister into rehab, and before the day was up, my mother would get her out."

Lucky hated to think that the girls had been through all of that. This woman could have maybe stopped it. Maybe. Then again, he was betting her sister wouldn't have just handed over custody, even to someone who was more capable of caring for her daughters.

"My mother didn't even call me when my sister died," Alice went on. "Nor when she got sick, so I didn't know about their deaths until the private investigator contacted me. Trust me, if I'd known those girls needed me, I would have been there for them."

The jury was still out on that, but she was certainly saying all the right things.

"My brother's getting married in a week," Lucky explained, "and Mackenzie asked if she could stay for the wedding."

"Of course," Alice said without hesitation. "I can adjust my schedule for that." Then she paused again. "I'm sorry, but I have another call coming in from Colombia that I have to take. But just tell the girls that

I'll see them in a couple of days. I can't wait to bring them to their new home in Phoenix."

When she ended the call, Lucky just stood there, staring at the phone.

"Are you okay?" Logan asked.

"Sure. This was exactly what we all wanted."

And he hoped if he repeated that enough, Lucky would start to believe it.

CHAPTER SIXTEEN

CASSIE SAT ON her bed, staring at the letter. It was silly not to just open it and see what her grandmother had written, but she wasn't sure she was ready to see those final words just yet. She wasn't anywhere close to a panic attack, hadn't been close in several days now, but this might push her back over the edge.

After all, she'd had a lot of edge-pushing things happen to her today.

That kissing session in the hayloft. The run-in with Andrew. The tornado of confusion going on in her head when it came to the girls, and the rest of her life. Now, this.

She was still staring at the letter when there was a knock at the door, and Cassie knew who it was before she even opened it. Lucky. He was there, no doubt to figure out if he had a reason to be concerned.

"You want me to stay with you when you read it?" he asked, tipping his head to the letter.

What he didn't do was come in, even though she stepped back so he could do that. Maybe because he was giving her some space. Too bad Cassie wasn't sure if space was the way to go.

"No. I'll be okay. I'm a little worried about Mackenzie, though," she said.

Lucky nodded. "I'm checking on her next."

And that was yet another reason why he probably wasn't coming in. Lucky was like chocolate—she wasn't to be trusted around it. Or him.

"Alice Murdock just called," he added a heartbeat later.

Mercy, was that the reason for his concerned expression? "And?"

He took a deep breath as if he needed it badly, and Cassie tried to steel herself for bad news. "She seems, well, great. It's hard to gauge someone from a phone conversation, but she seems to want the girls, seems to be have their best interest at heart."

"Seems?"

Lucky lifted his shoulder. "Seems is as good as I can get from what she said. She didn't seem anything like her half sister, though."

Cassie was going to take what he was saying as a red flag. Exactly what kind of red flag, she didn't know yet, but she wasn't just going to hand over the girls until she was certain this was the right guardian for them.

Except she might not have a choice.

The woman was blood kin so it was possible neither Lucky nor she would have any say in this. If Alice Murdock *seemed* suitable, then the courts would side with her. Not that it would come down to courts and such.

Her phone buzzed, and Lucky was still close enough to see Andrew's name pop up on the screen. "I'll go check on Mackenzie," he said, getting out of there fast. Probably because he thought she needed privacy for this talk.

But no privacy was needed. Not for the talk anyway. She shut the door after Lucky walked away, let the call go to voice mail and opened the letter. It was handwritten and dated the same as Mia's.

"Dear Cassie," it read. "I figure you're ass-kicking mad at me right about now. I knew it'd be a lot to ask, but I knew you'd do right by the girls. Right by Lucky, too."

That brought Cassie to a dead stop and she scowled. She turned that scowl to the heavens just in case Dixie Mae was watching her. Of course, no matter where Dixie Mae was in the hereafter, she probably wasn't watching. Her grandmother hadn't exactly been a sit-around-and-watch kind of person.

"No, I'm not matchmaking," Cassie continued to read. "I just think it'll help Lucky if he's got bigger problems than the ones festering in his own mind. Plus, he's easy on the eyes. Don't shake your head."

Cassie stopped shaking her head.

"You know he is," Dixie Mae had added. "Just don't let the problems festering in your own mind stop you from seeing that. Anyway, I love you to Pluto and back 'cause if you remember, to the moon and back was never far enough for us."

Cassie smiled. Yes, she remembered. And the feeling of that love came flooding back. In addition to being a nonwatcher, Dixie Mae hadn't exactly been sweet and cuddly, but she had loved Cassie, and Cassie had never doubted that love for a moment.

Well, maybe a moment when she'd first found out Dixie Mae had left Lucky and her with guardianship of the girls.

Dixie Mae had scrawled "Love, Gran," but that

wasn't the end of the letter. "PS. Try to make Lucky understand that his parents' deaths weren't his fault."

LUCKY KNOCKED ON Mackenzie's door and was surprised when she answered right away. Not with a scowl or a smart-mouthed response, either. She still looked plenty happy. At first, he thought that had something to do with Dixie Mae's letter, but she was clutching it unopened in her hand.

So this was no doubt some leftover happiness from his agreeing to that dance date. Something that Lucky hoped he didn't regret. However, for now he'd take that happiness. And even add some more.

"Your aunt Alice called, and she thinks it won't be a problem for you and Mia to stay for the wedding."

"Really?" Mackenzie didn't sound like goth moody girl now. She was fully smiling again, and she launched herself into his arms for a very unexpected hug.

And Lucky got an unexpected jolt from the warmth that went through him. Of course, none of this would last, but he decided to hang on to it for a while. But Mackenzie didn't hang on.

"I have to call Brody," she insisted, and practically shut the door in his face.

He had to smile, though. Apparently, she was a normal girl beneath all that anger and makeup. In fact, Mackenzie might just thrive with someone like Aunt Alice. That caused his smile to fade a little. Not because he didn't want her to be happy—he did. But it would have been nice to see both girls come into their own.

Lucky went back downstairs to check on Mia, but Della and she were tied up with a cookie-baking lesson, which meant he didn't have any excuses not to read the letter. He went to his room for that, though. He preferred not to have an audience for what could turn out to be gut-wrenching. Or just plain frustrating. Heaven knew Dixie Mae could be both in the span of two seconds.

"Dear Lucky," he read "I'll try to spell all the words right so you won't scowl. I suspect you're cussing me right now, but that's okay. It makes up for the times you wanted to cuss at me but were too much of a son to do it. Yes, I called you a son, because you were like that to me. That's why I wanted you to have the girls until something *permenent* could be worked out. I knew you'd do what was best for them because it would be like doing what was best for me."

Lucky had to admit she was right. And that part about his being like a son to her? That watered his eyes a little. But it would have watered them significantly more if she hadn't misspelled *permanent*.

"I didn't tell you about the girls sooner," Lucky continued reading, "because you were so busy with the rodeo stuff. I thought I'd have more time. More time to find their kin and get them settled before I passed. It was never my plan to keep them, even for a month, because let's face it, those girls deserve better than me."

Lucky wanted to disagree, but he couldn't. Dixie Mae wasn't the conventional mothering sort, and the girls needed someone normal and stable in their lives.

"Anyway, be good to yourself and Cassie," he read on. "And remember what I told you about rusting up your zipper a bit. Love, Dixie Mae."

He hadn't exactly planned on taking the zipper-rusting advice to heart, but it had worked out that way.

Thanks to Andrew's interruption in the barn. If he hadn't shown up, there might not have been enough rust in a junkyard to stop Lucky from finishing what he'd started with Cassie.

Lucky was about to refold the letter, but then he saw the PS at the bottom. "Make Cassie understand that that woman's death wasn't her fault."

And those were Dixie Mae's last words to him. They were good last words, too. Not like the bull remark she'd made on her deathbed. This was solid advice that he should start working on.

Like now.

He hurried upstairs, knocked on Cassie's door, and the moment she opened it, Lucky hooked his arm around her, hauled her to him and kissed her. Of course, Dixie Mae hadn't specifically told him to kiss Cassie. In fact, she hadn't said anything about a lip-lock, but Lucky figured it might help them both.

It was stupid logic, but that brainless part of him behind his zipper thought this was the cure to any and all world problems. Personal ones, too.

Cassie made a soft sound of surprise, a sound that got trapped in the kiss. A lot of things got trapped. Her hand. Her breasts. Basically the entire front part of her body ended up squished against his while he took the kiss to the next level.

It was the only way to make sure that Cassie knew this was a real kiss and not some peck of reassurance about their situation and those letters. And since it was a real kiss, Lucky made sure it went on for a while. That it involved some touching, as well. He kept kissing, kept touching, until air became a serious issue. He either had to break away from her or suffocate.

It took him several seconds to decide.

He finally pulled back, his eyeballs meeting hers. Cassie looked dazed. Aroused. And a whole bunch of other things that his hard-on wanted him to explore. But it wasn't the time or the place.

"Sometimes the bull doesn't win," he said.

Lucky didn't have a clue what that meant in this context. Didn't care. He walked away, smiling, and he was certain he'd just given Cassie something to think about.

MACKENZIE HATED TO leave a message for Brody. She wanted to tell him the news now, but the call went straight to voice mail. She mumbled a "call me" and hoped it wouldn't take him too long to get back to her.

She waited a minute. Then two. And since she didn't have anything better to do, she opened the letter from Dixie Mae and started reading.

Dear Mackenzie,

I hope you're behaving yourself and have found a good makeup remover. Clear skin really is one of the keys to a woman's happiness, though I'm sure you'll hear that love is. It can be, but you know firsthand that love can also be shitty. Yes, I know I shouldn't cuss around you, but it's hard to come up with another word for shitty, especially one that I can spell right off the top of my head. Probably should have taken that dictionary that Lucky was always trying to give me.

Anyway, just keep putting one foot ahead of the other. Never really did understand that since I'm not sure how you'd put two feet ahead with-

out busting your ass, but again I'm drifting off
point and cussing. Keep growing. Keep living.
Keep loving. One final thing: help Mia understand that life is more than the bucket of puke
you two have had so far.
Love, Dixie Mae.

Mackenzie couldn't help it. She smiled. Dixie Mae
was crazy, but crazy in a good way. Not like Mackenzie's mother. Probably not like Aunt Alice, either,
but at least her aunt had agreed to let her stay for the
wedding.

Her phone rang, finally, and she nearly dropped it
trying to answer it.

"Kenzie," Brody said.

God, she loved it when he called her that. Of course,
that's what Mia called her, but it sounded so grown-up
when Brody said it.

"I got your message," he continued. "Good news,
huh? But I got some more good news. Guess where I
am right now?" Brody didn't wait for her to guess. "I'm
in the barn behind the McCord house. There's nobody
out here but me, so why don't you come out? We can
hang out together."

"Okay," she heard herself say, though she knew
Lucky and Cassie wouldn't allow this. That's why
she had no intention of telling them. "I'll be down in
a couple of minutes."

The instant Mackenzie ended the call, she wished
she'd told him a half hour so she could pull herself together. Her heart was pounding like a gorilla on the
inside of her chest, and she could have used that time
to steady herself. She didn't want to go out there look-

ing like an idiot kid who'd never done anything like this before.

Even though she hadn't.

Sure, she'd done some sneaking out in the past, but it'd never been to meet a boy. A boy who liked her! It had usually been to get Mia away from their mom when she was high and acting stupid.

Mackenzie hurried to the bathroom to fix her makeup. That alone took a minute of that couple she'd given herself. On top of that, she couldn't just run down the stairs. She had to sneak, to make sure she didn't draw anyone's attention. Thankfully, there was no one in the front part of the house so she crept her way to the back door and slipped out.

Until she made it to the backyard, Mackenzie hadn't realized that the sun had already set. That was probably why Brody had picked this time to come. There were no ranch hands around, and it was already dark enough that she hoped no one would spot her. Wearing all black would finally work in her favor. And besides, Brody seemed to like it.

"Over here," Brody whispered when she got closer to the barn.

Good thing, too, because Mackenzie hadn't seen him at all. He was also wearing all black —maybe her taste in clothes had rubbed off on him—and he was standing in the shadows inside the barn.

"Hi," she said.

Brody took hold of her arm and yanked her into the barn, right into those shadows. "I don't want your watchdogs to see us," he said. "Because Lucky might not like me doing this."

And what he did was kiss her.

Brody smashed his lips against hers. It was rough, and Mackenzie nearly pulled away before she came to her senses. This was her first kiss, so how was she to know if this was rough or not?

"You taste like a birthday present," Brody whispered to her.

Mackenzie had never had a good birthday, certainly didn't know how one tasted, but Brody seemed to like it. He made a grunting sound and kissed her again. Mackenzie felt the warmth trickle through her, but she also felt something else.

His hand going up her top.

Again, it was rough. He had calluses, and they raked across her skin. He shoved down the right cup of her bra before she even realized what he was doing.

Mackenzie stepped back, her breath gusting.

"You're not quitting, are you?" Brody asked. "Because you don't look like a girl who'd quit to me."

"I don't quit," she said. In the past that was her answer to anyone who wanted to fight, but Brody must have figured out that she didn't want to fight with him. So what did not quitting mean to him?

Certainly not *that*.

"But maybe we can just kiss," she whispered.

Mackenzie couldn't see a lot of his face because it was so dark, but Brody still had his hand on her arm, and she felt his muscles tense. Then relax.

"All right. For now, we kiss," he agreed.

The relief flooded through her, along with a new trickle of heat when his mouth came back to hers. Not so rough this time. It was gentle, and strange. Strange because it made the heat trickle even more than it had when he was being rough. She wasn't sure why that would make a difference. Mackenzie wasn't sure of anything except that she wanted Brody to keep on kissing her.

And he did.

Until there was a bright flash of light. Not from overhead but from outside the barn. At first, she thought Lucky or Cassie had found them, but this wasn't anyone she recognized. It was some bald guy with a camera.

The flash went off again.

This jerk was taking their picture. But why?

"Hey!" Brody warned him. "You stop that now."

Well, the guy did stop taking their picture. But he didn't stop moving altogether. He took off running, taking the proof of the kiss with him.

Mackenzie held her breath, waiting to see if someone was going to come running out of the house. When that didn't happen, she figured that she'd pushed her luck enough for one night. If Lucky or Cassie caught her out here, they might not let her go to the dance.

On a date, she corrected.

Her first date. And there was no way she wanted to ruin that.

"Gotta go," she said.

Before he could say something to stop her, Mackenzie brushed a quick kiss on Brody's mouth and slunk back toward the house.

CHAPTER SEVENTEEN

CASSIE CAME DOWN the stairs and immediately had to dodge a cat that zipped past her. The dodging caused her to sidestep, and in turn she tripped over a basket of toy cars. Ethan's "flower boy" offerings no doubt. She hadn't needed another reminder that Claire and Riley's wedding was only three days away, but the stubbed toe now served as notice that the clock was ticking.

Too fast.

Business had made that time jet by even faster. First business on her part—Marla had made a return visit, this time to lament over whether or not her kneecaps were too saggy. A lover—Cassie didn't bother to ask which one—had mentioned it, and it'd sent Marla into a tailspin. Or rather straight to the airport. Cassie had calmed the woman down but then had suggested she might want another therapist. Marla had balked about that for hours until Cassie had suggested Andrew.

Success.

Marla was no longer on Cassie's client list. In fact, her client list was down to just a handful now, even though she did have two television appearances still scheduled for the end of the month. By then, the wedding would be over, the girls would be with Aunt Alice and Lucky's kisses would be a memory.

It was getting harder and harder for Cassie to hang

on to those memories. Mainly because Lucky hadn't exactly been around much to remind her.

Or kiss her again.

In fact, it'd been three days since he'd done that.

The business bug had bitten him, too, and he'd been forced to spend time in his San Antonio office to put out whatever kind of fires a rodeo promoter had to put out. Thankfully, Mackenzie had behaved herself even if she'd pretty much stayed in her room. And besides, the time spent not kissing Lucky had given Cassie a chance to hang out with Mia.

Which was both fun and exhausting.

She wasn't sure how parents did that day in and day out, but at least now Cassie knew if she ever had children of her own, she'd be able to handle it without going into panic mode.

That left the letter. Cassie wasn't sure how to deal with her grandmother's letter. Well, one specific part of that letter anyway.

PS. Try to make Lucky understand that his parents' deaths weren't his fault.

Cassie wasn't sure how Dixie Mae had expected her to fix that since Lucky wouldn't even talk about it. Worse, Cassie wasn't sure she wanted him to talk about it. That was how she'd gotten into trouble with Hannah. She'd encouraged the woman to open some old wounds that had apparently been so deep they'd caused her to kill herself.

Still rubbing her toe, Cassie made her way to the kitchen in the hopes of finding a second cup of coffee. Maybe finding Lucky, too, or the girls. But what she found was Andrew sitting at the table, drinking what appeared to be the last cup of coffee. The pot was empty, and Della was at the counter prepping lunch.

Since Andrew had been making daily appearances at the ranch to counsel the girls, it wasn't much of a surprise to see him. However, the fact that he had an open bottle of whiskey next to his cup gave Cassie a moment's pause.

"Uh, is something wrong?" Cassie asked.

Della glanced at her, giving her what Cassie could only describe as a sympathetic look. "I sent Mia to the sunroom to play with the cats," Della said. "Mackenzie's with her. I thought it was for the best." Then she excused herself and left the kitchen. Definitely not a good sign since she'd been in the middle of chopping an onion.

"Sit down," Andrew said, and it sounded like an order.

For that reason alone Cassie stood, and she huffed. "Look, Andrew, I'm grateful you were there after Hannah died. You kept me from falling apart—"

"You did fall apart," he argued.

"No. I had panic attacks, and plenty of people have them without having to stay in Sweet Meadows." It had taken her a while, too long, but now that she'd distanced herself from that place, she knew it hadn't been a good idea. "Being there made me feel as if I needed to be there."

That probably didn't make sense to him, but she wasn't sure she cared. What she did care about right now was a cup of coffee. The caffeine hit would help her headache so Cassie went to the counter and started a fresh pot. While she was waiting, she decided to wash her hands and finish chopping the onion for Della.

"Is there a reason for all this hostility I'm sensing coming from you?" Andrew asked. This time he sounded like a therapist. *Her* therapist. "Maybe there's something you'd like to tell me? You know, before I find out on my own."

That didn't sound like a fishing-expedition sort of comment. Of course, Cassie had been chilly to him so maybe he was picking up on the fact that she wanted him to leave Spring Hill.

"I know you're thinking about throwing your career away," he continued. "But I didn't think you'd trash mine in the process."

Cassie stopped, turned, and she was certain there was confusion and alarm on her face. On Andrew's face, too, but then she realized her eyes had watered from the onion and she was holding up the knife as if she were the star of a slasher movie. Cassie eased the knife back onto the counter.

"What are you talking about?" she asked.

"Don't play games with me."

She shook her head, causing him to huff. Apparently, he wasn't going to take her head shake as proof that she didn't have a clue what was going on. Then she rubbed her eyes and made the stinging and burning significantly worse.

"Use your words, Andrew," she snapped. Cassie also snapped a paper towel from the roll, dampened it and pressed it to her eyes.

"I don't need words because these pictures are worth a thousand of them." And Andrew slapped something on the table. Perhaps something he'd taken from his pocket, but with her having to blink ten times per second, it was hard to tell.

Hard to see what'd gotten him so riled up, too.

Hard to see, period.

Cassie went closer, blinking even more to get her eyes to focus, and she finally saw the photo clearly. At first she wasn't sure what she was actually looking at, and it took her a moment to realize it was Mackenzie and Brody. Kissing in the barn.

Sheez, Louise.

The photo was indeed worth a thousand words, and the word at the top of that list was *grounded*.

Since it was obviously dark in the picture, this meant Mackenzie had no doubt sneaked out to meet Brody. Cassie wasn't sure when the girl had done that, but she hadn't had eyes on her 24/7, mainly because Mackenzie had been so happy lately. Well, if happiness was graded on the Mackenzie scale anyway.

But that was only part of the problem Cassie had with the unauthorized smooching. It was the fact that there was a picture of it. A picture that Mackenzie and Brody clearly hadn't taken because they'd been too busy exploring each other's tonsils.

"Who took that picture?" Cassie demanded.

"The same person who took this one." Andrew reached into his jacket pocket and extracted another photo.

Not of Mackenzie and Brody this time. Of Lucky and that sleazy woman, Angel, who'd French-kissed him on the porch. Even though Cassie knew nothing had come of it, that Lucky had quickly gotten rid of her, the photo made it look as if they were making out in public.

"Who took these?" she repeated.

Andrew didn't answer that time, either, but he did

pull out a third picture. Another one that had been taken in the barn. It was a shot of Lucky and her. Snapped on the day that she was now referring to as the great chaps lapse.

Oh, mercy.

Lucky and she were doing some smooching, too. And he had his hand on her butt while leading her up the ladder to the hayloft.

Cassie groaned, but what she wanted to do was scream her head off. She hadn't caught even a glimpse of anyone taking their picture. Of course, that had been the last thing on her mind. What she'd been focused on was getting that orgasm from Lucky. Besides, the photo of Lucky and her appeared to have been taken with a long-range lens. Ditto for the one of Lucky and Angel. So it was possible that the photographer hadn't even come onto the ranch.

She couldn't say the same for the one of Brody and Mackenzie, though. That one had been taken up close and at night. There was no way they wouldn't have known about it.

Cassie's stomach knotted into a giant ball, and it was churning as if a basketball point guard were dribbling it. That didn't help her breathing, either, and her heart was thudding in her ears.

Breathe.

She refused to have a panic attack. Cassie tried to put this in perspective. No one was dead or even hurt. Yes, she'd screwed up again, but the damage wasn't anything like it'd been with Hannah.

She hoped.

"What's going on?" Mackenzie asked.

Cassie hadn't heard her, but the girl was right there in the kitchen, and her attention landed on the photos.

"Oh, God." Mackenzie's hand went flying to her mouth. She shook her head. "Who took that picture?"

That was a really good question, but it wasn't nearly as good as the one Cassie had for her. "What were you doing kissing Brody in the barn?"

And apparently Andrew thought he had the best question of all. "What were you doing kissing Lucky in the barn?" he asked Cassie.

Since Cassie didn't have anything near a good answer, she repeated Mackenzie's question. "Who took those pictures?"

"Theo Kervin, the reporter who's been sniffing around town for a story," Andrew said, but his huff and glare let her know that his question was still on the table—literally. That was where the picture of Lucky and her kissing still rested.

"Why would some stupid reporter take a picture of me?" Mackenzie asked.

Maybe it was that her eyes were still burning, or because she still had that headache, but it took Cassie several seconds to piece it together. "This Theo Kervin wants to paint me in a bad light because it'll hurt my reputation as a celebrity therapist. It'll be *news*."

"Bingo," Andrew confirmed. "I don't know all the details of what will be in the article in the Friday paper, but I know he's mentioning me as your spurned lover. It'll make me look like a fool."

"Ex-lover," Cassie corrected, though that was splitting hairs. She knew how tabloid journalism worked, and "ex-lover" wouldn't be nearly as tawdry as having her step out on a distinguished psychologist so she could make out with a cowboy.

All the while she was supposed to be parenting two children in her custody.

All the while one of those girls was making out with a wannabe cowboy.

If Theo had found out about Sweet Meadows, then he could seal the career-ruining deal by just mentioning it. And yes, that would hurt Andrew, too, because it would make it seem as if his lover was a sex-crazed lunatic with no regard whatsoever for the children.

Breathe.

The reminder wasn't working so Cassie put her head between her knees again. And that's how Lucky found her when he walked into the kitchen.

LUCKY HURRIED OVER to Cassie, lifting her head so he could see what was wrong. He saw her red eyes and whirled around to beat the shit out of Andrew for whatever he'd done to make her cry.

But then his attention landed on the photos.

Oh, man.

It felt as if someone had sucker punched him, and he instantly knew. Andrew wasn't the reason for Cassie's tears. He was.

"Theo Kervin took those?" Lucky asked Andrew. "Or did you?" While he was in the Q & A mode, his gaze shot to Mackenzie. "And what the hell were you doing kissing Brody?"

"Uh, kissing him," Mackenzie answered.

No smart-assery in her tone this time. She gave him a truthful answer that in no way answered his question. But Lucky would deal with her later. For now, he needed to stop Cassie from having a panic attack. However, when Cassie lifted her head again, she didn't seem to be in panic mode but rather anger mode.

"I'm going to sue Theo Kervin," she insisted.

"They'll be in the morning papers," Andrew added. "Including the local one here. I tried to stop it, tried to pay off the idiot, but he wouldn't take it."

Maybe because someone had already paid him— like Mason-Dixon. Of course, Cassie's father was more the type to extort money than to pay it, but if he'd wanted to burn Cassie and Lucky for the cats, then this would have been the way to do it. It wouldn't hurt Lucky's reputation. In fact, it would confirm what most people thought about him anyway, but it would hurt Cassie. Would hurt Mackenzie, too.

First things first, though.

"You're grounded," Lucky told Mackenzie. "I let the money thing slide with just an apology, but this isn't sliding."

"Grounded?" she howled as if she'd just been sentenced to be pecked to death by rabid ducks. "This isn't fair."

"Probably not, but you're not allowed to sneak out of the house and make out with boys. I'm just funny that way."

Mackenzie flung her hand toward the other pictures. "You made out with Cassie and that skank."

"Not to the skank. To Angel," he corrected. "Yeah, to Cassie. But Cassie and I are adults." Though it hadn't felt like it that day. Lucky could have sworn he'd felt a few raging teenage hormones himself when he'd been with Cassie.

Mackenzie huffed and puffed a few seconds while

she stared at Cassie, apparently waiting for a second opinion on the grounding verdict. But Cassie just shook her head. "You're grounded. We'll talk later."

After more huffing and puffing, Mackenzie spun around to leave. Lucky followed her a few steps to make sure she was actually going upstairs rather than heading out the front door. She not only went upstairs, he heard her slam her bedroom door.

Good.

Slamming was preferable to running. Heck, he might slam a door or two himself before this day was over.

"What can I do to fix this?" Lucky asked Cassie.

But she didn't give him a good answer. She only shook her head.

"You can't fix this," Andrew insisted. Not a good answer, either. "If you're the one who talked Cassie into giving up being a celebrity therapist, then the timing couldn't have been worse. There's no way she'll be able to build a new client base once this story gets out. Plus, how do you think the girls' aunt will react?"

Probably not well. Heck, Alice might get on the next plane to whisk the girls away. Of course, Alice's whisking was only days away anyway, but Lucky didn't want things to end like this. And speaking of whisking things away, that's what Andrew did to the photos. He stuffed them in his jacket pocket and looked at Cassie. "I'll be leaving for the airport in a few hours. If you have anything to say to me, then I suggest you say it now."

Lucky wasn't sure exactly what Andrew wanted to hear Cassie say. Did he want her to beg him to forgive her and stay? Did he want a goodbye? Cassie didn't give him either of those, though. She just sat there staring at the now empty spot on the table where the photos had been.

"Fine," Andrew snapped, and he hurried to the door.

And yep, he slammed it on his way out.

LUCKY STOOD IN the shower and let the scalding-hot water do its job. Not with the cleaning part. He could have accomplished that with a much cooler temperature. What he needed was some of the muscles unknotted in his back and shoulders.

The house was essentially on lockdown. Lucky wasn't sure if that was the right thing to do or not, especially since he'd have to leave in a couple of hours for Riley's bachelor party. He'd considered skipping it, but Della, Stella and Cassie had all assured him they'd keep an eye on Mackenzie.

That might not be enough, though.

But Lucky kept going back to bull logic. Some bulls were just harder to fence than others, and a few were downright impossible. They'd break fences no matter how strong. It was a bad analogy, but there might not be a fence tall or strong enough to keep Mackenzie from sneaking back out again.

Lucky gave up on getting relief from the shower. He toweled off, pulled on his boxers and jeans and headed back into his bedroom to get a clean shirt. And he stopped in his tracks.

Because Cassie was sitting on his bed.

Her eyes weren't red as they'd been in the kitchen, but she wasn't exactly sporting a sunshiny smile, either.

"Is Mackenzie all right?" he asked.

"She's still in her room. Mia's with Della, and the ranch hands are watching to make sure Mackenzie doesn't sneak out again."

Since that was about as good as they could expect right now, it didn't explain Cassie's "somebody died" expression.

Hell, unless somebody *had* died.

After all, that lunatic client had flown in the day before for another session. Had Marla done something? Or had Andrew? Lucky figured the guy was far too egotistical to end his life, but maybe he'd said or done something to hurt Cassie. Or to get back together with her. She hadn't gone running out of the house after Andrew, but that didn't mean she hadn't called him afterward.

"Are *you* all right?" Lucky asked, sitting down on the bed next to her.

Cassie gave a little laugh, definitely not from humor. "I'm fine. I'm worried about you, though."

"Me?" Lucky wasn't sure where she was going with this. "I'm not the one who'll lose clients or have my reputation ruined. Heck, I'll probably get some calls for dates after the story runs and they see me with both Angel and you."

He'd meant that as a joke, but Cassie must have thought he was serious because it put that troubled look back on her face. Then he noticed what she had in her left hand.

The letter.

She unfolded it for him to see. Lucky glanced through it, the PS snagging his attention right off, and he groaned.

PS. Try to make Lucky understand that his parents' deaths weren't his fault.

"Dixie Mae had no right," he snarled.

Cassie nodded. "And I suspect she had no right to give you a PS about me. Let me guess—she told you to make sure I understood that Hannah's death wasn't my fault?"

Since that was almost verbatim, Lucky just nodded. He was about to say Dixie Mae had no right to say that about Cassie, either, that it wasn't Dixie Mae's place. But hell, it sure felt like it was his place to try to help Cassie.

Without her trying to help him, of course.

Lucky frowned. He didn't want to be fixed. Didn't deserve it.

"I'll show you mine if you show me yours," Cassie said.

His mind, and body, immediately started to fill in the blanks, but he didn't think his dick was a blank in this. No, this wasn't something nearly as much fun.

"I'll start," she said, though he'd given her no encouragement whatsoever to do that. "I can't forgive myself for what happened to Hannah because I don't feel as if I deserve forgiveness."

Well, now. Since that, too, was almost verbatim what Lucky had been thinking, he had to wonder if Dixie Mae was somewhere in the spiritual realm making all of this happen. It didn't matter. Lucky still didn't want to play this game.

"I figure I deserve the panic attacks, too. Deserve my inability to commit because I haven't gotten past the baggage my parents left me." She paused. "And I have trouble having orgasms."

Lucky had tried to anticipate what she was going to say. That last one hadn't been anywhere on his list, and it didn't fit with the other things. Or maybe it did. Did she truly feel she didn't deserve orgasms?

"Really? Because you seemed to be doing okay with that up in the hayloft," he reminded her.

"I know. But that was a fluke. At least, I think it was."

And then Cassie did something else that would have knocked his socks off, had he been wearing any.

She kissed him.

Cassie took hold of him, dragged him to her and kissed him. Again, it didn't go with the first part of the conversation, but it certainly went with the second because it seemed as if Cassie was in search of that orgasm—right here, right now.

Lucky felt the kiss all right. Not just in the usual places, either. This was a head-to-toenails sort of sensation as if every bit of him had managed to toss back some shots of hundred-proof. It was an especially good feeling since he was already half-naked, and Cassie and he were on the bed.

So Lucky kissed her right back.

He kept on kissing her until she did something else surprising. Cassie moved away from him and stood.

"I just wanted to give you something to think about," she said as if that explained everything.

And Cassie walked out, leaving him there with that warm head-to-toe feeling and a raging hard-on.

CHAPTER EIGHTEEN

CASSIE WENT TO the window and checked again. No sign of Lucky. Of course, it was barely 10:00 p.m., and it was possible Riley's bachelor party would go into the wee hours of the morning. Still, she was hoping he would get home early just so she could explain herself.

Kissing him like that had been a bold move. Sort of throwing down the F-word gauntlet. And he would have known that, too. She wasn't a tease, and there was only one reason for her to kiss a man like that.

Because she wanted to F-word him.

Now that the fire in her body had cooled just a bit, she was feeling all the nerves beneath her skin. That was why she wanted to talk to him. Or preferably have sex with him. Sex wouldn't help with the PS from Dixie Mae's letter, but Cassie was reasonably sure it wouldn't hurt.

The knock at her door sent her racing to open it, and she tried not to look disappointed to see Mackenzie standing there. Because Cassie really wasn't disappointed. She'd tried to talk to Mackenzie several times since Andrew's photo bombshell, and the girl had clammed up. However, Mackenzie certainly looked ready to talk now.

"Mia's asleep," she said right off. "Can I come in for a minute?"

"Of course." Cassie ushered her in and shut the door.

"I'm sorry," Mackenzie said before she even sat down on the bed. It not only sounded genuine, it looked as if she'd been crying. There were some visible streaks in her makeup. "I didn't mean to mess up anything for you and your job. I just wanted to see Brody."

Considering Cassie was fighting her own hormonal impulses, she totally understood.

"I'm really sorry," Mackenzie added, and yes, there were tears now. Unlike her apology to Wilhelmina, it sounded as if the girl meant it.

Sighing, Cassie sat down beside her and slipped an arm around her. This time, Mackenzie didn't go stiff as she usually did when Cassie touched her. She actually leaned against Cassie.

"I just thought Brody wouldn't like me if I said no," she went on. "That's why I went to the barn. I didn't know he was going to kiss me, honest."

Cassie got that, as well. Of course, from the moment she'd seen Lucky walking toward her in the barn that day, she'd pretty much figured a kiss or something more would happen between them. But she was an adult, and she'd known the consequences of her actions. Her limits, too. Maybe Mackenzie didn't.

"You shouldn't say yes to a guy just so he'll like you," Cassie told her. "Because it might not stop at a kiss. He might want *more* to keep on liking you. Understand?"

Apparently, she did because Mackenzie's gaze darted away. "Brody wouldn't do that. He just wanted to kiss me."

"Maybe. Guys can be…complicated." But then Cassie shook her head. "Actually, that's not true. Many of them just want sex. I'm not saying that's true for Brody, but it's their hormones." Something she completely understood since her own hormones were in a tizzy over Lucky. "Plus, you have to consider that you might not be here at the ranch much longer. I know it doesn't seem that way right now, but it might be only a short while before you forget all about Brody because you've met someone else."

Mackenzie sucked in her breath as if horrified by that thought. Cassie was about to start drilling home that it was just the way these things worked, but that might not be true, either. After all, Cassie had had a thing for Lucky all these years, and that thing was stronger than ever. It might happen to Mackenzie— thirty years from now.

Mackenzie looked up at her. "I get what you're saying, but I just want to be with Brody. Even if it's only for a day or two. I know you don't owe me any favors, but I really want to go to that dance with him tomorrow night."

There it was. The megaproblem that Mackenzie had just dumped into her lap. If Cassie held firm and said no, it would break Mackenzie's heart. Temporarily. But to a thirteen-year-old girl, it would feel as if it were a permanent scar. On the other hand, if she said yes, then it could make her look like a wimp.

Mackenzie put her own hand into play. She opened her palm, and Cassie saw the gold star that Livvy had given her the day she'd arrived at the ranch. It had a little less gold on it now, and there was no way Mackenzie really believed it was magic. Still, it had sort of a magical effect on Cassie when Mackenzie gave it to her.

Cassie decided to go with being the wimp. It would be far easier for Cassie to mend her own ego than it would for Mackenzie to mend her teenage heart.

"Yes, but with rules," Cassie quickly added when Mackenzie started to squeal—yes, squeal—with enough excitement that you would have thought she'd just been granted every wish she'd ever wanted.

"Any rules are fine as long as I can go."

"Hear the rules first," Cassie warned her. "And I have to clear all of this with Lucky, understand?"

Even that didn't seem to diminish a drop of her happiness. Mackenzie nodded. Too bad she didn't have a second gold star for Lucky.

"We'll drive you there and bring you home," Cassie continued. "At no point will you slip off to be alone with Brody. We'll make sure of that because we'll be watching you."

Still nodding, she seemed surprised when Cassie didn't add any other conditions. "I don't have to, like, dress like you or anything?"

"No. You can wear what you want as long as it covers all parts of your body from here to here." Cassie pointed to her neck, then to her midthigh. "Now get some sleep."

"I will. Thank you, Cassie. Thank you." She hugged Cassie again and practically skipped out of the room.

After being given such a huge concession, she doubted Mackenzie would skip out of the house, but just in case she watched Mackenzie go into her room and shut the door. Cassie was about to do the same thing when she heard the footsteps on the stairs.

Lucky.

"You're home early," she said, and it was a good

thing she said it fast, too, because it was all Cassie managed to get out before he reached her.

Lucky hooked his arm around her waist, snapped her to him and kissed her. All in all, it was a lot better than him saying hello or responding to her comment. And he didn't stop there. It was like the loft ladder all over again. Kissing her, he pushed her deeper into the room and kicked the door shut.

Mercy, he smelled good. Tasted good, too. Cassie had expected him to smell like strippers and taste like tequila, but the only thing she was getting here was the heady scent of cowboy and testosterone. Lucky should bottle it.

But for now, no bottle required. He was giving her a full dose of not just the kiss but of body contact. His chest against her breasts. His left leg wedged between hers. He was working that leg, too, giving her just the right kind of pressure to go along with the kiss.

Lucky broke the contact only to reach back and lock the door. He came back to her, his mouth already finding hers. And then he said the exact thing Cassie wanted to hear.

"I thought about that kiss," he said, "and now I'm thinking it's time we did a hell of a lot more."

LUCKY WAS TIRED of debating with himself over whether this was a good idea or not. It wasn't. But some of the things that had turned out good in his life had started with not-so-good ideas.

Or at least that was the logic he'd used on the drive home from the bachelor party.

It wasn't necessarily good logic, but then who cared. Cassie certainly seemed willing to jump into this, and even if this was their one and only time together, that just meant Lucky had to make the most of it.

She reached behind him, groping. Not for his back, he realized, but for the light switch. Lucky maneuvered her away from that right off. He wanted to see her, along with tasting lots and lots of her body.

"You're used to being with hot women," she mumbled. "I'm not hot."

There weren't many things that could have made him break the kiss, but that did it. "You're hot."

And since Cassie screwed up her mouth and didn't look sure of that at all, Lucky went down on his knees, pushed up her skirt, yanked down her panties and put her knee on his shoulder so he could give her a kiss to make her body feel as hot as she looked.

It worked.

Not just for Cassie—she made a gasping sound of pleasure—but for him, too. Of course, he had been sporting a hard-on for days so he didn't need anything additional, but the taste of her gave him a nice buzz.

"I wasn't expecting that," she said, gasping again.

Good. It was nice to keep her a little off balance so that maybe those orgasms she said she had trouble with would sort of sneak up on her. Lucky helped with that. He added a little nip—the kind that would hurt so good—and deepened the kiss. Lucky took her to the brink.

Before he pulled her back.

She cursed him and called him a bad name when he stopped.

"Foreplay," he explained but since she'd brought up the subject of ass with her name-calling, he got to his feet, turned her and put her against the door.

Normally, this was the part where he would want her stark naked, but if that happened, the *fore* would leave the foreplay, and he'd fuck her brains out. He preferred a more controlled fucking right now, to test to see just how sweet the part of her he'd just kissed was.

He shoved up her skirt again, though it was already practically around her waist. The panties went. He pushed them to her knees, caught onto them with his boot and pushed them the rest of the way down. He raked them aside when she stepped out of them, and Cassie put herself against the door again.

Holding her in place, he managed to put on a condom, and he moved her legs apart so he could enter her from behind. Not deep. Just enough to let him know what he was up against. Kissing Cassie there was one thing, but his dick was a lot more sensitive than his tongue.

Oh, man.

He was in trouble. He shouldn't have waited this long to be with her because Cassie was tight, wet and yeah, hot. All the things that would end this much too fast. Good thing they weren't face-to-face because he would've been a goner if she'd kissed him. Or if he had been looking into her eyes.

She made that moan again and went still a second as if trying to steady herself. Lucky knew exactly how she felt—literally. He wasn't too steady, either, and he got even less steady when Cassie pushed herself against him, taking him deeper inside her.

Hell in a hurricane.

When he was a teenager he'd used a trick so he could last long enough to do things the right way, with both him and his partner getting off. He mentally quoted the recipe for his dad's barbecue sauce. Ketchup, brown sugar, vinegar and mustard. Yeah, it was stupid, but it always worked. Though when Cassie kept moving, kept pushing herself so that all that slick heat was sliding right against his hard-on, Lucky was forced to repeat the recipe three times.

"Vinegar?" she asked.

Crap. He hadn't meant to say it aloud, and that meant it was clearly time to take this to the next level. He pulled out of her, causing her to call him a name again. The woman did like variations with the root word of *ass* in them. She turned so that they were face-to-face, and she would have taken him back inside her if Lucky hadn't scooped her up and carried her to the bed. He put her on the mattress, her legs still spread, and he damn near lost his breath. Damn near came, too.

Maybe he should have turned out those lights after all.

Too late.

Things were moving very fast now, and despite the fact he still had on his jeans, Cassie pulled him down on top of her. It was as if his dick had a homing device on it instead of a condom because he went right inside her, pushing through all that tight heat until he was exactly where he wanted to be.

Cassie didn't groan this time. She stopped breathing, and for a moment he thought she'd fainted or something. But no. Lucky looked in her eyes and saw exactly what he wanted to see—a beautiful woman on the verge of a beautiful orgasm. And she wouldn't have to work for this one.

Lucky did it for her.

As a teenager he'd had a very good teacher, a girl

two years older than him who'd made him take exams of sorts on locating what she'd called her love button. Hours and hours of practice had made him particularly aware of how important it was to find any and all love buttons of his sexual partners. Cassie's was pretty easy to find, and he knew he'd hit pay dirt when her eyes practically rolled back in her head.

Lucky didn't have a choice about moving then. She caught onto his hips and helped him with that. Not that he actually needed help, but it was obvious that Cassie was on a mission to make the best possible use of his hard-on.

She moved.

He moved.

Faster.

Deeper.

Until recipe-quoting time was over. It was time to finish, and he made sure that's exactly what Cassie did. That was the nice thing about a woman's climax—all those muscles squeezing him until he wasn't sure of his own name, much less barbecue ingredients. Lucky let her love button do the rest of the work for him, and he let himself go.

Lucky collapsed on top of her, trying not to crush her, and as soon as he could get his body working, he flopped down on his back beside her like a landed trout. Cassie's breath was gusting, and she was making little sounds. Mumbling something.

And then she laughed.

He lifted his head to see what the heck was going on. Usually he didn't leave a woman laughing after an orgasm.

"You know it was great," she said, clamping her

teeth over her bottom lip for a second. "Don't look so pleased with yourself."

Did he look pleased? Probably. He'd just had sex with a woman who'd been causing his body to burn for years.

Cassie laughed again, turned her head and kissed him. Not the long, lingering kiss, though, of a woman who might want seconds. Seconds done the right way, with them both naked as jaybirds.

"I don't think I've been this relaxed in years," Cassie said. "All the muscles in my body are slack. You're a great stress reliever, you know that?"

He smiled.

Then he didn't smile.

A stress reliever? Was that what this had been for her? Yeah, he'd been a player most of his life, but for the first time, that was starting to wear thin. Maybe he was looking for more than being just a bull rider/player/screwup after all.

Well, fuck.

When had that happened?

CHAPTER NINETEEN

THAT WONDERFUL SLACK feeling hadn't lasted for Cassie. It had vanished shortly after Lucky had kissed her good-night and headed off to his room. And the vanishing act had happened only minutes after he'd given her that equally wonderful orgasm.

Cassie knew she'd blown it.

For someone who had been trained to deal with people's emotions, she'd sure missed the mark when it came to Lucky. Clearly, she'd hurt his feelings with her stress-reliever remark. Strange. She hadn't thought he would be sensitive about something like that, especially since they had known the sex was just that—sex.

Wasn't it?

Cassie had to shake her head. She wasn't sure about anything anymore, but she knew she had to talk this out with Lucky now that it was morning, and she wanted to do that before any of the wedding crew showed up. They weren't setting up for the actual wedding just yet since it was still two days away, but they needed to start clearing out the furniture so there'd be room for the chairs and flowers.

She checked on the girls first by putting her ear to their bedroom door. No stirring around in there so Cassie headed downstairs. Before she could make it to Lucky's room, though, she heard the voices in the living room. One was Lucky's, but the other Cassie didn't recognize. However, she immediately knew who the woman was when Cassie spotted her.

Alice Murdock.

She was tall, blonde and, well, stunning. She was wearing sensible traveling clothes that managed to look fashionable on her model-thin body. Alice stood the moment Cassie stepped into the living room, and with a smile on her face, she approached and shook Cassie's hand.

"I apologize for being here two days early," Alice said, her voice a whisper. "I rescheduled some work and took an earlier flight because I was so anxious to finally get here. I hope you don't mind. I was going to wait outside in my rental car for a while, but then Lucky saw me and invited me in."

Of course, they'd been expecting Alice but not until later that week. Cassie had wanted those extra hours to ready herself for this. Then again, readying apparently wasn't necessary. Alice certainly didn't appear to be a drug-addicted lowlife like her half sister.

"Alice and I were just talking about her job," Lucky said.

And they were drinking coffee. Judging from the fact that both their cups were nearly empty, they'd been chatting for a while.

"Oh?" Cassie settled for saying.

She hated to sound even remotely catty. Hated to feel it even more, but there was something about this that put her off. Maybe it was just jealousy. Not just because this woman would soon whisk the girls away but because of this cozy time she was having with the man who'd given Cassie an orgasm about ten hours earlier.

"You remember me mentioning that Alice heads up a nonprofit. It arranges for medical and dental care in third-world countries," Lucky explained.

"And Lucky told me all about his bull riding," Alice quickly added. "He even showed me the bulls he just bought. No way would I climb on one of those things." She chuckled. Then she looked at Cassie. "Of course, I've seen you on television, so I know what you do. It must feel good to be able to touch so many people like that."

It did, sometimes, and it was the perfect thing for this woman to say. Cassie settled for a nod.

"So, you live in Phoenix?" Cassie asked, sitting on the sofa. Not too close to Lucky, but it was close enough that another woman might notice she was marking her territory.

Sad, very sad, that Cassie felt the need to do that, especially since Lucky wasn't doing any territory marking of his own.

"I moved there about five years ago, after my divorce." Alice dismissed that with a wave of her hand. "The job was just too tempting to pass up. Our organization helps several thousand people each year."

"It sounds as if you work a lot of hours." Cassie tried to sound like she was making casual conversation rather than appearing as if she was fishing for anything negative.

"I do, but I know that'll have to change now. I'll need a new place, too. And a nanny, of course. Any idea how the girls do in school?"

"Mia hasn't started yet," Cassie answered. "She'll be going into pre-K at the end of the month. Mackenzie will be in eighth grade. Her grades took a hit when her mother died."

"But she's good in English," Lucky added.

Cassie hadn't even known that Lucky had checked on her school records, but it didn't surprise her. They'd both gotten more involved in the girls' lives than Cassie had originally planned. That's what made this meeting all the more difficult.

"So, you want children?" Cassie didn't even attempt the casual, conversational tone that time.

Alice nodded without hesitation. "I can't have children of my own." Had her bottom lip trembled? Heck, it had. "That's the reason my ex divorced me. I'd given up on the idea of being a mom, and when I got the call about Gracie's death, I was naturally upset, but I was glad to finally be able to do something to help her."

Before the woman had even finished, Cassie heard a familiar sound—Mia talking to the cats. It didn't take the little girl long to make it to the living room, holding one of the cats in her arms.

Alice got to her feet again. "Hi. You must be Mia. I'm your aunt Alice."

Mia looked at both Lucky and Cassie, maybe asking for some kind of signal that it was okay to go closer. Cassie nodded, and Mia took more steps toward Alice.

"This is Sassy," she said, introducing the cat. "Are you a nice lady?"

Alice chuckled again, apparently thoroughly enchanted. "I like to think I am. Do I look nice?"

Mia studied her a moment. "I guess so."

More footsteps, and Cassie knew Mackenzie was on the way. Cassie would have bet her favorite jeans that Alice's enchantment would diminish considerably when she saw Mackenzie.

But she was wrong.

Alice gave Mackenzie an equally warm smile and then pressed her hand to her heart. "You look so much like Gracie."

Mackenzie flinched as if someone had struck her. "Then I must not have put on enough makeup."

It was inches deep as usual, and it broke Cassie's heart a little not to have seen why Mackenzie put on this mask each day. She probably didn't want to be reminded of her mother whenever she looked in the mirror. Some therapist she was not to have picked up on that.

"Is it still okay for us to go to the wedding even though she's here early? I mean, we don't have to leave right away with her, do we?" Mackenzie said to Cassie. She tipped her head to Alice. Then she did a second head tip to Lucky. "And did you ask him about that other thing we talked about?"

"Of course, you can still go to the wedding," Alice assured Mackenzie before Cassie could speak. "I've reserved a room at the Bluebonnet Inn, and I figured we could all fly out on Sunday night. Or maybe Monday if that works better with everyone's schedule."

Cassie figured she couldn't ask the flight to be changed to next year.

"What are you supposed to ask me?" Lucky pressed.

Cassie had wanted to have this chat in private, but she really should include Alice in this anyway. "I didn't know her aunt would get here this soon so I told Mackenzie that if it was okay with you that she could go to the dance tonight." She didn't mention the part about Mackenzie being grounded. If Mackenzie wanted her aunt to know, then she could tell her. But Lucky would perhaps think that the grounding extended to the dance.

Judging from his expression, that's exactly what he thought.

A flatter look would have required Lucky getting his eyelids steamrollered.

"Of course, I'll chaperone," Cassie added.

"Please," Mackenzie begged, not sounding at all hostile or surly. She was the normal thirteen-year-old again, standing on the brink of what she no doubt considered to be a life-and-death matter.

"A dance?" Alice questioned.

Oh, no. If both Lucky and Alice were on team no, then Cassie wouldn't stand a chance of convincing them.

"It's at the town's civic center," Cassie explained. "All the local kids used to go to dances there when they were Mackenzie's age." Or at least she was sure Lucky had. Cassie had always had her nose in a book from the time she'd been able to turn pages.

"Brody still has plans to be there," Lucky practically growled, and it certainly wasn't a growl of approval. Alice followed up with a "Who's Brody?"

"Brody Tate," Cassie said.

"A friend," Mackenzie said.

"A boy," Mia said.

Alice looked at Lucky, apparently wanting his take on the situation. Lucky glanced at both Mackenzie and her aunt. Scowled. "Brody is someone who thinks he's Mackenzie's boyfriend, but he's not. He can't be because Mackenzie's too young for a boyfriend."

While his tone wasn't exactly friendly, Lucky hadn't mentioned the shovel or stun gun. That was something at least.

"I'll be late for chaperoning duties," Lucky said. "I thought the plans for the dance were out…because of the other thing."

He meant the grounding over the photograph. So obviously Lucky had mentally nixed the dance. Which was reasonable, but Cassie had just had such a hard time saying no after her talk with Mackenzie.

"Because I thought I'd be free, I've got that dinner thing tonight with Sugar and Wilhelmina," Lucky added.

Yes, payment for keeping quiet. The "date" had been postponed so many times that Cassie had forgotten about it. Apparently, Lucky had decided to kill two birds with one stone and wine and dine the women together. She was betting that wouldn't be a pleasant evening.

"I don't think both of us would need to be at the dance anyway," Cassie explained.

"I could do it," Alice volunteered.

"Uh—" Mackenzie said at the same time Cassie said "Huh?"

It wasn't that Cassie didn't want Alice there— All right, she didn't. Cassie also wasn't sure how Alice would take it when she learned Brody was older than Mackenzie. And that he had somewhat of a reputation. No way would Alice be able to get out of that civic center without hearing a boatload of gossip.

Including gossip about those photos that would be in the paper. Since Spring Hill wasn't that big, the local newspaper only came out three times a week, but the latest edition came out this morning, which meant people were probably looking at them right now.

Of course, Alice would hear about that soon enough anyway, but Cassie hoped she could put off explaining it until after the dance. If she told her now, Cassie doubted even the perfect Alice would agree.

"So I can go?" Mackenzie asked.

"If it's okay with Lucky," Alice assured her.

Now all eyes turned to Lucky. Even the cat in Mia's little arms was staring at him.

And he finally nodded.

Mackenzie squealed again, and she rushed to hug all of them. Including Alice and the cat. "I want to go try on my dress," she said, and she bolted for the stairs.

"I remember those years," Alice said, smiling. She touched her finger to Mia's nose. "Your years not so much. So will this kitty be coming with us to Phoenix?"

That got eyes back on Cassie. And like Lucky, Cassie nodded. Mia squealed.

Squealing aside, everything was falling into place.

Alice picked up her purse. "Let me see if I can get checked in to the inn. I'll be staying in the garden room. And then if it's okay, I'll come back and spend some time with the girls."

"Of course," Cassie mumbled. Lucky mumbled it, as well. Mia was still squealing and running around the room with the cat.

Lucky and Cassie followed the woman to the door. "I'm so sorry about losing my sister," Alice whispered to them. "But you can't imagine how much joy the girls have already given me."

There were tears in her eyes, and Cassie guessed

they were of the happy variety. Alice gave a little wave goodbye before she headed out.

Lucky and Cassie stood there in the doorway, waving back. Smiling. Until Alice had gotten in her rental car and driven away.

"Shit," Lucky mumbled. "She's perfect."

CASSIE HAD BEEN right about the gossip and those pictures. No one at the civic center was actually saying anything to her face—not to Mackenzie's or Brody's faces, either—but a lot of hands were being used in the dance hall to cover whispers. Cassie suspected that the whispering would increase significantly when Lucky finally arrived.

He'd gone on the payback date after all but had promised to get to the dance as soon as possible. He had also somehow talked Alice into not coming. Cassie wasn't sure exactly how he'd accomplished that, but she was glad he had. The wedding chaos would start again first thing in the morning since the furniture had been cleared and the decorating would begin. So these were likely her last few hours to spend with Mackenzie.

And fifty other teenagers.

The civic center was jammed, and even though Cassie had never attended a dance here, it was how she'd imagined it would be. Crepe-paper decorations. Toilet-paper roses. Dim lights. Really loud music. But Mackenzie didn't seem to notice any of that. She had her eyes locked on Brody as they danced.

Cassie's phone buzzed, and she took it from her pocket long enough to check the screen. It was her agent, who'd no doubt gotten word of the photos. He was probably calling to tell her that her reputation had been as sullied as Andrew had claimed it would be. Or heck, maybe this had put her even more in demand, sort of like those pseudocelebrities who did sex tapes.

Either way, Cassie didn't intend to find out what was going on until after the wedding. It wasn't very healthy to take the head-in-the-sand approach with something as big as this, but it beat having a panic attack.

She let the call from her agent go to voice mail. The very thing she'd done with Andrew's calls. And the one from her mother. The four from her father, too. She decided the only non-McCord/Compton call she might answer would be from a Girl Scout who wanted to personally deliver a case of Thin Mints. Everybody else could leave a voice mail.

"Enjoying yourself?" someone asked from behind her.

Deputy Davy.

He was in uniform, his thumbs hooked over his equipment belt, his legs apart as if he was ready to pounce on any situation that might require pouncing.

"So, did Lucky dump you already?" Davy asked.

There were so many things wrong with that question, and any way she tried to answer it Cassie would say more than she wanted to. So she didn't answer at all. "Why are you here?"

He gave his thumbs an adjustment. "To stop underage drinking. You can't trust these kids, and I figure somebody will try to sneak in some liquor."

Maybe, but since there were just as many adults there as children, it wouldn't be easy.

"It's all over town, you know," Davy went on. "Not

just those kissing pictures, but about the cats. Folks know that Lucky and you took 'em."

She grunted again. And considered a pretend gag. If Davy thought she was about to barf, he might move away from her and pester someone else.

"I went to the McCord building," he continued, "to search for those cats."

This time she grunted because her stomach got a sudden knot in it. Certainly Helene or Logan would have called if Davy had found the cats, though.

"Helene wouldn't let me in," Davy added. "Said I had to get a search warrant. I'm working on it, and once I have it, I'll go back and search that place from top to bottom."

She seriously doubted any judge would sign a search warrant for a building that Logan owned, but just in case, Cassie made a mental note to arrange to have the cats moved. Where exactly she didn't know, but she might have to fly them to California with her and kennel them for a while until she could find permanent homes for all of them. But that still wouldn't get her father off her back.

Or off Lucky's.

Heaven knew how long her father would hound Lucky.

And Cassie decided to try to fix that. "The next time you talk to Mason-Dixon," she said to Davy, "tell him I'll offer him fifty grand for the cats."

Davy looked at her as if her functioning brain cells had been killed with the loud music, but he finally nodded. Finally, he moved away from her, taking out his phone as he walked. No doubt to call her father.

With the deputy finally out of her hair, Cassie

turned her attention back to Mackenzie. And she immediately frowned. Yes, the light was dim, but she had no trouble seeing that Brody had taken hold of both of Mackenzie's wrists, and it didn't look like a dance move. He appeared to be "coaxing" her toward the corner, and he didn't look especially happy that she was putting up some resistance.

Cassie made her way to the dance floor, hurrying but trying not to look as if she were. On the outside chance she was misinterpreting Mackenzie's expression, Cassie didn't want to embarrass all of them. But the moment she reached Mackenzie, Brody let go of her as if she were an electric fence gone live, and he marched toward the drinks table.

"Everything okay?" Cassie asked her. Of course, she had to shout it. And of course, that was when there was a dip in the music volume, so Cassie hadn't managed to do this without drawing attention after all.

"Everything's fine," Mackenzie snapped, but then she huffed and led Cassie off the dance floor, toward Brody and the drinks table—though she stopped a good distance away from him.

"He's the only boy who's ever noticed me, all right?" Mackenzie threw out there.

There were as many things wrong with that comment as there had been with Davy's question about Lucky dumping her.

"You're thirteen," Cassie reminded her. "There'll be plenty of years for boys to notice you."

"Mom said she lost her virginity when she was thirteen."

Good grief. "There'll be plenty of time for that, too," Cassie assured her.

Mackenzie made a sound that might or might not have been of agreement. "Brody likes me, okay?"

"Okay. But that doesn't mean you have to give him your virginity. Or anything else for that matter." Cassie paused. "Did Brody force you to kiss him that night in the barn?"

"No. I wanted to kiss him," Mackenzie insisted. "Anyway, it doesn't matter. This is the last night I'll be with Brody like this, and I don't want to spend it standing here, talking to you." Her tone was sharp, but Mackenzie brushed her hand on Cassie's arm before she stepped away and joined Brody.

Even with the music still going, Cassie became aware of the hush that had come over the room. For a moment she thought it was because all eyes had been on Mackenzie and her, but then she noticed Lucky. He came in through the door, looking exactly like the hot cowboy fantasy that he was.

And she'd had sex with him.

Something that made her all tingly. And then it made Cassie frown. Because apparently everyone in town was aware of that and then had made the assumption—based on what, she didn't know—that Lucky had dumped her. Of course, maybe they thought that because Lucky didn't spend too much time with any one woman.

Cassie saw him glance around. Their gazes met, and he started to weave his way through the crowd to get to her. He was a different fantasy tonight. Not chapped and spurred but rather suited. He had on a dark-colored jacket paired with his jeans. Clothes for a "date."

"Everything okay?" he asked the moment he

reached her. But then Lucky glanced around the room. "Hell, what's everybody saying about us now?"

"That you dumped me."

He repeated that "hell," huffed and then kissed her. Not a friendly peck, either. He kissed her so long and with so much body contact that Davy called out for them to break it up. Probably not the best behavior for chaperones at a teenage dance where hormones were zinging, but it did start a new ripple of behind-the-hand whispers.

"Something for me to think about?" she asked.

"Something for them to talk about," he corrected.

Oh. So it hadn't been an invitation to go back to his bed. Cassie really did need to apologize for that stress-reliever comment.

"Is Mackenzie all right?" he asked.

Cassie nearly blurted out her concerns right there, but since everyone had their ears and eyes still turned in their direction, she motioned for Lucky to follow her to the side double doors. They were wide-open, mainly because the AC wasn't cooling off the room nearly enough and also because there was a steady trail of older teens coming and going.

Something Mackenzie definitely wouldn't be doing.

Of course, everyone inside probably thought Cassie was hauling Lucky off to make out with him, but she wasn't. Even if her body thought that might be a fun idea. Nope. She just needed to tell him that she thought Brody was pressuring Mackenzie and then hope Lucky didn't find a stun gun and shovel to use on the boy.

Since Gladys Ellsley, the minister's wife, was in their path, Cassie stopped a moment and asked Gladys to keep an eye on Mackenzie. It really wasn't necessary. If Mackenzie did anything, or even if she did nothing, Cassie figured she'd have a full report from at least a dozen people.

Lucky and Cassie stepped just outside the door and definitely weren't alone. There was a couple kissing, but they either didn't notice or didn't care that they had an audience because they didn't stop. On the other side of the doors were five teenage boys. They were huddled in a circle, their backs to Lucky and her, but a sudden breeze sent a familiar scent right at Cassie.

Booze.

No, Mackenzie definitely wouldn't be coming out here.

Cassie turned to Lucky to start the conversation she didn't want to have, but he was already moving away from her. He broke through the circle of boys like a bowling ball, scattering them and sending a bottle of cheap whiskey splatting to the ground.

"What the hell do you think you're doing?" Lucky shouted at the same moment one of the boys shouted something similar.

The boy was clearly drunk, and he threw a punch at Lucky. Lucky ducked, and in the same motion he put the boy against the wall.

"I said what the hell do you think you're doing?" Lucky's voice was even louder this time.

"Drinking," the kid snapped, sounding pretty cocky for someone who was being restrained.

Cassie hurried to help, not that the other boys were in fight mode. They were all backing away, and they backed away even farther when Deputy Davy came waltzing out. Davy repeated a version of Lucky's original question, and he nearly tripped on his own feet trying to get to Lucky and the boy.

"He was drinking," Cassie volunteered.

Though Davy no doubt saw the bottle on the ground. The other boys took off running, and Davy went in pursuit.

Cassie went to Lucky and, because his grip on the boy seemed a little too tight, she took hold of his hand to get him to let go of the kid. That's when she realized Lucky was shaking.

"Come on," Cassie insisted. "Let go of him, and we'll get out of here."

"No. Mackenzie—"

"Gladys is watching her, and we won't be long. We can go back in as soon as we've talked." And as soon as Lucky had had a chance to settle his nerves.

Lucky finally backed away, and even though the kid took off running as well, Lucky picked up the bottle and threw it against the brick wall. It shattered and sent what was left of the whiskey and the glass scattering around them.

She led him away from the kissing couple, who still hadn't stopped to draw breath despite the disturbance, and took him to a large oak. Not very private, but it was the best she could do. Suddenly, his head and back went against the tree, and his breath started gusting.

"Are you having a panic attack?" she asked.

Lucky shook his head. But didn't say anything else. Cassie decided just to wait him out because whatever was going on had gotten to him.

"I didn't stop him," Lucky finally mumbled.

"But you did. The boy was drinking, and…"

This wasn't about that boy. This wasn't about tonight. This was about his parents.

"The teenager who killed your mom and dad had been drinking," she said.

Well, according to the rumors he had been anyway. Cassie seemed to remember reading in the paper that he had a blood alcohol level that had exceeded the legal limit. Added to that, he hadn't even been old enough to drink.

"Brian Ducal," he said.

Yes, that was the boy's name. He'd been alone in his car and had swerved and hit Lucky's parents' vehicle in a fatal head-on collision. The only survivor had been Claire, who had been riding in the backseat because Lucky's parents had given her a ride home from a ball game. Cassie was away at college at the time, but she'd heard plenty about it from Dixie Mae.

"I saw Brian that night," Lucky continued a moment later. "He was drinking, and I was too busy making out with a girl to take the time to stop him."

Oh, God.

"I didn't stop him," Lucky repeated. He jerked away from the tree. Away from her, too. "I have to go. Please stay here with Mackenzie and make sure she gets home all right."

Lucky didn't give her a chance to say anything. Not that there was anything she could say that would help him right now.

Cassie just stood there and watched as Lucky walked away.

THE BULL RIDE hadn't worked for him. Not that Lucky had expected a good crap-slinging to erase his bad mood, but a ride usually jacked up his adrenaline enough for him to nudge the old memories into the back of his head.

Not tonight, though.

Even the Angus had seemed confused as to why Lucky was leading him into a gate this time of night. Hell, so had the ranch hand. Hank Granger hadn't complained, not out loud anyway, but then the man had worked for the McCords for nearly twenty years. He knew plenty of the things Lucky had done didn't make sense. After all, Lucky hadn't gotten the label of screwup by doing nothing.

Well, except for the nothing he'd done the night of his parents' death.

No nighttime bull ride was going to erase that.

Lucky heard the footsteps and knew it was Cassie before he even looked over his shoulder. He got that funny feeling in his stomach again, the one he always got when he saw her, but tonight neither the funny feeling nor Cassie herself were going to help.

Hank mumbled a good-night and said something else that Lucky didn't catch before he ambled off toward the guest cottage that he'd called home for the past decade.

"Did the ride help?" Cassie asked. She joined him at the fence where he was still watching the bull. The bull was watching him, too, and even though Lucky knew he was projecting, he thought the Angus was calling him an asshole.

Lucky didn't answer her question but instead went with one of his own. "Did Mackenzie have fun?"

"I think so. I think she floated up the stairs to her bedroom."

Yeah, he'd seen the light come on in her room, so he

figured she was back safe and sound. Safe and sound for two more nights anyway. After the wedding the day after tomorrow, the girls would be heading to Phoenix.

"I'm sorry about ditching you at the civic center," he said.

But Cassie waved him off. "Davy arrested a couple of the boys. Personally, I was surprised he was able to catch up with them, but he did."

Good. Maybe that would teach them a lesson about underage drinking. Of course, Lucky had gotten arrested for it once, and it hadn't stopped him, but what he'd never done was drink and drive. Brian Ducal had taught him that lesson quite well.

Cassie's phone buzzed, but she didn't even take it from her pocket to look at the screen. "It'll be from my agent, Andrew or someone else I don't want to talk to."

"Your agent?"

"He'll want to tell me that my career is over."

Hell. This wasn't making things better. "Is it?"

She shrugged. "Probably. At least my old career is finished. I doubt anyone will be calling me for TV appearances, but I guess I'll just do something else. Like you will when you get tired of having your vertebrae snapped and popped by a two-thousand-pound bull." Cassie paused. "Is that bull looking at us?"

"Yep. I think he's mad because I've kept him up past his bedtime."

She smiled. It was short-lived, though, because her phone buzzed again.

"Maybe you should at least see who it is," he suggested.

"Nope. The only person I want to talk to tonight is you."

It was going to be a short conversation, then, because Lucky didn't have a clue what to say. Or do. "I don't know if I'll ever get past this," he admitted.

Cassie made a sound of understanding. "I don't think you do. Sorry. I believe the scab just stays over the wound until something or somebody picks at it. Like tonight. That kid picked at it, and you bled all over again."

"Bled all over *you*," Lucky corrected. "I shouldn't have dumped that on you."

"I dumped my panic attacks on you. I poured my heart out to you about Hannah. Think of this as a tit for tat."

Ever since he'd been a horny teenager, the expression had always made him smile. Lowbrow humor usually did. But even that wasn't working tonight.

"So, how are you getting past Hannah?" he asked. And it wasn't just Dixie Mae's letter that had prompted him to ask. Lucky was hoping Cassie had a magic pill for this, or had at least figured out a way to stop her panic attacks.

"By trying to remember the good parts. Not that there were a lot of good parts with Hannah, but I had them with other clients. I think I helped some people. I just didn't help her. I don't believe I can ever completely forgive myself for what happened, but I'm finding some peace with it. I'm accepting that it wasn't totally my fault."

Peace. That was a good thing to have. Lucky was still searching for it in a couple areas of his life. Especially when it came to his parents. But like Cassie, he was getting there. Some of that soul-crushing guilt was easing up. Finally.

"And the panic attacks?" he asked.

"I haven't had one in weeks. If they return, I'll deal with them. Deal with my father, too. I would like for things to be different between us, but there's no fixing it."

No. Assholes weren't fixable, and Mason-Dixon was the king of assholes.

"So in the grand scheme of things," Cassie continued, "I failed with Hannah. I can never undo it, but I have some little dots of success surrounding it."

"I've failed at a lot more than saving my parents," he confessed.

"You mean your long string of lovers? Or maybe trying to push Logan out of your life?" she asked, causing him to frown.

He'd at least expected her to sugarcoat some bullshit. Apparently not. He was just going to get the shit tonight. And he deserved it.

Cassie patted his arm. "Lucky, you're not a screwup. You helped Dixie Mae build a successful business. You've won more rodeo buckles than you can wear in a lifetime."

Lucky dismissed both of those. "I didn't stay around here after my folks were killed. I left and allowed Logan to put everything on his shoulders."

"Logan wanted it on his shoulders. And besides, you're entitled to the life you want to lead. You didn't call Riley a screwup when he left to go into the Air Force. You don't call your sister a screwup, and she's off in Florida going to law school."

"They don't get drunk and sleep around," he pointed out.

Another sound of agreement from her. "It's because you're hotter than they are. Though Riley is pretty hot. I'd probably think Anna was hot, too, if I were a guy."

That got him to smile. A little. "Logan and I are identical twins," he pointed out.

"Yes, he's hot, too," she admitted. "It's just a burden you McCord brothers have to bear. But you got the looks *and* the charisma. It makes it easier to sleep around when women are throwing themselves at you."

Lucky wished he could be flattered by her description of him. "I could have dodged them. I didn't." Not many of them anyway. He looked at her. "You dodged me, though."

Cassie nodded. "Because I thought you'd break my heart."

She leaned in, kissed him. Not the hungry "I want you now" kind of kiss that led to sex. This was, well, sweet. And it sent up red flares in his head. Because it was exactly the kind of kiss that Lucky had spent his adult years avoiding.

The kind of kiss that meant something.

Lucky didn't move into the kiss. Definitely didn't deepen it because it already felt way too deep as it was.

"And now?" he asked when she pulled back and met his gaze. "Do you still think I'll break your heart?"

"No." Cassie smiled. The deep kind of smile that meant something, too. "I *know* you will. And I'm going to let you do it."

CHAPTER TWENTY

THERE WAS EXCITED chatter downstairs. People were working hard to pull everything together for Riley and Claire's wedding, which would happen in less than twenty-four hours. Everyone was thrilled.

Including Cassie.

Thrilled for Claire and Riley anyway, but that's where her joy ended.

The heart-to-heart she'd had with Lucky the night before had left her raw—and wanting more. She'd nearly stayed there by the corral. A few more kisses and it would have led them straight to bed.

Or rather to the hayloft since it was closer.

But Cassie hadn't stayed. She'd shielded her heart for one more night. It wouldn't help, of course, because the broken heart was inevitable. Even if she stayed in Spring Hill and ditched her entire life in LA, that didn't mean she would get Lucky. He wasn't exactly the type of man to settle down with one woman. And she wasn't exactly the marrying sort, either. Not after living through the disastrous relationship that her parents had called a marriage. And not after seeing the failed marriages of 90 percent of her clients. No, marriage was messy and painful and not for her.

She'd just have to deal with a broken heart, that's all.

Of course, the broken heart wouldn't just be because of Lucky. Losing Mia and Mackenzie would add to it. Thankfully, the girls hadn't seemed that sad about leaving. Of course, with the excitement of the wedding, maybe they hadn't had time to consider it. And wouldn't for a while. When Cassie had seen them last, they'd been in the sunroom with Livvy, helping her decorate.

There was a knock at her bedroom door, and like all the phone calls she'd been getting, Cassie nearly didn't answer it. Not until she realized it could be one of the girls. But it wasn't. It was Claire. Or least she thought it was. It was a woman holding a plastic garment bag.

"Can I put my wedding dress in your room?" she asked. Definitely Claire.

"Of course." Cassie stepped back so that Claire could squeeze the dress inside.

"Thanks. Livvy's taken over Anna's room with the rest of the decorations, and I don't have anyplace else to stash this dress where Riley won't see it. He'll peek if he gets the chance."

"Can I peek?" Lucky asked.

Cassie hadn't even seen him behind Claire, but then it was hard to see much of anything because of the dress.

"No peeking for you, either," Claire insisted, and she dropped a kiss on Lucky's cheek. Dropped one on Cassie's, too, surprising her. "Livvy got carried away with the whole idea of a fairy-tale wedding."

Yes, but Cassie was pretty sure Claire was loving every second of it. Claire draped the dress over a reading chair in the corner of the room and turned back around to face them. Cassie wasn't sure exactly what Claire saw in their expressions, but it had her frowning.

"Is, uh, everything okay between you two?" she asked.

Cassie glanced at Lucky to see how he was going to answer that. He didn't.

"I mean, what with the girls leaving soon," Claire added.

Cassie thought the quick breath that Lucky took was one of relief. "It's tough," Cassie settled for saying.

"Yeah." And that's all Lucky said for several moments. "I hadn't expected to feel this ache in my heart."

Claire nodded, took a quick breath of her own. "It'll be a bittersweet day. Hopefully more sweet than bitter, but I think we'll all be remembering the people who aren't here. My grandmother, for instance."

Cassie knew that it'd been less than a year since Claire had lost the grandmother who'd raised her, and from all accounts they'd been very close. Bittersweet indeed.

"I was hoping you'd give me away," Claire said, and when she looked at Lucky, there were tears watering her eyes. "I know I'm late asking. And that the wedding's so informal what with there not even being an aisle—"

"Of course I'll do it."

Claire's eyes watered more, and heck, now Cassie was feeling all teary and sentimental.

"I figured you'd want Logan," Lucky added.

Claire managed a smile. "I've always been a lot closer to you than Logan. And when you look at me, I've never seen any blame in your eyes. Not ever."

Lucky shook his head. Cassie also didn't understand.

"Because of your parents," Claire said.

Lucky just gave her a blank look.

"See?" Claire said as if that proved her point. "You didn't even think to be mad. But sometimes when Logan looks at me, I believe he blames me for what happened."

"What?" Cassie blurted out, though this was too personal a conversation for her to be a part of. She should just step out of the room and let them finish. But she didn't. Her feet seemed glued in place.

"Claire." Lucky put his arm around her, pulled her to him and kissed the top of her head. "That wasn't your fault."

She shook her head. "Your folks offered me the ride home from the game because it was raining, but I forgot my clarinet in the band hall and had to go back for it. If I'd left with them right away, or if they'd never waited to give me a ride, then they wouldn't have been on that part of the road at the exact second of the crash."

Lucky kissed her hair again. "That wasn't your fault," he repeated.

Claire nodded, pulled back and wiped the tears from her eyes. "See? You never blamed me. Riley, neither. But he blamed himself. He thinks if he hadn't been making out with Misty—" she paused, rolled her eyes at the mention of Riley's old flame "—then he might have stopped it somehow."

Cassie hoped all of this was sinking in. In a town the size of Spring Hill, every single person had probably thought they could have done something to stop them from dying in the accident. Not just his parents but the other driver, too.

"Sorry about that." Claire wiped away more tears.

"Talk about bringing up the worst subject possible. Anyway, thanks for agreeing to give me away." She brushed another kiss on his cheek and walked out.

Lucky didn't say anything, and Cassie wanted to give him some time to absorb all that. And hopefully connect the dots. But her darn phone buzzed again, and when she saw her father's name on the screen, she figured she should take it.

"I'll take this in the hall," she said, moving to do just that. Not that she wanted to talk to him, but it would give Lucky some privacy to think about what Claire had said.

"What do you want?" Cassie greeted when she answered.

"Well, good morning to you, daughter of mine." Mason-Dixon's tone was just as "friendly" as hers. "I thought you'd like to know that I accepted the offer you made to Davy. I'll take fifty grand for the cats. Transfer the money to me today, and Bernie will give you the ownership papers. They've already been drawn up."

Fifty grand probably seemed like a lot to most people for three cats, but at least this would put an end to something that had been very important to Dixie Mae. "You'll have your money as soon as I can arrange it. I'll have the funds sent to Bernie's office."

She hung up so she could call her investment manager and have him do a wire transfer ASAP.

"I can pay for the cats," Lucky offered when she finished the call.

He'd obviously heard her conversation, which meant he hadn't been using the time to think. Or maybe he had. He looked a lot more relaxed than he had in days.

Lucky reached for her, easing her to him, and Cassie

readied herself for a kiss. One of those scalding-hot ones that he was so good at giving. But the raised voices downstairs stopped him.

"Alice?" Lucky questioned.

Cassie turned her ear toward the voices and realized it was indeed Alice. And that the woman's voice was indeed raised.

"Cassie! Lucky!" Alice shouted. "I need to talk to both of you right now."

Even without that demand tacked on, Cassie knew something was terribly wrong. They hurried down the stairs and found the woman in the foyer. Della was there, too, along with the florist and two other people who were moving furniture out of the living room.

"What happened?" Lucky asked the woman.

"I just saw this." Alice lifted the newspaper for them to see. The two kissing photos on the front page.

Cassie hadn't thought the pictures could look any more tawdry than when Andrew had brought them over, but she'd been wrong. Whoever had arranged them in the paper had adjusted the lighting so that it appeared Cassie's breasts were actually heaving. And the adjustment made Lucky appear to be past the well-endowed stage when it came to male genitalia.

Mackenzie and Brody hadn't fared much better in the other picture. Their kiss looked more like a zombie attack with Mackenzie playing the role of the zombie.

"Are these pictures real?" Alice demanded. She wasn't the cool, composed woman that'd visited the day before. In fact, she hadn't brushed her hair and had clearly thrown on her clothes in a hurry. Her breasts were heaving, too, but Cassie was betting it wasn't from lust. It was because she was breathing so hard she might hyperventilate.

"They're real-ish," Cassie admitted. "Obviously the reporter took a few liberties with the shots."

But that *obviously* wasn't obvious to Alice at all. Her mouth dropped open and she grabbed the entry table so she wouldn't pitch right over.

"My niece is thirteen," Alice said, stating the obvious. "And I'm assuming this is the same boy you let her take to the dance last night. Since the newspaper came out yesterday that means you knew about the photo before you let her go."

There was no way around that; both Cassie and Lucky nodded. "But Cassie chaperoned the dance," Lucky added.

"She shouldn't have been allowed to go at all!" Alice was shouting again now. Well, as much as she could shout considering her breath was vanishing fast. "And I won't even address the other picture." But she did address it. "You're both adults. What kind of an example does this set for impressionable young girls? Girls who have had their lives turned upside down?"

Cassie wanted to give Alice a really good explanation for all of this, but she didn't have one. Lucky and she hadn't made out in front of the girls, but it didn't matter. They could see the photograph. Heck, anyone could.

And that wasn't even the worst of it.

Lucky and she had done all of that when they should have had their focus on Mia and Mackenzie.

Alice shook her head. "I can't believe neither of you told me about this before now."

Neither could Cassie. "I'm sorry. I meant to tell you,

but it slipped my mind." It shouldn't have, and Cassie wanted to kick herself. "There are a lot of gossips in this town, and I figured even if you didn't actually see the newspaper, then someone would let you know."

"The maid at the inn did. She gave me a copy and said the photographer, Theo Kervin, even sold the pictures of Lucky and you to one of the big LA tabloids."

Great. Cassie groaned. Now all of her friends, business associates and clients had seen it, as well.

"The maid told me about you, too," Alice went on, her attention on Lucky now. "Apparently, you do this sort of thing all the time." She stabbed her finger at the picture but probably wasn't aware it was on Lucky's photographed crotch. "You are not the kind of man who should be around my nieces."

Since Lucky wasn't defending himself, Cassie decided to step up. "Lucky's a business owner. And a McCord. They're a prominent family around here."

"He's also been arrested several times. And he went on a date last night with two women. One of them was a stripper. Did you know about that?" Alice didn't give Cassie a chance to answer. "Of course you did, because the stripper works for your father."

Obviously, the gossip had made its way to the garden room of the Bluebonnet Inn.

Cassie wanted to tell Alice that she had no connection to her father and the Slippery Pole, but that wasn't exactly true. She had been there to steal the cats, and she'd just had a phone conversation with him that some could have construed as bribery. Hardly good bargaining examples to use to profess her innocence.

"And then there's your job," Alice went on. "I thought you were a real therapist. But you just appear on those terrible TV shows where people air their dirty laundry. How can that be good for the girls?"

"Cassie's an excellent therapist," Lucky spoke up.

Cassie appreciated him coming to her defense, but she doubted anything could change Alice's opinion of either of them.

"I want you to get the girls ready," Alice insisted. "Because I'm taking them away from this house—and away from the two of you—*right now.*"

LUCKY OPENED HIS mouth to say whatever it would take to keep Alice from taking the girls. But then he realized he was on the losing side of this. Everything Alice had said was true. Except for the part about Cassie. Though if he was being honest, even that had some truth to it.

Cassie must have come to the same realization because he heard the sigh leave her mouth. It was the sound of surrender.

"Now!" Alice repeated. "I don't want them here a minute longer."

Cassie nodded, and Lucky and she started toward the sunroom. Of course, Mackenzie and Mia were going to be upset about missing the wedding. Ditto for Mackenzie not being able to see Brody, but Lucky had known right from the start that this was temporary.

Well, temporary had come to an end.

Alice didn't follow them to the sunroom. Maybe because she didn't want to step another inch inside the house, but Lucky was glad for the small reprieve. This way, they would get a chance to break the news and have time for a short goodbye.

Or not.

When they got to the sunroom, they found Mia wearing a tiara and dancing around like a fairy princess while Livvy strung twinkling lights around the windows.

"Here to help?" Livvy asked. She was grinning, but the grinning came to a quick end when she saw their expressions.

"Their aunt is here to pick up the girls now," Cassie told her.

Mia stopped in mid–dance step. "We gotta go?"

Lucky nodded, not trusting his voice.

Livvy nodded, too, and she hiked her thumb to the door. "Mackenzie went out to see the bulls."

"I'll find her," Lucky volunteered, and he turned to Cassie. "You can help Mia start packing."

"We gotta go?" Mia repeated, and Lucky nearly lost it when he saw her big eyes get all shiny with tears. Her bottom lip started to tremble.

He went to her, going down on his knees so he could pull her into his arms. Lucky wanted to assure Mia that this wasn't a real goodbye, that he'd see her again, but after the way Alice had just reacted, he'd be surprised if the woman didn't try to file restraining orders against Cassie and him. Not that she had actual cause to do that, but their behavior might not sit well with a custody lawyer.

"Everything will be okay," Lucky told her, and he prayed that wasn't a lie. Mia deserved the best. Mackenzie, too.

Lucky stood, meeting Cassie's gaze. The sadness he saw in her eyes matched his own. He brushed a kiss on her cheek and headed out to find Mackenzie for what would no doubt be an even more emotional encounter than the one he'd just had with Mia.

Mackenzie wasn't by the corral, and he didn't see her in the pastures. However, Lucky did hear something in the barn. It sounded as if some kind of struggle was going on. Lucky ran toward the noise and rage filled him the moment he reached the barn.

Brody had Mackenzie pinned to the wall. From what Lucky could see, Brody was trying to kiss her. And Mackenzie was resisting. She had her hands on his chest and was trying to push him away, but Brody was shoving right back.

After that, all Lucky saw was red.

He charged toward them and caught onto the back of Brody's shirt, and Lucky slammed him against the barn door so hard that it rattled. Lucky figured Mackenzie would jump to defend this dickhead.

She didn't.

Mackenzie stood there, shaking, with tears in her eyes. The red that Lucky had seen before was a drop in the bucket compared to what went through him now. It didn't get better.

"She wanted me to kiss her," Brody snarled. "She wanted a lot more than that."

Obviously not. Lucky gave Brody another slam and had to rein in his rage to keep himself from ripping off the guy's arm and beating him to death with it.

Lucky's teeth were clenched so tight his jaw was throbbing. His fist, too, but that was just because he'd never wanted to punch someone as much as he wanted to punch this kid. And he forced himself to remember that Brody was indeed a kid.

"You have two options," Lucky managed to say.

"You can go to the police, turn yourself in and admit to attempted assault, or I beat the shit out of you. Your choice."

Lucky was really hoping Brody picked option two.

"Assault?" Brody howled. "I barely touched her."

"Barely is enough, asshole. When a girl says no, she means no. Even if she doesn't say it, if she's trying to get away from you, the answer's still no." Lucky hadn't even realized he was yelling until Hank came running into the barn.

"You need some help, Lucky?" Hank asked.

"I think I might. Brody's either going to need to go to the hospital or the cops. And I'll need someone to escort him."

Brody's glare turned to a stare. Then he looked away from Lucky. "The cops."

Lucky forced himself to back away, and Hank took over from there. He waited until Hank had Brody out of earshot before Lucky looked at Mackenzie.

"Are you going to tell me that I overstepped my boundaries—" he started. But he didn't get to finish.

Mackenzie hurried right into his arms. "I was so scared," she whispered through the broken sobs.

That did two things to Lucky. It made him want to give Brody that shit-kicking he deserved, but it also crushed him to think of Mackenzie afraid while a bully groped her. Part of him knew he should lecture her about never risking anything like that again, but Lucky could tell from her tears that it was a lesson she'd already learned.

"I wish I could promise you that you'll never run into another guy like Brody," he said, brushing a kiss against her temple. "I can't. But if it ever happens again, just call me. Or better yet, just knee the idiot in the balls."

She nodded and kept crying. So Lucky just stood there, feeling like shit because he hadn't been able to protect her from this. However, he also felt something else. He felt what it was like to be a father.

Hell.

This wasn't any fun at all, but the fact that Mackenzie was here, crying on his shoulder—literally—also made him feel, well, loved. Too bad the feeling wasn't going to last. Also too bad he still had to tell Mackenzie about what else had gone on.

"Your aunt saw the pictures in the paper," he explained. "She's upset about the one with Cassie and me. And she should be. We didn't set a very good example for Mia and you."

Mackenzie pulled back and looked at him. "You're wrong. You and Cassie did okay."

Coming from her that was high praise, and Lucky felt that L-word again along with another round of getting his heart crushed.

"Your aunt's insisting you and Mia leave with her right away," Lucky added.

The tears hadn't stopped yet, but that put a fresh batch of them in her eyes, and Mackenzie took off running toward the house. Lucky wasn't sure if that meant she was ready to get out of there—a strong possibility after what'd just happened to her—or if she was upset about having to leave so soon.

He hurried after her, but she didn't go through the sunroom. She went in the back door and headed straight for the foyer. Cassie and Mia were there, and Mia's suitcase was beside her. She had her little hand outstretched, and Lucky could see the gold star that she was offering to her aunt.

"You let her believe it was magic," Alice said, shaking her head. Clearly, the woman had something else to be pissed about now. "Put that away, Mia. And Mackenzie, get your things. We're leaving now."

"Please, no," Mackenzie begged. "Just let us stay for the wedding. Please."

Alice huffed. "This is about that boy, isn't it? The one in the picture—"

"No, that's over," Mackenzie assured her. She exchanged a glance with Lucky. A glance that Cassie noticed. He'd tell her all about Brody soon, but he had no intention of mentioning what had just happened in front of Alice. If the woman heard anything about it, it would come from Mackenzie.

"Well, good," Alice answered. "But there's no reason for you to stay here. Not with these people."

"But I gonna be a star girl," Mia said. "I'm gonna throw gold stars and wear a princess crown."

"And Claire wanted me to be an usher," Mackenzie added. "Please. The McCords have treated us good. Like family. We want to stay for the wedding. After that, we'll leave with you." She added another please. Mia chipped in a couple, as well.

Lucky could see the debate going on in Alice's head. Could also see her displeasure anytime her attention landed on Cassie and him. Thankfully that displeasure wasn't for the kids, though.

"All right," Alice finally said. "We can stay one more day for the wedding. But not here. Get your things and you can stay at the Bluebonnet Inn tonight.

I'll bring you back for the wedding, and we'll leave right afterward."

All four of them mumbled a version of "thank you." Mia even hugged Alice. Then Lucky and Cassie. It wasn't goodbye, yet, but Lucky knew he had less than twenty-four hours before he'd have to say a real one.

Mackenzie and Cassie went upstairs to get her suitcase, and Lucky was about to assure Mia that everything was going to be okay, but his phone buzzed and he saw Bernie's name on the screen. It was instant hope.

Stupid hope, too.

Because for just a couple of seconds, Lucky thought the lawyer might be calling with some kind of info that would stall Alice from taking the girls.

"I know you're probably in the middle of wedding stuff, but I need Cassie, you, Mia and Mackenzie to come to my office first thing tomorrow morning," Bernie said the moment Lucky answered. "I don't normally go into the office on Sundays, but it's important." That sure didn't sound like the kind of news that would give Cassie and him some extra time with the girls.

"What's this about?" Lucky asked.

Bernie cleared his throat. "Dixie Mae's will. Per her specific instructions, it's to be read at eight in the morning. Brace yourself, Lucky. There are some surprises."

CHAPTER TWENTY-ONE

CASSIE WAS SO not in the mood for a girls' night, but this was for Claire. A last-minute bachelorette party. Claire more than deserved something like this the night before her big day, but Cassie just wasn't up to a celebration.

The only redeeming thing about it was that it was small—just Claire, Livvy, Helene and her—and it was in the sunroom at the ranch. It meant Cassie could put in an appearance and then excuse herself.

So she could go to her room and cry.

And pack.

Which would only result in more tears. But by tomorrow, she'd be ready to cry again. She always cried at weddings, and this one would be a tearjerker because shortly afterward Lucky and she would have to say goodbye to the girls.

The house already seemed way too quiet without them. And that was saying something since Livvy was doing the "Boot Scootin' Boogie" to the popular Brooks & Dunn song.

"This would have been so much better with strippers," Livvy insisted, tossing back another glass of wine.

"No, it wouldn't have," Claire replied. Both Helene and Cassie agreed. Helene probably for a totally different reason than Cassie, though. Helene didn't appear to be the stripper-watching type.

Claire had apparently had very specific instructions. No male strippers or anyone else that Livvy might try to sneak in to liven things up. Claire had instead wanted wine, cheese and girl talk. Other than the dancing and the Brooks & Dunn, Livvy had abided by that.

"I understand you're the owner of three more cats," Claire said to Cassie.

She nodded. "I bought them from my father. Had Bernie draw up ownership papers that I signed this afternoon. It's all official now—I'm the owner of six cats." Of course, on the way to the lawyer's office, Cassie had parked in front of the Bluebonnet Inn hoping to get a glimpse of the girls. She hadn't, though.

"And I'm happy to say that after the wedding, the cats will be brought here," Helene explained. "Not that we weren't happy to have them at the office, but some of the clients are allergic."

Cassie thanked Helene again for taking care of them and assured her she was already working out something more permanent. With a single phone call, she'd put her LA condo up for sale and had asked her Realtor to look for a place that allowed more than two pets. However, the idea of taking six cats still seemed a little daunting.

"Cats?" Livvy huffed. "That's what we're going to talk about tonight?"

"No subject is off-limits," Helene said.

"Except for the kids. Sorry," Livvy immediately added.

"That's okay," Cassie assured her. "They're on my mind whether we talk about them or not."

Which was a serious mood killer.

This time Livvy groaned. "Can we at least talk about sex, then?" Livvy asked. "Dirty sex," she qualified. "The nastiest sex you can think of. How about I start? Blow jobs—yea or nay?"

Cassie laughed, causing the other three to look at her.

"Something you want to tell us about Lucky?" Claire said.

That stopped her laughing. "No."

Clearly they wanted more, but Cassie didn't have more to give them. Lucky and she had had sex, but it hadn't involved a blow job.

"Then Helene can tell us," Livvy insisted. "Since Lucky and Logan are identical twins, it'd be pretty much the same account anyway."

Helene smiled and sipped her wine. "A lady doesn't talk about such things."

Too bad because Cassie wanted to hear. It was silly to want details, but it felt deliciously naughty doing this. And it got her mind off the girls for a few seconds. Too bad her mind kept going back to them, though.

"I've got a sort-of BJ sex story," Claire volunteered. "Not about Riley, though. About Logan and Lucky."

That got their attention, and even Livvy stopped dancing so she could rejoin them on the sofa.

"Logan might have told Helene about this and, Cassie, you might remember," Claire went on, "but when Lucky and Logan were seniors in high school, Lucky was seeing Darla Jean Nederland. *Briefly* seeing her."

Cassie had to shake her head. Helene shook her head, too. By her senior year, the only thing on Cassie's mind had been getting a high score on the SATs, and she had especially shut her ears whenever there was talk about Lucky.

"Well, anyway, Lucky wanted to break up with Darla Jean, but every time he'd try, she'd cry and carry on," Claire continued. "So Logan lost some bet to Lucky, can't remember what about, and the payoff was that Logan would pretend to be Lucky and do the breakup. Logan was a lot better at that sort of thing anyway."

All of them made a sound of agreement about that. Logan wouldn't have had any trouble ending a relationship, even with a Nederland.

"So Logan dressed up like Lucky and went to Darla Jean's house to tell her it was over. But when he opened the door, she was standing there stark naked, and she tackled him. Even after she kissed him, she still didn't know it wasn't Lucky and tried to give him a BJ." Claire patted Helene's hand. "Don't worry, Helene. It didn't work."

Helene dismissed that, too. Clearly she wasn't worried about her man. And shouldn't be. Logan and she had been together a long time and seemed perfect for each other.

"Then what happened?" Livvy pressed.

"Darla Jean was, is, quite aggressive. And strong. She managed to get Logan unzipped, but Logan was finally able to get away from her. The next day at school, Darla Jean told everyone that Lucky was impotent."

Livvy laughed like a loon. "As if." But then she blushed. "Sorry, Cassie."

Cassie waved her off. "I know Lucky's had a lot of

lovers. And besides, it's not serious or anything be-tween us."

There was no mistaking the look all three of them gave her. Skepticism. A big dose of it, too.

"Uh, Cassie," Claire said. "I'm pretty sure Lucky's in love with you."

Cassie choked, not on the wine but the huge gulp of air she sucked in. She wasn't sure what surprised her more—that Claire had said that or that Livvy and Helene made sounds of agreement.

Good grief. They had all lost their minds. Lucky wasn't in love with her. And vice versa. And this wasn't a conversation she wanted to have. Nope. She was already on the path to a good heart-stomping, and if she added even a smidge of the notion that the no-rings-attached Lucky had real feelings for her, then she might give him too much of herself.

Her heart might never recover.

It was time for a subject change. "I can't believe Darla Jean couldn't tell the difference between Lucky and Logan," Cassie said.

"I know," Helene agreed. "They're nothing alike. She should have been able to tell the second she opened the door."

Definitely, and that gave Cassie something to think about. For a second or two. But her stupid brain kept going back to Claire's L-word remark. And to the skep-tical look the others had given Cassie.

"You know, Lucky's in his room," Livvy whispered to her.

Mercy, was she that obvious? Apparently so. Be-cause Claire and Helene nodded. "We won't talk about you behind your back if you want to sneak out and see him," Claire offered.

"Oh, yes we will." Livvy laughed again. "But your choices are us, sex talk, wine and cheese—or Lucky. I'm thinking that's not really a choice."

Livvy was right. It was sort of embarrassing to duck out when the women obviously knew the reason for the ducking. And when one of those women had been Lucky's previous lover. Still, that didn't stop her.

Cassie finished off her wine, gave her best wishes to Claire and walked to the other side of the house to Lucky's room. She knocked once, then opened the door before she could change her mind. Not that she had time to change it anyway because Lucky was right there.

"What the heck took you so long?" he asked and pulled her to him and kissed her.

She'd intended to bring up Claire's comment in a roundabout way, but that kiss stopped Cassie from saying anything, and after a few seconds of being in Lucky's arms, she wasn't sure she could think, much less speak. In fact, she didn't want to speak. Cassie wanted to be swept away, and sweeping away was Lucky's specialty.

However, the sweeping stopped almost as fast as it had started.

"Are you okay?" Lucky asked her.

Cassie knew he wasn't talking about that kiss. This was about the girls. "I miss them already," she admitted.

"Yeah." That's all he said for several long moments, though he did push her hair from her face and kiss her again. Not like the knee-weakening kiss from before, but it was still a kiss.

"Stay with me tonight?" he asked.

"What the heck took you so long to ask?" she countered.

He smiled. It was that "I'll make you melt" smile. Of course, he'd already seduced her so it wasn't necessary to bring out the big guns, but a dimple flashed in his cheek.

Despite the smile, there was a sadness around them. One that Cassie felt bone deep. So maybe their being together right now didn't have as much to do with the scalding attraction as it did with needing to be with someone who understood.

Of course, the attraction was a big part of it.

No use trying to fool herself about that.

Cassie stepped back into his arms and right into another kiss, and she tried to prepare herself for the onslaught. For the fierce intensity that'd happened the other time she had been with him.

But no fierceness.

Lucky kissed her as if he had all the time in the world. Slow. And easy. He didn't even press her to him. He kept an inch or so of space between their bodies, just enough room for her breasts to occasionally brush against his chest. Cassie hadn't expected this from Lucky. Wasn't even sure she wanted it. Fast and frantic didn't give her time to think. It only gave her time to feel, and that kind of swept-away feeling was exactly what she needed now.

Or maybe not.

The long, dreamy kiss continued. No pressure. He definitely didn't take it up to the French stage. And then something happened to her. Cassie started to relax. She started to move into the kiss without actually moving into him. It reminded her of those long-lost innocent days when she'd first been kissed. A time when there were no other expectations but to feel, to be in the moment.

So that's what she did.

She took a mental trip back to high school, and even though she'd never kissed Lucky then, she knew this was how it would have been. Cassie wasn't sure how long it went on. The time just slipped away. But not the need. Lucky was building the fire slowly inside her, making her want him even more.

"Where next?" he asked her. He must have doused himself with pheromones or something because that two-word question sounded sexy as hell.

She glanced at the saddle. Lifted her eyebrow.

"Well, I've never used it as a sex toy," he said, "but if it's what you want…"

Cassie considered it. Dismissed it. For now. "My neck," she settled for saying.

Of course, it wasn't really where she wanted him to kiss her. She wouldn't have minded him getting on his knees again and giving her another of those special kisses, but Lucky was creating a mood here. Best not to spoil it with a blatant request for oral sex.

He didn't kiss her neck, though. He stared at her, his right eyebrow lifted. "You can do better than that," he challenged.

So maybe blatant was okay here after all. And maybe she could create her own mood. Cassie pinned him against the door, unzipped him and went to her

knees. Lucky managed a hoarse sound of surprise before she took him in her mouth.

There.

Challenge accepted.

Cassie was pretty sure he had not expected this, but
since the next sound he made was one of pleasure, she
thought maybe she'd hit the right chord. She took and
tasted until the pleasure was hers, too.

She never would have done this in high school.

Cassie continued for several more seconds before
Lucky gutted out some profanity, caught onto her
shoulders and hauled her back up to him.

"I'm not getting off with my clothes on this time,"
he insisted. "And you're not getting off unless you're
bare-assed naked."

Cassie wanted to tell him not to expect too much,
that her body in no way qualified as hot. Especially
compared to the kinds of bodies Lucky was no doubt
used to seeing. But then he pulled off her top and her
bra and went after her breasts with his tongue, and she
no longer cared if she looked hot. Because she was hot.
Her body was burning.

Mercy, the man was good.

For once, she was seriously glad he'd had all that
experience because Cassie wanted to benefit from it.

Since he was kissing her and ridding her of her
jeans, Cassie got to work on making him naked. That
gave her a moment's pause, though, and she suddenly
wanted to slow things down again. She'd fantasized
about seeing Lucky naked for a long time, and she
wanted to appreciate every moment of this, every inch
of him.

Even though she was standing there, topless and

with her jeans and panties pooled around her knees, Cassie stopped him, then had to stop him again when he tried to kiss her. The kiss would be amazing. But it would nix the peep show she had planned.

Cassie started with his shirt, opening it button by button and slipping it off his shoulders. Of course, he had a six-pack. Of course, he was perfect.

"You're amazing," he said, his gaze shifting over her body.

She thought maybe she said, *Thank you but that's BS.* Or maybe she just said it in her head. That's because her mouth was occupied with kissing his chest. He tasted as good as he looked, and she would have made her way back to his erection if Lucky hadn't stopped her.

All this stopping and starting made her want to scream. Or just screw him. Cassie was leaning heavily toward the latter option.

But Lucky was no longer in fast-screw mode. He went gentle on her again, sliding her jeans and panties the rest of the way off. She did the same to his pants and underwear and got that peep show.

It was really easy to have an orgasm with a man who looked like that. Of course, he didn't have to rely on his looks for it. For a mouthwatering man, he had certainly taken the time to learn the ins and outs of a woman's body.

He kissed her again. Used his tongue. And then nipped her lip with his teeth. Cassie thought she was floating, but Lucky was actually moving her. Slowly again, but not wasting a second for a chance to kiss her.

Lucky wasn't just a pretty face—he was limber, too, and could kiss her breasts and back her up to the bed at the same time. They landed on the mattress, him on top of her. Between her legs. They nearly had acciden- tal sex, but he moved out of the way, fished through his nightstand drawer for a condom and put it on.

The seconds it took him to do that felt like an eter- nity.

Followed by the pleasure of Lucky pushing into her. He wasn't gentle. Which she didn't want anyway. Cassie wanted a full dose of Lucky McCord. And that's exactly what she got.

Every inch of him.

Inside her.

Oh, mercy. For a woman who had a hard time achieving an orgasm, the one Lucky gave her hap- pened way too fast. Just a few strokes. And while the pleasure racked through her, wave after wave, Cassie couldn't help but want him all over again.

Immediately.

How could that be? How could she want him this much? How could she feel this much?

How could she have been so stupid as to play with such fire?

She gathered him close, lifted her hips and helped him reach his own release. She felt the climax rack through him, too. Felt his body relax, then tense.

"What the fuck did you just do to me?" Lucky asked.

Cassie had no idea because minus the F-word, it was exactly what she'd wanted to ask him.

LUCKY WAS CERTAIN he could have handled their latest round of mind-blowing sex better. Clearly, he hadn't made it end on a romantic note.

What the fuck did you just do to me?

She didn't answer, but with the way he'd growled that out, he was surprised she didn't state the obvious.

That she'd F-worded him.

And that he'd F-worded her right back.

Instead, Cassie got all quiet, maybe regretting the amazing thing that'd happened.

The shitty thing that'd happened, too.

He wasn't supposed to feel this way. A good fuck was supposed to make him relax, make him quit thinking. Sex was his drug of choice. But it hadn't worked this time. Instead of numbing his mind and body, it was as if Cassie had flipped a switch in his head, and everything had come flooding into him.

Losing his parents. Losing Dixie Mae. Losing the girls. Now losing his mind.

It wasn't as if he was opposed to having feelings like this. Especially feelings for Cassie, but the problem was, Lucky didn't know exactly what he was feeling. And even if it was the thing that normal, unbroken men felt, what the hell was he supposed to do about it? He sucked at commitments, sucked at staying in place.

Sucked, period.

Still naked, still rosy and glowing from the orgasm, Cassie leaned over and kissed him. Then she got up, and while he watched her, she dressed. Slowly, like those kisses he'd given her earlier. It was like a strip-tease in reverse.

If he'd been a teenager, watching her would have given him an instant hard-on, but he needed at least ten minutes to recover.

Five, Lucky silently amended when she bent down to pick up her panties.

Two, he amended again when she shimmied into those panties.

But Cassie probably wasn't ready for another round so soon. He figured this was the part where they were going to have the talk. *Where is this going? How do you feel about me?*

But Cassie didn't say anything close to either of those things. When she'd finished dressing, she came back to the bed, kissed him.

"I love you," she said.

And then she walked out, closing the door quietly behind her.

CHAPTER TWENTY-TWO

LUCKY WASN'T SURE what he was supposed to say. Or how to act. So he decided to stay quiet and let Cassie take the lead. The problem with that?

No lead.

She didn't mention a word about her bombshell as they drove to Bernie's for the reading of Dixie Mae's will the next morning. And Lucky wasn't sure he should even push it. Not with Bernie's warning flashing in his head.

Brace yourself, Lucky. There are some surprises.

As if he hadn't had enough surprises already. There were a few good ones, though. The hug from Mackenzie in the barn. Sex with Cassie. But Lucky was afraid any surprises Dixie Mae had in store for them now would not be of the good variety.

Nor was Cassie's *I love you*.

Hell, he hadn't meant for that to happen. He sucked at relationships, and the last thing he'd wanted was for her to fall in love with him. Or for him to feel this way about her.

Which he still wasn't exactly sure about.

This was new territory for him, and Lucky thought if his life would just settle down for a couple of minutes, he'd be able to figure it out. Unfortunately, a settled life wasn't going to happen until at least after the will reading and the wedding. Then he'd have to say goodbye to the girls—he didn't want to know how long it would take him to get past that.

Maybe never.

Lucky parked in front of Bernie's office, a reminder of the last time he was there. No doubt a reminder for Cassie, too, judging from the heavy sigh that left her mouth.

"I don't want to cry in front of the girls," she insisted, as if saying it would prevent it from happening. Heck, maybe it would, but Lucky knew Cassie was hurting just as much as he was.

Cassie reached for the door but didn't open it. "Della said Brody confessed to assault and that he's going to have to do community service. Anything you want to tell me about that?"

Lucky hadn't intentionally withheld the incident from her. They just hadn't had a chance to talk, with the exception of the conversation they'd had pre- and postsex.

I love you.

Yeah, that and Cassie's quick departure from his room had pretty much put an end to open communication.

"Brody was trying to kiss Mackenzie in the barn." Maybe trying to do more, but since it made his blood boil to think of that, Lucky went with the sanitized version. "Mackenzie resisted, I stopped Brody, and I told him to turn himself in to the police or else. He opted against the *or else*."

Judging from the way Cassie put her hand on her chest, Lucky's explanation had gotten her heart pumping. "Is Mackenzie all right?"

He nodded. "She hugged me afterward."

The corner of her mouth lifted. "Good. She needs to know the world isn't filled with assholes."

She did. But there were other assholes out there. Too many of them, and Lucky wouldn't be around to protect her from them. Nor would Cassie. Since that made the knot in his stomach even tighter, Lucky got out of the truck. Cassie, too, but they hadn't even reached the front door to Bernie's office when someone called out her name. It was a sweaty-faced, middle-aged man getting out of a car parked just up the street.

Cassie groaned. "That's Simon Salvetti, my agent. What the heck are you doing here?" she asked as the man approached them.

He took her phone from her hand, made a show of pointing to it. "This is an amazing talking device, but when it makes a ringing sound, dings or plays a song, that means you should answer it because someone likely wants to communicate with you."

"I didn't want to *communicate* with you. Or anybody else from LA. I knew the newspaper photos would get around. I knew what that would do to my career, and I didn't want to hear a lecture from you."

"No lecture. What I was calling to tell you is that my talking device has been ringing nonstop with TV and radio shows who want to book you. Those pictures are freakin' gold, Cassie. You've got work lined up for the next two years." His attention finally landed on Lucky. "And this is the cowboy who made that possible."

Lucky sure hadn't kissed her to help her career. It had been for a more basic reason than that—lust. But he was glad it hadn't *hurt* her career, though work lined up for the next two years no doubt meant he wouldn't be seeing that much of Cassie after today.

That knot in his stomach was tightening like a vise.

"Anyway, since I wasn't able to talk to you," the man went on, "I hurried through one of the contracts and brought it with me for you to sign." He handed her a folder. And a pen.

Cassie glanced at the folder, Simon, then Lucky. She frowned. "Look, uh, Simon, there's a lot going on today—"

"Yes, the wedding and the reading of your aunt's will. I was out at the McCord Ranch, and the house-keeper told me about it, told me you'd be here. It won't take long for you to sign them, and then I can be on the next flight out."

She made another glance at the folder. Another glance at Lucky. As if she were trying to make up her mind about something. Was she thinking about turn-ing down the jobs? Because Lucky certainly couldn't offer her anything better.

"Simon, I can't do this now," she finally said. "I'll take a look at the contract after I'm finished here."

Her agent opened his mouth as if to argue, but Cassie gave him a stern look, and with the folder clutched to her chest, she went inside the office.

"You're not trying to convince her to stay here, are you?" the guy asked Lucky.

"No." It was the truth. A truth that made Lucky want to do something really unmanly, like puke.

Simon tried to tell Lucky why it would be a bad idea for Cassie to stay, but Lucky tuned him out and went into the office. Thankfully, Simon didn't follow.

Wilhelmina was there behind her desk, and her

feathers were no longer ruffled. She was back to batting her eyelashes at Lucky.

The puking feeling eased up a little when he saw Mia in the waiting room. She was hugging Cassie. Even though the wedding was still hours away, Mia was wearing a pale pink fairy-princess dress, complete with tiara, and she had a huge basket of gold stars clutched in her hand.

"Livvy's doing," Cassie said to him.

Lucky nodded in approval and made a mental note to thank Livvy. He'd thank Alice again, too, for letting the girls stay for the wedding. And speaking of Alice, she was right there next to Mia, and she wasn't in much of a festive mood. Her mouth was still tight. Her body, too. And she didn't soften even a little when Mia rushed to hug Lucky.

"I'm a star girl," Mia proudly announced.

"I can see that, and you look beautiful." He kissed the top of her head and turned to Mackenzie to tell her the same thing, but Lucky nearly tripped over his tongue.

Not his goth girl today, but rather a wedding girl. She was wearing a pink dress. Probably still too short. Of course, part of him wanted her to cover up from head to toe like a nun. And her hair wasn't spiked and black. It was pink to match the dress. She looked thirteen instead of twenty. Something he'd take to the grave because he doubted any thirteen-year-old girl actually wanted to look her age.

"I wanted to try something new," Mackenzie mumbled, looking uncomfortable. Did she think she was selling out? Not a chance.

"You look amazing," Lucky told her, and he also

gave her a kiss on the head. "But then, you looked amazing before, too." Before, however, it'd just taken him a little longer to see through the makeup.

"I understand the wedding is at two o'clock," Alice said, standing. She had her purse in front of her like a shield. "The girls and I will be leaving immediately afterward so if you could please bring them outside to the car then, I'd appreciate it."

Talk about killing the mood. Or rather what little mood they had. Even Mia's shoulders dropped. Too bad. Because seeing the joy on her face might be exactly what Lucky needed to get through the next few hours.

"You can come to the wedding, too," Lucky offered Alice.

"No, thank you," she jumped to say. "The girls and I are already packed to go."

Yes, she'd made that abundantly clear.

"I told her we wanted to stay with you," Mackenzie said, springing to their defense.

"And I told Aunt Alice I'd give her my cat if we could stay," Mia piped in.

Those two sentences warmed Lucky's heart. And crushed him. Because Alice wasn't going to take those things into consideration. She had already made up her mind.

But Lucky had been a master of mind swaying for years.

Lucky looked at Wilhelmina. "Could you go ahead and take the girls back to Bernie's office? I'd like to have a word with Alice."

Wilhelmina nodded, then ushered Mia and Mackenzie away, and Lucky made sure they were out of hearing range before he continued.

"I'm either going to insult you," he said to Alice, "or make your day. But I'm offering you a million bucks to sign over custody of the girls to Cassie and me."

Alice rolled her eyes. Obviously, his offer insulted her. "Cassie already offered me money." She huffed. "Do you really think my nieces are for sale?"

"Of course not," Cassie and he answered in unison. It was Lucky who continued. "But you heard what they said. They want to stay here. I believe they're happy at the ranch, and I think Spring Hill would be a good place for them to be raised."

"With Cassie, you and your family." Alice made them sound like fungi.

He wasn't sure Cassie would be in that equation, but he hoped she knew she was welcome, too. Well, welcome as long as he didn't have to deal with her hit-and-run *I love you.*

"My family would be a good support system for the girls," Lucky explained. "There'd be no need for a nanny since we have Della and Stella. My brother Riley and his soon-to-be wife live just minutes away—"

"Cassie brought up all of this when she called me this morning," Alice snapped. "But what both of you seem to be forgetting is that you're not fit to be parents."

"Bullshit." Lucky hadn't meant to curse, but he didn't take it back. "Cassie and I love the girls. We're not lowlifes like their parents. And we want them. That makes us fit."

He was clearly losing this argument since Alice

was making sounds like a riled rodeo bull. "This discussion is over."

Maybe, but Lucky wasn't giving up. "Do you love the girls? And I don't mean the kind of love that happens just because they're blood kin. Do you love them?"

The bull sounds turned to more glaring and staring. "I'm sure I will once I get to know them."

Yeah, she would. But Lucky doubted she'd ever love them as much as he did.

"Uh, Lucky and Cassie?" Wilhelmina said from the hall. "Bernie says you two should go on back for the reading."

Alice didn't even ask to go with them, and while Lucky wouldn't have refused her, he was glad to have a few more minutes with the girls away from her. Yeah, Alice was perfect all right, except for being pigheaded. Of course, Lucky wasn't even sure it was right to blame her. He hated to admit it, but if their situations had been reversed, he'd be pigheaded, too, if doing so would protect Mia and Mackenzie.

"Thanks for trying," Cassie said, giving him a pat on the back.

"Thanks for trying, too. How much did you offer Alice?"

"Everything in my savings account. Not as much as you, though. You really have a million dollars?"

He shrugged. "I think I do. I haven't touched my trust fund. And yeah, I have a trust fund," Lucky added almost defensively. "Never felt I deserved it so I didn't touch it, but using it for this seemed the right thing to do."

She nodded, paused outside Bernie's door. "I don't suppose Alice would budge if we pooled our money?"

Lucky had to shake his head. "I don't think money will do it. Nor a pound of flesh."

But what would exactly?

Obviously, Alice seemed to have the girls' best interest at heart, so what would make her believe that Cassie and he would be the best thing for her nieces? A few ideas came to mind—contributing to her charity, vowing chastity, joining the priesthood.

"We could get married," Lucky threw out there. He wouldn't dare tell Cassie that the notion had come in fourth—after chastity and the priesthood. "Then we could make our own petition for custody."

Cassie didn't exactly jump at the offer—his first marriage proposal ever. And it wasn't as if they were strangers. They'd had sex twice. Great sex, too. Then there was that part about her saying *I love you.*

"Marry you?" she questioned.

Since she had sort of a sneaky look in her eyes, Lucky just settled for a nod.

She nodded back. It was sort of sneaky, as well. "If you want me to even consider marrying you, you have to do one thing." And she reached for the doorknob to Bernie's office.

"Wait a minute. What one thing?"

The sneaky look intensified. "When you figure it out, you can ask me again."

Well, hell. It was one of those riddles, and he hated riddles. When she reached for the door again, Lucky stopped her.

"You want me to say I love you?" he tried. It was the only answer on his list of possible answers.

But Cassie shook her head. "When you figure it out, just let me know," she said and then opened the door despite his still trying to stop her.

"Are you two getting married?" Mackenzie immediately asked.

"Thin door," Wilhelmina grumbled, and she walked past them as she headed back to reception.

"And yes, your trust fund is worth more than a million," Bernie said to Lucky. "If you want to know the exact amount, I can look it up for you."

Lucky shook his head.

"Did you pay enough money for us?" Mia asked. "What one thing do you haveta do to marry Cassie?"

"No, we're not getting married," Cassie answered Mackenzie.

Lucky had to give the same no answer to Mia coupled with a "heck if I know" to her second question. And Lucky was glad everybody had read his thoughts in addition to hearing every word he'd uttered in the past five minutes. Hell, he was already flustered and frustrated, and the meeting hadn't even started.

And the meeting got even worse when he spotted Mason-Dixon.

The man was sitting in the corner, literally as far away from the rest of them as he could get. Of course, it was his right to be there since Dixie Mae was his mother, but if Dixie Mae did come back as a ghost she might try to kick her son's butt right out of the room.

Cassie and Lucky took a seat next to the girls when they went into the office. Bernie was wearing jeans and a Beatles T-shirt today. Probably because he was planning to head to the Founder's Day picnic later. Lucky would still have to make an appearance at that as well, something else that would no doubt be flustering and frustrating. Painful, too, because it would push his memory buttons about his mother.

Well, maybe.

After Claire had said how she felt guilty about the accident, Lucky was starting to see things in a slightly different light. Yeah, he was still responsible, but it had still been an accident.

"You said there were surprises," Lucky prompted Bernie when he just stood there, will in hand, and stared at them.

Bernie took a deep breath. "For the record, I tried to talk Dixie Mae out of this."

Shit.

This was going to be *bad*. Bernie began to read.

"I, Dixie Mae Weatherall, revoke all previous wills made by me and declare this my last will. And we're not even going to get into that monkey crap about me being of sound mind because all that's somebody's opinion. Just in case it's brought up, though, especially by my so-called son, I've given Bernie a copy of a psych eval to prove I'm not crazy, just mean and opinionated."

Lucky concurred on all points. Sane, mean, opinionated.

Bernie paused, looked at them. "I'm omitting some of the curse words, but they're here in writing if anyone wants to see them for themselves." He glanced at Mason-Dixon. "She called you a few choice names."

"I'll bet," he snarled. "Just tell me what the old bat left me."

Bernie took another deep breath and continued.

"To Mia and Mackenzie Compton and my grand-daughter, Cassandra Weatherall, I leave my half of Weatherall-McCord Stock Show and Rodeo Promotions, which will be divided into thirds among them. My partner, Austin McCord, will maintain majority percentage in the company and act as the trustee until the Compton minor children are each twenty-one. Also in accordance with my wishes, Cassandra, Mia and Mackenzie will remain in the state so they can better deal with the operation."

Judging from the way Cassie, Mia and Mackenzie stared at the lawyer, that was one of those surprises. But not to Lucky. This was exactly the sort of thing Dixie Mae would pull, and he wished that it was the magic bullet to keep them all here. But a will couldn't force something like that, and he was betting Alice wouldn't care a rat about Dixie Mae's will or wishes.

"What does it mean?" Mia asked, tugging on her sister's arm.

"It means we own part of a rodeo."

Mia grinned. "Do I get to own a bull?"

"About 17 percent of each bull," Bernie provided.

Mia's grin widened. "Cool. I want to own his leg. And Scooter's clown nose."

Mackenzie gave an irritated shake of her head and an eye roll that only a big sister could have managed.

"'In addition to the part ownership of the business,'" Bernie read on, "'I leave Mia and Mackenzie Compton the sum of two hundred thousand dollars each to be placed in a trust fund and used for their college educations.'"

Lucky was glad Dixie Mae had obviously gotten so close to the girls and had provided something for them. Plus, the rodeo business would give them some solid income, too.

"Keep reading," Mason-Dixon snapped.

Bernie smiled. The look on his face was too accommodating. It was sneaky like Cassie's earlier one. "'As for my residuary estate, all my money and personal items will go to the person who has ownership of my six cats.'"

Yeah, it was a sneaky smile all right. Lucky didn't just smile, he laughed, and Cassie giggled right along with him.

"What?" Mason-Dixon howled. "She left those cats to me."

"And you signed over ownership to Cassie." Bernie held up a copy of the document. "Her ownership means she inherits the remainder of Dixie Mae's estate, and it's valued at…" Bernie paused, fighting back a new smile. "Nearly twenty million dollars."

Cassie stopped laughing. Perhaps because she was in shock at her grandmother being worth that much. But no. Her eyes watered, and Lucky knew that she would trade every penny to have Dixie Mae back.

"What does that mean?" Mia asked.

"It means Cassie's rich," Mackenzie explained.

"It means you're rich, too," Cassie told Mia, "because I gave you one of the cats."

Mia thought about that a second. "Do I still get the bull leg, though? And the clown nose?"

Mackenzie rolled her eyes again.

"That hellhound can't just write me out of her will!" Mason-Dixon yelled.

"There's more," Bernie said, and he continued to read. "'For my son, Mason-Dixon Weatherall, I bequeath him a truckload of merchandise that will be delivered to his place of business today.'"

Bernie stopped and motioned for the three adults to join him at the desk so they could read the last line of the will for themselves. Mason-Dixon made it there ahead of them and tried to push Cassie aside. She held her ground. Then, she broke down in hysterical laughter when she read the last line.

Lucky had to laugh again, too, and he blew a kiss up to Dixie Mae.

"The merchandise consists of one thousand jumbo-size dildos," Dixie Mae had written. "Which my son can then use to go fuck himself."

CHAPTER TWENTY-THREE

"Uh, I'm not sure I can fit through the door," Claire said, studying herself in the large mirror.

Cassie wasn't sure of that, either. The wedding dress was as wide as Claire was tall. It was beautiful, though, with yards and yards of pearl-white organza and netting, but Cassie wasn't sure even the aisle of a cathedral would have been wide enough to accommodate it.

"It'll fit just fine," Livvy insisted. She wiped away another tear as she looked at Claire.

Cassie blinked back some tears, too. It had been an emotional morning what with Dixie Mae's will and Lucky's half-assed marriage proposal, and it was only going to get more emotional between attending the wedding and then saying goodbye to the girls.

"Riley'll be gaga when he sees you," Livvy said. She was fussing with the veil some more when there was a knock at the door.

"No one with a dick can come in," Livvy called out.

The woman opened the door and stuck her head in. "Good thing, then, I left my dick in Florida."

Anna.

She'd made it despite what had apparently been a couple of flight delays. It had been years since Cassie had seen her, and it was obvious that Lucky's little sister was all grown up. Cassie could see bits of all three of her brothers in that beautiful face, but that was hands down a genetic copy of Lucky's smile.

Anna eased into the room, shutting the door behind her before she hurried to Claire for a hug. Or at least she tried. "Air kisses and hugs only," Livvy insisted. "You'll ruin her hair and makeup."

Anna obliged, making a show of the air kisses and hugs. And of the real ones she gave to Livvy. Then Anna turned to Cassie. Cassie wasn't even sure she'd remember her, but she obviously did because Anna pulled her into a hug.

"I understand Lucky proposed to you," Anna said.

Cassie froze, but since Claire and Livvy didn't, she could only guess that this wasn't the first they were hearing of it. Cassie dismissed it with a wave of her hand.

"Lucky only did that because he thought it would help get custody of the girls."

Anna nodded as if that were old news, too. Livvy nodded, as well. Claire shrugged. Cassie dismissed the shrug. Because after all, Claire had been the one to say that Lucky was in love with her, and clearly he wasn't. If he had been, he would have done more than just give her a blank stare when Cassie had told him that she loved him.

"Is it true you said you'd marry Lucky if he'd do just one thing?" Anna asked. "But then you wouldn't tell him what that one thing was?"

Sheez. Wilhelmina had blabbed everything. Thin doors and a blabbermouth were a bad combination.

Anna, Claire and Livvy all stared at her, obviously waiting for an answer. An answer she didn't have to give because there was another knock at the door.

"If you got balls, you can't come in," Livvy said this time.

"I own a bull's leg," someone answered. "And a clown nose."

Mia.

"Oh, God. Sorry about that," Livvy added.

Horrified that Mia might have heard what Livvy said, Cassie hurried to open it, and there they were. Mia and Mackenzie. Thankfully, they didn't seem as appalled as Cassie was over the balls comment. The girls looked perfect. Of course, she'd already seen them in their wedding clothes, but it was just as special to see them a second time. Cassie gathered them into her arms and kissed them.

"You two ready for this?" Livvy asked them.

Mia nodded. "Kenzie's been putting people in the seats." She lifted her basket filled with gold stars. "And I'm going to throw these at people." However, the moment Mia said the words, she glanced down at the stars. "There's a lotta magic wishes in here."

Claire smiled. "And everybody will get at least one today. Especially me. Can we just get downstairs and do this before Riley changes his mind?"

There was zero chance of Riley doing that, but Mia took off as if to make sure that didn't happen. Mackenzie looped her arm through Cassie's. "Come on. I'll take you to your seat."

They stepped into the hall, and Cassie nearly smacked right into Lucky. He, too, gave Mackenzie a hug and kiss. And Cassie got a look from him. A long, appreciative one as his attention slid from Cassie's head to her toes.

"There you are," Livvy said, catching onto Lucky's

arm and pulling him into the room. "Now, here are some things you need to remember when you walk Claire down the aisle…"

That was Cassie's cue to get moving. Mackenzie and she went downstairs where there were guests milling around, making their way into the living room for the ceremony.

"What's Mia doing?" Mackenzie asked.

The little girl wasn't hard to spot with her sparkly tiara, but Mia was racing out the front door. Alarmed, Cassie went after her with Mackenzie right behind her. Cassie doubted Mia was running away, and she wasn't. Mia hurried to a silver car where Aunt Alice was waiting.

Mia took out one handful of stars, as many would fit into her tiny hand, and gave the basket to Alice. "Magic wishes," Mia told her. "I want to use them so Kenzie and me can stay here with Miss Cassie and Mr. Lucky."

Alice's gaze flew to Cassie, maybe because the woman thought Cassie had put Mia up to it, but there must have been something in Cassie's expression that let Alice know otherwise.

Mia looked at her hand. "I gotta save these to throw at people." Then she gave the basket another look, picked several more stars from her hand and added them to the hundreds that were already in there. "And I can give you my bull's leg and clown's nose." She pulled off her tiara, added it to the basket.

"I can give you the money Dixie Mae left me," Mackenzie said.

Her aunt shook her head. "I don't want your money.

Or the stars." She handed the basket back to Mia. "I just want my sister's children to live with me."

There it was. Alice's bottom line—again.

"But what if we really, really, really wanna live here?" Mia asked. "What if being here makes us really, really happy?"

Another head shake from Alice, but it also looked as if she'd swallowed hard. "I can make you happy, too."

"Yeah, but you can't do it really, really, really." Mia looked ready to cry, but she took several of the stars and put them in Alice's hand. "I'll give you magic stars anyway."

Great. Now Cassie was crying again. This time in front of the girls, something she'd sworn she wouldn't do.

"Hurry up," Livvy called out from the front door. "We're about to start, and we need the star girl."

Mia took off running, jiggling the basket and leaving a trail of magic gold stars behind her.

LUCKY WAS PRETTY sure he'd never seen Riley happier. Claire, either. And there had only been one mishap during the ceremony, when Ethan had tossed one of the toy cars a little too hard and it'd smacked Livvy on the forehead. Other than a few drops of blood, the wedding had been perfect.

But now perfect was over.

The thirty or so guests were already filing out of the house, all heading to the picnic grounds for the reception. Lucky and Cassie would soon follow, but first they had to say goodbye to the girls. Something they'd do as soon as the photographer finished taking pictures.

Della walked over to him, watching as the photographer posed Mia and Ethan in front of Claire and Riley. It was slow going because Riley and Claire kept kissing. Ethan kept trying to play with the cars he'd retrieved from the floor. Mia was darting out to retrieve gold stars, too. Cassie and Mackenzie weren't in the shot, but they were helping Livvy arrange the flowers around the couple.

"An engagement ring," Della said to him.

"Huh?" Lucky figured he had spaced out and had missed whatever she'd said before that.

"An engagement ring," she repeated.

So he hadn't missed it after all. "Am I supposed to know what that means?"

"It's the one thing you've got to do before Cassie will marry you," Della clarified.

Oh, that. Lucky should have known. Clearly the gossip mill had worked overtime getting out the news of what Cassie and he had discussed outside Bernie's door.

If you want me to even consider marrying you, you have to do one thing.

Maybe he needed to build a room with concrete walls for his next chat. If there was a next chat, that is. After all, Cassie's agent had brought her all of those offers.

"A bunch of people already suggested that," he let Della know. "In fact, it was the second-most suggested answer."

"What was the first?" Della asked.

"Saying I love you."

"I just assumed you'd done that."

He had, but Cassie had let him know that was

wrong. He'd been doing a lot of wrong things lately and hadn't done much of anything except fail to fix any of this. He was losing all of them.

"Getting down on one knee?" Della went on. "I heard that talked about a lot as a possibility."

So had he. Lucky wasn't opposed to that, but not for a marriage proposal. He'd rather spend time on his knees kissing Cassie in all the right places. Or rather one special place anyway.

Cassie turned, smiled at him, and he could have sworn that she had ESP or something because enough heat zinged between them that he almost forgot about having to say goodbye.

Almost.

Cassie finished whatever she was doing and made her way to Lucky. "They're a beautiful couple," she remarked, and the silence—and the heat—settled between them for several moments. "Everyone knows what we talked about at Bernie's office."

He nodded.

"And for the record, the right answer is *not* for you to wear chaps and spurs," she added.

Lucky frowned. "Who suggested that?"

"Livvy. She said it could be the tipping point, that it always gets women hot."

"Does it?" Automatic question. He would have been kicked out of the male club if he hadn't asked it.

"It worked for me," she admitted, smiling. Then, frowning, added, "But it's not the right answer."

Of course. It was just another bad suggestion, but it beat Hank's. The ranch hand had told Lucky that the thing he had to do was to knock Cassie up. All in all,

Lucky had gotten some of the absolute worst advice of his life from people who were family and friends.

"Can I talk to you?" someone asked from behind them.

Alice.

Lucky had no idea how long she'd been standing there, but he hoped she'd missed out on the getting-hot-over-chaps chat. "Of course." Both Cassie and he turned toward her.

Alice looked at the girls, smiled, but it wasn't the smile of a victorious woman who had just gotten exactly what she wanted. She opened her hand to show him the gold stars.

Lucky wasn't surprised to see them. What with the way Mia was flinging the stars around, every inch of the living room floor seemed to be covered with them. They were in people's hair, on their clothes. He figured some of the little glittered bits had worked their way into places he didn't want to know about.

"I suppose you'll be leaving town soon?" Alice asked, and it took Lucky a moment to realize she was talking to him. "Gossip," she added in a mumble. "The consensus is you don't stay here much."

"Not usually, but I'll be around for a while."

Another nod. "Because of those bulls you're buying. The clerk at the inn said you'd want to work with the bulls yourself, that you're picky about that sort of thing."

Now it was his turn to nod. If Alice knew that, then she probably also knew about the rift that had formed long ago between Lucky and his twin brother. Except it no longer felt like much of a rift. Logan had his business to run. Lucky had his. There was no reason they couldn't run those businesses in the same town.

"And what about you?" Alice asked Cassie. "You'll be going back to LA?"

"No. I'm selling my condo, though, so eventually I'll have to go back for the closing. But not for work. I've, uh, decided to pass on some recent business offers so I'll be staying around here. I might open an office here in Spring Hill since there's not another therapist in town."

Finally, there was something the gossips hadn't gotten hold of yet. Probably because Alice and he were the first people she'd told. But that meant there was a silver lining in all of this. Cassie would be around so they could continue having sex.

And whatever the heck else was going on between them.

Alice's gaze drifted to the girls again, and she motioned for them to come closer. She didn't say anything until she had an arm around each of them. "I didn't reach this decision easily, and I'm still not sure it's the right thing to do. But if Cassie and Lucky are here, together, then I'll consider allowing you to stay with them. As long as it's what you girls *really, really* want."

Lucky was so lost in the thought of sex with Cassie that the words didn't sink in at first. Even when they did, he was certain he'd misheard the woman. Until he saw the tears in Alice's eyes.

"It's what we want. Really, really, really, really." But Mia didn't just say it. She said it while jumping around, squealing and eventually adding more *really*s.

No squeals of delight or jumping from Mackenzie, but she did bob her head in agreement.

"They were willing to give up everything they have to stay here," Alice went on, speaking to Cassie and him now. "If that isn't love, I don't know what is. I love them, but they obviously love the two of you a lot more."

"We do love them," Mia volunteered. "But we love you, too," she added.

Another head bob from Mackenzie.

Alice tried to blink back tears. "Just promise that you'll visit me often. Every summer. School breaks. And promise me that I can come and see you whenever I want."

"Promise," Mia said, using her free hand to cross her heart. She left a trail of gold stars there as well, stuck to her fairy-princess dress.

"I promise," Mackenzie agreed. Heck, she also crossed her heart.

Lucky wasn't sure he could breathe yet—the air was caught in his lungs and throat—much less speak, so he nodded. Cassie nodded, too. And yes, she was crying. Hell, he was crying. He was really going to get kicked out of the man universe now.

"The magic stars worked," Mia whispered to Lucky.

As a responsible adult, Lucky should have probably tried to dispel the notion of magic, but shit, maybe it was magic. He scooped Mia up, kissed her and passed her to Cassie so she could do the same. Then he pulled Mackenzie into her arms so they could share a group hug. Mackenzie didn't even give a protesting grunt.

Mia caught onto Cassie's face. Kissed her. "We gonna get to stay and run seventy-teen percent of the bulls. And the clowns."

"Yes, we are. Personally, I think we'll do a great job. What do you think?" Cassie asked her.

Mia giggled behind her hand. "I think we should give Kenzie all the bulls' bootees. She can own them."

"No bull bootees," Mackenzie grumbled, but she smiled a little.

When Cassie put Mia down, Alice gave both girls hugs. "I'll get your suitcases from the car," she added, then looked at Lucky and Cassie. "If they need anything, call me, and I'll stay in touch with them daily through calls and emails. Just make sure I'm a part of their lives."

Lucky nodded, and because it looked as if Alice needed it, he hugged her. "Of course. You're part of their lives. Ours, too. You're family now, and you're welcome here anytime."

That put some fresh tears back in Alice's eyes, and after another set of long hugs, more muttered good-byes, she pulled away from the girls, her clothes and face sparkling from the stars.

Mackenzie folded her arms over her chest as Alice slipped out. "So, I guess you're, like, stuck with us now," she said to Cassie and him. The attitude was goth girl, and Lucky was a little surprised to realize he'd missed it.

"Seems like it." Man, his heart was about to burst, but it would probably scare the hell out of them if he started jumping up and down and whooping like an idiot. A happy idiot, though.

"Of course, that means we're stuck with you, too," Mackenzie said. "Am I still grounded for all that mess that happened with Brody?"

"Absolutely," Cassie said, and at the same time

Lucky added, "You bet. And you can't talk to any boys at the picnic today unless they're your age or younger. Preferably younger. In fact, Ethan will make perfect company for you."

Mackenzie lifted her shoulder, obviously expecting that.

From the corner of his eye, he saw Alice set down the suitcases just outside the door. Lucky mouthed a thank-you, but it didn't seem like nearly enough. Of course, nothing would ever be enough to thank her.

"So, are you and Miss Cassie getting married?" Mia asked him after Alice left. "Because Miss Cassie said you had to do one thing." She paused. "What's the one thing?"

To hell if he knew.

But Lucky went with his gut. "I love you," he told Cassie.

After all, those were magic words. Or so he'd been told. However, they didn't seem to do the trick here.

Cassie gave him a flat look. Mackenzie huffed. Mia tugged on his sleeve again.

"You gotta say it like you mean it. Like this. I love you." Mia stretched out the words, smiled and then hugged his leg.

Since Mackenzie didn't huff this time and Cassie's look didn't go flat, Mia might be onto something.

"Mia and I will get changed for the picnic," Mackenzie said. "Don't mess this up," she whispered to Lucky. "Say it like you mean it."

Was that it? Was it really that simple? Well, heck. Then he'd been close all along—even though he'd just realized it.

He pulled Cassie to him. Kissed her. A kiss that

was too long and deep considering the minister and his wife were walking by them.

"I love you," Lucky said, and he didn't just sound like he meant it because he did mean it.

When the world didn't collapse and a lightning bolt didn't hit him, he said it again. And again.

Cassie gave it right back to him. "I love you, too."

Lucky smiled. "So, that was it, huh? I just had to say it like I mean it?"

She shook her head. Put her mouth right against his ear. He felt some tongue. "You have to say it tonight while wearing those chaps and spurs."

Oh, man.

This love shit was going to be fun.

* * * * *

*Be sure to check out the third McCord story,
featuring responsible brother Logan,
when BLAME IT ON THE COWBOY
goes on sale in October 2016.
And for more from* USA TODAY *bestselling author
Delores Fossen,
look for SIX-GUN SHOWDOWN,
in August 2016
from Harlequin Intrigue.*

Read on for a special
THE McCORD BROTHERS
bonus prequel
from
Delores Fossen.

Cowboy Trouble

COWBOY BUTTS.

Not what Rico Callahan wanted to see when he came out of one of the barn stalls. Yet there they were.

Four Wrangler jeans faced him like some kind of stock picture that got posted on the internet. And none of those jeans-covered butts were moving, something that darn sure should be happening since there was more manure that needed shoveling and fences that should be checked.

"Is there a reason I'm the only one on bullshit detail?" Rico snarled.

No answer. All four ranch hands just stood there gawking. So help them if they were ogling Anna McCord sunbathing again in the backyard, he was going to kick some of those butts. One of Anna's brothers, Logan, was Rico's boss and the head of the McCord Ranch, but Rico thought of her like a kid sister, too.

Using the hay strewn on the barn floor, Rico wiped off some of the muck from his boots and made his way to the others. Along the way, he stopped by the tack room and snagged a bottle of water from the fridge. He drank half and poured the other half over his head. The water snaked down his face and back.

It didn't help.

"Hey, Rico, you'll wanna take a look at this," Shane called out. He was butt number two from the left in the line of gawkers.

When Rico reached them, he followed their gazes. Not to a sunbathing Anna. Or even to another livestock delivery they were expecting any minute now. They were staring at a sleek silver sports car, as expensive as they came. And it was parked on the side of the McCord house.

The driver's door of the car was already open, but thanks to the tinted window and the door itself, the only thing he saw of their visitor was a foot. Not just any old foot, though. One wearing a four-inch sexy heel that was almost the same color as the car. That heel and the accompanying shapely ankle grabbed Rico's attention.

It was like watching a striptease. A delicate hand slid over the top of the driver's-side window and door. Perfectly manicured nails—the color of ripe raspberries—gripped the glass and metal. The other foot touched down on the ground. Graceful. Like a dancer getting ready to strut her stuff.

Rico felt like fanning himself, and it wasn't all a result of the July heat. It'd been a while since he'd taken the time to appreciate a good-looking woman. A reminder that he needed a life outside the ranch and shit-shoveling.

Inch by inch the top of their visitor's head came into view as she rose from the seat. Honey-blond hair. It looked touchable, and he could almost feel his fingers sliding through it. It'd probably be like silk.

She had a well-shaped forehead. Sleek sunglasses

that curved just above her high cheekbones. Blush-touched cheeks, and he was willing to bet it didn't totally come from a bottle or a tube.

But then the striptease came to a kick-to-the-nuts halt.

Rico's gaze landed on her mouth. A full, sensual mouth covered with just enough gloss to make it noticeable. And notice it he did. It was a mouth he hadn't seen in twelve years, and it belonged to the last person on earth he wanted to see.

Natalie Landon.

His ex-wife.

Shane and the others cursed, obviously realizing that their fantasies had been ill-placed, as well. They all knew Natalie, of course, even though she no longer lived around here. Everybody knew everybody in Spring Hill, both past and present residents, and the gossips soon filled in the newcomers with all the delicious details.

Gossipy details about Rico and their visitor.

Like the fact that Natalie had been slumming twelve years ago when she'd married Rico, the ranch hand. The fact that she'd dumped the ranch hand, too, when her daddy hadn't approved. And the final fact was that most folks thought Rico hadn't gotten over her.

They were dead wrong about that.

Probably.

With seemingly no effort, she used her elbow to push the car door shut, eased off her sunglasses and started toward the barn. No hurried footsteps for her. Just the long, easy stride of a woman who had a mountain of confidence.

A change for Natalie.

She wasn't exactly the mountain-of-confidence type. Or the type to wear sex-against-the-wall heels like that. His Natalie—when she had been his, that is—was more of a jeans-and-cowboy-boots kind of girl. Her daddy had often joked that cowboy boots and princess tiaras didn't go well together.

Neither had princesses and cowboys.

But she was definitely more in the princess wheel-house today. The muggy breeze flirted with her turquoise-colored skirt, fluttering it around the tops of her knees. Rico obviously wasn't the only one to notice that, because Brandon mumbled something about being "in lust."

Rico understood completely.

Even now, he felt the lust. He wanted to punch himself hard for feeling it, and he wanted to punch all four Wrangler butts for feeling it, too. Thank goodness that lust was tempered with a hefty dose of reality. It didn't matter how good she looked, he definitely didn't want to go another round with Natalie Landon.

Now, the question was—did she want to go another round with him?

If so, it'd be a shocker, considering she hadn't even bothered to call him once since she'd walked out on him twelve years ago after their one-week marriage. No, it probably wasn't for round two. After all, she'd been the one to leave.

By the time she'd made it to the front of the barn,

her deep violet-blue eyes slid in Rico's direction. Their gazes met. And held.

Natalie didn't smile or offer him an acknowledging nod, even though her mouth did that little quivery thing where her bottom lip trembled just slightly. This time it was maybe from nerves, but it happened other times, as well. She probably didn't know she did the same thing just seconds before reaching an orgasm. He knew. Because Rico had been on the giving end of those particular orgasms.

And that was something else he really wished he hadn't remembered.

Rico stayed put but watched as she made her way past the line of butts. The barn was littered with hay, feed and equipment. The air was heavy not just with heat and humidity but with manure and dust. Hardly a fitting place for Natalie, not dressed like that anyway.

Not smelling like that, either.

She was wearing perfume that screamed "I'm expensive." Ditto for the earrings. Diamonds, of course, that dripped down like raindrops on tiny gold threads. The only thing that didn't mesh was the small silver heart that she'd pinned, well, over her heart.

Natalie stopped right in front of him, and her attention went from his hair, which was still soaking wet, down to his unbuttoned shirt. Also drenched. Not just drenched from the water he'd poured over his head, either, but from an ample amount of sweat. If she'd been any other woman, Rico would have wished for a shower and a shave before facing her.

But she wasn't any other woman.

There was no need to impress her.

"Lost?" Rico asked, just so he could make sure his mouth was moving and not gaping. "Because you're a long way from Austin."

"No, not lost. But believe me, it'd be better for both of us if that's why I was here. Is there someplace we can talk? In private?" she added, sparing the hands a cool glance.

Hell. This couldn't be good. Rico wanted to refuse, but that would just make him look petty. Besides, he was curious, and since he wasn't a cat, maybe that curiosity wouldn't kill his ass.

He led her through the barn. Through the crap and hay. No doubt messing up those girlie shoes. Rico took her to the bunkhouse and his office there. Such that it was. It was barely big enough for one, so Rico had to work hard to keep some personal space between them. He leaned his shoulder against the metal filing cabinet, folded his arms over his chest and generally tried to look surly. With the heat and her impromptu visit, it wasn't a hard look to accomplish.

He hoped.

"Well, you don't appear to have a flat tire," he commented.

A reminder, or rather a jab, of how they'd first gotten together. In a downpour, no less. She'd had a flat tire on her vintage candy-apple-red Mustang. One look at her, and he'd stopped to help. And the rest was history. Within three days, they'd become lovers. Secretly. Within three months, they'd become engaged.

Also secretly.

Ditto for the elopement and marriage.

It'd been a whirlwind romance by anyone's standards. But when the whirling finally stopped, Natalie opted out of her promise to love him forever and went back to dear old Dad.

"No flat tire." And from the way she pursed her mouth, Natalie was remembering that fateful day, as well.

She pushed aside some papers on his desk and propped her right butt cheek on the corner. She probably did that to give herself some more space as well, but the simple gesture caused her skirt to shift slightly, and he got another glimpse of her thigh.

That cooled down the surliness and brought on the fantasies again.

Hot fantasies of him sliding his hand right up her thigh and into her panties. Which were almost certainly silk and lace because even when Natalie had been a tomboy, she'd had great taste in underwear. Then he could sink his fingers into that moist, slippery heat and give her an orgasm they'd both remember.

Oh, man.

What the hell was he thinking?

Or better yet, what was he thinking with? Of course, he already knew the answer to that. He was thinking with that brainless part of him that was causing a three-ring circus in his jeans.

"This is your office?" she asked, her gaze landing on the framed photo on the file cabinet of him and his mother. She sounded surprised. Maybe because she hadn't thought of him as the office-having sort.

Rico nodded and nearly added that he was a top hand now, that he supervised the gawking butts. But that wouldn't impress Natalie because simply put, he was still just a cowboy.

"Why are you here?" Rico came out and asked at the same moment Natalie said, "Are you, uh, seeing anyone?"

Rico was certain he scowled. Natalie scowled, too, huffed and stood. Or rather she tried. But she got off-balance in the small space and wobbled. It likely would have stayed just a wobble if she'd been wearing cowboy boots, but the needle-thin heels didn't give her much support. She reached for the filing cabinet to steady herself.

She caught on to Rico instead.

Specifically, his thigh. She clamped her hand over it. That didn't help him in the dirty-thoughts department.

"Sorry," she grumbled, snatching back her hand and hitting him in the crotch in the process. He winced, cursed. But she cursed, too. "These damn shoes."

Bingo. Natalie was still a cowboy-boots girl. "Please don't tell me you wore them to impress me?" he asked.

She blinked and stared as if he'd just suggested they fly to Pluto on a hay bale. "No." Natalie paused. "Maybe," she amended, swallowing hard.

Hell's Texas bells. Now he was the one with that "fly to Pluto" look of disbelief. "You're not here for ex sex, are you?"

"No," she jumped to say. But then she hesitated, nibbled on her bottom lip. "Are you seeing anyone? Engaged? In love?"

None of the above, but Rico didn't answer. He went with a repeat of his question. "Ex sex?" And he was about to tell her there was no way that would happen. However, Natalie spoke before he could get his mouth working.

"We'd have to be exes for ex sex," she said.

Because Rico was already confused, it took longer than normal for those words to sink in. Even when the sinking was done, they still didn't make sense.

"What are you talking about? We've been divorced for twelve years." He was about to add all that old baggage about her buckling under to her daddy's demands, but again Natalie got a word in first.

One very important word.

"No," she said.

"No?" he questioned, only because Rico didn't know what the hell else to say.

"No," she verified. "The district clerk messed up and didn't file the papers properly. We're still legally married."

Then Natalie did something else that nearly shocked Rico's boxers off. She slid her hand around his neck, dragged him to her and kissed him.

CHAPTER TWO

THIS WAS A textbook example of playing with fire. Or being just plain stupid. But Natalie had to find out if kissing Rico still felt as if she'd just been dropped into a scalding-hot vat of lust. After one second, she had her answer.

Yes.

Mercy. That wasn't the answer she wanted.

Even if every part of her body did. Her mouth was especially eager about this experiment. It was the same for her lady place. In fact, her lady place wanted a whole lot more than just a kiss from him. And for a moment, she thought she just might get more, too. Then Rico pulled away from her and looked at her as if she'd sprouted a couple of extra noses.

"What the hell are you doing?" he snapped. "And get back to explaining about us still being married."

Natalie drew in a long breath, which she would need. Not just to recover from the kiss, but because Rico was asking a mouthful. She went with the second part because it was actually easier to spell out. Easier than admitting she'd come there to test the old flames.

"The divorce decree that I got doesn't appear to

be in order," she told him. "The judge's signature is missing."

He cursed, scrubbed his hand over his face and cursed some more. "Well, the signature can just be found."

She doubted that profanity was because he'd reacted in some small way to the kiss. Or rather in some big way, she mentally corrected, when she glanced at the front of his jeans.

She didn't smile. Not with this riled mood he was in. But, yes, he'd reacted all right.

Natalie wasn't sure why that pleased her. It certainly didn't help things other than falling into the "misery loves company" department. Even if it was obvious Rico didn't want to be married to her, there were parts of him that still wanted her. That meshed with the parts of her that still wanted him, but Natalie was reasonably sure there'd be no meshing today.

Or any other day, for that matter.

Still cursing and shaking his head in disbelief, Rico kept tossing scowls and glares at her. He probably didn't know that he was hot when he scowled. Even more so than when he smiled. Of course, with those looks—the black hair and steamy blue eyes— Rico always fell into the hot category. It was why she hadn't been able to resist him twelve years ago. It was why she'd made a fool of herself and kissed him today.

It took him a couple of minutes to quit cursing and shaking his head, and the scowl stayed in place when he looked at her again. "Why were you even looking at the divorce decree anyway? And how do we fix this?"

That required another deep breath. Best for her to be vague on that first question, though. "I just happened to come across the decree and finally read it from start to finish. As for how to fix it, I can refile the paperwork, of course. Today, in fact. But I'll need you to go with me to the lawyer and then the courthouse." Natalie paused. "I was hoping to keep it quiet." And she really hated to tell him the rest of this. "My father doesn't know about the snafu."

The scowl morphed into a flat look. "Right." With just that one word, he managed to spell out their entire relationship. Or his version of it anyway.

There were some things Rico didn't know, either.

Things that sliced at her even now, all these years later.

That thought cooled down some of the fire inside her and reminded her that she'd been an idiot to come here like this. She couldn't do anything about that kiss, but she could do something about the blasted shoes. Natalie plopped back down on the desk and took them off so she could massage her toes.

Which had possibly fused together.

"So, can you come with me now, to the lawyer's office?" she asked. "I made the appointment with Bernie Woodland here in town so that you wouldn't have to travel far." It was less than a half mile away. "I made Bernie promise to keep this quiet. And you could ride with me. When we're done, I can drive you back."

Rico didn't exactly jump on any part of that offer.

"How the hell did this happen?" At that exact moment, he wiped his mouth—or perhaps his upper lip—with the back of his hand, so Natalie wasn't sure if they were talking about the kiss or the divorce debacle.

"People screw up," she settled for saying. "The clerk did. I did," she added. "With that kiss just now," she tacked on to her added comment. Though she could include the marriage in that screwup, as well.

Oh, she'd loved Rico all right. Of course, he would never believe that. But she had. And it had crushed her heart to sign those divorce papers. For all the good it'd done. Fate was laughing its butt off about right now because their signatures had meant nothing. She was still married to this hot, sweaty cowboy.

A hot, sweaty cowboy who was pissed off. "Why didn't you follow up on the paperwork?" he snapped. "Why didn't you make sure the divorce went through?"

Natalie opened her mouth. Closed it. And repeated that process a couple of times. "I got what I thought was a legit decree. Plus, I had some things going on in my life," she settled for saying. Things that were still going on.

Things she didn't want to get into with him now. Maybe not ever.

"Why didn't you follow through?" she countered. "Didn't you notice that the judge hadn't actually signed it?"

His eyes narrowed. "I had some things going on in my life," he tossed right back at her.

Touché. He was probably referring to the fact that

he'd been shaken up. Hurt. Even more pissed off than he was now. In a "things going on in my life" contest, she'd win.

But it wasn't a victory title Natalie wanted.

The heat from the kiss had cooled a little now. Enough for the other memories to come poking into her mind. Always the memories. She'd caused so much pain. Too much. And that was yet another reminder of just how stupid that kiss had been.

"Well?" she prompted when he didn't say anything.

He glanced around as if deciding whether to agree to go with her or curse. Then his gaze landed on her mouth, and she wondered, briefly, if he was considering another kiss. Maybe his way of testing if the old flames could still be fanned.

However, no kiss.

He went with more profanity and another scowl. "You really wore that outfit and shoes for me?" Rico asked.

They were back to the her-sprouting-more-noses tone, but it was a question she hadn't expected. Maybe it was a safer topic for him than discussing why neither of them had made sure they'd actually gotten a divorce.

"I wore it for you and my father. He prefers me to dress this way because it looks more professional, and I didn't want to show up here today looking like..."

His eyebrow rose. "Me?"

Natalie studied his clinging gray shirt and then his jeans that were snug in all the right places. She often wore jeans, but they never looked that good on her. Heck, they wouldn't look as good on an underwear model as they did Rico. He'd sewn up the hot-cowboy clothes market.

"I didn't want to look like someone you were glad to be rid of," she corrected, then waved him off before he could say anything about that. "It doesn't make sense. I just wanted to know I was still, well, attractive to someone other than...well, to anyone."

If his flat look got any flatter, she'd be able to use it to make pancakes on it. "Of course, you're attractive. That was never the problem between us. Neither was that." He glanced down at what was left of his erection. "The problem was your *daddy*."

He said that last word as if he was discussing navel lint. Which in his mind, her father was. But then, she fell into the navel-lint category, too, because she'd given in to her father's demands. For all the good it'd done. She was still married to Rico, still trying to make sure her world didn't implode.

And speaking of imploding, that might happen on a more personal level. She tugged at her body-shaping underwear in the hopes that it would give her a little relief. It was like wearing a boa constrictor, and it was possible her intestines had fused together, as well.

"Your dad wants you to dress like that?" Rico snapped.

Apparently, they were still on the subject of the outfit that had taken her five hours to choose. She nodded. "I do PR for his real-estate company. I need to look professional and approachable." That was according to the stylist her father had hired for her several years back.

"Approachable?" Rico repeated. He'd taken the navel-lint tone up a notch.

Natalie didn't ask him if she'd succeeded because she wanted to get this conversation back on track. "Will you go with me to Bernie's office?"

He stared at her. A long time. And then he did something Natalie certainly hadn't been expecting.

Rico got naked.

Well, almost. Actually, he stripped off his sweaty shirt, tossed it onto the chair and grabbed another one from the small closet that was behind his desk. Natalie figured she should turn away and not stare, but her eyeballs seemed glued to him.

He pulled off his boots, reached for his zipper but then stopped. "You can watch if you want, but I'm about to drop my pants."

Yes, so he could change into a clean pair of jeans that she saw hanging in the closet. And yes, she should turn away.

She did.

But not before she got an eyeful of his toned and perfect backside.

Oh, the ache came. It always did. That tug deep within her that made her want to go to him, drag him onto the floor and ride him hard. As good as that would be, and it would be good all right, it would come with complications. Complications that Natalie wasn't sure she was ready to face. A kiss to test old waters was one thing, but sex could cause her to make a decision she shouldn't be making. That was why she turned around and shut her eyes for good measure. Too bad she couldn't shut her ears, too, because she could hear him dressing, and her imagination was filling in the blanks.

"Thank you for doing this," she said.

No answer. Maybe he didn't want her thanks. Heck, maybe he didn't want to talk about it at all, but she wished she knew how he felt about it. Natalie already knew how he felt about her.

She'd seen the disdain in his eyes. The lust, too. She figured he saw the same thing in her own eyes.

"We'll need to make this quick," he growled, moving ahead of her. Of course, that meant sliding against her as he went to the door. But it seemed as if he took his time. And as if he were enjoying it a little too much.

"Payback?" she mumbled.

The corner of his mouth hitched. Then immediately lowered. Probably because he knew that kind of payback came with consequences.

Natalie checked the time. Just past one o'clock. If all went as planned, they could pick up the papers from Bernie, sign them and drop them off at the courthouse. It could be a done deal by three o'clock. Well, except for the waiting. The law required the papers to be on file for sixty days before the divorce was finalized. Maybe during that time, the news wouldn't make it back to her father. He already had enough on his plate without adding more from her.

"We'll take my truck," Rico said as he walked out the door. "I don't have spare boots here, and I doubt you'll want cow shit in your car."

It already had shit. Her riding gear was in the trunk, but Rico didn't give her a chance to explain that. He headed straight for a dark blue truck that was parked at the side of the barn.

They didn't make it far.

She spotted Logan McCord making his way toward them. Or rather making his way toward Rico. Logan spared her a glance and then did a double take.

"Natalie," he said. Not exactly a warm and welcoming greeting. He knew her, of course, because they'd gone to high school together, and Natalie had occasional business contact with his longtime girlfriend, Helene.

Logan was part of the superior gene pool known as the McCord brothers. There were three of them. Lucky and Riley were the other two. But he was the least friendly of the bunch. Of course, probably none of them would be friendly to her, since they'd be on Rico's side.

"Is everything okay?" Logan asked, volleying his attention between Rico and her.

"Rico and I are just catching up," she jumped to say. She'd sworn Bernie to secrecy and didn't want to have to do any more swearing today, especially since just her mere presence would cause tongues to wag. Spring Hill was the mecca of tongue-wagging.

Logan's expression was a prime example of a skeptical expression. For a moment she thought he might press for more, or even the truth, but thankfully, this was Logan and not one of this brothers. From everything she'd heard, Logan wasn't the sort to want to know more unless it pertained to business.

"I'm here to check on the livestock shipment," Logan continued, proving that the gossips had indeed gotten it right about the business-minded CEO of McCord Cattle Brokers. He hadn't lingered on potential rumor fodder at all.

Rico shook his head. "Hasn't arrived yet. I called about an hour ago, and the calves should be here soon."

"Good. I've already got a buyer for them, so we shouldn't have to keep them more than a week." He glanced at the truck keys that Rico had taken from his pocket. "You going somewhere?"

"Just into town for a cup of coffee," Natalie volunteered, earning her a fresh scowl from Rico. Maybe because he didn't like lying to his boss.

Rico glanced over his shoulder in the direction where the hands had been earlier, and so did Natalie, but the four were nowhere in sight. Probably back to work since the boss had arrived.

"Natalie and I need to take care of some paperwork," Rico explained to Logan.

Logan really had that skeptical look down pat. "Anything I can do to help?" But that sounded like man-code for *You want me to get rid of your ex?*

"No. I won't be long, and if the calves arrive before I get back, Lucky's inside, and he can sign for them."

"Lucky's home?" That sent Logan's attention toward the sprawling house. "I didn't see his truck."

"He left it at the pub. I gave him a ride here. But he'll be leaving before long because he said he's got a rodeo up in Dallas."

Logan made a sound of disapproval. "Is he with someone?"

Someone meaning a woman. The gossip was ripe

about that, too. Lucky was apparently as devoted to women as Logan was to the business.

"Lucky was alone when I dropped him off," Rico answered. Of course, that didn't mean he was alone now.

Logan mumbled something, maybe a goodbye, and he headed in the direction of the house. Thank God he hadn't pressed for more info, which meant she'd just dodged a bullet.

But another bullet quickly came her way.

She heard the sound of an engine, and a moment later a car pulled in behind hers. A car that Natalie immediately recognized.

No.

Not this, not now.

"A problem?" Rico asked her when she cursed under her breath.

"Yes," she verified when the man stepped from the car. She hurried toward him as fast as her fused toes and boa-constrictor underwear would let her move. "What are you doing here?" Natalie demanded.

He flashed a smile that could have dissolved multiple layers of rust, and he extended his hand to Rico. "I'm Marcus Jacobson, Natalie's fiancé."

It felt as if Rico moved in slow motion. Not to return Marcus's handshake. But to slide his gaze toward her. That glare could remove not only the rust but also the metal beneath it.

"And you are?" Marcus asked Rico.

The corner of Rico's mouth hitched, letting her know he was about to dish out some crap. "I'm Rico Callahan. I'm Natalie's husband."

CHAPTER THREE

"I CAN EXPLAIN," Natalie jumped to say.

Rico seriously doubted that. Hell in a handbasket. She'd come here wearing that outfit, kissing him, and all the while she'd been engaged.

"He's not my fiancé," she said to Rico, then snapped toward Marcus. "And what are you doing here?"

Her sharp tone and explosive look didn't deter the blond-haired lover boy. He smiled as if this were as right as rain and leaned in to kiss her. His smack landed on her cheek, and Natalie's hand landed on his chest.

"You're her ex-husband," Marcus corrected, and he put a lot of emphasis on the *ex* part.

Obviously, Marcus was clueless. Probably an idiot, too. Rico was about to set him straight, but Natalie spoke before he could say anything.

"Why? Are? You? Here?" she repeated to Marcus, but this time it was more of a snarl than a snap.

Marcus shrugged. "Your assistant said you were coming to Spring Hill, and I thought it was my chance to see the town where you grew up."

She made a circling motion with her fingers when

he paused. "And how did you know I'd be here at the McCord Ranch?"

Another shrug, but this one didn't look as casual as the first. That might have had something to do with the fact that Rico slid his arm around Natalie. Lover Boy's forehead bunched up.

"Uh, what's going on?" Marcus asked. "I mean, it's one thing to come and see your ex, but it's another thing for him to say he's your husband. And for him to be holding you like that."

"I am her husband," Rico answered. Yeah, it was downright petty, but she deserved some payback for that blasted kiss.

Marcus huffed, and his hands went on his hips. "Natalie, is there something you want to tell me?"

"No." But then she was the one who huffed. She also glanced around as if to make sure no one could hear this. "The paperwork got screwed up, and Rico and I have to refile for the divorce. That's where we're headed now."

Marcus's mouth didn't drop open, but it was close. He certainly looked as if someone had knocked him upside the head with a shovel. Rico knew the feeling because he'd been hit, too.

"So, is this guy your fiancé or not?" Rico asked her. "Because that seems a little like semi-bigamy to be married to me while engaged to him." He didn't bother taking the stank off the *him* and the look he gave Lover Boy.

"No, he's not." Natalie repeated it when she turned to Rico. "He's my ex-fiancé."

That didn't sweeten things for Rico much at all.

Of course, nothing was going to seem sweet at the moment. Except for another kiss.

And he wanted to neuter himself for even letting that thought pop into his head.

"But it's only a matter of time before we make things right again," Marcus went on. He somehow managed to scrounge up a smile even though this sure as hell wasn't a smiling situation. "It's what Natalie's father wants."

That put an end to any further thoughts about kissing.

"Your daddy wants you to marry this guy?" Rico asked, but he didn't bother listening for an answer.

Of course Dermott Landon wanted his princess to marry someone like this. Someone who wore a suit that cost more than a prize-winning Angus bull at the state fair. Someone who didn't smell as if he'd just shoveled up what the bull had left in the holding pen.

"I think it's a good idea if we go ahead and meet with the lawyer," Natalie said, though he wasn't sure how she could speak with her jaw that tight. "Marcus, don't say a word about this to anyone. We'll talk when I get back to Austin."

Rico was betting that chat would happen as soon as humanly possible because she practically ran to his truck. Well, she ran until those heels spiked into the soft ground, and she got stuck. She flailed around like the rubber inflatable air dancer outside the used-car dealership.

Marcus moved as if planning to help her, but that would only cost them more time. Of course, Natalie and he had ended their marriage twelve years ago, but it suddenly seemed urgent to Rico to end it again—officially.

"Natalie, are you sure you don't want me to go with you?" Marcus called out.

"Positive. I'm so sorry," she added to Rico when he was closer to her.

Again, in the time-saving vein, he scooped her up and carried her to his truck. Probably not the best idea he'd ever had, since it squished her left breast against his chest and her butt against his arms. But sadly, it wasn't the worst idea he'd had, either.

And the worst ideas just kept coming.

When he deposited Natalie on the truck seat, he saw several things he didn't want to see. First, her bra when the side of her top slipped down. Not the barely there things she used to wear, but even a granny-bra glimpse from Natalie fired his blood. However, the firing didn't last because the other glimpse was of her eyes before she put on those sunglasses.

She was crying.

Crap.

He hated seeing a woman cry. Any woman. It kicked at his old baggage and reminded him of seeing his mother cry after his dad had walked out on them. Rico never considered himself the warm-and-fuzzy type, but a woman's tears—especially this woman— could bring him to his knees.

"I keep screwing up," she said. There was a sob in the middle of that, and it was obvious she was trying to put a quick end to the boohooing.

She was failing, though.

Rico grabbed a tissue from the glove compartment,

buckled her in and drove off. No need for Lover Boy or anyone else to witness Natalie's meltdown. It was going to be hard enough to put a lid on the gossip as it was. When he got back, he'd need to threaten the hands with a good butt whipping if they breathed a word of what they'd seen or heard.

"I swear he's my ex," she went on after another sob. Her phone buzzed; she glanced at the screen and turned it off. "And yes, my father wants me to marry Marcus, but that doesn't mean I will."

Yeah, it did. Natalie had done pretty much everything her father had ever wanted, so she'd eventually give in. Once she'd divorced him, that is.

Rico didn't hurry. It was only a short drive to the lawyer's office, and he wanted to give Natalie a chance to compose herself. Ten minutes ago, he might not have cared if folks had seen her like this, but those tears changed everything.

And she noticed the change in him, too. He didn't want to know how bad his expression must have been for her to notice that.

"Oh, God. I'm sorry," she said, yanking off the shades and wiping her eyes. "I know you hate these tears. Your mother," she added in a mumble.

He was surprised that she'd remembered. Equally surprised that he'd told her in the first place. She was the only person who knew, and it rankled him that her remembering could hook into his emotions. Thankfully, he got an eyeful of something to help with that.

The rest of her underwear.

Her skirt had ridden up, and he could see that she wasn't wearing some kind of granny panties after all but rather something that resembled thin, mesh bicycle shorts. They stopped just above midthigh, high enough for him not to have seen them when the breeze had fluttered her skirt.

"Oh, God," she repeated when she followed his glance. She fixed her skirt. Frowned. And it seemed to help with the tears. It didn't help with her anger, though. She got a new dose of that. "I've put on weight, all right?" she snapped.

"Okay," he answered after a long pause. He wasn't sure whether to say the extra pounds looked good on her—they did—so he decided it was a good time to keep his mouth shut.

"Stress," she went on. "And chocolate to help with the stress. I went riding this morning, and my mare groaned when I climbed into the saddle."

The laugh came before he could stop it. Sweet merciful heaven, he should have stopped it because it made her smile, and it was a moment he didn't want to share with her.

"We'll get this over with fast," he grumbled.

But it obviously wasn't what she'd wanted to hear because her mouth turned downward. "I know you think I'm spineless," she went on. "But I have my reasons for most of what I've done."

"You have a reason for accepting Marcus's proposal in the first place? Because you must have accepted if he's now your ex."

She stayed quiet a moment. And the moment turned to several moments before Rico realized she wasn't going to answer. Natalie just pinned her attention to the window and watched as he drove down

Main Street. Not that there was anything for her to see, really. Other than Logan converting the old Victorian inn into an office building and loft, the town had pretty much stayed the same.

So, her silence was his answer. She probably had loved Marcus. Maybe still did. And maybe she'd broken things off with him when she'd realized she was still married. Well, Rico was about to remedy that.

He pulled to a stop in front of the lawyer's office, gave Natalie a moment to powder her nose. Another moment to make sure her underwear was all out of sight. Good thing, too, because the moment they stepped into Bernie's office, they came face-to-face with one of the biggest gossips in Spring Hill.

Wilhelmina Larkin, Bernie's receptionist.

Rico figured he stood no chance of getting Wilhelmina to agree to secrecy, so he took a different angle. "Did I hear that you have a date with Hank?" he asked the woman. Hank was one of the hands at the McCord Ranch.

She blushed. The reaction he wanted. "He told you."

Not really. Rico had heard Hank's side of the conversation when Wilhelmina had called the man to make the date. Hank hadn't actually wanted to go, but Rico planned to keep that to himself.

The blushing didn't last long, and Wilhelmina's attention quickly landed on Natalie. Oh, no. The questions were about to come. Questions about why they were there and why Natalie had been crying.

But there no questions.

Hell. That meant Wilhelmina knew. So much for Natalie telling Bernie to keep this quiet.

"Don't you two look so good standing there together," Wilhelmina went on. "So much better than Rico's last girlfriend. She was a cocktail waitress from one of those bars in San Antonio where the girls wear next to nothing." She lowered her voice as if telling a secret.

Of course, it wasn't anywhere near a secret. Everyone in town knew he'd gone out with a woman whose uniform included a tank top and skintight orange shorts. Well, apparently everyone knew that but Natalie. She gave him a funny look. Not jealousy exactly, but she seemed to be questioning his choice in women. Well, he gave her a look right back, questioning her taste in men like Marcus.

"It was one date," Rico clarified, though he wasn't sure why he needed to explain.

"Well, it was more than once with Shari Deever," Wilhelmina corrected. She turned back to Natalie and lowered her voice again. "She's the kindergarten teacher at the elementary school. They dated for nearly a year before Shari broke off things. Word has it that she figured out that Rico just wasn't ever going to settle down. And there was the problem with his laundry detergent."

Rico cursed. Good grief. He was about to cut Wilhelmina off, but the woman just kept running on like a dentist's drill that'd gotten stuck. And was just as annoying.

"Shari got a rash whenever she'd sleep on Rico's sheets," Wilhelmina provided. And her gaze combed over Natalie as if she expected to see a rash on her exposed body parts.

Wilhelmina continued with the stuck-drill chatting pace. "Rico was accommodating and changed detergents, but Shari just kept on getting a rash. Personally, I think it's because she knew he wasn't right for her." Wilhelmina smiled. "I think the only woman right for him is the one standing beside him now."

Judging from Wilhelmina's widening smile, she thought that would please them. It didn't.

"Uh, Bernie is expecting us," Natalie threw out there.

Wilhelmina nodded. Glanced around as if expecting someone else in the room to respond to that. But there was no one else. "Bernie's over at the courthouse. There's a problem, and he said I was to tell you two things."

Rico went with another mental *Hell* and waited for Wilhelmina to continue.

"You know Spring Hill has one of the lowest divorce rates in the state?" Wilhelmina asked. She didn't wait for an answer, but yes, Rico knew. It was one of the brags the mayor threw out every year at the town's annual picnic.

Rico huffed. "Is there a reason you're mentioning that?" Because he hoped like the devil that Bernie and Wilhelmina weren't going to try to talk Natalie and him out of this.

"Ruby Fay Barker's been working as the district clerk for the county for going on twenty years now, and she's from right here in Spring Hill," the woman continued. "Well, she has a problem with divorce since she wants to keep up the town's reputation." Her mouth tightened. "Personally, she's a busybody who puts her nose in all kinds of places." She paused. "And this time she put her nose in your place."

Rico definitely didn't want Ruby Fay's nose in any place of his, and he thought he knew where this was going. "Is Ruby Fay responsible for a judge not signing some paperwork Natalie and I filed?"

Wilhelmina nodded. "Yours and apparently several others. That's why Bernie's over there now. There'll be an investigation. Ruby Lee might go to jail."

Rico wasn't sure who groaned louder, Natalie or him. Because this didn't sound like the speedy start to a divorce.

"Can Rico and I at least get the papers Bernie drew up for us?" Natalie asked. "Then we can sign them and file them with whoever's replacing Ruby Lee."

Wilhelmina was shaking her head before Natalie even finished. "No paperwork'll be going through until the cops figure out just how deep this goes. Bernie said he'll give you a call as soon as he knows something. But I gotta warn you. They're bringing in the Texas Rangers to investigate. Maybe even the state attorney general. This is going to be even bigger news than when you two eloped."

It wasn't just the delay that had Rico groaning. It was the fact that there was no way Natalie was going to get her wish about keeping this a secret.

"You should go ahead and call your father," Rico suggested. "Before he hears it from anyone else."

Natalie nodded, looked as if she'd rather walk barefoot with her already-sore feet through Lego blocks but she took out her phone.

"Are you about to call Dermott?" Wilhelmina asked. "Because if so, there's no need. That's the second thing I'm supposed to tell you. Your daddy's waiting for you in Bernie's office."

CHAPTER FOUR

NATALIE THOUGHT SHE might be able to hear a whistle. The one from the freight train that was about to smash into her.

Good grief. This was exactly what she had been trying to avoid.

She debated what to do. Running was out of the question. Not only because it would be cowardly but also because she wouldn't get ten feet in the shoes she'd chosen for this occasion. Her toes were numb now and in possible need of amputation. Plus, running in the body-shaping panties would create so much friction that she might light her thighs on fire. There was only one thing to do.

Suck it up and seize the bull by the horns.

However, that didn't mean Rico had to deal with the bull or his horns.

"I'll take care of this," she told him. "You can go ahead back to the ranch."

Judging from the way Rico looked at her, she might as well have suggested that he wear a thong made of sandpaper. Natalie considered arguing, but she decided to save her breath for the real argument that was about to come with her father. Of course, she stood little chance of winning that one, either.

"Bernie's office is that way," Wilhelmina said, pointing up the hall.

Natalie dragged in a long breath, wishing she had time for a strong margarita, and she headed there. Rico was right behind her and even passed her up along the way. That meant another body bump from him as he slid around her, and despite the circumstances, it gave her a cheap thrill. It was also a reminder that in the future, she probably needed a more appropriate way to get her cheap thrills.

The door was already open, so when she walked into the room, she spotted her father right away. He was an imposing man, looking a little like Brando as Vito Corleone in *The Godfather*. Sometimes, he acted that way, too, making those offers that people just couldn't seem to refuse. Her father had a way of, well, getting his way.

She wasn't sure what kind of reaction she'd get from him, but Natalie was rendered speechless when he went to her and kissed her cheek. Then he took her by the shoulders and gave her a loving, supportive look.

"I'm sorry," he said. "We'll get this all sorted out." Then he turned to Rico. "That *I'm sorry* extends to you, too. This must be upsetting."

Natalie waited for the other shoe to drop. But apparently this wasn't going to be a shoe-dropping kind of moment. The loving look stayed on her father's face.

Unlike Rico's.

No loving look for him. He was as suspicious as she was. That probably had something to do with the last time he'd seen her father. There'd been heated words hurled around. Like *no way in hell will you stay married to my daughter*. Other things had been said like *white trash, gold digger, cowboy loser* and *hot*. Of course, Natalie had been the only one who'd used the *hot*. Because it was true.

Hot had been enough argument for her to stand up to her father. Not her mother, though.

"How'd you find out the divorce hadn't gone through?" Rico asked her father.

"I overheard Natalie's phone conversation with Bernie. It was by accident, I promise," he quickly added to her.

Maybe. But even if it wasn't, it didn't matter. He knew, and that rid her of one less clown in this particular circus. She would have had to tell him eventually, and he was taking it far better than she'd ever expected.

"I checked to make sure you hadn't remarried," her father continued, speaking to Rico again. "Good thing you hadn't or what a mess that would have been. It's the same for Natalie. She was within a breath of saying 'I do' to Marcus. When she called it off, I thought she'd lost her mind, but I can see now that it was for the best."

And now the other shoe would drop.

It didn't take long.

"Marcus and Natalie are perfect together." Her father volleyed his gaze to both of them when he said that. Then he shrugged. "Of course, you both know you were wrong for each other, so I'm preaching to the choir."

If her father had seen that kiss earlier, he might believe the choir needed a longer sermon. But yes, she did know that she and Rico were wrong for each other. Just not the way her father meant.

The images of her mother came, giving Natalie a sucker punch of emotion that she didn't need. She was already battling enough and tried to push those memories aside.

"Are you okay?" Rico asked.

It took her a moment to realize the question was for her. Those damn memories had leaked through again, and he could no doubt see them on her face. She quickly tried to right her expression.

"I'm fine," she lied. Rico probably saw through the lie. Apparently intense physical attraction had an ESP side effect.

Her father continued looking at them, as if trying to figure out what wasn't being said here. He also likely decided those were things he didn't want to know. Instead, he took something from Bernie's desk.

"I had Bernie go ahead and finish the papers," her father explained. "I paid him, too, so there'd be no reason for you to have future dealings with him. You can file for the divorce in Austin."

Well, there was a third shoe dropping, and it sounded more like a steel-toed combat boot in her head. Her father was taking charge, the way he always did. He handed her the papers.

A pen, too.

"You can both sign them now, and I'll drop them off for you," he added.

She looked at Rico. He looked at her. And after

all the looking, Rico shook his head. "I want to read the papers first, just to know what I'm signing. My lawyer should also take a look at them."

Her father didn't seem so happy with that. "Your lawyer? Why would a ranch hand need a lawyer?"

"Because I own property. Because I have investments, a decent income. I need to make sure that's all protected."

Natalie could have kissed him again. Not because she didn't plan on signing the papers. She did. But she wanted to sign them on her own terms, not her father's.

"Anything that you own is a drop in the bucket compared to Natalie's net worth," her father growled. And yes, it was a growl.

Rico shrugged. "I still want to hear what my lawyer has to say."

She could have sworn little lightning bolts zinged through her father's eyes. He turned to her, probably expecting her to force Rico's hand on this. Since she was feeling raw, squeezed and congested from the crying, Natalie had to dig deep to find her backbone. It was something she frequently had to do with her father.

"I can wait until Rico's had a chance to do whatever he needs to do with the papers," she said.

More lightning bolts in her father's eyes, and even though she hadn't noticed it before, a scowling jowl just wasn't very attractive. "Fine." He stretched the word out through semiclenched teeth. "Then you come with me while he does that. I'll give you a ride home."

"Natalie's car is at the McCord Ranch," Rico spoke up. "She can't leave it there because it's blocking the driveway."

The driveway was large enough for twelve cars, so Rico had just lied to her father. Good. She wasn't sure she could find her backbone again right away and needed some breathing room.

The jowls reacted, tightening, but her father must have realized this wasn't a battle worth fighting because he gave a crisp nod. "Fine, then." The crispness stayed in place when he turned to her. "I've got meetings all afternoon, but I'll be home at six. I'll expect you to come for dinner. I also expect the papers to be signed by then. You can call your mother afterward and have a nice chat."

Rico and she stood there, watching her father walk out after delivering that decree. If she didn't show, there wouldn't be a horse's head in her bed in the vein of Vito Corleone, but he could play the guilt card.

And would.

Too bad the guilt card—aka her mother—worked. So, the bottom line was that she would indeed show for dinner. First, though, she needed some steeling up.

"I could use a margarita," she said. "A strong one."

Rico glanced at his watch, frowned. "It's not even two o'clock yet." That seemed to be a reminder that it was too early for alcohol. It was, but then he shrugged. "Come on. I could use one, too."

TAKING NATALIE TO his house wouldn't be too big of a mistake. But the moment Rico thought that, he had to frown. It was a sad day when a man started lying to himself.

Of course it was a mistake.

A whopper, really, but they both did need a drink, and Calhoun's Pub wouldn't be open for hours. That left him with either getting the bottled margarita cocktails from the convenience store/gas station or making them at his house. Since he figured they'd be spotted in the parking lot—which would only fuel the gossip—the house option was the lesser of all evils.

Natalie stepped into the house, taking off her shoes first and then looking around. She'd come here a couple of times when it'd still belonged to his grandparents, but it had been pretty much a wreck then. He'd remodeled it from top to bottom. It wasn't grand like her daddy's house, which seemed all marble and glass. Rico had kept the original hardwood floors and the pine ceiling beams.

"Very nice," she said, not sounding surprised. Which pleased him.

He hadn't wanted her to think he'd been lying to her father about having property. Especially since he'd lied to the man about having a lawyer. As a general rule, ranch hands didn't need lawyers.

"The kitchen's this way." He led her in that direction, and she repeated her *very nice* as she ran her fingers over the butcher-block countertop. That was also where she placed the divorce papers, right next to the stove. "I'll mix us up a drink and then I can take you back to the ranch for your car."

Of course, when he returned to work he'd have to listen to the jokes about him and Natalie stepping out for an afternoon delight. The jokes would be raunchier when coupled with the news that they weren't really divorced. No way would Wilhelmina let that stay quiet for long.

He took out the mixings, his gaze meeting Natalie's, and he saw something in her eyes. Literally. They were watering.

"Are you, uh, crying?" he asked.

"No." She dropped her shoes on the floor and pulled at the waist of her skirt. "It's this body-shaping underwear I have on. They're called Skinnies. Because you feel as if you've been skinned when you take it off. Anyway, I thought I'd only have it on for about two hours or so, which is my max level of tolerance for it." She paused. "I want to take it off."

Now, normally this would have been something a man would love to hear. But nothing about this was normal.

"I don't have any spare underwear with me, but I was hoping you could lend me a pair of boxers," Natalie added.

For some stupid reason the thought of her getting into his boxers gave him a hard-on. Or maybe that was just the idea of her stripping down while under the same roof with him.

"Sure," Rico said. Not easily. But he finally managed to get out the words. He also kept the lower half of his body hidden behind the counter. "I can get you a pair."

"No, just point me in the right direction. I'll find them. I need you to get started on those drinks."

Sadly, he understood that particular need and

hoped in this case that tequila would soften him up a bit. In more ways than one.

Rico pointed toward his bedroom. "There are boxers in the top drawer of the dresser. And socks." Because he doubted she wanted to put those painful-looking shoes back on until it was time to go.

Which should be soon.

Rico figured that three drinks would do it. Two for her, one for him, and then if he gave her some food, she'd still be good to drive in a couple of hours. He'd be good for work as well since he wanted to check on that livestock delivery.

He put the margaritas in the blender, took out some eggs to scramble. Not exactly the meal of champions, but eggs wouldn't test the limits of his cooking skills. He put some bread in the toaster while he was at it.

"I'm thinking about burning these Skinnies," he heard Natalie say.

He looked up. And he was sure his tongue landed on the floor. Crap. He was in trouble here.

Natalie had put on his cotton boxers and a pair of his gray socks. She'd also taken off her skirt. The boxers covered a lot since they hit her just below midthigh, but the fabric clung to her curves as if holding on for dear life.

Rico knew how the cotton felt.

He was clinging to the spatula he was using to scramble the eggs. Clinging to his eyeballs to keep them in his head. Also attempting to cling to his will-power.

"I know," she said, looking down at the garb. "It's not the dress-to-impress outfit I showed up in."

She took off her earrings and watch as well and slipped them into her purse. Apparently, they weren't comfortable, either.

"This will give me an hour or two before I have to regear and go home," she added. "I tried putting the skirt on over the boxers, but it just bunched up everything."

Then she noticed that he was staring at her.

"Is this too much? Did I overstep the limits of your offer to make me a drink? And eggs," she added, glancing into the kitchen. "And toast."

"You didn't overstep anything," he mumbled, and Rico forced himself to turn around and take the eggs from the skillet before they burned to a crisp.

Natalie came up behind him and searched the cabinets for glasses. She found mason jars and filled them with the margaritas. She started in on hers, and since she seemed determined to finish it as quickly as possible, Rico dished her up some of the eggs and toast.

She didn't touch the food, but she carried her margarita to the floor-to-ceiling windows that flanked the stone fireplace. The windows had a good view of the creek and the surrounding woods. Just as Rico had designed it.

"I can see your handiwork in every part of this house," Natalie said. "I can see *you.*"

It was the best compliment anyone could have paid him. Funny that it'd come from his ex. Well, his wife who should have been his ex had it not been for a judgmental county clerk.

"You brought me here that night you fixed my flat tire," she continued. She kept her back to him. Kept sipping the margarita. "Because I was soaking wet and didn't want to go home like that. Your grandparents were asleep, so we had to be quiet. And you lit a fire. In the fireplace," she amended.

When she looked at him over her shoulder, he could see something he didn't want to see. More of her thigh, for one thing. And a smile. The wrong kind of smile because they weren't talking about fireplace heat right now.

She turned slowly and walked toward him. With the backdrop of the windows and the Mason jar dangling from her hand, she made a picture.

A bad one.

Because that wasn't a princess look in her eyes. That was the naughty-cowgirl-in-boxer-shorts look.

"Natalie," he warned her, and since he was damn certain he was going to need it, he downed some of his own margarita.

He did need it.

Because when she got closer, he knew she was going to kiss him. Rico did something about that. By kissing her first.

Yeah, this was a thousand gallons of stupid, but that didn't stop him. Nope. He just slid his hand around her nicely curved butt, hauled her to him and kept on kissing her. It was scalding, of course, until some of her margarita spilled on him. It gave him a jolt and should have knocked some sense into him.

It didn't.

Rico continued kissing her, hard and deep, just the way he liked both kisses and sex. It must have been the way she liked kisses, too, because Natalie practically threw the margarita glass onto the counter. Did the same to his when she wrenched it from his left hand. And she coiled her arms around him, pulling him right smack-dab against her. All in all, it was a good place to be.

She made a sound of pleasure that fired him up even more. Not that he needed any more firing. She was doing a good enough job with her breasts pressed against his chest and her leg sliding against his.

It didn't take long for them to start jockeying for position. Trying to get closer. Trying to deepen the kiss even more. Trying to do something to relieve the heat and the need. Which really shouldn't happen.

Rico repeated that.

Repeated it again.

Then he cursed when he tore himself from her.

"Natalie, this could muddy some waters that need to stay clear," he reminded her.

She stared at him. Her breath gusting. Her breasts reacting to those gusts. His body reacting to her re-actions.

"You're right," she said.

So, that was it. They were stopping. No ex sex or one last hookup before they filed for the divorce again. Natalie was going to do the sensible thing here. That was why it shocked Rico when he didn't.

Hell.

"I'm all up for a little mud," Rico drawled, and he snapped her right back to him.

CHAPTER FIVE

NATALIE HAD SEEN the last kiss coming, but she still hadn't been ready for it. Certainly hadn't been ready for that rush of fire to any and all parts of her body. Leave it to Rico to have her feeling that heat all the way down to her toes.

Her lady place had the most feeling of all, though. And it wanted to feel even more. Thankfully, Rico knew how to give *more* because he caught on to the back of her knee, lifting her leg until their bodies were aligned in the best possible way to make her want to finish this. That could happen in the bedroom or right here on the kitchen counter. Location was irrelevant.

But Rico stopped. And he blinked as if trying to focus. "How much is that margarita playing into this?" he asked.

"Zero." Her head was spinning a little, but Natalie was pretty sure that was from the kiss. From the touching, too. Rico gave her a little nudge with his erection that had her seeing double.

He made a sound that seemed as if he wasn't quite buying that. He also gave her a skeptical look to go along with that sound and continued to stare down at her.

"Don't overthink this," she insisted. Natalie certainly had no plans for that. Yes, the divorce papers were just a few feet away. Papers that they needed to sign, but if they had sex, then…

Heck, she was overthinking this.

To remedy that, she kissed him again. Really kissed him. She added some body nudges, too, and just in case he was still able to think straight, she slid her hand down into his jeans. That took care of the skeptical look and sound. Took care of her overthinking, too, because she took hold of what would put a great finish to all of this foreplay.

Rico cursed, turned her and pinned her against the counter. What he didn't do was let her keep her hand in his jeans. Natalie was about to protest, but he yanked down her boxers and put his own hand to good use. His fingers sank into her while he continued to deliver some of those wildfire kisses. Not just to her mouth, but to her neck.

Then her naked breasts.

Rico had absolutely no trouble locating them. He'd somehow managed to shove up her top, pull down her bra and lower his head to her nipples, all without stopping his magic fingers. It was perfect.

Almost.

Even though the pleasure was making her senseless, she still figured out a way to get her hand in his jeans again. "This would work even better than your fingers," she pointed out.

He grunted, that painful pleasure sound of a man who was aware she'd just stated the obvious. Rico knew very well what to do with that particular man-part of his.

"This will take the edge off so you can think straight," he said. Whatever the heck that meant. Natalie wanted the full Rico treatment. Every hard inch of him.

He moved her hand away again. She opened her mouth to protest, got a French kiss instead. It not only hushed her, but it also gave Rico's fingers enough time to make her incapable of protesting even if her mouth hadn't been otherwise occupied.

Natalie came so hard and fast that her legs buckled. It was nothing like mere fireworks when she was with Rico. It was more like a solar system exploding. It wracked through every nerve, every part of her. Thankfully, Rico held her in place, pinning her not only with his hand but with his erection right behind his hand.

"The edge is off," Natalie managed to say when she could remember how to breathe. She pushed his hand away so they could rebuild that edge with what he had behind his zipper.

Once more, he stopped her. Despite the amazing orgasm that was still rippling through her, Natalie scowled.

"You know you want this," she said.

"Yeah," he verified right away. "But what I don't want is for you to have so many regrets about this that it'll make you cry. I especially don't want you to do that when there's any chance the tequila might be calling the shots here. Because tequila is rarely a good shot-caller."

Since her mind was still clouded with lust, it was hard to come up with a logical response to that. "I might cry if I don't have real sex with you." It was a bluff, of course, but she was still feeling a little desperate.

Looking very pained, he took her by the shoulders, moved her away from him and then fixed her clothes. Natalie didn't want her clothes fixed. She didn't want to talk. She wanted sex.

But Rico brushed a very chaste kiss on her mouth and headed in the direction of his bedroom. Natalie was about to follow him, but she soon realized Rico hadn't exactly issued her an invitation.

He shut the bedroom door.

And he locked it.

RICO TOOK A shower. A cold one. So cold that he felt like a block of ice, but even that might not be enough.

What the hell had he done?

Clearly, he hadn't learned anything from his breakup with Natalie, and he had rocks in his head. Rocks in his nether region, too, since he was still hard even after all that cold water. Despite the hardness, and the ache—man, the ache was bad—he got dressed and forced himself to go back out there and face her. It was time to discuss those divorce papers and sign them so they could both get on with their lives.

He practiced a little of what he was going to say to her. Then forgot every single word of it when he ran right into her as he came out of his bedroom. Suddenly, she was in his arms again and plastered against his body. Rico would have remedied that if she hadn't held on.

"Just listen to me," she said. But she didn't say anything. Not right away. Natalie stood there, her arms wrapped around him, their gazes connected. The lower part of her body was connected to his permanent erection, too.

An erection that she noticed because she glanced down between them.

That slow, evil ride-'em-cowgirl smile appeared again. "I can fix that."

Yes, he was very familiar with Natalie's means of fixing. But as much as he wanted to take her up on the offer, Rico shook his head. "We need to talk," he insisted.

She groaned, the smile vanished, and probably as a way of punishing him, she stepped to the side, the pressure of her body so well-placed that he damn near came. Her smile returned, but she kept it brief, no doubt because she knew he wanted to ring her neck right about now.

"So, no real ex sex?" she asked.

Rico hesitated. He shouldn't have. Because it got her mouth moving as if she were ready to smile again. And reach for his zipper.

"You know you'll regret this," he started. "Because you'll sign those papers, marry Marcus and be the good girl that your daddy wants."

Obviously, he hadn't practiced that enough. It sounded mean, mean enough to make Natalie look away from him. She mumbled something he didn't catch and went back to the kitchen for her margarita.

That was when he noticed she'd practically finished the entire pint jar.

Hell.

She'd had even more than that because the blender was empty, too. Rico doubted that she'd poured it down the sink, which meant she wouldn't be going anywhere for a while longer.

"What if I don't regret it?" she asked.

Good question. He didn't have much of a good answer. "Is that the margarita still talking?"

She shook her head. "I didn't regret it before I even started it."

"But you will." He grabbed his own margarita and went to the sofa. "Obviously, you've got some things to work out." One of those things immediately popped into his mind. "Earlier at the ranch, you said you just needed for someone to find you attractive again. What the heck was that all about?"

Natalie lifted her shoulder, followed him into the living room, but she didn't sit next to him. She took the chair across from him. "Marcus doesn't come right out and say it, but he's always hinting that he wants me to lose some weight."

"What?" And in his head, he didn't just say that word. Rico yelled it. Not that he'd needed any evidence that Marcus was a dunderhead, but that proved it. "Screw him. Not literally. But tell him to screw himself. You look great."

She frowned. "That's your erection talking."

"Maybe, but my eyes agree with it."

His mouth did, too. But yes, his hard-on did have a say in this. Always would when it came to Natalie.

Because no matter how rocky their past, the attraction just walked right over those rocks and found its way into his boxers. Just as Natalie had done.

Now that Rico was satisfied there was no way Natalie should marry her daddy's choice in mates, he went on to the next thing that was bothering him. "While we were in Bernie's office, your expression changed when your father mentioned your mother."

Natalie didn't exactly skitter away from him, but it was close. She got up from the chair and walked over to the windows. She stood there with her back to him.

"Sorry," he said. "Is that off-limits?" Rico didn't wait for her to confirm that. "But the rumor mill says that your mom left your dad, and you, because you married me."

She didn't confirm that, either. In fact, she stayed quiet for so long that he thought maybe she was ready to leave. Not dressed like that, of course. And not while still sipping that margarita, but she wasn't thinking straight, so there was no telling what was going through her head right now.

"I messed up a lot before you," she finally said. "I made some very bad choices. I got arrested for underage drinking. I got suspended from school for skipping. I sneaked out of the house—many times to meet you."

He knew all about that, even the parts that hadn't personally involved him. Small town, big mouths. "Hell, half of Spring Hill has been in trouble for things like that or worse."

"Half the town doesn't have my parents." She let that hang in the air for several long seconds, and even though he still couldn't see her face, he could have sworn her shoulders slumped.

Rico wanted some air clearing, but this didn't feel right. Not after the against-the-counter hand job.

"My mother didn't just leave Spring Hill," Natalie finally said. "She tried to kill herself. Sleeping pills. And that happened because I sent her over the edge."

Rico could have sworn his heart skipped a couple of beats. "She did that because we got married?"

Natalie shrugged. "It didn't help. She was already...delicate. And I kept getting into trouble. For her, public appearance was everything even if it was a facade. When the facade was gone, she just couldn't handle it."

Things suddenly became a whole lot clearer. "So, that's how your father has kept you in line all these years."

She didn't deny it. "My mother is in a mental hospital just outside of Austin. Of course, it's top notch, more of a country spa with lots of daily therapy. She has no intention of leaving—ever."

Well, hell. Rico had wanted to know. And now he did. But how the devil was he supposed to deal with this?

"Are you okay?" It was something he wished he'd asked a whole lot sooner.

"Yes." She nodded, repeated it. Natalie even scrounged up a smile. "I can't fix the situation with my mother, but at least I've worked out some things in the last hour or so. I'm not losing weight. I'm burning those Skinnies. And I'm buying some comfortable shoes."

Rico made a sound of approval. All of those were good, but that issue with her mother would always be a dark cloud. And in their case, that dark cloud was hanging right over their heads.

"I'm also going to tell Marcus that I can never marry him," she went on. "That way, he can get on with his life and find someone thinner who's right for him."

He made a sound of approval to that, too.

Natalie made a corresponding sound and continued, "Of course, I'll have to make my father understand, as well. Because I've messed up so many things, he thinks he knows what's best for me. But he doesn't." She paused again. "One final thing. I want to have sex with you."

Rico made another sound of approval before those last words sank into his head. A head he was already shaking.

"Muddy waters," he reminded her. Because while she wasn't marrying Marcus, that didn't mean she'd stay married to *him*.

And Rico wasn't sure he wanted that anyway.

"You'll always be daddy's princess," he added. "I'll always be a ranch hand."

He frowned. Because he wasn't just a ranch hand. He was in charge of managing the other ranch hands for one of the most profitable cattle brokers in the state. And Natalie was more than just a princess. She was apparently a capable businesswoman with questionable taste in undergarments.

Unlike before, she didn't come to him, so Rico got up and went to her. He turned her around so he could tell her to her face exactly what she didn't want to hear.

She tipped her head to the papers. "I'll sign them. I'll even file them. But I want one last afternoon with you."

He doubted she was talking about margaritas and scrambled eggs, either. No. This was about what they'd been skirting around since she'd stepped from her car at the ranch.

Even though Rico was pretty sure this was a mistake, he no longer cared. He pulled Natalie to him and started something that he intended to finish. And not just do a half-assed job, either.

Rico intended to finish this the right way.

CHAPTER SIX

DESPITE WHAT RICO had just told himself, *the right way* got off to a wrong start.

He lowered his head to kiss Natalie at the same moment that she raised hers to kiss him. Their faces sort of collided, her cheekbone slamming into his nose. It felt as if a boxer wearing iron gloves had punched him.

Rico probably would have disgraced himself by howling in pain if Natalie hadn't followed through on the kiss. It only took a few seconds of her mouth on his to cure the pain. It cured other things, too, like any remaining doubt and common sense. But then, he'd never had much common sense when it came to Natalie.

She slipped right into his arms. And into the kiss. Of course, it didn't just stay a kiss, either. Not with their bodies already pressed against each other. Since there weren't any condoms in this part of the house, Rico scooped up Natalie and headed toward his bedroom.

Rico got another jolt of pain when he slammed his shoulder into the doorjamb. He wasn't usually this awkward with sex, but the stakes suddenly seemed sky-high.

Like maybe this would be the last time he'd ever be with Natalie.

That froze him for a moment. Because it was true. This would almost certainly be a onetime deal. It should have been a whopping red flag flapping in the breeze. Not that he was opposed to onetime sex deals. In fact, he'd been a willing partner in them on several occasions. But it just didn't seem right when it came to Natalie.

That didn't stop him.

Mainly, though, because when they landed on the bed, Natalie immediately started trying to undress him. Or maybe she was trying to give him a hand job. It was hard to tell which. Either way, it was a huge distraction, and thoughts about onetime deals flew out of his head.

Rico stopped her undressing attempts by flipping her onto her back and pinning her hands to the bed. That way, he could kiss her neck, and her breasts, without the distraction of an imminent orgasm.

Man, she tasted good. Tasted *right*, too. There it was again, the word that kept finding its way into his lust-hazed mind. Since the word just kept coming, Rico made it his mantra, and he kissed her right, as well.

He circled her nipples with his tongue.

Natalie seemed to like that a lot because she called him a bad name and used her knee to slide against his crotch. All in all, that was right, too. For a couple of seconds anyway, but then it became too right and would have put a faster end to this if Rico hadn't stopped it. If this was going to be a onetime deal, then he wanted more than a blink of foreplay.

He flipped her again, this time with him on his back so that she wouldn't be able to give him a knee-job.

Bad idea.

Really bad.

Natalie pinned his arms to the bed, and with that naughty glint in her eyes, she went after his neck. It was a very sensitive spot for him. Not as sensitive as the spot she chose next. His chest. She yanked open his shirt and had a go at circling parts of him with her tongue, too. Rico gritted his teeth, tried to steel himself for the onslaught of sensations. He was winning.

Until her mouth went to the front of his jeans.

Except it was really the front of his boxers since Natalie had managed to get him unzipped. Yeah, there was a millimeter of cotton between him and her hot mouth, but Rico still felt it as if they were bare-assed naked.

Which happened next.

Foreplay sucked when it was time for sex, and he got his hands free so he could do another flip. So he could also strip off her clothes. Natalie laughed like a loon, battling his clothes as if this had turned into a race.

Rico won.

But that was only because his cowboy boots slowed her down. However, it did create an interesting body position with Natalie's head on his boxers while she tugged at the boots.

Rico didn't help her. He had his own chore to do.

While she wriggled him out of his jeans, he maneuvered himself to the nightstand and fished through the drawer to get a condom. By the time he opened the wrapper, Natalie had rid him of his boots, his jeans, his boxers.

And she kissed him in the best place.

Except it was wrong. Because he was already primed and ready to go, and her mouth would put a much-too-quick end to this. That meant more maneuvering, another flip with her on top of him. He barely got the condom on before she slid down onto him.

And the world tipped on it axis.

Yeah, he remembered this, but he still got that jolt of surprise. The word came again.

Right.

Sex was usually good, no matter the partner, but with Natalie, it was *r* word.

It was selfish of him to let her do all the work, but watching her was spellbinding along with mind-blowing. The way she looked when she slid against him. Her eyes partly closed. Her mouth partly open. And that little smile.

Maybe this was the *r* word for her, too.

Rico caught on to her hips. Not that she needed help. She knew exactly what to do. And even though he'd been the one to start this, Natalie was the one who finished it.

Natalie finished things for both of them.

NATALIE OPENED HER eyes. And she nearly screamed because she thought she'd gone blind. There was also a tingling sound in her ears.

Rico's bedroom was pitch-dark, not even a thread of light coming in through the curtains. That was when she realized there was no blindness involved. It was night. There wasn't anything wrong with her ears, either. It was raining on the house's tin roof. A relaxing sound under normal circumstances.

This wasn't normal.

She rolled over, checked the clock on Rico's night-stand—8:30 p.m. Where the heck had the day gone? She'd only intended to rest for a couple of minutes after their second round of sex. Instead, she'd crashed for hours.

Groaning, she got up. Or rather she tried to, but Rico just hooked his arm around her and pulled her back to him. Natalie didn't put up much of a fight. Though she should have. She should squeeze back into her clothes, have him drive her to the McCord Ranch so she could get her car and go home.

"It's late," she whispered. "And it's raining. I need to leave because it'll take me even longer to get back."

His response was to kiss her, the very thing that had started this afternoon marathon of sex. Natalie gave in to it for a moment longer, but as usual, oxygen became an issue. So did the burning attraction that just wouldn't cool down. She would have thought that three orgasms would have done the trick, but she still felt that "edge." Of course, that probably had something to do with having a butt-naked Rico next to her. Hard not to be edgy with a hot body like that around.

All those muscles.

Not from exercise in a gym, either. Rico had a cowboy's body chiseled from years of hard work.

Work that he hadn't been doing since he'd been in bed with her.

"Won't Logan be wondering where you are?" she asked.

"No. I texted him a couple of hours ago when I went to the bathroom. Lucky handled the livestock delivery." But then she felt his muscles tense. The very muscles she'd just been admiring. He sat up, flicked on the lamp. "But what about you? Shouldn't you be…somewhere?"

He meant home, where her father had demanded she be for dinner. Which she'd obviously missed. Even if she left at this very minute, it'd be after ten o'clock by the time she got back to Austin.

"I need to text my dad just so he won't worry." It wouldn't stop him from being pissed, though. That ship had already sailed.

She started to get up again, but like the other time, Rico kissed her. This one wasn't long and lingering. In fact, he cut it short, pulled back and looked at her.

Uh-oh.

Now that the lamp was on, she could see more than heat in his eyes. Natalie could see the questions. Well, one question anyway.

What now?

Natalie didn't have a clue. The sex had been great. Better than great. But she already knew from past experience that she couldn't build a marriage on that alone.

Especially not with Rico.

To build a marriage with him, she'd have to do the impossible and rewrite the past. Talk about a de-

pressing thought. It really killed the mood. Well, until
Rico kissed her again. Apparently, that was the way
he was going to deal with those questions in his eyes.
Temporarily anyway. He pulled back, gave her that
look again. So, Natalie just threw something out that
would help them with this gorilla in the room.

"You've got your wedding ring in the nightstand
drawer," she said. "I was surprised that you'd kept it
all these years."

It was as if his expression stuttered. "You looked
in my drawers?"

She lifted her shoulder. "Let's call it what it is. I
snooped. I felt the sheets, too, just to see if I was allergic to the detergent like the kindergarten teacher."

He groaned and was probably making a mental
note to hire a hit man for Wilhelmina. Bernie's secre-
tary just didn't have any boundaries. But then, neither
did she because she'd gone through his nightstand—
mainly to make sure he had some condoms. He had,
but just one. Natalie had then gone through his medicine cabinet to see if there were backups.

There had been.

Good thing, too, because they'd needed them.

"I'm betting you got rid of your wedding and engagement rings," he said.

That was a bet he'd lose. Well, sort of.

She felt around on the floor beside the bed and
came up with her top so she could show him the heart
pin. It looked silver, but it was actually white gold.

"My wedding band went missing, but I had a jew-
eler make the engagement ring into this," she explained.

Judging from the way Rico stared at her, he wanted more information. Like why the heck had she done that? And what did it mean?

Natalie was still trying to figure that out all these years later.

"I couldn't just give the ring away," she said. "Or toss it the way some people do. But it didn't seem right to wear it, either. If the wedding band had ever turned up, I would have had earrings or something made from it. But I looked everywhere and couldn't find it."

He kept staring at her.

"I wanted to keep them, all right?" Natalie snapped, and she realized she sounded pissed.

Which in a way she was.

She didn't like explaining that it had felt good to keep the ring, in some form or another, close to her. She definitely hadn't shoved it away in her nightstand drawer so that it was out of sight, out of mind.

"You wear the pin a lot?" he asked.

All the time. In fact, she told everyone it was her good-luck charm. "Whenever it matches my outfit," she said. Thankfully, it matched everything.

Rico stared at her a moment longer. Then he mumbled some very bad curse words and dropped his head back onto the pillow. "If the ring was important, why didn't you get in touch with me at least once during the past twelve years?"

"I did." Oh. This would lead to another confession. "I called you but would then hang up because I didn't know what to say." After all, there really wasn't much she could say. "I did that for a while, but then you changed your number."

"Because I thought I was getting crank calls. Your name wasn't on the caller ID."

"I used one of those disposable phones when I made the calls. My phone is part of the company's business accounts."

"And you didn't want your dad to see my number and know you'd contacted me," he finished for her. He cursed.

"Well, you didn't exactly call me," she argued.

He stayed quiet a moment. "No, but I did go to see you."

She practically snapped to attention. "When?"

A muscle flickered in his jaw. "About a year after you left. I drove to Austin and saw you walking out of your dad's office building with another guy."

Natalie shook her head, clearly not able to remember that specific time. She exited that building at least once a day.

"The guy was tall, looked like a body builder," Rico provided. Judging from the slightly narrowed eyes, he remembered it in nth detail. "He was wearing a bright blue suit."

"Trent," she quickly provided. "He's my assistant, and he's married with four daughters. Trust me, Trent and I weren't involved."

"He had his arm around you."

Natalie didn't have to think hard to recall why he would have done that. "I was having trouble walking in my heels." She huffed. "A year after I left, I wasn't ready to look at another man. I didn't get involved with Marcus until four years after that, and the truth is, I was never really involved. Sadly, Marcus is just another outfit that my dad wants me to have."

There it was. All spelled out. Her life without Rico. Of course, she was never really without him. Not in thought anyway. Since she was just now realizing that, it made her seem more than a little pathetic.

"Yeah, having sex with you today didn't muddy the waters at all," he snarled, his voice heavy with sarcasm.

"It doesn't have to," Natalie threw out there. Like the pin/ring discussion, he was clearly going to want a whole lot more.

More that she didn't have. But she did have an idea, one that would probably send his common sense into cardiac arrest.

"Why can't we just be sex buddies?" she asked. "We're obviously good at it. And it's not as if we're having sex with anyone else." Her own common sense stalled a little when she realized that might not be true. "Are you?"

He gave her the flat-look treatment. "No." Then huffed. "You really think we can have more sex and not screw up…things?"

He meant their lives. Their hearts, too.

Even with the stakes that high, Natalie nodded. Again, her decision was highly influenced by having a naked Rico just a few inches away from her. Those inches were too far, she decided, and she moved in for a kiss.

There were plenty of nice things about kissing Rico, but the best one was that it caused them to stop thinking. Natalie didn't want to think right now. She wanted to have him one more time before she had to go home. Rico seemed to be on the same page with that, and he pulled her down to him. All in all, a very good place to be.

Until Natalie heard the two sounds.

Sounds that she didn't want to hear.

First, there was a knock at the door. A very loud one. In fact, it wasn't a knock at all but more like a bang. That put a stop to their kissing. So did the voices that followed the banging.

"Natalie, we need to talk right now," her father called out.

Crap. Crap. Crap.

"Yes, we have to talk," Marcus piped up.

Both of them. Great. Natalie repeated a few more of those *craps* while she scrambled out of bed and hurried to dress. Rico got up as well, but not at the same breakneck speed she was moving. However, he was cursing under his breath.

Another bang on the door. Another shout from her father. Another plea from Marcus.

And then Natalie heard something that brought her breakneck pace to a full halt. Another voice. One that she certainly hadn't expected to hear.

"Natalie? Can I please come in?" the woman said.

Oh, God.

It was her mother.

"Is THAT WHO I think it is?" Rico asked. He, too, was in scramble mode now, trying to get dressed.

Natalie nodded. Even though Rico had only talked

to her mother a couple of times, he obviously remembered her voice.

"What's your mother doing here?" he added.

She had no idea. Well, she did have an idea, actually. A bad one. Her father had brought her here to make sure that Natalie didn't do something *he* would regret. Like stay married to a ranch hand.

"Give me a second," Natalie called out so that her father would hopefully stop pounding on the door. The sound was going right through her, and her nerves were already raw enough as it was.

She had to squeeze back into the Skinnies because it was the only way her skirt would fit, and despite the franticness of their situation, Rico looked at her while she shimmied them on.

"Yeah, you should burn those things," he said, frowning.

Natalie would, and buy bigger clothes, but she hoped for now that she didn't pop out of the Skinnies like a container of canned biscuits that had given way to the pressure.

Even though the seconds were just ticking by, and her father was still pounding on the door, Natalie took a moment to check herself in the dresser mirror. And she nearly screamed. She looked as if she'd been having sex for hours.

Crap.

Rico didn't do a mirror stop, and that was why he reached the door before she did. That was not good but he was too darn fast, and he threw open the door before she could get there.

And there they were.

Her father's face was so close to the door that Rico and he practically bumped noses. Marcus stood to her father's left while her mother stood to his right. Marcus and her father were both obviously in a snit and were glaring, but her mother gave a polite smile.

"Why didn't you answer your phone?" her father snapped. "I've been calling you all afternoon."

"Sorry, but I forgot that I'd turned it off." It was true, but he wouldn't believe that.

Rico stepped to the side, motioned them to come on in, and they did, one by one. Her father and Marcus kept their attention nailed to her while tossing a few glares at Rico. Her mother looked around the way a prospective buyer might.

"Thank you for inviting us into your home, Rico," her mother said, clearly remembering her manners. Unlike her father.

"You were supposed to be back in Austin," he snarled. "And you damn sure weren't supposed to be…doing whatever the hell it was you were doing with him."

"Sex," Natalie provided. No use even attempting to hide it. Rico looked as post-orgasmic as she did.

Apparently, neither her father nor Marcus were pleased with her truthful answer, though, because they were having some kind of scowling contest. At the moment her father was winning.

"You have such a lovely home," her mother added.

"Thank you," Rico told her. "Would you like to sit down? Or I can fix you some coffee."

"That would be nice," her mother answered at the same moment her father said, "We don't want to sit down, and we damn sure don't want any coffee. I want Natalie to come with us now. I've already arranged for someone to pick up her car from the McCord Ranch."

But her mother ignored him, went into the living room and sat on the sofa. Again, as if this were a social call. Since things were about to get even uglier than they already were, Natalie went to her, took hold of her hand while Rico flipped on the automatic coffeemaker.

"Mom, are you all right? Is it okay for you to be here?"

"You mean because I should be in my special place." Her mother smiled just a little, and it seemed slightly different from the smile at the door. "I can leave anytime I want, but it's just easier there, you know?"

Yes, Natalie did know. Easier because her mother was sheltered from things that would upset her. Like this situation with Rico. But her mother didn't seem upset.

"She's on her meds," her father quickly provided. "A larger dose than usual because I thought she would need it."

Rico frowned, and after he came out of the kitchen, his hands went on his hips. "You overmedicated your wife all so you could bring her here to guilt-trip Natalie into coming home."

It wasn't a question. Not in Natalie's mind, either. That was exactly what her father had done, and it was lowdown and dirty. Still, she didn't want her mother to have to pay the price for her father's manipulation tactics.

Natalie kissed her mother's cheek. "It's really good to see you, but I'll be by Sunday for my usual visit. I'd love for us to have a long chat then."

"Of course." So polite. But Natalie didn't know how much was real and how much was the medication.

"Mom, do you understand what's going on between Rico and me?" Natalie asked.

"Sex," her mother provided in a whisper, repeating Natalie's answer that she'd given to her father. "I'm old and on meds, but I do remember sex." Another smile. "Sometimes, it helps clear the head. Sometimes not. Which was it for you?"

"Both." It was the truth, and Rico made a sound of agreement.

Strange, but this was the first time she and her mother had discussed sex in any way, fashion or form. And it was in front of a room full of men. Men who, judging from their scowls, weren't in a sex-talking mood.

Natalie stood and looked at Marcus next. "Could you go ahead and take my mother to the car? I need to say some things to my dad."

Marcus shook his head. "But you and I need to talk, too."

"No, we don't. I'm not marrying you, not ever. So there, that's done."

Marcus opened his mouth, no doubt to argue.

Natalie nipped that in the bud. "It's over. Now go."

She checked to make sure this wasn't sending her

mother into a tailspin. It wasn't. Her mother had gone to the window next to the fireplace. There were security lights out there by the creek, and despite the rain, the view was still incredible.

"Mom, why don't you go with Marcus?" Natalie asked her.

Her mother nodded, stayed a moment to continue looking before she finally came back toward them. She stopped, though, when she spotted the divorce papers on the counter. Natalie tried to take them from her, but it was too late. Her mother was already reading them.

"It's true? You really aren't divorced?" she asked.

Natalie wasn't sure how much her father had told her, so she tried to keep things simple. "The courthouse clerk messed up the original paperwork. I'm sorry," she added, only because she should be adding something.

"Your father will fix this," her mother said like gospel, and then she turned to Rico. "Thank you for having me in your home."

God, it cut at Natalie to see her like this. Of course, the alternative would have been for her mother to be having a freak-out episode. Thankfully, the only suicide attempt she'd had was twelve years ago, and Natalie wanted to keep it that way.

Rico nodded, managed a "You're welcome." Her mother lingered a moment longer in the kitchen and went with Marcus so he could take hold of her hand.

Later, Natalie would need to apologize to Marcus for being so abrupt with him. Or maybe not. He might take her apology as an opening to try to renew their relationship.

"You shouldn't have brought her here," Natalie said to her father the moment her mother was out of earshot.

"You gave me no choice."

"Choice?" Rico repeated. Oh, no. This was going to get ugly. "You're trying to manipulate Natalie, the way you've always done."

"I'm trying to protect my wife. You don't know what she's been through—"

"I told him," Natalie interrupted.

Her father snapped back his shoulders. Clearly surprised. Probably because she didn't discuss her mother with just anyone. Of course, she didn't just marry and have sex with anyone, either. Rico was, well, special.

That didn't change things, though.

Her mother was perhaps still teetering on the brink of another suicide attempt, and Natalie had to make sure that didn't happen.

"Dad, wait in the car," Natalie insisted. "Please," she added. "I just need to talk to Rico for a couple of seconds."

Rico didn't say a word. Neither did her father, but he knew that he had won.

And Rico knew that he'd lost.

Other than her weight, things hadn't changed in the past twelve years, and they wouldn't.

Her father walked out, not in that same angry way as when he'd stormed in, and he left Rico and her standing there. Staring at each other. Natalie had no idea what the right words were to say to him because there was no way to fix this.

Apparently, Rico knew that, too.

"Goodbye, Natalie," he said. Rico brushed a kiss on her cheek and walked her to the door.

Natalie managed to hold back the first tear until she made it outside.

CHAPTER SEVEN

Rico cursed the heat and the long-assed day he'd just had, which included going through a mountain of paperwork and tracking down some calves that'd gotten through a fence that Shane should have fixed. That resulted in more cursing—aimed at Shane that time.

Of course, Rico had to admit he'd been cursing a lot lately, so just about anything and anybody set him off. Now he had to go home, where there'd no doubt be more opportunities to dole out some *damns*, *hells* and worse swearwords. Because there'd be memories of Natalie everywhere.

Of her naked.

Of the sex they'd had.

Memories of her walking out, too.

Those memories were the very reason he'd been staying at the bunkhouse at the ranch for the past three nights. In fact, he'd left right after Natalie had, and he hadn't gone back. Until now. But he was tired of being under one roof with a dozen snoring men, because that was also causing its own share of cursing.

Thankfully, he'd left some lights on, so he didn't have to curse the darkness, too. He pulled off his boots and shirt on the porch. No sense carrying that stench inside. Once they'd aired out a bit, then he would clean them. He'd have to do the same to his house.

Or not.

He frowned when he didn't see a mess in the kitchen. There should have been scrambled eggs, toast and leftover margaritas—the things he'd fixed for Natalie. But the only "mess" on the counter was the divorce papers. Someone had obviously cleaned, and he doubted there were fairy-maids or neat-freak burglars who'd do that.

"Mom?" he called out though his mother never just showed up unannounced. Even if she had, she certainly wouldn't have cleaned.

Rico glanced around for a note from a neighbor or one of the townsfolk who'd heard about his second breakup with Natalie. No note, but he heard the sound of footsteps coming from his bedroom. The door was open, and the room was dark, so it took him a moment to see anything. When he did, Rico thought maybe every drop of air had vanished from the planet.

Because it was Natalie.

And she was naked. Well, almost. She was wearing just a barely there lace bra and panties. He pinched himself to make sure this wasn't some sort of hallucination. Or a ghost. If it was, the ghost was wearing Natalie's perfume.

"We seem to communicate better when I'm not dressed," she said, as if that explained everything. It explained nothing, but Rico was so spellbound by the view that he didn't point out the flaw in her comment.

"Uh, how did you get in?" All in all, it was a really dumb thing to ask her, especially when he had more important questions on his mind.

Like *Why are you here?*

Or *Why are you practically naked?*

And *How soon are we having sex?*

That last mental question latched on to what was left of his brain and held on.

"The door was unlocked. I parked in the back because I wanted to surprise you," she answered.

Mission accomplished. He was so surprised, it was a wonder he hadn't dropped to the floor.

"I've been here since this morning," Natalie continued. She came closer. What she didn't do was smile, and he could tell her nerves were there just beneath the surface. He was feeling some nerves, too. And confusion.

Lots of confusion.

"I burned the Skinnies," Natalie added before he could get his mouth working. "I also made sure Marcus knows that it's a no-go with him."

That sounded, well, good, but Rico still didn't know where this was leading. "Why exactly are you here?"

She didn't answer. Not with words anyway. Natalie hooked her arm around him and kissed him. Not a wimpy kiss, either. This was the real deal. French and everything.

"Things are so good between us when kissing and nudity are involved," she said.

Yeah, they were, and Rico hoped he didn't get booted out of the man club for saying this: "But we can't stay naked and kiss forever."

She looked at him as if she might challenge that and then sighed. "Should I put on some clothes, then?"

"No." He probably should have given that some thought, but what the hell—he wouldn't change his mind even with thought and plenty of talk. He really did like having a half-naked Natalie pressed against him. In fact, the only thing that would have made it better was for him to take off that bra and panties. First, though, he really did need some answers.

"What about your father?" Rico asked.

Since Natalie was only a couple of inches from him, he saw her flinch a little. Then she kissed him again, and the flinch, the question and what shred of common sense he had left flew right out the window. When she pulled back this time, Rico was ready to haul her off to bed.

But no bed. Instead, Natalie held out her hand, putting it right in his face. Since it blocked the view he really wanted—of her and that skimpy underwear— Rico nearly pushed it aside.

Until he saw the ring on her finger. A ring that he recognized because he'd given it to her the night they'd eloped. Unless she'd managed to buy an identical one.

"You found it?" he asked.

Natalie shook her head. "My mother had it all this time, and when I visited her this morning, she told me she'd left it on the counter the night she was here."

Now it was Rico's turn to shake his head. "Why did she have it? Better yet, why did she leave it?"

"She took it that day when I went home to tell them we'd eloped. Remember, I went alone."

Only because Natalie had insisted on that. Rico hadn't thought it was a good idea for her to do it solo. And he'd been right. Things had gone to hell after that.

"Anyway, after I told my parents we were married, my dad had a blowup, my mother retreated to her bedroom, and I went out to ride my horse so I could clear my head. I left the engagement and wedding rings on my dresser because I was afraid of losing them. When I got back, my mother had taken the overdose of sleeping pills. She'd taken the wedding ring, too."

Rico hoped just talking about this didn't bring back all the painful memories for Natalie. But then the bad memories, like the good ones, would always be there. There was nothing she could do about that.

"Why did your mother take the wedding band?" he asked. Because this still didn't make sense.

Natalie lifted her shoulder, which created some fascinating movement in the lace bra. It was distracting. And damn interesting. But Rico tried not to notice it because this conversation was important. Well, maybe it was. And maybe it wouldn't ever be possible to understand the mind of a mentally ill woman.

"My mom said that whole day is foggy, but she was afraid my father would throw the rings away. Which he might have done if he'd spotted them." She drew in a long breath, and it caused her breasts to move again. "As for why she only took the wedding band and not both, we might never know."

Rico thought he might have an idea. "Maybe it was her way of saving the more important of the two rings for you." If so, it'd worked. "Except she didn't try to save herself."

Natalie made a sound of agreement. "But our elopement didn't have as much to do with what happened as I thought. She said she just gave in to the depression. That's why she wants to stay where she is, but by keeping the ring, that was her way of saying, it's okay."

"But it's not okay with your father," Rico reminded her.

She shrugged again. "No, but he's like the Skinnies. He's holding me in and not in a good way. If I keep letting him do that, I might pop. Also not in a good way," she added. Then she added a sly smile.

Despite the serious chat, the air was still zinging between them, and yeah, it felt as if something might pop. Something felt right, though, too. Rico was still in the cautiously optimistic department when he kissed her. As always, Natalie tasted like all the sweet things in his life rolled into one. That taste hummed right through him.

Until he remembered that he should add a reminder to all this. Hard to do, though, because he had to wait for her to finish giving him her own kiss.

"We might still suck at this," he said with his mouth against hers.

"Probably. Some of the time anyway. I think that's the way it's supposed to be, though. I don't think anyone can avoid total suckage."

She was right. This wasn't all sex and kisses, but it was a nice part of it. Nice holding her, too. And looking at her. Hell, there were a lot of nice parts.

"I need to thank the county clerk," she continued. "Her screwup was the best thing that could have happened because it brought me back to you."

It had, and Rico wanted to add his thanks for that. However, there was one more issue to be worked out. "You live and work in Austin, over an hour away from the ranch."

"I can work from home most days, commute on the others." Obviously, she'd given this some thought. She kissed him, which always made everything better.

Rico had one other point of possible contention. "My boots will always have cow shit on them."

She gave him a serious look. Then smiled. "Good. It's exactly where I prefer cow shit to be."

It was the right answer. The right woman, too. If he hadn't known that twenty minutes ago, he certainly knew it now. Of course, another kiss helped with that reminder. A nudge of her body against his did the trick, too.

That left Rico with just one last thing to ask. "Natalie, do you want to stay married to me?"

Her smile widened, and she caught on to his belt and yanked him to her. "I do."

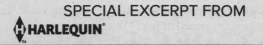
"Paige?" Jax whispered.

He could have sworn everything stopped. His heartbeat. His breath. Maybe even time. But that standstill didn't last.

Because the person stepped out, not enough for him to fully see her, but Jax knew it was a woman.

"You got my message," she said. "I'm so sorry."

Paige. It was her. In the flesh.

Jax had a thousand emotions hit him at once. Relief. Mercy, there was a ton of relief, but it didn't last but a second or two before the other emotions took over: shock, disbelief and, yeah, anger.

Lots and lots of anger.

"Why?" he managed to say, though he wasn't sure how he could even speak with his throat clamped shut.

Paige cleared her throat, too. "Because it was necessary."

As answers went, it sucked, and he let her know that with the scowl he aimed at her. "Why?" he repeated.

She stepped from the shadows but didn't come closer to him. Still, it was close enough for him to confirm what he already knew.

This was Paige.

She was back from the grave. Or else back from a lie that she'd apparently let him believe.

For a *dead* woman, she didn't look bad, but she had changed. No more blond hair. It was dark brown now and cut short and choppy. She'd also lost some of those curves that'd always caught his eye and every other man's in town.

"I know you have a thousand questions," she said, rubbing her hands along the outside legs of her jeans. She also glanced around. Behind him.

Behind her.

"Just one question. Why the hell did you let me believe you were dead?"

Don't miss SIX-GUN SHOWDOWN
by USA TODAY *bestselling author Delores Fossen,*
available in August 2016 wherever
Harlequin® Intrigue books and ebooks are sold.

www.Harlequin.com

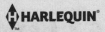

INTRIGUE

EDGE-OF-YOUR-SEAT INTRIGUE, FEARLESS ROMANCE.

Save $1.00

on the purchase of
SIX-GUN SHOWDOWN
by *USA TODAY* bestselling
author Delores Fossen,
available July 19, 2016, or on any
other Harlequin® Intrigue book.

Available wherever books are sold, including most
bookstores, supermarkets, drugstores and discount stores.

Save $1.00

on the purchase of any Harlequin® Intrigue book.

Coupon valid until October 31, 2016.
Redeemable at participating outlets in the U.S. and Canada only. Not redeemable at
Barnes and Noble stores. Limit one coupon per customer.

52614024

Canadian Retailers: Harlequin Enterprises Limited will pay the face value of this coupon plus 10.25¢ if submitted by customer for this product only. Any other use constitutes fraud. Coupon is nonassignable. Void if taxed, prohibited or restricted by law. Consumer must pay any government taxes. Void if copied. Inmar Promotional Services ("IPS") customers submit coupons and proof of sales to Harlequin Enterprises Limited, P.O. Box 3000, Saint John, NB E2L 4L3, Canada. Non-IPS retailer—for reimbursement submit coupons and proof of sales directly to Harlequin Enterprises Limited, Retail Marketing Department, 225 Duncan Mill Rd., Don Mills, ON M3B 3K9, Canada.

5 65373 00076 2   (8100)0 12194

U.S. Retailers: Harlequin Enterprises Limited will pay the face value of this coupon plus 8¢ if submitted by customer for this product only. Any other use constitutes fraud. Coupon is nonassignable. Void if taxed, prohibited or restricted by law. Consumer must pay any government taxes. Void if copied. For reimbursement submit coupons and proof of sales directly to Harlequin Enterprises Limited, P.O. Box 880478, El Paso, TX 88588-0478, U.S.A. Cash value 1/100 cents.

® and ™ are trademarks owned and used by the trademark owner and/or its licensee.

© 2016 Harlequin Enterprises Limited

DFCOUP0616

Same great stories, new name!

In July 2016,
the HARLEQUIN®
AMERICAN ROMANCE® series
will become
the HARLEQUIN®
WESTERN ROMANCE series.

Connect with us to find your next great read,
special offers and more.

f /HarlequinBooks
🐦 @HarlequinBooks
www.HarlequinBlog.com
www.Harlequin.com/Newsletters

HARLEQUIN®

A Romance FOR EVERY MOOD™

www.Harlequin.com

HWR2016